TALES OF THE
SHADOWMEN
Volume 14: Coup de Grace

TALES OF THE
SHADOWMEN
Volume 14: Coup de Grace

edited by
Jean-Marc & Randy Lofficier

stories by
Matthew Baugh, Adam Mudman Bezecny, Nathan Cabaniss, Matthew Dennion, Brian Gallagher, John Gallagher, Martin Gately, Micah S. Harris, Travis Hiltz, Paul Hugli, Matthew Ilseman, Rick Lai, Nigel Malcolm, Christofer Nigro, Frank Schildiner, Michel Stéphan, Artikel Unbekannt
and **David L. Vineyard**

translation by
J.-M. & Randy Lofficier, Michael Shreve

cover by
Florine Rétoré

A Black Coat Press Book

ISBN 978-1-61227-696-0. First Printing. December 2017. Published by Black Coat Press, an imprint of Hollywood Comics.com, LLC, P.O. Box 17270, Encino, CA 91416.

Table of Contents

In the 1960s, Zenna Henderson's stories about "The People" used to grace the pages of the French edition of F&SF. *There was even a rather enjoyable and faithful 1972 made-for-TV movie entitled* The People *starring William Shatner and Kim Darby that adapted a few of the original stories. While Henderson's characters have appeared in a Darkover crossover in one of the MZB anthologies, they have never graced our pages before—that is, until now...*

Matthew Baugh: *The Lights on Haint Mountain*

North Carolina, Late Summer 1959

The silver strings of my guitar rang through the quiet room as I sang...

Way up on Haint Mountain
The lights dance and play
There's a music that calls me
From far, far away.

There was some scattered applause from the patrons of the Stony Creek Café as I finished. One dark-haired woman in the back signaled me to come over and sit with her, which I did. She was pretty, a bit past college age, with the kind of features that might be Asian, or Cherokee, or maybe something different from either. She introduced herself as Mari and we commence to talking.

"That's a lovely song," she said. "Is it about a real place?"

"So I've heard tell," I replied.

"What does the name mean?"

"Haint Mountain? Well, it isn't a mountain as most folks would see it; more a high ridge back amongst the hills. Haint's a word folks hereabouts use for a ghost or a spirit. They call the mountain that because of the ghost lights you can see dancing on it some nights."

"Have you seen it?"

"I haven't yes, but I mean to," I said. "Maybe once I've seen the lights, I'll have more verses for my song."

"I'd like to see them myself," she said. "At least, if Haint Mountain is the same as what my map calls Witch Mountain."

She unfolded a USGS map with the town circled in red and a line leading to the ridge in question.

"That's the same spot, all right," I said. "I guess there's some who call it one thing and some who call it the other. Does this mean you're looking to see the lights too?"

She smiled and nodded.

"I'm part of a scientific team from the Atomos Institute. We've come up here to study the lights. If they're real, and not just swamp gas, or reflected headlights, or some other common phenomena, they could be of great scientific interest."

"I wish you best of luck."

"I'm hoping you can do more than that." She licked her lips nervously. "We need a guide and none of the locals are willing. They get quiet when I even mention we want to go there. But since you're already going there…"

I had to grin at that.

"Like I said, I've never been to Haint Mountain myself, but I know my way around this kind of country pretty well. I guess I'd be proud to help you."

The camp that Mari showed me was different from I'd imagined. They had a couple of Jeeps and an army-style truck, all with the same logo stamped on the doors. It was the words *Atomos Institute* with a series of loops around them, like a diagram of electrons circling the nucleus of an atom. The tents, which had the same logo, were laid out neat as could be. When she had told me her team wasn't used to this, I'd expected the usual clutter you see from folks unused to living outdoors. This looked more like an army campsite.

It was getting on sundown, and I could make out five men, all from some-place in the Far East by the look of them. One man strode out to meet us; a compact but strong-looking fella with short-cut hair and the walk of a soldier. He gave a stiff little bow when Mari introduced me.

"Isao Matsumoto," he said offering his hand. "I'm the head of this expedition. My companions are Kano, Mitsui, Demura, and Ishiyama."

"You folks are all Japanese?"

"Yes, mostly," Mari said. "My father was American and my mother Japanese. I should probably have mentioned that the Atomos Institute is based out of Nagasaki University, though it has recently opened a branch in America. I hope this doesn't affect your decision to help us. I know, for some people, the War was not that long ago."

"I'm not much for holding grudges," I said.

"Thank you." Mari looked relieved and Isao give a curt nod.

I spent the last of the daylight getting to know Mitsui and Demura. They were playing a game with cards that had the pictures of flowers on them. After a bit, they invited me into the game. Neither of them spoke a lick of English but they gave me some matchsticks to bet and soon I had a right fair understanding of the game.

Dinner was rice and some vegetables, cooked up real nice. Everyone ate real quiet and serious. After, Mitsui broke out a little bottle of sake and some little cup, and, mister, that was some potent stuff!

"Could you play the song I heard earlier?" Mari asked.

"I'm proud to be asked." I broke out my old guitar and tuned it up.

"The strings are different than I have seen before," Isao said. "They shine."

"Silver wires," I replied. "I melted down some times awhile back to make them."

"Why?"

"Silver's heavier than steel, gives 'em a richer sound. 'Sides, folks around here figure silver's a good charm against evil."

He grunted and nodded.

I've heard that ghost-singing
And the song's touched my heart
Someday I'll climb Haint Mountain
Never more to depart.

I strummed the last chord looked around. They gave me polite applause and Mari had a wistful look on her face. She turned to Isao and asked him something. It was in Japanese, so I didn't understand, but her voice was soft and urgent. His reply was neither of those things. He barked out a single word and I didn't need any interpreter to tell her it meant, "No!"

She asked again… or maybe, it was a different question that sounded like the first. This time, he gave that affirmative grunt.

"*Domo,*" she said, making little bow.

Then she rose and moved to the tents.

"I did not learn much about the mountain from your song," Isao said, turning to me.

"It isn't really a song about the mountain," I said. "It's a song about wanting to go to the mountain."

He took that in for a minute before he spoke again.

"Perhaps you can tell us what the locals say about the lights on the mountain."

"Mainly they say the lights are ghosts," I replied. "Some say they're the spirits of Cherokee widows, carrying torches is the search for the bodies of their husbands slain in war. Others hold that they're the ghosts of settlers, searching for a woman who was spirited away by night."

Mari rejoined us; she was pushing a wheelchair that held a whip-thin little girl, about twelve years-old, her legs tightly wrapped in a blanket. She had dark eyes and the kind of complexion folks call olive, but her hair was a pale blonde. She surely wasn't Japanese, but I couldn't guess just who her kin might be.

"This is Hannah," Mari said. "She is the other reason we want to go to the mountain. She's an orphan, and she doesn't remember where she comes from, but we have reason to believe it's the mountain."

"Miss Hannah," I said, offering my hand.

9

Her eyes got big, and her expression made me think of a frightened fawn.

"Hannah doesn't speak," Mari said. "She's also very shy, especially around strangers. I thought she would enjoy your music."

I had the suspicion there was a lot more to this than they were telling me, but there weren't anything for it but to sing, so I gave the girl warmest smile I could and picked up my guitar. I started out with some lively tunes to cheer her, playing *Flower Blooming in the Wildwood, Mole in the Ground*, and then switched up to *This World is Not my Home*.

Hannah leaned forward at that one, her eyes shining. Everyone else went real quiet and watched her, all anxious like. She noticed, and shrank back into herself, though the men continued to stare at her, expecting, I didn't know what.

As I finished the song, I searched my memory for something to break the tension. The tune came to my fingers before it came to my mind, a Japanese song I learned during my service in the Korean War. It had a bright bouncy feel. The men stared at me, their mouths hanging open, all except Isao, who continued to watch Hannah. Mari had tears in her eyes. After a moment, she began to sing in a voice that wasn't trained but was sweet as mountain honey.

Teru-teru-bozu, teru bozu
Ashita tenki ni shite o-kure
Itsuka no yume no sora no yo ni
Haretara kin no suzu ageyo

Teru-teru-bōzu, teru bōzu
Ashita tenki ni shite o-kure
Watashi no—

The song was cut off by a terrible howl from one of the tents. It sounded a little like the biggest bear ever, but I knew somehow that the voice was human.

Isao snapped something at Mari, who flinched as if she'd been struck. She dropped her eyes and bowed, then hurried toward the tents. As she entered one, the howling died away.

"Lord of mercy," I said. "What was that?"

"It is none of your concern," Isao replied in the same tone he had used with Mari.

My hackles were already up but that raised them even higher.

"Your business is your own," I said, "but it's my business if I don't care to guide you anymore. I'll be taking my leave."

"Wait! Is it a question of money?"

I shook my head. It didn't make me like the man any better that he made an offer like that.

"Please," he said, his voice much softer. "I did not say anything because I did not want to shame Mari. That sound is her brother. He is… different and she cares for him."

As I see things, there's no shame in being different, but I didn't say anything. I just nodded and sat back down.

Mari stepped out of the tent and trotted toward us. Isao spoke to her as she reached us.

"I told your friend about your brother," he said. "He knows Ken is not well."

Her face was blank for a moment, then she forced a smile.

"He has these fits. I'm afraid the music upset him."

"I'm sorry," I said. "Maybe I should pack it in for the night."

"No!" Isao said. "You should continue playing."

I looked to Mari.

"It is all right," she said. "It's just, the song you played is one Ken and I heard as children and it brought back memories."

"But, if you play songs from this place…" Isao gestured at the woods around us, "…surely that will not disturb Mari-san's brother."

"I think your music was helping Hannah," Mari said. "Could you, please?"

"Well," I said, "there are some more songs I'd purely like to sing."

I sat back down and played *Little Black Train* and *Barb'ry Ellen*, but when I moved into *I'll Fly Away*, I saw a change in Hannah's dark eyes. She leaned forward with a look of such longing that it near to broke my heart. Her lips moved; no sound came forth but it looked to me like she was mouthing the words, *The Home*. Her expression faded as I played the last chord, but not completely. Isao and the others had been watching her. Now he stepped forward and grabbed her by the upper arm.

"Did you see it, girl?"

I set aside my guitar and stood. The other men tensed and I expected I might be in for a good beating. It didn't matter none, though. I'm not a one to stand by and see a young girl manhandled without doing something.

"Wait!" Mari stepped in between us before Isao or I could move. She spoke to rapidly in Japanese. He nodded as she finished and met my gaze.

"I apologize. The girl's memory was returning and I became too excited." He gave me a bow that I took as an apology.

"Can you play another song like that?" Mari asked. "I think it will help her."

"There's a lot going on here that you aren't telling me," I said.

"I can tell you more, later. For now, could you play, please?"

I sat down again and plucked at the silver strings. I tried to think of a song that would match that expression of yearning on Hannah's face. On inspiration, I launched into the old church hymn, *I Wonder As I Wander*. Sure enough, something about that high, lonesome sound caught her the same as before. When I finished I shifted into *Wayfaring Stranger*.

I'm just a poor wayfaring stranger
Traveling through this world below
There is no sickness, no toil, nor danger
In that bright land to which I go
I'm going there to see my Father
And all my loved ones who've gone—

I stopped then for I could not believe what I saw. A look of rapture had spread across her face, and Hannah rose. She didn't just get up from her chair, she levitated into the air. The blanket around her legs fell away and I saw that she wore blue jeans underneath and her legs were bound together with canvas straps. They'd been keeping her a prisoner in that chair and now she was free. I knew then what the words to *I'll Fly Away* had affected her and wondered just where she meant to fly to. For the moment she simply drifted above us, twirling like a dancer, and I swear, I have not seen anything more beautiful in this life.

"Stop her!"

The men reacted to Isao's shout, drawing some odd-looking pistols from inside their jackets. I launched myself at Matsumoto, who was the first to draw a bead on Hannah. I caught him with a hard tackle that slammed him to the ground and sent his gun flying away. When I looked up, I saw Kano fire his pistol. A thin beam that looked like blue-white lightning shot from the muzzle. It crackled through the air and struck Hannah between the shoulder blades. She went limp and fell about twenty feet to the forest floor.

I rose slowly, stunned both by the strangeness of the weapon and what it had done. Balling my fists, I strode toward Isao with a purpose, not hesitating even when he drew his own pistol and pointed it at the center of my chest. A bolt of blue light struck me, sending a painful electric tingling out to the ends of my fingers and toes. I fell and, when I tried to move, found that I was completely paralyzed.

I was conscious but unable to move or speak or do anything more than breathe as they carried me into one of the tents and bound my wrists and ankles with the same sort of straps they'd used for Hannah. They left me to lie there for a while. I'm not sure how long, but it was full-dark when Isao, Mari, and Kano came to check on me. The men stood near the door while Mari knelt by me to check my pulse and breathing.

"He's nearly recovered," she said, then to me, "Can you speak?"

I tried and my mouth moved but no sound came out. My lips and tongue could move again, but they were sluggish.

"Here." She held a canteen to my lips and I gulped down a couple of mouthfuls. It helped a lot and I found that I could manage a few words.

"What happened?"

"You were hit with a paralysis ray," she replied. "The effect should wear off completely in a few moments."

"The little girl? Hannah?"

"She is not as big or strong, so it will take her longer to recover. She doesn't seem to have been hurt in the fall, at least not seriously."

"What is all this? Who are you people?"

A look of regret crossed her face.

"I must leave any answers for Isao-san." She rose. "I must go to check on Hannah now."

When she had left, Isao picked up a folding stool from the side of the tent, opened it, and sat down next to me. I gave my muscles a push, without any result. I wouldn't be able to bust free of those straps; not even with my full strength.

"I would not have chosen to treat you like this," he said. "Your music had a stronger effect on the girl than anyone could have foreseen. We knew she had psychic abilities, but had no idea that they were so powerful, or that your music would unlock them. We only hoped you could stir her memories."

It was starting to come together in my mind.

"You didn't need a guide," I said. "You wanted a musician?"

"Truthfully, we wanted both. The girl has responded to taped music, so Mari thought live music would be even better. We also need a guide."

"What does Hannah have to do with Haint Mountain?"

"That is no concern of yours. All you need to know is that you will continue to be our guide until we achieve our goal."

"What happens after that?"

"You will be paid and sent on your way."

"And the girl?"

"She will be well-cared for."

"So, as long as I don't make trouble, everything will be all right?"

Isao nodded and gave one of his grunts.

"It is regrettable that we had to treat you roughly. If we had let the girl slip away, she could have been lost or hurt."

"In that case, I expect you'll be letting me loose of these straps?"

"I cannot do that. If you were to slip away and tell the locals, it would threaten our mission. They are simple people, given to superstitions."

Isao went away, but he left Kano just outside the tent to guard me. My pack and my guitar sat on the other side of the tent, a dozen feet away but it might as well have been a hundred. I figured the only way I could get there would be to flop on my belly and hump along like an inch worm.

I lay there for a bit, contemplating my situation. I didn't trust Isao. He might not be planning on killing me, but I'd lay money he wasn't going to let me go to tell folks what I'd seen. I didn't have any idea what their plans were for Hannah, but I was pretty sure they were for the Institute's benefit and not hers. That still left me with a load of questions. As much as I tried to sort them out, they eluded me.

After about an hour, Mari came into the tent, pushing Hannah in her wheelchair. The poor girl was still so groggy that her head lolled to the side when they hit a bump.

"How is she?" I asked.

"She is fine, aside from a few bruises," Mari said. "She's lucky not to have broken anything."

"She didn't fall by her own design."

"No, she did not. "Mari's voice was soft and she cast her eyes down.

"Why are you helping these men?" I asked. "I can tell you want to help Hannah and me."

"I can't."

"Why not?"

"You heard my brother earlier?"

I nodded, remembering that inhuman howl.

"We were born in Hiroshima, twins. We were only toddlers when the bomb fell. I was out of the city with my father, but Ken-chan was sick and stayed with the nanny. He did not die of the radiation as so many did but it... changed him. His body is twisted, grotesque. Our father was ashamed and hid him away."

I couldn't help but feel for her as she spoke. It was clear she loved her brother with that special sort of closeness you see in twins.

"After the surrender, things were very bad in my country. We had relatives in Seattle who had not lost everything in the internment camps. They helped us to emigrate to America. Unfortunately, my father had not escaped the effects of the bombing. There was a black rain that fell after the blast, carrying radioactive particles with it. It clung to everything, contaminating the ground, the water, the people. My father eventually recovered from the radiation poisoning, only for cancer to claim him.

"I was sixteen when he died. I left high school to get hey a job. Then, less than a year later, Madame Yoshimuta contacted me. She is the founder of the Atomos Institute and the most brilliant scientific mind in the world. She offered me an education and promised to help Ken."

"Did she keep her promise?"

"Yes," she said, but I could hear hesitation in her voice.

"Yes?"

"Ken-chan would have died without the surgeries she did. She installed mechanical devices to support his heart and other organs, and to increase his strength."

"Sounds like there's a 'but.'"

"She has not helped him to look more human. Also, Ken is in constant pain and she has not found a way to relieve that. But she has promised to keep trying. I owe her more than I can repay."

"So, you're loyal to her, right or wrong?"

Mari's face hardened.

"I just wanted to make sure you were all right," she said. "Matsumoto-san has promised that neither you nor Hannah will be mistreated."

"That's good to hear. You wouldn't mind cutting these straps as a kind of gesture of good faith, would you?"

Without another word, she turned and left through the tent doorway. She didn't stomp, mind you, but it was clear she was fit to be tied.

Kano came inside when she left and sat on a camp stool, watching us. He still wore his light jacket against the chill of the night, and I could see his ray pistol in its shoulder holster. After a time, he drowsed off, but when I scooched my feet, trying to inch a little closer to my pack, he was awake and alert quicker than the wink of a cat's eye. After a few moments, his eyes closed again, but I didn't think he was any more asleep than he had been. I gazed at the knife in the top of my pack, feeling frustrated.

Then the knife started wobbling. I wondered if some critter, maybe a mouse or a raccoon had gotten behind the pack, but there didn't seem to be anything. The knife toppled off and fell but there wasn't no *plop* when it hit. Looking closer, I saw it was hovering like a hummingbird just an inch from the tent floor. I glanced over at Hannah. She had her eyes closed and sweat had broken out on her brow. Now the little tool zipped toward her, never touching down. When it reached her, it hopped right into her hand, nice as you please.

There was a band around the girl's upper arms but her hands and forearms were free. She popped the blade open right quick, and cut herself free. Then, moving quiet as a mouse's shadow, she slipped over to me and cut my bonds too.

I rose and moved toward where Kano slept. I was quiet as I knew how to be, which is pretty darned quiet, but he must have heard something. When I was halfway to him, Kano opened his eyes. He leaped to his feet, his hand reaching for the pistol and his mouth opening to cry out. I shut his mouth with an uppercut that came up from so low, my knuckles near dragged on the ground. The blow landed true and stretched him out on his back.

While Hannah watched, I bound him with the straps they'd used on us, then gagged him with a pair of socks from my pack. While I did that, Hannah gathered up my pack and guitar and passed them to me.

I cut a slit in the back wall of the tent and we slipped out into the woods. We hadn't gone more than a hundred yards when she stumbled and fell.

"Are your legs hurt?" I asked.

She shook her head, but it was just a few steps before she stumbled again. I felt her skinny legs, looking for sign of injury and found that her calves were flaccid. They must have bound her up in that wheelchair for so long all her muscle tone had left her. Scooping her into my arms, I headed into the woods again.

I stopped when the eastern sky first started to lighten. We'd come a far piece with nary a sound of pursuit. The Atomos people had wanted a guide, which probably meant none of them was a tracker. Hannah was sound asleep, so I laid her on the ground not far from a little creek, then began looking around. We didn't have any supplies and she was going to need to eat, weak as she was. I set a few snares then set about foraging.

I gathered up some dandelion greens, wild scallions, wood thistle and was lucky enough to find the big mushrooms folks call chicken of the woods growing shelf-like out of the side of a hickory tree. I took the lot back to where Hannah slept and laid it out on a rock near her, then went to check the snares. As luck would have it, there was a nice little cottontail caught in one. I pulled out my knife but a noise startled me. It was Hannah. She must have woken when I'd returned and followed me. Now she rushed past to place herself between me and the rabbit. Her eyes were dark with fright and her lips silently formed the word, "Please."

It took me off guard, mostly because I hadn't heard anything until she ran past me. I thought about it a moment, then gently pushed past her. She watched in horror as I reached my knife out, but burst into tears when I cut the twine from the critter's leg and set him free.

If I had any doubt that they were tears of gratitude, it ended when she threw herself against me and hugged me tight.

"Where are you from?" I asked over our breakfast of greens and mushrooms.

Hannah shook her head.

"Do you think those folks might be right, that you maybe come from Haint Mountain?"

She spread her hands in a helpless gesture.

"Where were you heading when you set me free?"

Hannah shook her head and lowered her eyes.

"No idea? Well, my best thought is to go on to the next town. They ought to have a sheriff or a town constable we can talk to."

Her eyes got big with fear and she shook her head.

"Why not?"

She looked around for moment, found a stick about a foot long, and used it to write in the dirt:

NO. THE POLICE ARE ON THEIR SIDE.

"What do you mean?"

I RAN AWAY BEFORE. POLICE SENT ME BACK.

I pondered on that for a moment as I chewed on a big piece of mushroom.

"If they did that, that must mean they've got some powerful influence and probably a lot of money to go with it. But that doesn't mean they can influence police everywhere."

She wiped out what she'd written with her foot and wrote some more:

NO POLICE. PLEASE!

"OK, but if we aren't going to them, where do you want to go?"

She shook her head, looking sad, then wrote on the ground:

THE HOME. IF YOU PLAY. I CAN SEE IT.

That sounded better than anything I could come up with, so I picked up my guitar and started in. Now that I had a feel what kind of music worked, I started right into *Wayfaring Stranger* then segued into *Great High Mountain*. I didn't sing, just put all the feeling I could into the music. I was so caught up that I barely noticed when Hannah rose into the air

Then she started singing; I can't say how, seeing as she had no voice, but I heard it clear. It was a lonely song, fully of beauty, and it felt ancient as the mountains themselves. My fingers, all on their own, started following her tune. I'd never played such music before, but it felt as if it was had been buried deep in my soul and I was just now remembering it. I saw a beautiful place in my mind, lush fields of silvery grain stalks under a pale blue sky. In the distance I saw a forest of trees in bloom and brightly colored birds flitting around them. The scene was illuminated by two suns, one setting and the other still high in the sky, the combination of their light gave the world a golden glow. But what world was it?

Then Hannah's singing stopped and she drifted gently back to earth wearing a bright smile.

"What I just saw," I said, "was that the Home?"

Her eyes widened and her mouth formed an "o" of surprise. I guessed she had no idea I'd seen it too.

"It was a pretty field, but the plants weren't any I'd ever seen before, nor the trees, nor the birds. The sky was a real pale blue and there was two suns in the sky."

Her eyes widened even further and she nodded.

"Have you ever sung like that before?"

She shook her head.

"I think that, somehow, your singing showed all that to me."

She smiled at that, then her expression turned serious and she bent to write on the ground:

AM I A WITCH?

"No, leastaways, you're not one the way people in these parts talk about witches. The way you rescued that rabbit. You're unearthly, but I guess you got a lot more kindness and goodness in you than anything hurtful or dark,"

The skin betwixt her eyebrows crinkled and she tilted her head to one side.

"I said, 'unearthly' because of what you can do, and where you come from. Ain't no place on God's green earth that has two suns like that."

She blinked a couple of times, then raised her eyes to the deep blue of the morning sky, then I saw her lips trace out the words: *From out there?*

"Does that make sense to you?"

She thought about that a moment, and a look of delight slowly bloomed in her face. She nodded.

"I guess it does to me too. At least, I can't think of no better explanation. Course that still leaves us the question of what to do with you. I think you're right about the law. Even if they aren't in the pocket of the Atomos Institute, they would purely hand you over to the government to study."

Hannah nodded.

"Maybe Mari and Isao had the right idea. If there's some connection between you and Haint Mountain, going there might give us a way to find the Home."

Hannah shook her head and I saw the tears forming her eyes. She scrawled again in the dirt.

THE HOME IS GONE. I CAN NEVER GO BACK

"I'm right sorry about that," I said. "I truly am. Still, it's best we get moving, and I don't know of a better destination; do you?"

She shook her head.

From what I remembered from the map, ahead of us lay a rocky ridge, near impossible to climb. We could skirt around through the woods to the east, though that would take days. The road to the next lay only about five or six miles to the west. It was the fastest way, but it was also most likely where is the Atomos crew would be looking for us. In the end of the choice was easy. The deep woods could be dangerous but it was a danger I was well used to, not like a crew of men with ray-guns and Lord knows what else.

We headed to the base of the ridge, then turned east. We'd only gone a little ways when we heard a terrible howl from the woods ahead of us.

Monster, Hannah mouthed.

I wasn't so sure I agreed, but I did not want to meet up with Ken. He sounded big as a bear and twice as mean. We turned around and started heading west as fast as we could. Hannah slowed me down considerable. As we ran, I saw sunlight flash off of something straight ahead of us. I climbed a tall sugar maple to get a better look. Several hundred yards ahead of us, two men in Atomos Institute jackets were crossing a glade as they came our way. I scanned the south and didn't see anything, but I was willing to bet cash money there was another group coming from that way too. I'd underestimated them. Just because they had no woodcraft didn't mean they weren't smart. They'd sprung a trap and pinned us against that ridge, nice as could be.

I dropped out of the tree.

"We're in some trouble," I said. "Don't worry though, I think I can get us past it. You need to hide here while I lead them off. When they follow after me, you head back south as fast as you can. Can you find your way back to town by yourself?"

She stared at me like she didn't understand my words.

"Listen, we got no time! You need to do as I say."

I could see two things in her eyes; the beginning of tears, and iron-strong determination. Abruptly she flung herself at me and wrapped her skinny arms around my waist. I caught her wrists and was about to peel myself loose from her grip, when I felt my feet leave the ground. I almost cried out as Hannah and me, guitar, pack, and all, rose up past the treetops, almost skimming the face of the high granite ridge. In just a few seconds, we lighted at the top, a hundred feet or more above where we had just stood. As I looked down, I heard a mournful bellowing, and Ken came crashing into view below us.

The sight of him was something I reckon I'll never forget. I hadn't been far wrong when I'd thought he sounded big as a bear. I'm an inch or two over six foot, but I'd only have come chest-high on him. He was hump-backed and scarred, without a lick of hair on him. His legs were short and thick and, by the way he moved, I judged one was shorter than the other, but he compensated by using his huge arms to move along, ape-like. Those arms looked more powerful than the rest of him. One appeared to be flesh and bone while the other was metal and jointed like the arm from a knight's armor piece of armor. He raised his scarred face at us and let out a howl that made my innards quiver. Hannah gripped my arm tight with both hands.

My heart went out to Mari, caring for that creature as she did.

A bolt of blue, so bright it hurt my eyes crackled past my head as the two Atomos men came into view. I recognized them at a glance: Isao and Kano, both with pistols drawn.

"That's sure going to slow them up," I said. A glance showed that Hannah was pale and sweating heavily. Lifting us both had been hard on her.

"Miss Hannah, are you okay?"

She gave a weak smile and nodded but I could see her arms and legs trembling.

"I figure it's my turn to do the carrying," I said.

She closed her eyes and leaned her head on my chest. I started out at a slow trot heading north.

The next day, Hannah was stronger, especially after breakfast. I was up before the sun and managed to spear a couple of fish to add to our moss, greens, and mushrooms. I didn't know if her tender-heartedness would apply to small-mouth bass, so I made sure they were cleaned and cooking before she caught sight of them. She didn't complain none, and ate her portion with relish.

The day's hiking was long but not too difficult. We took frequent rests, but Hannah took to the woods like she was born to them. The air was brisk but the sun was warm and the day cloudless and beautiful. Hannah's trick at the ridge seemed to have slowed our pursuers better than I'd hoped, though I didn't have any illusions that they'd given up.

We caught our first sight of Haint Mountain come sundown. It wasn't much to look at, but I could see Hannah twitching with excitement.

Let's go! She mouthed.

I shook my head.

"I'm itching to see it too, but not enough to try to go up that ridge after dark. We'll make camp here and be there by mid-morning tomorrow."

She nodded, but I could tell she was disappointed.

Dinner was sparse and we lay awake afterward. Hannah was too excited to sleep and I didn't want to doze off first, so I stayed up with her to watch the stars come out. It was just after full-dark that we saw the lights.

There were maybe half a dozen, though it was hard to count, the way they appeared and vanished. They looked like balls of pure yellow light close to the top of the ridge where they bobbed and danced like toy balloons. I couldn't tell if they really were made of light or brightly shining solid objects. They moved in a different way than anything I had ever seen and were wonderful to watch.

Hannah grabbed my hand and tugged.

Do you hear? she mouthed.

"Hear what?"

Singing

Her ears must have been some better than mine for I didn't hear anything. Even the crickets had gone silent. I closed my eyes and concentrated, and then I heard music. It was so soft, I thought it might be my imagination. As I listened, I decided that my imagination couldn't have produced such a haunting tune. It was played on fiddle, dulcimer, and some instruments like none I'd ever heard. The sound of it was heartbreaking but with an undercurrent of hope, like Hannah's song, but as different as a symphony is from a child's lullaby. Hannah began so sing, in a voice that was high and clear. I tried to follow the words this time, but it was no language I'd ever heard.

Then, quick as that, the music stopped and the lights blinked out.

Hannah turned her face to me. She looked as if her last friend in the world had just died.

Why? she mouthed.

"I don't know."

My people?

"Seems to me they must be. I don't know why they'd up and disappear like that, with you so close. I guess we can ask them about this when we get up there tomorrow."

She shook her head as tears ran down her face. I felt for her, coming so far, only to find rejection when she was so close. Even if she was ready to give up, though, I wasn't. I'd made up my mind, if they were going to reject her they'd have to tell me why, face-to-face. And if they did reject her, I was going to find a place where she would be safe, and welcomed, and loved.

She huddled against me, my arm around her shoulder, until she was cried out. When she lay down to sleep, I took my guitar and played an old Welsh lullaby.

Sleep my child and peace attend thee, all through the night
Guardian angels God will send thee, all through the night
Soft the drowsy hours are creeping, hill and vale in slumber sleeping,
I my loving vigil keeping, all through the night...

I drowsed off with my back against a stump and my gaze on the ridge. I hoped that the lights would come back, but they didn't before my eyes finally closed.

I woke with the sense we were not alone. The night was still dark and, by the position of the crescent moon, I judged it was nigh on three in the morning. Hannah still slept, so I rose quietly, as not to rouse her. What I saw were six forms standing about a dozen yards from us. I moved toward them and quickly made out that they were people, dressed as farmers, four men in overalls and two women in long skirts.

"Hello," I said, as I stopped a few feet before them.

"Neighbor," the man in the front replied. He was tall and lean with a bushy beard. I took him to be about sixty, though he stood and moved like a much younger man.

"I'd offer you dinner, but I've been abed for some time," I said.

"That's good of you, but we aren't here for any such thing," he replied. "We've come for the child."

"It's just the two of them, Jeremiah," the younger of the women said. "He is wary, but not hostile."

"Are you the people from up yonder? The ones with the lights and the music?"

"Our ways are our own, and we don't share them with outsiders," one of the other men said. His words were challenging but his tone was matter-of-fact.

"Daniel," the older woman said in mild reproof. Then she spoke to me. "You must have some idea of who we are, having been with the child."

"Some idea," I admitted.

"What are your thoughts?"

"You're the ones folks hereabouts call witches, but you aren't, are you? Leastaways, not how they mean."

"No," Jeremiah said. "We are not."

"But you do have abilities; special things you can do. Folks here don't understand them, so they name them witchcraft. But where you're from, I guess they're as natural as breathing."

"Where do you think that is?"

"The girl, Hannah, she showed me a different world... a place with two suns. I reckon it's out in space somewhere, far from the Earth."

"She showed you the Home?" the younger woman said. "That is a great gift."

I felt someone clutch my shirt from behind. Hannah had wakened and now stood there, peeking around my body at the strangers.

"Hannah," the older woman said, "we've come to take you home."

I felt Hannah's grip tighten. Now that we'd met these mysterious people, she didn't know what to make of them any more than I did.

"We've been waiting for you for a long time, child." Jeremiah glanced up at me. "When we came to your world, our arrival was chaotic and we lost track of many of the lifeboats we deployed. We believe that Hannah's lifeboat crashed in California where it was partly salvaged by the Atomos Institute. We are grateful to you for helping her escape, and bringing her here."

"You know about them?"

"A little. They are very secretive, but we have learned a few things. Their leader is a brilliant woman named Kanoto Yoshimuta whose spirit was badly twisted by the bombings of Hiroshima and Nagasaki. She is working to create even greater weapons of destruction to use against the United States as an act of vengeance."

That thought made my insides go cold.

"And now she's got your people's technology?"

"She was only able to salvage a little from the crash. We believe that is why her people were bringing Hannah here. They hoped she could lead them to the rest of us, and that she could force our secrets from us."

"Someone's coming!" the younger woman said. All of them became more alert, though I could not hear anything.

"They're approaching from two directions," Jeremiah said.

After a couple of minutes I heard a sound, like the whooshing of a jet engine, only much softer. Lights appeared, two on each side of us. They looked like the headlamps on motorcycles, but they moved more smoothly over the rough ground than anything with wheels could have done. They came close enough that I could see they were some sort of sleds, round and small enough to carry two people each. I reckoned they must have been what the big truck had carried. They landed and I could see the Atomos people. They all had their pistols drawn. All, that was but for Mari, who left hers holstered and Ken, who didn't need one.

"You must be Hannah's people," Isao said stepping toward Jeremiah. "Don't worry, we have come to take all of you to a safe place."

"We are not interested," the older woman said.

"You should be. I'm sure you know what would happen if the American government discovered you. We mean to take you somewhere no government can ever touch you."

"You offer is generous," Jeremiah said, "but we decline."

"We cannot permit that. These weapons will not harm you, but they will persuade you to comply."

"Hold up!" I said. "You aren't going to use your guns on these people."

"Are you going to stop us?" Isao's chuckle raised my hackles.

"You bet I am!"

"Thank you," the younger woman said. "But there is no need for you to fight. Their weapons do not threaten us."

"No?" Isao raised his pistol and pulled the trigger.

I moved to put my body between the blast and the woman but nothing happened. With a puzzled expression, Isao pulled the trigger again, with no result. The next moment, the weapon jerked out of his hand and rose into the air. The pistols of all the others also pulled free and rose to join it. Then the guns just kind of came apart and rained over us in little pieces.

"Ken!" Isao shouted.

With a howl, the big man-monster made a beeline toward Jeremiah. The old man turned and raised his hand. The next moment, Ken rose from the ground. He thrashed his powerful arms and legs but there was nothing he could do to break free of that invisible force.

Then the engines on those hover-sled things started up. The Atomos folk watched with expressions of awe that changed to terror when the vehicles shot toward them. For the next few moments, the men ducked and dodged to stay out of the way of the careening craft. The vehicles didn't hit any of the Atomos men, but did scatter them into the woods like a flock of chickens with a brace of foxes after them.

As the sounds of pursuit faded, I saw that only Mari and Ken were left with the rest of us.

"What shall we do with you?" Jeremiah said, looking up at the giant.

"Please, don't hurt him," Mari said.

"You didn't complain when you thought he might hurt us," one of the men with Jeremiah said.

"Please!"

"He is in terrible pain," the older of the women said. "If you let him down, I can sort him."

The old man looked at me.

"He threatened you before. What do you say?"

That wasn't too hard for me. As frightening and dangerous as he was, Ken was like a little child.

"If you feel you owe any kind of debt to me, I'll count it as settled if you help him," I said.

"And you, Hannah?" Jeremiah asked. "Do you want to let Jerusha sort him?"

The girl answered with a firm nod of her head.

Jeremiah lowered his hand and the giant drifted to earth. He stood there, looking from one of us to the other, uncertain what to do next. Jerusha moved to his side and held out her hand. With a growl, Ken moved away a step.

"Don't be afraid," she said. "I'm not going to hurt you."

Ken growled again.

Mari went to Ken and he placed her hands on his massive arm. She spoke to him softly in Japanese for several moments. He growled again, but this time it reached out his hand for Jerusha to take. The woman closed her eyes for a long time and there was scarce a noise as we all watched. Finally, she opened her eyes and withdrew. Ken patted himself in places with his big hands, making noises of surprise and pleasure. Mari asked him question in Japanese, to which he nodded his head and a smile appeared on his distorted face.

"Thank you!" Mari was crying harder now. She went down both knees, clutching Jerusha's skirts.

"There has been a great deal of damage done to his body," Jerusha said. "I can heal much of it, but it will take time."

"She came here as an enemy," Jeremiah said.

"She come here as a sister who loves her brother," I said. "She was loyal to the Atomos people because she thought they were his only hope. I can't tell you what to do, but if it was me, I'd trust her."

Jeremiah looked around at his people, then nodded.

"If they choose, the two may come to live with us. You may also, if you want."

"I'd be proud to come visit, especially if I could learn your songs. I haven't got again me to settle in one place, though."

"Then fare thee well," Jeremiah said.

They started to go, but Hannah turned back. She ran to me gave me a hug it was fierce and tight, then she looked into my face and mouthed the words, *I'll miss you.*

I hugged her back and whispered that I'd miss her too, which I surely would.

I sat there that place for a long time when they'd gone. After a bit the lights appeared on the ridge, and the music returned. This time it felt like the tune was meant for me:

I've heard that ghost-singing
And the song's touched my heart
Someday I'll climb Witch Mountain
Never more to depart.

Most of the SF works of the great pioneer of French SF Maurice Renard (1875-1939), translated by Brian Stableford, have been published by Black Coat Press, with the notable exception of his 1920 classic The Hands of Orlac, *easily available in other English-langage editions. Amazingly, this story about a pianist on-to whom Dr. Cerral grafts the hands of a murderer, was filmed five times: four movies (1925, 1935, 1960, 1962) and a recent 2013 French TV adaptation. Adam Mudman Bezecny deals here with the many-limbed (!) ramifications of...*

Adam Mudman Bezecny: *The Curse of Orlac*

1954

The house of Orlac was a relic of an older time, and it reflected that fact on every board. Time had had its way with the old place, and now, on stormy nights like this, the rain got in. Soon, the house would be washed away entirely, its wood left to rot, along with all of its contents. The rain had claimed all of the pianos, which didn't matter—their owner had lost his passion to play them.

The owner of the pianos, and the house, was also a relic of an older time. He had seen his prime at the dawn of this 20th century, until that terrible day in 1918 when he had lost his hands. From there, he had seen nothing but horror and misfortune. The glory days were over, and now thirty-six years of suffering had passed. That he had invited his guest here, to the crumbling old house, was only feeble defiance against what he wanted to avenge.

The guest of Stephen Orlac, brought back to France to find the truth, was yet another relic. Orlac had been surprised to learn that the Sâr Dubnotal was still active in 1954, but then, the so-called "Great Psychagogue" was said to be immortal, wasn't he? Preserved by the magics and occult secrets that he wielded, he hadn't aged a day when he had first started making news nearly fifty years ago. He was supposed to be a detective as well as a mystic. Orlac had tried hard to dismiss the supernatural since the incident with his hands, and yet he had turned to it when conventional detectives had been unable to answer his questions. Questions, plural, was perhaps an inaccurate word, for he had one simple question: where had his hands come from?

He was supposed to know the answer. Dr. Cerral had told him that the hands had come from the executed criminal Vasseur, and that had been at the core of the murders that Orlac thought he himself had committed. If he had the hands of a murderer, was it not possible that he would become a murderer himself? Yet they'd proven that theory wrong—the true villain had faked Vasseur's fingerprints. That had been the end of it. Or so it seemed...

Stephen Orlac told the Sâr how he had killed again. He'd done it so many times, in those thirty-six years, never being caught once. Slowly, the head injury he'd sustained in the accident that had taken his hands had healed, and he had regained full awareness of his actions. It had been in an unclouded state of mind that he had killed. He remembered every detail of it, how the hands had tingled as he'd done it, filling him with an odd pleasure—soon replaced with horror once it was over, of course, but it did not help the fact that he couldn't resist when the hands called to him.

Ordinarily, the Sâr would have imprisoned Orlac on his island for this, but when the former pianist first approached him, he had said to the mystic:

"If you do not believe me, *El Tebib*, you may read my mind."

And in that search of his mind, the Sâr had seen that, if Stephen Orlac did not hate the act of killing, he was good at hiding it. The psychic scan also confirmed that the feeling of compulsion that seized the pianist was not natural. A spot of evil had formed on his soul, and indeed, the Psychagogue could see that it *was* the hands that were causing it—this discovery was the undoing to the happy ending of the mystery he'd braved years ago, which had distinctly *disproved* the possibility of a supernatural element. But the death of Orlac's wife had already reversed his sense of good fortune.

The Sâr could not turn away from an evil growing in strength, and from helping a man whose life was now ruled by fear. Using means both material and metaphysical, he had searched high and low for the original owner of the hands.

Now the Great Psychagogue was presenting his findings. His eyes tracked sweat beads on the forehead of the pianist.

"Ease your mind, Mr. Orlac," the Sâr said. Then he inhaled sharply. "I was fascinated by your case, initially because of my knowledge of medicine. Medical experts are only now learning the secrets of your Dr. Cerral and his transplants, so we are just crossing the first threshold of the concept of transplant rejection. That your body didn't begin turning on and consuming your new hands indicates that they came from someone who was related to you."

The pianist was taken aback, but didn't take long to find his voice. "You had to look into my genealogy? I pity you," Orlac said bitterly. "I know nothing of my parentage—I was raised an orphan, though I have a certificate of birth."

"I was able to locate your family," the Sâr replied simply. "And you have a troubled background indeed."

He raised his hand, and gently beckoned for Orlac to close his eyes. Orlac had seen a demonstration of the psychic powers of the so-called "Napoleon of the Intangible," and so, within his mind, he saw a regal-looking man, wearing the clothes of a Russian aristocrat of the Napoleonic Era.

"The earliest forefather of yours I could find was Count Feodor Orloff. Your branch of his family changed the name to Orlac, as you might expect. Count Orloff was a pawn of the Czar during his attempt to take control of the country of Czernova, until he was stopped and seemingly killed by an English soldier named Paul Cressingham and the Czernovan Princess Barbara. The Orlac family split off in the wake of this disgrace. But the Count left a son, who was raised in England, who would grow up under the name of Dr. Dionysus Orloff."

The image of the Russian Count changed suddenly to a man with a frog-like face, clad in the Victorian outfit of a black suit and top hat. Orlac saw some slight resemblance between himself and this man, moreso than he had with Count Feodor.

"Dionysus Orloff was a particularly long-lived man, and before I discuss what he did in this long life, I must explain that he was an occultist like me. That is how he prolonged his life. But an occultist is not like a wizard. He was a scientist, as I am, as well as a purveyor of the mystic arts, like the alchemists of old. Combining magic and surgery gave him many minor but strange talents.

"In any event, he was protective for most of his life of a girl named Melissa, his daughter, who had been disfigured and put into a coma by a fire. This display of fatherly affection, however, was not a heartwarming one. In 1888, the doctor was implicated in the Jack the Ripper case under the Anglicized name of 'Dennis Orloff,' though I know from personal experience that Orloff was not *the* Ripper. That does not change the fact that he did truthfully kill several women. The reasons why came to light in 1912, when an operation he was conducting was exposed."

"What was it?" Orlac asked, keeping his eyes closed. He spoke the words even though he didn't want to know.

"He believed that stealing the skin of these women and grafting it onto Melissa would restore her health—that's why he targeted the most beautiful and youthful of girls to make his victims. His notes on the matter have seen recent revival via the controversial writings of a certain Dr. Genessier, though Genessier's notes are not Orloff's own. They come from two of Orloff's pupils, a Dr. Conrad Jekyll and a Dr. Mason Zimmerman. Returning to the 1912 case— Orloff didn't perform these later killings himself. Instead, he employed a servant named Morpho for his murders. These crimes were subjected to a police cover-up."

Orlac had a brief glimpse of a tall, pale man, who stared horribly forward with eyes that appeared to have been mutilated.

"How did you learn about these events if they were hidden?"

"I am friends with the son of Inspector Tanner, who stopped Orloff. William Tanner was also a policeman, and he asked for my help on the Viscount Lebanon case from about twenty-five years ago." The sorcerer's eyes became wistful then. "I was introduced to his nephew, now a teenager. His wife's sister married a wonderful man named Kelton and young Paul seeks to follow in his uncle and great-uncle's footsteps."

"What happened to Dr. Orloff and Morpho?" asked Orlac. "Or Melissa Orloff?"

"William told me that they all perished in the confrontation with the police, but five years later, an English doctor named Harker, or Hacker, reported the death of his old professor, a man identical to Orloff named Erik Usher, who was in the company of Orloff's killer, Morpho. I learned from there that, at some point, Orloff posed as a relative of the American Usher family in order to obtain money from them to fund his research—and to bribe off those who would report his murders. He returned to this alias in his final days, when he died from the collapse of the castle he took refuge in. It appears as if Orloff, his daughter, and Morpho all perished without ever restoring Melissa's face or health.

"Dionysus Orloff had more children besides Melissa. A friend of mine who served in the RAF during the War, has met a young woman named Tania Orloff—she may be the doctor's descendant. A prominent Soviet officer with the family name may also be his son or grandson; he is paralyzed by a rivalry with a certain Captain Gogol. But one person who is surely his son is the scientist known as Feodor Orloff II—named for the doctor's father."

"Is he the donor of my hands?"

"I do not yet know. Feodor II would be a distant cousin of yours. There are nearer relatives."

Orlac breathed a sigh of relief. "You've left me filled with anticipation. I believed that you were being cruelly suspenseful, leading into revealing that I was the son of this murderous Dr. Orloff."

"Receiving his hands would be no small burden in itself, Stephen. Regarding your branch of the family, however, there were three possibilities I investigated. The first was an actor from the 1930s named Byron Orlac—he certainly possesses both of his hands, and all one has to do to confirm that is see one of his films. Next I looked for Leonard Orlac, or Orlok, an ex-Nazi scientist who curiously resembled Dionysus Orloff. He was known to have an interest in a certain project which he called *Alphaville*, but I have been unable to locate him in this dimension."

"In this *dimension*? What do you mean?"

"Do not panic, Mr. Orlac. You remember that you recruited me for my psychic talents. I possess a higher knowledge of the nature of reality than you. I have seen much that it is best you do not understand. That knowledge will be necessary to drive the darkness from your soul. Unfortunately, my third lead went nowhere as well. I went to Mexico to confront a Dr. Orlac who was using robots to kidnap people to experiment on. I put him in prison, but he has both of his hands."

"I have a diverse family—who were these other men? My... half-brothers?"

"Half-brothers, nephews, cousins... It must be someone well and truly named Orloff who gave you your hands."

Orlac leaned back. His skull was pressed tight again the skin of his aged face—he ran a bony hand through the thin white hair. He was staring almost enviously of the Sâr's preternatural youth. His hand stopped partway through sliding through his hair, and his eyes fixed on the old white scar on his wrist where the hand had been sewn on.

"Feodor II is the only one left, then, I take it," he whispered.

"Feodor Orloff II has taken many aliases. He was once known as Professor Dearborn, but has also been called George Lorenz, Richard Marlowe, and Eric Vornoff. In that latter guise, that of Dr. Vornoff, he employed a Morpho-like servant named Lobo, who has appeared independently of Vornoff in at least one other case."

Here, the Sâr Dubnotal leaned back in the aging chair in Orlac's leaky parlor.

"If you desire, Mr. Orlac, we can take leave of this place, and go to where Vornoff is currently hiding."

The look on Orlac's face was not unfamiliar to the Great Psychagogue—decades had never dulled the joy of bringing surprise to someone's expression.

"What location do you mean?"

"Across the Atlantic, in the United States, there is a party occurring in just a few hours at the home of the late Dr. Richard Vollin, hosted by a Dr. James Underhill. There are several other musicians performing there, so we'll blend in. The guests are scientists from the fringes of their respective communities. This Dr. Underhill seems to enjoy entertaining... outcasts."

Orlac stood up, then. "As a murderer, I am most certainly an outcast. You, at least, still have some public popularity."

"Not for eternity. Tastes change, and my mantle will have to change with them. The world of magic is like music, Mr. Orlac—always in motion, and usually never repeating too much."

Orlac looked his guest over, taking in his appearance for what was truly the first time. The rich brown beard and sparkling dark eyes and dusted white turban fit well with his long coat and prim tie. From one of the breast pockets of the coat was something that betrayed his exotic origins, a handkerchief of some kind which blazed with garish colors. As a warm but faint smile split the occultist's face, he gestured this handkerchief, and Orlac observed that even in the darkness of the rotting house, the colors were moving. They were shining, too, with an internal light that was growing and growing. Orlac had heard stories that the Sâr Dubnotal was a hypnotist—but he didn't want to be hypnotized, not now. But as the colors swelled and obscured the whole of his vision, he realized this wasn't hypnosis. He was leaving the old house behind, perhaps forever.

And then they were elsewhere.

Standing under a sunset, where it wasn't raining. They were on the lawn of a very large house, which was ringed by a polished marble wall. Beyond a wrought-iron gate, so much like the gate that had once adorned the front of Orlac's own house, several cars were pulling in.

The Sâr had caught onto Orlac's suspicions of hypnosis. "If I have to use my abilities to give us access to this party, I trust you will not be disturbed."

"My mind is... admittedly still catching up with me, sir. Remember, I am an old man..."

"As am I, Stephen."

"I won't be disturbed. But remember that I have seen and heard much to-day. My... uncle, or cousin, is a murderer, apparently a very grave one. What can you tell me about his... son? The man we're trying to run into."

"As Professor Dearborn, he pulled in a good deal of blood money by mur-dering subjects of bad life insurance policies. He employed a blind servant named Jake, an equivalent of his father's Morpho, to kidnap the people he mur-dered. And like his father, he used up at least two of his aliases extracting some life-giving essence from people in order to rejuvenate women he was in love with, when he operated as George Lorenz and Richard Marlowe. What he learned about hormones as Lorenz, he applied to his present goal of creating a race of super-men. Vornoff, as he calls himself now, is dangerous, but he's just another guest at this party. There are going to be many conflicting interests..."

The Sâr and Orlac moved themselves from the lawn to the house. If the Great Psychagogue had used his aforementioned hypnotic talents to blend in with the party, he did so silently and with only glances. Looking at him for too long brought a chill to Orlac's heart, even as he seemed friendly to the incoming guests. Once more, using glances, he communicated what he felt of each of the passing guests to Orlac, as if Orlac was a youthful student that he kept by his side. The pianist knew there was no whimsy in this: the Sâr, unreadable as he was, knew they were effectively behind enemy lines, and he was skilled at using his face to pass on what needed passing on. He seemed positive over the woman named Jan Compton, but not her fiancé, Dr. Bill Cortner. Another woman, named June, was apparently just as sinister as her husband, a man named Dr. Paul Talbot, and Orlac recalled that an occult expert like the Sâr would naturally be averse to the name Talbot. Finally, there was lonely Alberto Levin, yet an-other holder of a doctorate, who instantly filled even Orlac with revulsion.

They had all naturally migrated to a large living room, where there was champagne and a beautiful buffet spread. Orlac couldn't resist food like that, and with the interest of gathering information at the back of his mind, he wan-dered towards the other musicians, who were conferencing to discuss the pro-gram. One of them he recognized. He hoped that these men were too young to remember this infamy, and the face that went with it. He sat himself at the piano and played a selection of the one of the compositions of the man whose face he knew.

"My name is...Vernon Paris," Orlac said. He remembered using the name before, when word of his murders spread. "I guess I'm joining you gentlemen tonight. May I learn your names?"

"Duncan Ely," said the man he already knew, quietly. The soft-spoken man was sometimes known as "the Great Ely." He seemed charmed by Orlac's re-membrance of his piece.

"I'm Damien Ludlow," the other man said. He had a sinister look to him, and the name rang a bell for Orlac, but fortunately Ludlow chose to explain why: "I can see the look in your eye. Yes, my uncle was Eugene Ludlow, the murderous sculptor. I resemble him almost perfectly...it has not gone unremarked before."

"There are no worries between us pianists, Mr. Ludlow," Orlac said. "Our families do not define us, usually. You're not a killer—you're a musician—right?"

"Correct." There was a gleam in Ludlow's eye. "And tonight my skills will be needed to play something to accompany Dr. Marlowe's game. I certainly hope you, Mr. Paris, can produce something...atmospheric."

Orlac tried to force himself to grin. Dr. Marlowe—that had been one of Orloff's aliases. "Dr. Marlowe's game?"

Across the room, Sâr Dubnotal was sipping his drink to cover his surprise at the words he was hearing. Mrs. Talbot, face lined with age, simply couldn't believe that the Sâr hadn't known that the party was Dr. Marlowe's. "After all, Mr. Dubnotal, are you not supposed to be the Napoleon of the Unknown or something? Couldn't you see who was hosting the party you were attending with a crystal ball?"

"I'm afraid there are some things that are beyond even I, Madame Talbot," the Sâr replied. He was using his second sight to peer into Talbot's body, along with that of Dr. Levin, who had joined the two of them upon recognizing the Sâr. "Such as the fact that I was under the impression that this party was hosted by a Mr. Underhill."

"I don't know where you could have gotten that, Mr. Dubnotal."

The Sâr blinked. He found himself straining to remember where he *had* gotten it, and he didn't know why. He felt like it was tied to the fact that somewhere had spent a lot of money adding onto the Vollin house—when its owner died, it had lacked the wall and gate outside. It was the money of an aristocrat, he felt, for some reason. Perhaps Mr. Underhill was the source of Orloff's apparent wealth? Thinking about that gate, he allowed himself a moment to travel on the astral to the gate outside. A few more strangers were coming into the house, but someone had taken pains to lock the gate from the outside.

"What is Dr. Marlowe's game?" he asked, echoing Orlac's question.

"I'm sure it's something terribly exciting," Mrs. Talbot replied, shooting a glance over at her husband, who had already had too many drinks in the proximity of Mrs. Compton. "Dr. Marlowe is very mysterious. Did you know he was once into voodoo?"

"How curious. I'd certainly enjoy discussing it with him. I wonder what *loa* he prays to—perhaps Baron Samedi? I presume if that's the case that he has a sizable collection of rum, to offer to him. Perhaps we'll be lucky enough to share in such a gift." He noted that if he was onto something with that, he

"I should hope so; I do like coming to parties held by the wealthy, so that I may taste such things," Dr. Levin confessed. "Maybe the game will be like a treasure hunt—and there'll be some sort of prize at the end."

"The best games yield a prize of wisdom," the Sâr said. "I am still puzzled by my confusion of the hosts; I hope that such a prize comes to me soon."

"I'd be glad to give you easy fulfillment," came a voice then.

It was a voice lilted with an accent of Europe's east, full of many years. The entire room turned to face its source.

With a widow's peak fronting the slicked-back gray hair, there was a grandfatherly nature to "Richard Marlowe." Stephen Orlac could see that they were of the same blood, and because of that connection, he could see a chilling evil within the shrunken old scientist.

"Good evening. I am your host."

He and the Sâr shared a glance, and in that glance they communicated everything.

"As some of you have already gotten wind of, we are going to play a game tonight. It seems as if Dr. Levin and Sâr Dubnotal have deduced the point of it. You will have full access to the rum below this house if you can only find the key... but beware! There are many frightful dangers in an old house like this."

The party had swollen from those external others, and quickly the many associates of "Marlowe" scattered in search of the way to eternal booze. *El Tebib* wondered how so many persons had forgotten that, under the identity of Richard Marlowe, Orloff, or Vornoff, or Lorenz, had killed people. They acted as if they were under a spell, reduced to flimsy attractions to cheap celebrities. They were so casual around him, too—it nearly hurt his pride. Once more he considered how mystically sterile the 1950s seemed. And yet, he could not shake the idea that a terrible occult evil was at the root of things.

Probably in a literal sense. Orloff exited, trying to avoid the suspicion of mocking Dubnotal or some such thing. Dubnotal hurried across the living room to Orlac, and he whispered to him:

"We don't need a key. Let's get moving now."

"You..." And once more, fear choked Stephen Orlac's voice, even though he tried to fight it. "You think the answer's down there?"

"It has to be. Observe: Dr. Orloff still has both his hands."

Orlac had no experience in voicing what he wanted to say next: he wanted to ask if there was any point in sweeping the house to check the validity of Orloff's "frightful dangers." But before he knew it, there was a sensation that began coming over him... he began to feel a tingling in his hands.

The Sâr wasted no time in locating the entrance to Orloff's basement. With his talents, he could take shortcuts others couldn't—he knew the whole layout of this place without having to go farther than the lawn and the living room. There was no time to see if the eeriness of his directness was alarming to Orlac. Soon the two of them were going down the cramped stairs to the wooden door that hid Orloff's secret.

But Sâr Dubnotal would admit that he did not anticipate what happened next. He hadn't expected the growth of the cancer in Orlac's soul, nor the strength of those hands, which, being from a dead man, seemed frozen in time, immune to the aging that claimed their possessor.

Soon they were looped around his throat, and his physical strength failed to get him loose from those hands. They pressed tight, so that he couldn't order the man to release him. Uttering a few phrases in his mind, the Sâr swatted his hand at Orlac's wrist, and a flash of white sparks emerged. But Orlac didn't even flinch. Closing his eyes, the mystic produced enough air to speak a verbal hex, and his hand started on fire, lighting the dark staircase.

Trying not to burn Orlac, he moved his burning hand to the pianist's wrists. His eyes widened with amazement as the musician refused to flinch, until his sleeve was on fire. Dubnotal jerked away as the flames burst into life, his neck sore and bruised.

"Orlac!" he shouted then.

He could see the pianist's face: he yearned to deal with the redness bubbling up on his arm, but the hands wouldn't let him. His agony was a mental one, too.

"Go... Dubnotal..." he whispered, holding back tears. "The evil knows that I'm here..."

He was right—and that meant the evil was moving fast. It was strong, so strong that the Sâr was shocked that he hadn't detected it before.

When he walked through the door, he began to recognize what he had stepped into. This was no wine cellar, stocked with rum. It was a small, dusty chamber, lit by candles. And at the far end of it was a coffin, leaning upright against the wall. Sâr Dubnotal fixated on this, to the point where he ignored what was on the dark floor. When he reached the center of the room, the coffin began to open from within.

The creature inside wore a strange resemblance to Dionysus Orloff, though the Sâr knew he was someone else. He was dressed in a wealthy costume—one suited for an aristocrat.

"James Underhill." Of course. It seemed like something *he* would call himself: disguising him and yet still hinting at the truth. Just like turning his name backwards. Even as the thing in the coffin opened its eyes, and curled its lips back to expose its pearly fangs, Dubnotal spoke its name:

"Dracula..."

The vampire stayed within his coffin, staring out with bestial eyes at the Great Psychagogue.

"*El Tebib*," Dracula hissed. "Your presence is easier to attract than I first imagined."

"This is one of your other selves, isn't it? One of your alternate bodies?" The wise voice stayed strong, even in the presence of such a powerful entity.

"Yes. But these other bodies, which do my bidding, contain much of my strength. I am trapped here, in this chamber, but I could influence the outside world with my mind—I was the one who planted clues for you to find, regarding the Orloff family, which would cause you to lead Orlac here. Where my mind failed, I had the fortunes of Wallachia to aid me."

"You built up this house so it could trap Stephen Orlac. Why?"

"I built up everything... because I need his hands."

There was a pounding, now, at the locked wooden door. The hands Dracula referenced were pounding on the wood, with the spirit of the man they'd once belonged to obeying the will of the vampire. Dionysus Orloff's hands served Dracula—but why?

Dracula spoke again: "I need a surgeon. I have sustained... this."

And he pulled over the antique suit he was wearing, to show part of his pale shoulder. The frog-like face was aged and the body more so, but creeping across the shriveled flesh was a thick patch of swampy green. In an individual who was not undead, it would resemble an infected scab. But the cold bodies of vampires couldn't be corrupted in such a way. They remained vital even if their bodies were not alive.

"An enemy of mine spent much time studying my kind," Dracula intoned. "He was able to inflict this. I cannot heal from it, and this body is waning. I do not intend to lose control over it. Orlac will heal me, and then, before I destroy the one who injured me, I will take preemptive steps for my further plans by destroying you."

Sâr Dubnotal went into action, his mind moving before his body. If he could find a stake, or conjure one, then it would be over. Whatever had burned Dracula *was* serious, and it would keep him down until he could deliver the killing blow. Dracula had wanted to trap Orlac, but he had merely trapped himself.

But the Sâr couldn't move, because he hadn't noticed the sigil that had been drawn on the chamber floor.

He noticed it the same time that he noticed the knocking at the door had stopped. Now, there was a key at the door—the key that the guests above were sent looking for. Slowly, the door slid open, and Feodor Orloff II crept inside. Stephen Orlac followed, being dragged along by his hands. They walked so as to stand before Dubnotal, flanking Dracula's coffin.

"Don't be afraid, Orlac," Dubnotal said. "I can't move—aside from my mouth—but I don't need to move to do what I do."

Orlac once more couldn't speak—his voice was smothered by heavy breathing.

"Sometimes everything can be taken away from you in an instant," Dracula said. "It was just a single vehicular accident that took away Orlac's hands and opened him up to being a monster. All because Dr. Cerral happened to have the preserved hands of the awful Dr. Orloff and obsessive, half-mad plans for them. Now you will see your downfall, after all these decades, simply because you chose to dedicate your time to him." The vampire lurched forward, barely able to take a step forward. "This was supposed to be a minor case, wasn't it? The spot on his mind wasn't that large or that dark, was it?"

"What are you babbling about, Dracula?"

The vampire took his time in answering.

"The key to the puzzle, to the game, is the fact that centuries ago, I tried to manufacture... a duplicate of myself," intoned Dracula. "The result was a twisted monster, barely resembling me in form and yet sharing my curse, my thirst for blood. It was even more savage. I couldn't give it any other name than Orlok. A guttural, ugly name for a guttural, ugly thing. Nonetheless, this thing was like my son." The aged face was serious and yet still somehow reflected humor. "When I say that Orlok was capable of reproduction with ordinary humans, you certainly understand what I want you to infer. It is not too much to expect that over a few generations the name could shift from Orlok... to Orloff."

Feodor Orloff had evidently already known this, but Sâr Dubnotal and Stephen Orlac were unaware. More than any other time, the Sâr wished he could move his body.

"In trying to duplicate myself, I additionally learned the secret of weaving homunculi," Dracula said. "These artificial servants, often blind or mindless, and always brutish, I have spread throughout the world. The names Lobo and Morpho are carried by many of them. Even the accursed Frankenstein employed one of the men named Morpho at some point."

"That does not matter now," Dubnotal said suddenly. "Everything falls into place—Stephen, you must fight back. It will be a hard fight, for you fight against the blood of the King of Vampires... but you can't become like him! Do not let your ancestor seize you, and don't aid the monster in his recovery."

"Ignore him, my child," the vampire interjected. "Come to me... I know of your secret liaisons with dark powers. Dubnotal was not the first you approached. You spoke with Julian Karswell and Hazel Hexen, and they taught you that the power in your hands would lead you to great things..."

"No, Orlac!" Dubnotal cried. "You are not those hands. You are not Orloff. You are an artist, a player of instruments..."

"He's right, *El Tebib*," Orlac said then. "I learned the secrets of black magic. I did so deliberately. I began to understand, as a result of my ordeal, that I was a killer. And I began to take sincere pleasure in killing. It's like I told you— I simply lied about being remorseful. I could not resist Dracula offering me a fresh young body, to replace this old and mismatched flesh, so I could play my music again... and so I can be better suited to resume killing."

The Sâr was shaken to silence.

"This is the end for you," Dracula said. "My knowledge of the mystic arts can revive the spirit in Orlac's hands, and the late Dionysus Orloff will operate on my injury. Orloff was a surgeon who could operate on injury caused by the sort of powers that can harm vampires... after all, it was his study of ancient secrets that allowed him to survive his long century on this world. Orloff's son will aid in the operation. Then I will kill you, and with the spells I *drink* from your corpse, pry from your blood, I will destroy the one who did this to me—the cursed Frankenstein."

Dubnotal saw his chance: Dracula was speaking too often. There were other incarnations of the Vampire King he'd met, who never spoke and instead only growled like beasts. He had a preference for them in this moment. Orlac was gone—given over to the curse within him. There was nothing in his soul now that could be used against him.

But Feodor Orloff II had something. Dubnotal could sense it. He didn't want to weaponize it—ordinarily he wouldn't. Here he had no choice.

Feodor Orloff heard a voice behind him, then, coming from beside the coffin. "Father?"

He turned, and suddenly, there was another object in the room. How he had not noticed the cage before, he did not know—how he had not recognized that his son was trapped inside it, either, was a mystery. "Feodor!" He exclaimed. Indeed, Feodor II had also named his son Feodor. "What are you doing here? You're supposed to be training in our homeland with the Communist space program."

"Help me, father!" the young man exclaimed. He appeared to be on the verge of tears—Orloff II could see that his son had marks on his face, deep cuts. The scientist and murderer looked at Sâr Dubnotal, and frowned. An idea appeared in his head.

"Why have you done this?" he asked his ancestor.

He never heard what the vampire objectively said in reply: instead he heard him say, "Even my descendants must be kept in line."

"Kept in line? I have been your humble servant for years now. That is why you allowed me the use of Lobo."

Orloff could not see that Dracula was vehemently denying these nonsensical accusations, but the old man could see only his progeny in torment. "You betrayed my trust, by losing Lobo... even if he was easy to create, I am offended by this loss. I shouldn't squander even my scraps on filth like you." And Dubnotal kept weaving the image, so that the vampire leaned forward: "I found great pleasure in torturing your son."

He couldn't let his own guilt stain the image. To pervert someone's family was cruel, but he knew what Orloff kept in his pocket, just in case. He removed it now.

With a savage cry betraying a strength beyond his years, Dr. Orloff charged at Dracula, and with a single swift motion, plunged the small wooden stake into his heart.

For a second it seemed like it was all over. But then Sâr Dubnotal found he still could not move. It hadn't been Dracula's power that had kept him trapped in this floor-sigil—it had been Orlac's. Now Orlac moved towards Dr. Orloff, even as the illusion of Feodor Orloff III vanished. Before Dubnotal could stop him the possessor of the dead man's hands placed those hands on his relative's neck. "Now I'm going to make up for what that octopus didn't finish." And with a sharp jerk, he broke the old man's vertebrae.

Sâr Dubnotal could no longer hesitate. He stretched out with his mind, and performed a very old technique. Recently, he had begun meeting members of the so-called "Uncountables"—the *Incomputare*. They maintained that all things could be simplified into perspective; how one viewed the mystic world determined the rules of magic. Along these lines, there was a spell that relied on perceiving the source of one's life as a small lamp-bulb. A glass sphere full of a soft light, delicate.

Because he perceived this light as his life, it *was* his life. When he broke it, as easy as crushing a handful of snow, his body could not keep living. It was painless—nearly unnoticeable, in the moment. Nearly.

Far beyond the room full of corpses, Mrs. Talbot, Dr. Levin, and several of the other scientists were on the front lawn of the house of Richard Vollin. What a miserable old place. Now it crawled with hordes of pale creatures who had wasted no time in feeding upon the warm blood of the others who'd come here. As they panted in this brief pause before they made their escape, some of them caught a glimpse of a flash of light as Sâr Dubnotal blew open the door to the cellar. He emerged slowly, and the friends and family of the King of Vampires prepared to do battle with him. Most of the guests did not stay to see such a battle, but those who had heard of him forgot their concept of him as an idle celebrity. He would win this day, as he always did.

June Talbot turned to see that someone, someone she *did* recognize for celebrity, had also escaped. "Mr. Ely!" she cried to the pianist. "I-it's good to see that a man of your talent got away from those... those..."

But before she could finish, she saw what she was sure to be the weirdest thing she'd ever see in life. The Great Ely gave a wide and enthusiastic grin, and brushed past her. In doing so, he nearly knocked her over, until Dr. Levin took her hand.

"Did you see that?" she asked. Her mind swirled. Things that like, thing she couldn't explain, were becoming commonplace. Maybe her mind was going—maybe Paul was right, and she *was* getting old.

Time would pass, and most of these people would forget their horror. Trauma changes everyone, and in many people it takes away memory. Others change different.

As he turned the keys of the Great Ely's car, Stephen Orlac felt younger than ever. He had found his passion again.

This charming historical vignette by Nathan Cabaniss takes place right after President Monroe invited Lafayette to visit the United States to celebrate the nation's 50th anniversary. The Tour was a grand and glorious affair, ending with Lafayette celebrating his 68th birthday on 6 September at a reception with President John Quincy Adams. Lafayette took back with him some soil from Bunker Hill, to be sprinkled later on his own grave. Congress, at Monroe's request, voted him a grant of $200,000 and a tract of public lands in Florida, which was later deemed invalid and reclaimed.

Nathan Cabaniss: *Hero of Two Worlds*

August 1824

Gilbert du Motier, Marquis de La Fayette,later to be known simply as "Lafayette, shifted on the bed in his cabin to soothe the ache in his knees, but each rock of the mercantile ship he traveled upon only served to further aggravate the pain. It was a constant now in his life as an old man. If it wasn't his knees giving him problems, it was his back, or his fingers. Pain was a frequent companion for Lafayette, an old friend he could never quite fully leave behind. He was familiar with pain and its many permutations. As a young man, his father was taken from him, killed by a British cannonball on the field of battle while he was still in the crib. Roughly forty years after that, he lost his wife, Adrienne, to illness on a chilly Christmas morning. He had led men in war, had been injured by muskets and swords alike, and had been imprisoned and defamed... Several lifetimes somehow condensed into one. All these years and all that struggle, and what did Lafayette have to show for it? Nothing but aches and pains, and naught but a handful of drops when he got up to make his water on fitful nights.

Frustrated by his aches, Lafayette pulled himself from his bed. His joints popped and flared as he stretched, burning alight with new flames of pain, but at least they briefly dulled the persistent ache deep in his bones. He grabbed an overcoat and made his way above-decks. He braced himself for the smell of dead fish and brine, but the sea was fresh and almost sweet-smelling. The sky was clear as well, with nary a single cloud hanging between the canopy of stars spread like diamonds tossed on a black velvet rug.

He paced the ship from bow to stern countless times, shifting his gaze from the endless night sky to the quivering black mirror beneath. He was setting sail for America, returning for a grand tour of the colonies (no, that's not right; of the *states*) for the young country's fiftieth anniversary as a nation unto itself. Fifty years, half-a-century... had it really been that long ago?

Lafayette remembered the first time he had set sail to the fledgling nation's shores; so eager he was that all he could do was to keep himself from jumping into the sea and paddling ahead of the ship. Was he so restless because he believed in the cause of freedom and liberty, or was he merely seeking revenge against the British for the death of a father he had never known? All these years later, and he couldn't say for certain. He would like to believe it was the former, but he also recognized the darkness in himself, the part that—on some level—relished the idea of battle. Walking the razor's edge of life and death, meeting his opponents and determining if they could tread upon that fine line as well, or be pushed permanently to one side.

He shook his head, as if to rid himself of the very thought. He was too old for any of that now. Of course, he had thought himself too old before, and had attempted to retire to a quieter life. But for whatever reason, he had constantly been pulled back in. There was always a revolution, always more cries for freedom and justice, and he could never fully resist it. Once, he had felt it was his true calling. Now, it felt like a never-ending cycle. A wheel that turned endlessly and ground him beneath its tread until all that was left were old bones and unfulfilled promises.

Lafayette ceased his pacing, and turned his gaze skyward. What wouldn't he give to float upwards to the Heavens, see his father and mother and wife and all those whom the wheel of time had taken from him... What wouldn't he give to be free of that wheel, and finally know peace in his time.

A red twinkle in the sky caught his attention. He thought nothing of it at first, but soon found that he couldn't look away. The sight transfixed him, freezing him where he stood on the bow of the ship. He felt the strangest sensation, almost as if something were pulling him. Some invisible hand reaching out of the sky and lifting him upwards, rushing across vast distances towards the red diamond floating in the sea of stars.

He felt faint for a moment, and caught himself on the guard-rail, but still his gaze held on the red diamond. Suddenly, he felt the ship drop right out from under him, followed by the sea and the very Earth itself. His consciousness shot like a ball fired from a cannon, hurtling up toward the infinite black abyss and the red diamond at its center...

Lafayette awoke with a start, lying face down in red sand. He was in what looked to be a mountainous desert, a rust-colored collection of dunes and rocky outcroppings that was at once familiar, and yet totally alien. Had he passed out on the ship traveling the Atlantic? Crashed onto the shores of some strange American land as yet undiscovered? That couldn't have been possible: there was no ocean in sight, no bodies of water of any kind. No evidence that anything living had been anywhere in this vicinity in some time. He looked up at the night sky, the stars that had held his attention so raptly before, but something wasn't right. Their position was vastly different. The stars themselves were different.

He pulled himself up from the sand, expecting a war against his own body as he struggled to rise, but there was no pain. He felt no flare in his knees, no ache in his bones, no fire in his lungs at the exertion. He stood upright with alarming ease, never having felt better. Lafayette looked down at himself, and was alarmed to see not the body of a 67-year-old man, but that of someone much younger. He still wore the housecoat and pajamas he had on his back from the ship, but he quickly threw them over his head, standing naked in the strange desert of red sand. His stomach was fit and trim, his legs limber and powerful. Lafayette hadn't been in such shape in over thirty years. His heart raced in his chest, pumping blood throughout his newfound body, filling him with strength and vitality. Where was he? What was this marvelous, alien place?

Before he could ponder his situation anymore, a sound caught his ear. He turned in time to see the point of what looked to be a spear rocketing at the space between his eyes. Without thinking, he reacted: leaping backwards, knowing the distance wouldn't be enough to escape being skewered like a fish at the end of a harpoon. Except that the distance was more than enough to dodge the spear's tip. Before he knew it, Lafayette had cleared ten feet of ground in the blink of an eye.

Astonished at his new-found abilities, he wasn't able take the moment to enjoy it, for now he got a good look at what held the spear so intent to skewer him to the ground. His breath was stolen at the sight. A massive, four-armed creature sat upon an eight-legged steed. The rider was a brilliant green, with massive tusks jutting out from its alien mouth. It had no clothing other than various harnesses and straps, from which swords and daggers of all sizes were stored. It stared at Lafayette with bug-like eyes that moved independently on either side of its head, confounded at its new prey that leaped from one end of the landscape to the other with the deftness of a grasshopper.

Lafayette himself was confounded, enough to distract him from noticing the four-armed rider clearing the distance between them in no time, the point of its spear once more aiming for the Marquis as the creature held it like a knight at a joust. In an instant, Lafayette's battle-hardened instincts kicked in, and he leapt into the air with alarming speed. The spear passed just underneath, barely missing him as his body shot up and over the massive creature riding its alien steed. Not eager to continue dodging lunges of a spear from a physically-greater opponent, Lafayette reached down as he leapt, grabbing the spear as it passed beneath him. He pulled it up with him as he arched through the sky, ripping the four-armed creature from its mount, which kept on running until it was out of sight.

Before the creature could regain its footing, Lafayette hurled the spear back at it. He had no other weapons, but the missile was nearly three times Lafayette's own height, and would have been otherwise useless to him in combat. His aim was true, but the creature was swift—it swung all four arms in a cross swipe, shattering the spear in mid-air. Visibly angry now, the creature drew a sword from one of its many straps, and bounded for Lafayette.

Its sheer size meant that it only took a few steps to reach him. The Marquis leapt again, bounding over the creature's head with the ease of a bird taking flight, but the creature was wise to his game now. It dashed the sword upwards, and Lafayette nearly found himself skewered again. He deflected the sword with his forearm, trying to hit the blunted side but still drawing blood in a thin cut.

Lafayette's feet barely touched the ground before the four-armed creature was at him again, sword gleaming against the strange and unfamiliar sky. It was only years of hard-won intuition that kept Lafayette from losing his head; he ducked right as the creature's sword carved a crescent moon in the air above him. If Lafayette were to survive this encounter, then he himself would need a weapon. Looking at the various blades strapped to the four-armed creature, Lafayette had an idea of where he could get one.

The creature swiped the air again, and Lafayette dove between the creature's legs. As he slid beneath, he reached up and grabbed the hilt of a weapon that jutted from the creature's belt-harness. It was a differently-styled sword than the one the creature was using, long and thin and not unlike a rapier. It was unbelievably light, allowing Lafayette even greater speed. He dashed the blade across the creature's back, and it let out a wail.

The creature swiped the air behind it, but Lafayette had already leaped a distance of several meters. The Marquis gave a few quick strokes of his sword, before raising the hilt to his face. Lafayette might as well have been born with a sword in his hand--no matter how tall the creature was, no matter how many limbs it had, it now had to prove itself against *him*.

The creature didn't immediately rush to attack as before. It paused for the first time in their battle, raising upright and reaching its remaining three hands to the belts and sheathes strapped to its body. It drew three more blades: another long sword, a short one and a dagger. It lunged at Lafayette, blades glimmering in a hurricane of flashing metal—testing the very limits of the Marquis' expertise. Were it not for his increased speed and agility, he would have been carved into many pieces by the creature's four blades.

Their duel lasted for what felt like time untold. Neither opponent found any advantage over the other, and thus the blades clashed endlessly, causing sparks to alight against the night sky. A lucky cut found the wrist of the four-armed creature, causing it to drop one of its long swords. The tide of battle shifted in Lafayette's favor just so, and the Marquis advanced with everything he had, jumping from one side of the creature to the other, raining down blow after blow in an endless fury. He worried the exertion would tire him out more quickly, but it had the opposite effect: Lafayette felt more vital and alive with each swing of his sword.

Another slash against one of the creature's hands sent its short sword spinning through the air. It was beginning to tire out, and Lafayette didn't relent. He thrust his sword through the creature's other wrist, causing it to drop its last long sword. Lafayette then ducked, and with two quick strokes, slashed the soft parts of the creature's ankles. It howled, and fell to its knees, bringing the massive creature almost to Lafayette's eye-level.

Defeated, Lafayette paused to let the creature gather itself from the ground, hobble away and lick its wounds. But the thing was either too stubborn or too stupid: it lashed out its arm with its only remaining weapon, the small dagger. In a flash, Lafayette whipped his sword forward and found purchase in the space between the creature's eyes. The bug-like orbs dulled as blue blood dribbled down its face and chest. Lafayette placed his foot against the creature's shoulder, and pulled his sword free. The thing fell to the ground with a heavy thud.

The rush of blood throughout his body began to wane. It was something he never truly got used to, no matter how many times he had lived through it to tell the tale afterwards. He felt conflicted, killing the thing so coldly; Lafayette had always fancied himself a gentlemen. But the thing was so monstrous, and it had attacked him so viciously and without any other provocation. And he had given the creature the chance to flee, only to be assailed again for his troubles. If the tables were turned and it was the four-armed creature standing over a wounded Lafayette, it would have not hesitated in dashing his brains against the red sand, surely.

No... that was no reason to meet it with equal savagery. He shook as light crested the horizon, turning everything blood-red with the morning dawn. Violence had been with him so long that it was hard to see life through any other lens. He remembered the young man who fled his home country to take part in a fight he had no real stake in. Leaving his equally young wife and child behind; disappointing his family and countrymen. Desperate to prove himself, no matter how many bodies gathered in his wake.

He was that young man again, his youth restored through whatever strange means had brought him to this place. The rush it brought with it turned within him, twisting into something bitter and anxious. The duel had stirred something inside Lafayette... something that had been dulled and hidden away with age. He could deny it all he wanted, but the truth was plain: he *relished* the fight.

He surveyed his surroundings, baffled at the barrage of impossible phenomena that had occurred in such a short span of time. There was no explanation to account for how he had gotten to this strange and alien land, or even where this strange and alien land was in the first place.

"*You're on the fourth planet from the sun,*" a voice called out.

Lafayette turned with a start, sword at the ready, but was halted by the sight behind him. It was a young man clad in an advantageous manner with the most handsome face in the world: a privileged physiognomy, a tender gaze and an affable expression which prejudiced Lafayette in his favor from the outset; at the same time, the grandeur and majesty of this person inspired respect and confidence in him.

"*The red planet,*" it continued. "*Barsoom. Malacandra. I believe you call it Mars.*"

Dumbfounded, the words barely escaped Lafayette's mouth. He raised his sword, hesitant. "What... what is this? Who are you?"

"*There is no need to be alarmed. I mean you no harm,*" it said. "*I have many names, but the beings of this planet know me as Zachiel, guardian of the pathway between the worlds.*"

Unbelieving, Lafayette let his sword drop to his side, but still held firm to the hilt. Zachiel may have indeed meant him no harm, but Lafayette kept his guard up all the same. "I'm on... Mars? How is such a thing even possible?"

"*There are many pathways to the red planet... some yet to be discovered by your kind. But it was I who brought you here.*"

"You?" Lafayette asked.

"*I am one of the genii—beyond time and beyond age. My abilities are vast and wide within this place,*" Zachiel explained. "*The true question is not how, but rather... why?*"

Lafayette cocked his head, puzzled. He turned to the four-armed creature, sprawled on the sand. "You did all of this? Restored my youth, brought me across the stars to this place?"

"*Essentially.*"

"For what purpose?"

There was a pause. Zachiel's face seemed to darken while he considered his answer. "*I seek to give solace to those who are troubled, or frighten those lacking decisive instincts into action. I provide environs to such souls for them to conquer what ails them.*"

"And what is it that ails myself, in your opinion?"

"*You are conflicted within. A hero of two worlds.*"

Lafayette's blood rose again. "Oh, really? And just how did you come to that conclusion? How do you presume to know me or my inner self? I would remind you that my first experience at war resulted in the freedom of a country from the most powerful military force on my world, so have a care how you address me, Sir."

"*As it was in your youth, your haughtiness acts as nothing more than a mask to hide your fears. Hide behind it all you want, but you'll never hope to face your fears if your own face is covered.*"

Lafayette began to offer another, even more fiery retort, but stopped himself. Deep down, he knew Zachiel was right. He inhaled sharply to calm himself. God, being young again made one susceptible to the baser instincts. The movements were so quick and easy, the emotions so amplified and powerful. It was equally intoxicating and maddening.

"I... apologize. This is a lot to take in at once." Lafayette paused, looking towards the Martian horizon. He was still annoyed, but had a better hold of his temper. "I assume that, instead of simply telling me the reason you've brought me here, you want me to discern it for myself."

"*A truth holds more power if arrived at through no other faculties that one's own.*"

"All right, then," Lafayette replied. "I assume this charade is meant to teach me something on the importance of pressing on. To remind myself that life is a constant struggle, and surviving it requires constant motion."

To this, Zachiel said nothing. He remained still, hovering on the hillside as the radiance engulfing him touched the night sky.

Lafayette continued: "The only problem is I've been in constant motion for almost my entire life. I longed for the struggle, for the fight... for something, *anything* to give my life some measure of meaning. God, I never—"

He stopped, choking back tears. Images flashed through his mind, visions of his family: his father, marching proud on the battlefield, his military garb immaculate and pristine. Except, he had never known his father. He could scarcely recall what the man looked like. The image he had was one he created from the time he was a boy, and had held onto for all these years. An image that had never really existed, for all he knew.

The sword slipped from his grasp, and Lafayette fell to his knees. "I never stopped to appreciate all that I had. I was always moving towards the next thing, always looking for what I thought I'd lost, I never saw what was right in front of me all along. If that was the 'lesson' you wished me to learn, then job well done. Consider it learned."

Having remained silent for some time, Zachiel finally spoke:

"*I do not seek to teach lessons or pass judgment. I care not to offer forgiveness or absolution, nor could I even if I wished to. My only aim is to help those struggling in their journey.*"

"How is any of this helpful?" Lafayette said, just barely above a whisper.

"*It's true that you have a dark and terrible drive inside you, but it's that same drive that's propelled you to whatever greatness you have achieved. You are the hero of two worlds, and thus, there are two worlds within you. The light and the dark.*"

With that, the world around Lafayette began to fall away. No, it was Lafayette himself who was falling, tumbling through a bottomless void. He caught one last glimpse of Zachiel, and continued falling.

Lafayette awoke with a start. He was back in his cabin on the merchant ship. He saw his own face when he looked up, almost as if he were staring directly into a mirror.

"Father? Are you well?"

Lafayette rubbed his eyes, vision still foggy from sleep. When he opened them again, he saw the face of his son, Georges Washington. The boy (no, the man... his eldest son was rapidly approaching fifty) looked worried.

Lafayette shook his head, waving his son away. "Fine, fine. Fitful sleep, as always."

Georges Washington sighed, looking greatly relieved. It was maddening how everyone made a fuss over Lafayette now, all merely because he was older. His son's mood quickly changed, as he smiled from ear to ear. "Hurry and dress yourself. We've just made port at Staten Island!"

Lafayette nodded, and his son left the cabin. The Marquis pulled himself up to a sitting position on his bed. The old pain flared up again, but somehow, it wasn't as bad this morning. It dulled into something familiar, something that was as much a part of him as old memories and the fingers on his hands.

He studied the cabin surrounding him. It felt real enough. Surely this wasn't another dream... if what he had experienced the previous night was in fact a dream. He wasn't sure. It had felt so palpable and real in the moment. Sitting in his cabin now, he could remember the smell of the Martian atmosphere, and the feel of red sand between his toes. That strange being, Zachiel, had called himself the "guardian of the pathway between the worlds."

Lafayette wondered...

But no matter. he stood from the bed, feeling more spry with each successive movement. He stretched, burning alight with new flames of pain, but it didn't bother him as it did before. He felt as if a great weight had been taken from his shoulders, and now he could stand tall like he used to.

Lafayette stood at the precipice of the stage, staring at a blank curtain. On the other side stood a crowd of eighty thousand gathered in the streets of New York, all shouting his name. He could scarcely imagine it, a crowd of that size. The number seemed as impossible as a voyage to Mars.

He hesitated in opening the curtain. The Marquis had led men into battle, had stared down angry mobs and their guillotines, had won them over at the last second with a quick wit and a bit of luck. So much he had accomplished in this life. Was there anything left still to do? He didn't know the answer. Perhaps one day he will take the stage for the last time. But that would not be today.

For he was the Marquis de Lafayette, and he was not done with living just yet.

Matthew Dennion has often speculated about the mysterious figure of Colonel Bozzo-Corona, the preternatural, and seemingly ageless, leader of the Black Coats, that vast, criminal organization invented by Paul Féval. None of his earlier tales, however, have been as challenging as the one which follows...

Matthew Dennion: *A Case of Mistaken Identity*

Paris, 1985

Teddy Verano shook his head as he pulled into the Charles de Gaulle Airport international terminal. He still could not believe that man he was going to pick up had willingly agreed to let himself be put into the situation that he had described to him.

Teddy saw the man he was going to pick up standing on the curb outside of the American Airlines gate. He was of average height and build, with silver hair, and wore a long, brown trench coat that covered most of his body. Teddy had described his Peugeot to the man, so that when he pulled over to the curb, the other simply walked over, opened the door, and stepped inside the car.

Teddy's detective skills kicked in and he scanned the man for any information that he could gather. When he had been trying to track him down, he'd researched all that he could find about him, but despite his best efforts, the only thing he'd found was his address, phone number, and the fact that he was an antique dealer. The man's movements did not betray much, other than he was hiding something almost a meter long under his coat.

Teddy pulled away from airport and began talking to his passenger.

"Are you sure that you want to go through with this exchange? I mean, the group that we are talking about is comprised of the most dangerous criminals in the world. The likes of the DGSE, MI6 and the CIA are not able to touch them."

The passenger shrugged and replied with an odd accent that Teddy was unable to place:

"The Black Coats are of no concern to me. As an organization, they have no interest in me. It is only their head, Colonel Bozzo-Corona, who desires to see me."

Like his father before him, Teddy had investigated and battled many bizarre and dangerous entities in his time as a detective, but none of them made his spine shiver like the near-mythical Colonel Bozzo-Corona.

The passenger closed his eyes and took several deep breaths. Teddy asked, "Are you OK? Do you have a headache or something?"

The man shook his head.

"Something like that, but there is nothing that can be done about it." He opened his eyes and looked at Teddy. "Tell me again about how your friends came across the Colonel. I am interested in that other individual that they mistook him for."

Teddy shook his head. He wondered if the man he had contacted, picked up, and was likely driving to his death, was mentally challenged. Usually, when Teddy told people about some of the strange, almost supernatural cases that he had investigated, they either didn't believe him, or thought he was joking. His passenger seemed to believe everything that he told him without question.

Teddy took a deep breath and retold the story of his friends' capture as earnestly as he could.

"My friends Mike Pearson and Reggie Bannister are known as 'Hunters' in the United States. They hunt supernatural creatures and dispose of them as they come across them. While most Hunters travel across the county, disposing of ghosts, demons, vampires and various other creatures, Reg and Mike have been hunting a strange creature known as the Tall Man for the past five years. The Tall Man is difficult to define. He is a large Caucasian man with stark white hair and he is seemingly immortal. Reg and Mike have inflicted damage on him that would kill a normal human. They have shot, stabbed, and even run him over with a car on numerous occasions, but despite the damage done to his body, he quickly recovers from whatever injuries have been inflicted on him."

Teddy waited for his passenger to say something, but the man simply continued to stare out the front of the windshield. Teddy shrugged and continued his tale: "They have also uncovered evidence the Tall Man was alive as far back as 19th Century. To be honest, they have no idea how old he truly is."

Teddy stopped talking for a moment as he turned a corner. After he had completed the turn, he continued: "The Tall Man also has other strange powers and abilities, including an array of flying spheres with various weapons in them the he can control somehow and an army of strange creatures that do his bidding."

Despite the claims that Teddy was making, his passenger simply continued to sit quietly and take in everything that he was saying. Teddy's stomach tightened up as they drew closer to their dark destination. "The American Hunters work as sort of a loose-knit organization. They exchange information on certain supernatural phenomena and sometimes work together. When Mike and Reg were on the trail of the Tall Man, they briefly worked with a hunter who is a friend of mine named John Winchester. I have known John for several years. When he was in Paris, he hired me to help him track down a Yellow-Eyed Demon who was feeding his blood to young boys and burning their mothers alive. When we worked together, I told him about some of the strange things that I had come across, including Colonel Bozzo- Corona. When Reg and Mike were talking to John about the Tall Man, he pointed out the similarities to them between the two. Reg and Mike were obsessed with finding the Tall Man and John put them in touch with me.

"When I met them, we discussed both the Tall Man and the Colonel. I do admit there were some similarities between the two. They both appear to be older men who, despite their age, are in tremendous physical shape. They have both seemingly lived for a very long time and may well be immortal. They both control strange and devious organizations. While I was not convinced by the evidence that they were one and the same person, I agreed that the similarities between the two were enough to warrant further investigation. I gave them the address of one of the locations in Paris that I suspected may have been a Black Coat safehouse. I suggested that we could stake it out for several days and then decide what to do next. However, they exhibited that typical American bravado of charging into a situation without fully understanding it..."

Teddy looked over at his companion, "No offense."

The man shrugged, "I am not an American. I simply live there for now."

Teddy sighed, hoping that his passenger would catch the part about not fully understanding something before rushing into it, but the idea seemed lost on the man. Teddy pulled into the parking lot of what appeared to be an empty warehouse as he finished up his story:

"Reg and Mike took off without me to storm this place with nothing more than shotguns and chainsaws. The Black Coats easily overpowered them, but rather than then kill them, the Colonel took them hostage when he found out that they were connected to me. He then contacted me and said that he knew of my detective skills and suggested that, if I was able to find you and convince you to come Paris, he would trade Mike and Reg for you. I protested saying that I would not trade an innocent man for anyone, but he said that you were far from innocent, and that you would willingly accept the trade."

Teddy tapped the man on his shoulder so that he was looking at him in the eye, "I think that trading you for Mike and Reg is a death sentence. Why are you willing to do this for two people you don't even know?"

The man's piercing gaze held Teddy's eyes in place as he replied:

"Colonel Bozzo-Corona and I have been on a collision course for a very long time. I had thought to face him at much later date, on more neutral ground, at a time when I would be stronger than I am now. If the Colonel is able to kill me, he will become the most powerful man on the face of the Earth. With his organization, he could likely place all of humanity under his control. Your friends and the information they possess on this Tall Man also intrigue him as much as it does me. The Colonel knew that, once you told me about the Tall Man, I would have to accept his challenge in order to obtain information on this other immortal."

The man looked away from Teddy and opened the car door.

"Come on. It's time that we got your friends back and ended the Colonel's power play."

Teddy shrugged and followed the man to warehouse door. The man knocked on the door and Teddy took a step back when a gigantic figure opened it. Teddy had never seen the Marchef in person, but from the tales he had heard of the Colonel's high executioner and personal bodyguard, the detective was sure that this was him. Seeing a huge blade at the Marchef's side, Teddy reached for his handgun, but the man in the trench coat held up his hand.

"That will not be necessary, detective. This man will not harm you. At least, he won't harm you until my business with his superior has been concluded."

Teddy's hand moved away from his gun and the Marchef motioned for them to follow him. They followed the giant down a dark corridor to a large black door. The Marchef held up his hand for the two men to stop and then he pointed at the man in the trench coat.

Teddy shook his head, "No! Not until we have Mike and Reg!"

The Marchef nodded and then walked through the door. The door opened and, a moment later, Mike and Reg came running out of it. Teddy looked past his friends to see the Colonel sitting in a chair in the center of large, empty room with a sword placed across his lap.

The Marchef came through the door next and once more pointed at the man in the trench coat. Teddy looked over at him and said:

"MacLeod, I don't know what's going on here, but I can't just let you go in there to be executed." He looked at Mike and Reg. "Together the four of us might be able to fight our way out of this."

Teddy took half a step toward the door when MacLeod's left arm shot out and blocked him. With his right arm, MacLeod pulled a sword out from under his coat. He looked at Teddy and said:

"Take your friends and wait in the parking lot. If I survive this battle, I will need to question them more about this other immortal."

MacLeod stepped forward and opened the door. As the door was closing, Teddy saw the Colonel stand up from his chair with his sword in hand as MacLeod held his sword over his head and stated:

"There can be only one!'

Brian Gallagher continues to chronicle the adventures of Marie Nizet's Captain Liatoukine—from her ground-breaking 1879 novel Captain Vampire, *Black Coat Press, ISBN 978-1-934543-01-6)—moving forward in time. While each story can be read independently, the sequence is most impressive, starting with "City of the Nosferatu (Vol. 10), "The Trial of Van Helsing" (Vol. 11), "The Stake and the Sickle" (Vol. 12) and "The Berlin Vampire" (Vol. 13). Here is the latest installment...*

Brian Gallagher: *The Death of Von Bork*

August 1979

In her catsuit, the intruder effortlessly clambered back out of the window of the French Riviera mansion she had just robbed. Bag slung across her back, she paused to ensure that the security camera would have a picture of her. She pretended to fumble with her mask; she let the outside camera take a shot of her face. She jumped to the ground—a feat that would have broken the legs of any normal human—and bounded out of the drive. She could hear the alarms going off. Splendid! She could have robbed the wealthy family of their precious jewels without setting off any alarms. However, she wanted to make sure that she was seen. She bounded off down the drive, and merrily jogged down the road, startling some passers-by. Turning a corner she climbed up a wall—seemingly effortlessly—and onto a roof and was seen no more.

Just a few minutes later, a rather elegant black-haired lady carrying a couple of shopping bags got into a nearby black Lotus Esprit and drove off, heading towards Monaco. At the wheel, she laughed and laughed. She enjoyed driving. She often used her private chauffeur to drive her around. However, for this work, that was inadvisable. And she did rather enjoy these night rides. Tonight, she was going a bit fast. A police motorcyclist waved her down. The policeman strolled up to the car window.

"Good morning Madame. You understand that you were breaking the speed limit just now?"

"Was I?"

She had intended that to be charming, but unsurprisingly the policeman was not amused.

"Please step out of the car," he said.

Now here was a thing. Should she kill him for his impertinence? No, of course not. Killings would bring a lot of unnecessary attention to the area—any linkage with the theft of the family jewels last night would not be good. Not that she would be recognized as the thief, she had a different face on right now, but nothing should be left to chance. Her other talents would have to be used.

"Officer, everything is in order surely?" she smiled her most winning smile and showed her license.

The young policeman looked at it, and back at her, and was suddenly overwhelmed. He would do anything for this woman.

"Of course, Mrs. Adler, I just wanted to make sure you were having no problems."

"Thank you for your concern, officer, but I am fine. I must go now."

And then she drove off, taking care to not to speed again. Best not to push her luck. The policeman himself stood dazed for a moment. He shook his head, and got back on his motorcycle to resume his patrol.

The next day, she was in her own mansion in Monaco, her booty laid out on a coffee table in front her. She also had the late editions of the newspapers. They had held the presses for this story. *France-Soir* had the banner headline *Irma Vep strikes again!* And there was a picture of her from last night. At that moment, she did not look like the picture. She could do that. She was delighted with all the coverage—even more so than the actual robbery. She looked up at the TV news. They, too, were discussing the robbery in fevered terms. They were pondering how could Irma Vep be committing such robberies in 1979? Had the once-famous criminal gang of the Vampires reformed? Could this be some descendent of Irma Vep, its most notorious female member?

She knew the answers to all of these questions: No. Not least because Irma Vep had died in 1916. Her being like the original was no more real than the identity of wealthy young widow, Mrs. Adler, she used for everyday purposes.

She looked at a copy of the *International Herald-Tribune*. Too late to cover the robbery. She turned to the arts pages and was delighted to read about the opening of the new Soviet-French Cultural Center to be opened in Nice in a couple of weeks' time with an exhibition of Russian historical treasures. Would the security be strong enough, given the robberies committed by Irma Vep, it asked.

The so-called "Mrs. Adler" smiled. Yes, this would be her next, irresistible target. She had some Russian business that needed attending to, and she was very much looking forward to taking care of it.

At a cafe on Dubrovnik's Stradun, the Adriatic city's popular main street, Boris Liatoukine was reading the same edition of the *International Herald-Tribune*—but focusing on an article about the situation in Afghanistan. The place was clearly not very stable. As a KGB colonel, Liatoukine was, of course, more aware than most of that fact. His superior, the notorious spymaster Von Bork, was especially keen to get involved there. Von Bork was old, dreaming of more glories. He was keen, in particular, to send Liatoukine there, with a couple of specialists to assist the communist government. The higher ups—KGB Chairman Yuri Andropov in particular—were convinced of the need for full, military intervention, and were prevailing upon General Secretary Leonid Brezhnev to agree to it. Brezhnev was no longer the man he had been, so might be persuaded to do it. These were the machinations of old men, whose time was passing. Even in this state—Yugoslavia—dictator Tito was not in the best of health.

This Afghanistan thing made Liatoukine uneasy, however. The Soviet Union had happily invaded other countries, and he had participated. He had helped crush anti-Soviet elements in East Germany, Hungary, Czechoslovakia... He was all in favor of subjugating other peoples. He himself was older than all of the rulers in Moscow put together. However, his body was young and thus his mind was as sharp as ever, with the benefit of experience. Such was the advantage of being a vampire. His mind went to the past. He had been to this Croatian city before, in 1806 when Russia and Montenegro savagely besieged the city during the war against Napoleon. Despite the damage wrought, in particular outside the city walls, the fortifications of the city did their job and remained to this day. The city in many ways looked the same now as it did then.

His thoughts moved back to the reason why he was here. He had an excellent view of the café opposite. He had been watching a British diplomat drinking coffee there. Liatoukine knew that someone else would be joining him soon; he was that person he wanted to know about. The evening was starting to draw in. Like a number of vampires, Liatoukine was able to exist in daylight, albeit with reduced supernatural powers. The twilight would help his heightened senses.

Within minutes, another man joined the British diplomat. He was in his early 30s and looked, in fact, rather like a younger version of his superior, Von Bork. Which is what Liatoukine had expected. He was aware that Von Bork had grandchildren, with a grandson in the military. Von Bork was always discreet about his family, but Liatoukine had made sure he knew about all of them, including their appearances. Despite his resemblance to his superior, however, this man was not one of Von Bork's relatives.

The two men sat together for a few minutes, discussing the delights of Dubrovnik in German, including its impending UNESCO recognition as a World Heritage Site. The diplomat then bade him good night and left, leaving behind some papers under a discarded copy of *The Times*. All a bit obvious, and Liatoukine wondered if MI6, possibly Tito's notorious UDBA[1], were behind this.

However, looking around, the vampire could not detect any surveillance, and, with his senses and experience, it was probable he would have detected any if there were. He strolled over to his target.

"May I?" he asked.

---

[1] The Yugoslav State Security Administration

The man looked surprised, casting a glance at the empty table next to him, essentially saying, "Why can't you sit over there?" The Russian vampire ignored that and simply said, "Thank you," and sat down. It was fortunate that it was the diplomat who had left rather than this fellow. It made things a bit easier, despite it being rather public.

Liatoukine spoke in Russian. "Good evening, Comrade." The other man sat bolt upright at that. Very poor, thought Liatoukine. "Guten Abend" his interlocutor said, in German. That was even poorer. He should have feigned complete lack of understanding rather than answer in German. Liatoukine continued, "Comrade, I believe we work for the same employer."

The man started making his excuses and clearly was about to go. It was time, Liatoukine thought, to use one of his special talents. He fixed his eyes on the man. "Please," said Liatoukine, "stay... have a drink with me." The man looked into the eyes of the Russian vampire. They were like a cat's. He then decided, that yes, he would have a drink with this charming fellow. "Of course, it would be my pleasure," he replied—in Russian.

Liatoukine summoned the waiter and ordered a slivovitz for both himself and his guest.

"Tell me, what is your name and who do you work for?" asked Liatoukine.

"My name is Pyotr Suvorin. I work for the KGB."

"What is your current mission?" Liatoukine asked.

"I am working here in our embassy here under the assumed name of Von Bork."

Von Bork! This was certainly not Von Bork, and Liatoukine had a good idea what was going on. The rest of the conversation informed Liatoukine that this "Von Bork" was an officer of no real connections suddenly deployed in a new role under the assumed name. At this point, he was handling a mole in the UK embassy in Belgrade, meeting in this Adriatic city. Liatoukine looked over the photocopied papers the diplomat had given Suvorin, much of which seemed to be routine diplomatic material.

Liatoukine told Suvorin to go away, and to simply think he had had a pleasant drink with a tourist after his rendezvous. Then he sat a while. There was much to consider. What he had seen was familiar. As an immortal vampire, he had had to replace himself in Russian society with a fake son, or occasionally another relative, after faking his own death. The fake would then effectively replace him, looking younger. Sometimes he used others for those purposes, under mesmerism, and discarded them just prior to his "death." However, he had a splendid ability—albeit one he barely understood—to create a duplicate of himself, which appear as a "younger" version of himself prior to his "death." Naturally, this was not foolproof, but those who were suspicious would either be no longer so after a spot of mesmerism, and the more difficult ones would simply die of the usual "natural causes" or have an accident of some kind.

Clearly, Von Bork was preparing the same ground—if a little crudely, given that this Suvorin had only a resemblance. Any inquiries as to who this relative taking over Von Bork's post would find a trail of sorts, and further inquiry would probably lead to the death of the curious. Suvorin would either be liquidated, or reassigned to somewhere like Siberia.

But Von Bork was not a vampire. He was an old man who had refused the *dark kiss*, which would have meant to be under the thrall of another vampire. That was something he would never countenance, and he had made it clear many times that he would die a human. So something had changed, and this did not suit Liatoukine at all. He intended to take over the control of the KGB's supernatural division after Von Bork passed.

He finished his slivovitz and decided he had to return to Moscow at once.

A few days later in Nice, "Mrs. Adler" had the opening of the Soviet-French Cultural Center to attend to. She drove to the entrance and someone took her vehicle to the car park. The banners around the Cultural Center were large and clear, heralding *The Treasures of Russia*. This would be the first exhibition at the Center and consisted of various jewels and treasures that had belonged to the Tsars and the wealthy noble class. The Soviet state had appropriated the items after their takeover.

Security was tight. Everyone was concerned. Would this new Irma Vep strike again? It was thought that the exhibition was too high profile for her. "Mrs. Adler" smiled inwardly at that. That might be true, but she had certain inside knowledge to help her. She had every intention of robbing the exhibition, albeit not today. Today was for her to be seen at a major society event. And yes, a spot of early reconnaissance. She walked up the steps to the entrance. There seemed to be a commotion in front of her. A tall, haughty redhead with that American sounding accent that some Europeans have whilst speaking English was arguing with the doormen, with a couple of plainclothes guards hovering nervously nearby.

They may well be nervous, "Mrs. Adler" thought. This lady was none other than the Polish Countess Irina Petrovski. She would have received no invitation whatsoever.

"No, I am not on your invitation list," she was saying, waving her arm at the guards who were as likely as not French police.. "But I have every right to come inside. The Petrovski Cameo is here. It belongs to my family not these... communists!"

"Mrs. Adler" stood patiently behind. She knew Petrovski, but the Countess would not recognize her. Indeed, she had met her only a few weeks before—as Irma Vep—in order to discuss her next theft. The Countess was a sort of neighbor; she lived in Monaco as she could hardly do so in communist Poland.

The Countess continued with her tirade. "That cameo belonged to my grandmother. She lost it in a rail disaster in 1906 in your country. It was retrieved years later by godless communists and has since been held onto by them rather than being given back to my family!"

A couple of other staff came out to see to the other guests. "Mrs. Adler" went in to the Center. Yes, The Petrovski cameo was one of the smaller attractions of this exhibition. But her stealing it for the Countess, for a suitably agreed-upon sum, would have the splendid effect of showing Irma Vep as being not merely a thief but a restitutor of property back to its rightful owner. Her legend would grow, she would make profit—and there was still another certain aspect to consider, too...

Liatoukine left his Moscow office for a meeting with Von Bork. He had to play this very carefully. What was Von Bork up to? Outside his superior's office, Von Bork's secretary buzzed him. No reply. She buzzed again. Again, no reply. This was happening with more frequency of late. The secretary got up and went to the door. She knocked loudly and went in. Presently, she came back out. "He will see you now," she said to Liatoukine.

As Liatoukine went in, he took a look at the photographs on the wall: mostly, his superior pictured with various Soviet notables. There was one with Lenin, one with Khrushchev. There was a recent one—Brezhnev. The Trotsky and Stalin pictures had, of course, long gone. Von Bork had kept a low profile in the past when necessary, but, at this point, the photographs produced the desired effect on some visitors that he was not without some degree of influence. Von Bork had wanted advancement, but being in charge of this supernatural division—officially titled the Special Logistics Directorate—had certain disadvantages due to the distrust some felt towards it. They had dodged various purges by ensuring that anyone wishing them harm would be dissuaded or simply liquidated. The powers at their disposal—they employed a number of supernatural beings as agents—gave them an advantage in survival that millions of others had not. However, whilst effectively autonomous, they were unable to exert the influence that they wanted.

Liatoukine then looked at the figure behind the desk. An old, bald man slouched in his chair. Advanced in years—was he approaching one hundred? He had likely been dozing when his secretary had buzzed him. He remembered the young, proud man of old. Von Bork had created this division out of nothing. It had served the Soviet Union well. Guarded itself against Stalin, against all odds. And yes, Von Bork had defeated him, the great Boris Liatoukine, and made him work for him. Von Bork gestured him to sit.

"How was Prague?" asked the German spymaster.

Liatoukine had officially not been to Dubrovnik at all. His cover was that he spent those couple of days in the capital of Czechoslovakia.

"It went very well. The local StB [2] afforded me every help. The reports we had of Golem activity turned out to be nothing, let alone the thing's sighting. We did however, find a West German—a private citizen—looking into the same reports. We were unable to capture him for interrogation, and he spirited himself out of the country with the help of the BND [3] the moment he realized he was under observation. It is possible that the man was part of some private network in West, working with their secret service. It's all in the report," he pointed to a file on the desk. He wondered if Von Bork had even read it. It was all true, however. Liatoukine had the power—which Von Bork knew about—to create duplicates of himself. That was what Liatoukine had sent to Prague. In the past, this technique could only be used at short distances, with a limited lifespan. Over the years, however, the Russian vampire had worked hard on developing this unusual skill. His duplicates could now operate for days, with autonomy, and at greater distance. It did require, however, a considerable intake of energy from Liatoukine. He had carefully ensured that Von Bork knew nothing of these improvements.

"Germans?" asked Von Bork.

"Yes," said Liatoukine. "It appears that the BND are continuing their limited interest in supernatural matters. We have always suspected that they took over the Austro-Hungarians' resources decades ago. Their continued interest perhaps indicates that they didn't all fall into the hands of the British and the Americans at the end of the war."

Von Bork snorted. "The BND need Prussians to do the job. Only we have the right mentality. But we were not appreciated." He paused. "*I* was not appreciated," he said bitterly.

Liatoukine was slightly startled by this. Von Bork would not deny being a German *per se*, but it had been decades since he had heard him refer to himself as a Prussian.

"*They* appreciated me," Von Bork, continued, pointing to a picture of Lenin on his wall. The Russian knew what he meant. Von Bork had been unmasked as a German spy in Britain in 1914 by the private detective Sherlock Holmes, later even blamed by British propaganda for starting the First World War. He returned to Germany in disgrace and was rejected by the Kaiser's government, whereupon the Communists lost no time in recruiting this embittered man. He had since served them rather well, despite being German.

Von Bork looked at the file. "No, my old friend. Let us not think of those to whom we have already brought socialism. We must think of the future, as Lenin did. Kabul, old friend, Kabul! Our comrades there need our help."

Again, he speaks of Afghanistan, thought Liatoukine. He decided to try and dissuade him from thinking about this. "Comrade Von Bork, there is not

---

[2] Czechoslovakian state security service.
[33] The West German Federal Intelligence Service.

much for us to do there. Our reports of supernatural activity are somewhat scant and..."

In a surprising burst of energy, Von Bork cut him off. "Supernatural activity has been scant since the Great Patriotic War, and especially since Stalin destroyed the Vampire City with an Atom bomb!"

Liatoukine remembered that well. It had been kept from him for a time.

"We have a role in using the talents of this directorate to further the liberation of the working classes around the world," the spymaster continued, "and to defend the Soviet Union and hear allies from threats at home and abroad." He pointed at the Russian vampire. "Never forget, Liatoukine, that we bested you in the end, and your sudden conversion to communism has always been closely monitored by me."

That was true. Von Bork had found in him in Paris in 1928 and gave him a choice: work for Moscow or taste a silver stake. Liatoukine had a surge of resentment against this impertinent German addressing him—a former Imperial high Russian—in such a manner. But he suppressed his annoyance. He was playing a long game, intending to take over when Von Bork died. However, things were coming to the surface. A conclusion was perhaps coming into view?

The Russian vampire decided to soothe Von Bork. "I have served the cause well, Comrade. You are correct; I will send Comrade Ivanov to Kabul to assess how we can be of assistance to our fellow KGB officers already there. Perhaps we can run an assassination program against reactionaries and counter-revolutionaries?"

Von Bork looked pleased. "An excellent idea; however I would like to make a small change. It would be best if you were to lead the group. The KGB has a formidable presence there already, but I believe that soon we will be sending much greater assistance. General Secretary Brezhnev has been listening to the wise counsel of Comrade Andropov. We will save Afghanistan as we saved the German Democratic Republic, Hungary, and Czechoslovakia! We will normalize the situation, and the world will see our strength. Sending you, my top aide, will be a clear signal that our Directorate fully intends to play a powerful role in Afghanistan. If only I were younger, I would join you, but I have other duties."

Liatoukine was about to say something, but Von Bork was waving him away with his hand and clicked on the intercom. "Colonel Liatoukine is just leaving." His secretary came in and gently ushered Liatoukine out. Glancing back, he could see that Von Bork appeared to be dozing again.

In his own office, the Russian vampire considered the situation. Something was clearly going on. Von Bork was setting up a replacement for himself. Further, he was sending him well out of the way to Afghanistan. It could only mean that Von Bork was intending immortality for himself. What had changed? Perhaps Von Bork had somehow changed his mind on the matter? Had he found a way, some method of immortality, that did not involve vampirism?

The Vampire colonel had a way of finding out. The KGB Special Logistics Directorate Von Bork commanded had many defenses against the supernatural built into its facilities and indeed upon individuals themselves. One would have to be very foolish to try to mesmerize Von Bork, even in his advanced years. Such defenses extended elsewhere of course, to protect the Soviet Union. Quite deliberately, such defense responsibilities were not given to Liatoukine. However, over the years, he had quietly probed them. He could not overcome them, but had found a weakness or two.

Later, he boarded a train on the Metro and walked past a young lady sitting down. He stopped and spoke to her. "Good evening Elena!" She was a typist, whom he knew worked for Von Bork's secretary.

She seemed taken aback. "Good evening Comrade. I did not know that you took this route home."

She was entirely correct, he did not. However, they had met like this a number of times before, not that she would remember. "I am on the way to see a friend," he lied, sitting next to her.

There were no people around them, which was fortunate, as it meant he did not have to waste time walking with her out of the station to where there might be fewer people. He gazed at her intently, draining her very slightly of energy. This was merely to weaken her will. He turned on his mesmerism facilities, at a low level. "How are things in the typing pool? Von Bork keeping you all busy? He certainly does me!"

They both laughed. "Well, we are typing up the orders for your going to Afghanistan in a couple of days' time." She was not supposed to discuss such matters in public, but it was hardly a secret and no one was in earshot. Where was the harm?

Liatoukine laughed again, "Yes, I look forward to that! What else is he up to to make our lives a misery?"

Elena leaned forward conspiratorially. "He is off to Nice for a few days— as part of a cultural trip."

"A cultural trip?" asked the vampire. He knew that Von Bork did go on a number of these, to examine the "decadent" West at close quarters.

"Yes, he is due to attend a reception connected to an exhibition of some of our precious artifacts—probably a lot of drinks are involved!"

They laughed again. Liatoukine had heard enough—he would find out the rest. It was best not to probe too much, in order to leave only minimal psychic traces. "This is my stop Elena. You look tired, please forget you saw me tonight and sleep a little until your stop." Which she did.

The next day, in his office, Liatoukine mapped a strategy. He had heard of the Soviet-French Cultural Center being established in Nice, but had no idea that his superior was planning to go there. This was unusual—Von Bork was usually not secretive on such matters. He was to leave for France the very next day after Liatoukine was due to go Kabul, which was tomorrow. Nice was clearly the key.

Upon further research, he discovered that the Petrovski cameo was part of the exhibition. This could well be part of it. There was a notorious incident in 1906, an "accident" involving the Trans-Siberian express. But it was not an accident. There had been a creature from beyond this world running amok on board. Indeed, it had been Liatoukine in Moscow who had given the orders to destroy the train. The locals had not wanted to go anywhere near the wreckage which had been difficult to retrieve, having gone over a sheer incline. It was the Army, under Von Bork's direction, who had retrieved what lay below, several years later. Amongst what was retrieved from a safe that had survived were the valuables belonging to two passengers—Count and Countess Petrovski. This included a cameo of the Countess herself. It was going on display in Nice, as a property of the Soviet state, much to the chagrin of her descendent. However, Von Bork had access to the Cameo if he wanted, and indeed it was he who had ordered the release of such items from the KGB vaults.

There was another more intriguing possibility. Across Europe, in the Côte d'Azur in particular, there had been a recent number of high level thefts, paintings and jewelry. The perpetrator was referred to by the press as "Irma Vep." The original Vep had been part of a notorious French gang that had called itself The Vampires, and which had terrorized the country in the early part of the 20th century. They had committed quite a few strange and ingenious crimes, killing a number of people along the way. They were not actual vampires, however. Liatoukine recalled that a number of true vampires in the Sepulchre had thought them impertinent and sworn that they should be dealt with. None had tried, however. This criminal gang was not be trifled with, even by the undead. They were brought down by humans in 1916, with Irma Vep being shot and killed in the process.

Liatoukine looked at the feature on this new Irma Vep in a recent copy of the *International Herald-Tribune*. The original had been known to occasionally dress in a black catsuit, exactly as the current one did. More relevantly, a picture or two of the thief showed her exact likeness to that of the original. She clearly had been posing; she wanted her picture taken. And the same with a video at another theft. Plastic surgery by a current woman thief was a popular press theory to explain this "resurrection."

But could the original Irma Vep have achieved immortality in some way in 1916? The third leader of the gang of the Vampires had been a master-chemist named Venenos. Could he have created some immortality formula? The press—most of it, anyway—would not entertain that theory, but the Russian vampire knew that such things were not necessarily far-fetched. If Irma Vep had become a real vampire, she would have long been exposed at some point. An immortal human, however, may not have come to the attention of those such as he—if they were being careful enough.

Liatoukine's strategy was clear. He would quietly go to Nice and find out what exactly Von Bork was up to. He would also send his double to Kabul—it would have full autonomy.

"Mrs. Adler" returned home early from the opening ceremony of the exhibition. She had seen enough. Security was too tight to risk a theft, but she had a certain advantage. She got to her door and hesitated, to make sure the man who had followed her all the way from the exhibition was still doing so. She entered, leaving the door open for him. Stupidly, he just walked in after her.

She whirled around and picked him up by the neck. She took him into an adjacent room. Glaring into him, she used her power of mesmerism to the fullest. "Who sent you, and for what reason?" she demanded, although she had a pretty good idea.

He was struggling not to speak, and succeeded. As one of Von Bork's agents, he had been well trained in such resistance. She repeated the question two more times, and then broke through. "I was sent here by Von Bork," he gasped, "with instructions to locate Irma Vep to see if the elixir of life she claimed to have was real—and to steal it if possible."

Having established control, she put him down. "How did you locate me?" she then asked.

He faltered slightly, still resisting control, but spoke again. "The methods you set up to communicate with us were not as secure as you thought. We determined that one of your messages had been sent from this neighborhood. Of all the local residents, we found out that only you were scheduled to attend tonight's opening. We decided to follow you and see what connection, if any, you had with Irma Vep."

She nodded and asked, "Von Bork did not think to send a vampire or some other supernatural agent of his?"

"No, such resources are few at the moment, and many are earmarked for Afghanistan."

That made sense to her. The destruction of the Sepulchre in 1953 had reduced the vampire population somewhat. Things were clearer now. She—as Irma Vep—and Von Bork had been discussing the exhibition, its security arrangements in particular. They had a deal—one which Von Bork had clearly reneged on.

She got a few more details from the man. Then, she walked him back to his car, where she ordered him to drive to a secluded spot out of town, with her following him. There, she left her car a little way off, and walked over to where he was parked. He was still sitting in the driver's seat. She shot him in the head with a pistol through the window. She peered through the shattered glass to make sure he was quite dead, then went back to her own car. The body would be soon discovered, but having been killed in a human fashion. Let Von Bork continue to think he was dealing with a human, albeit an immortal one. His little gambit had failed. He would have to give her what she wanted in return for immortality. Which she would give him, and which would be her greatest prize.

The flight out of Moscow towards Kabul was uneventful. The duplicate of Liatoukine was seated on in the hold of the Antonov-12 with a number of troops. These were human Spetznaz—Soviet Special Forces troops—especially trained to work with the Supernatural division. There had been some discussion of what was to happen in Kabul. A headquarters for them had been set up, with the cover for the troops being that they would guard Soviet facilities. Their real objective would be to assassinate targeted rebels, investigate anything supernatural threats, and even liquidate the local communists who were seemed less than reliable. Although this Liatoukine was a duplicate—albeit one without the full powers of the original—somehow, he was still part of the same consciousness.

He looked over to the soldiers; they were examining their weapons and the crates. Aside from regular weapons, Kalashnikov weapons and so on, there were the usual special weapons, such as silver bullets, stake guns, gallons of holy water, etc. The soldiers finished what they were doing and broke open a bottle of vodka, taking swigs from it, laughing and joking. The officer in charge came over to him with the bottle. "Join us, comrade colonel!" he said, offering the bottle to him. It would not do to refuse. Over the many years, Liatoukine had remained a true soldier and knew that it was a good idea for an officer to be seen as one of the men from time to time. And he could not refuse a drink from a brother officer.

The vampire took a swig from the bottle. His mouth burned! He spat it out. Holy water! They had given him holy water! Something smashed into his shoulder. A wooden stake—they had fired a wooden stake into him! But it had missed his heart—an error that would cost them dearly. He was splashed with what seemed to him like acid, but was simply more holy water. He ignored the agony, effortlessly snapping the neck of the soldier who had gotten too close with the bucket of the water.

Liatoukine knew he was trapped. There was only way out—he would have to jump out of the aircraft. Unlike some other vampires, he could not fly. However, he may be able to survive the fall. He lunged towards the door. And then he saw something protruding from his chest. It was a silver spike. It was the same silver stake that Von Bork had made years ago. It had been used effectively on others many times even though Liatoukine knew that it had really been constructed especially for him. He was not dead yet, though! He grabbed the stake and tried to push it backwards and out. Perhaps, if he succeeded, his heart might regenerate...

"Die, damn you!" he heard the officer who gave him the drink shout. It was clear he was holding the stake in place. Liatoukine twisted, and then lunged forward. He was splashed all the while with holy water, burning him all over. He was free, but others grabbed him again. His arms flailing, he grabbed with one hand a pistol that had been secured on the bulkhead. With what remained of his strength and speed, he somehow got the safety off and started firing wildly. The Antonov lurched - the bullets had hit something important. That was the last thing he felt. He was now a burnt creature, and he disintegrated, strange energy dissipating with skull and bones falling to the aircraft floor. He was dead. The officer grabbed the skull as it rolled with the lurch of the aircraft, before realizing the aircraft's trouble was quite serious.

In Nice, the original Liatoukine was in an apartment with a good view of the sea. It was not a KGB one, but simply a private one that he had rented out through his own means, that he had covertly developed over the decades. It was well that he was in it, for the attack on his duplicate self on the Antonov suddenly took over his thoughts. He felt the moment of his double's death, feeling the same agony that the other had felt.

Suddenly, it was over and Liatoukine had all the memories of his duplicate. He collapsed on his bed, drained of energy. Von Bork wanted him dead; this could make sense, if the spymaster were to gain immortality. The German had correctly reasoned that he, the legendary "Captain Vampire," would not accept working for him forever. Von Bork was old and had become careless. Now, Liatoukine was no doubt already officially "dead," as well as being undead. This gave him a supreme advantage; Von Bork would hardly be expecting him when the vampire liquidated him.

Also in Nice, at a fashionable café on the rue Saint François de Paule, Countess Irina Petrovski was sitting and chatting with Irma Vep. They were two beautiful, sophisticated women, hardly out of place on the French Riviera.

"You are taking a bit of a chance sitting out here in the open, aren't you?" asked the Countess.

"Not really," her companion replied. "As you can see, I am differently attired from the pictures you may have seen in the press." She pointed to her flowing white dress. "And I don't have my 'silent film' look. People are not expecting to see Irma Vep sipping coffee!" What she did not say was that her low-level mesmeric powers pushed the curious away. It was a risk; but one of many she enjoyed at this time.

"You will soon retrieve my family's cameo?" asked the Countess.

"Yes," replied Vep. "Your fee is most adequate, and, of course, I shall be pleased to be seen to have retrieved the rightful property from the hands of communists. But how will you deal with all the legal implications of how the cameo got back to you? Surely the police will be wanting to speak to you?"

"The established chain of how it got back to me will have no direct connections... Certain anti-communist groups will announce they have procured it by underground means and returned it to me as a gift. The French have come to an agreement with the Soviets about dealing with such items for the their little cultural Center—owners cannot claim back their property from such displays. But the cameo will find its way to the United States, which do not recognize such laws. There, it will be returned to my family—not here or in Monaco. I will have had nothing to do with the robbery itself, and the cameo does, after all, belong to me, as US law recognizes"

"And this Center will have taken a great blow to its prestige, having only just opened," Vep said.

She knew very well about the Countess's crusade against communism, being determined to free her Polish homeland from it. The Countess nodded her head agreeably, observing Vep. Was she just a jewel thief with an uncanny resemblance to a legendary criminal, or something more? She and others had a private interest in such matters, which had begun with the 1906 incident her grandmother had been involved in. Not a matter for just now, however.

During the day, Boris Liatoukine was busy in Nice. As an energy vampire, he took the living essence from people. Sudden deaths and complete disintegration were possible in this process, but might have attracted some notice, and he could not afford any undue attention. The death of his duplicate had left him drained. Consequently, he needed human energy. He visited many places in the city, the Place Massena, the Place Garibaldi, the Naval Museum and Galerie des Ponchettes among others. He grabbed small bits of energy off as many people as he could. They would only feel weak for short while. This would hardly be the amount of energy he really needed, but it would see him through the next 24 hours, which he knew would be crucial. However, it would not be enough to create a new duplicate of himself, which was a disadvantage.

He had to get to Von Bork and liquidate him. He knew he would be at one of the receptions organized to celebrate the opening of the Soviet-French Cultural Center, off Place Massena. He needed more information though. And this proved simpler than he had thought. He went to where he knew the KGB had rented an apartment. He entered easily, and found one of Von Bork's personal guards, a vampire called Ivan. He was one of those who had great difficulty with daylight, and he found him asleep on a bed. Ivan had been a low-level dissident marked for death. Instead, he had been forcibly given the *dark kiss* by one of Von Bork's vampires and thus came under her control. Then, she had disappeared, and Ivan had been confined for some years. It was assumed that she had been killed in the destruction of the Sepulchre. Ivan was purposefully created weak, so that he could pose no threat. Von Bork only had a few such vampires created, and by different vampires, lest they be used against him someday.

With the one who turned him dead, Ivan was susceptible to the power of Liatoukine. He woke him up. The weakened vampire started in terror at Liatoukine. "Captain Vampire!" he said.

Liatoukine was amused by the use of his old nickname. "Colonel Vampire now, my dear Ivan, surely? Now, please, tell me all about Von Bork's plans here in Nice."

Which he did. Liatoukine had guessed correctly. Irma Vep did have some elixir of life to sell to Von Bork. He was to make it easier for her to rob the museum of its most valuable items, much of which had belonged to the Tsars such as Faberge eggs, and so on. They had tried to double-cross her, but she had killed their agent and upped the amount of material she was to steal. This would all take place at 10 p.m. tonight, at the Center.

It all seemed a bit risky for both sides, thought Liatoukine. Still, the rewards would be high. However, he would be there to deal with matters. "Go back to sleep now, Ivan, and forget this conversation," he told him.

There was much back slapping at the reception at the Cultural Center that evening, with all the guests being permitted a view of the exhibits—the controversial Petrovski Cameo being of particular interest. This was a largely diplomatic affair, Liatoukine noted, when he saw people start to file out at around 9 p.m. He had mesmerized Ivan into leaving a ground-floor window open for him.

In her catsuit, Irma Vep entered the building though an open skylight, which had also been left open on purpose. Soon, she was in the main hall. There, next to the Petrovski cameo, was Von Bork, Ivan standing a few feet away.

She took her mask off, revealing her face. Not her true one, but the Irma Vep one. For now. "Well, Comrade Von Bork, we finally meet. I do hope you are not going to try and kill me again." She waved a glass phial at him. "Otherwise this will get smashed for a start."

"Your Russian is excellent," said Von Bork.

"Oh yes, I've had plenty of time to learn languages. All thanks to Venenos, the leader of our gang back in the 1910s. He was a genius. Sadly, he was killed before he could test on it on himself. So I took it. I've always had a bit more." She had a rather large bag, which she dropped on the floor. "I take it your man here means me no harm?" she asked.

"None whatsoever," said Von Bork.

She looked at Ivan. "You won't harm me, will you?" Ivan made no response.

She gave him the spymaster the phial. "Just drink it. It will take only a short while."

He gulped the phial down. "Tastes like water," he said.

She nodded. "It is water."

Von Bork looked confused.

She was pleased, it was going well. "Don't worry, Comrade. You are going to become immortal. Just not quite as you thought."

"Ivan!" he snapped and pointed to her. But Ivan did not move.

She laughed. "He won't harm me. I was the one that turned him." She smiled at Von Bork, who was gazing at her in both confusion and fear.

Her face started to change. And some of her teeth grew to become vampire teeth. Now, Von Bork recognized her.

She grabbed his head, pushed it back, sunk her fangs into her neck and drank deeply. She then let him go. He staggered around, and then he started to change. He straightened up. And there was not the aged KGB official of 1979, but the German spymaster of 1914, young and vigorous again. He opened his mouth to reveal fangs. Dead—yet undead!

He stood up, now straightening to his full height—the first time in years!—stretching out his arms, testing his rejuvenated body. He laughed.

Irma Vep laughed too. "I have given you immortality as promised."

"Yes," he said, "but under vampiric control. Not part of my plan. However, I know who you are now."

She smiled at him. "I am your master now. Do not fear, Von Bork. I intend that you carry out your ambitions for power and influence in the Soviet Union in the way you see fit—unless I disagree, which may happen now and again. I will always be the one whom you will obey, but you will simply be an asset I may wish to use from time to time. Let us begin at once with our plan. Ivan, will you please activate the video cameras."

He dutifully moved to do so, whilst her face returned to that of Irma Vep. He was an excellent servant, she thought. He had already purged all evidence pertaining to her "Mrs. Adler" alter ego from the KGB files, and only Von Bork and he knew about her.

Then followed a staged presentation of Irma Vep entering the hall, masked in her catsuit, delicately opening the cabinet with the Petrovski cameo. She took it out, pulled off her mask, held the cameo up to the camera and then walked off. She enjoyed the notoriety of being 'Irma Vep'—as important to her as obtaining wealth and influence.

Von Bork and Ivan returned to the gallery. Von Bork seemed puzzled. "Is that all you are taking?" he asked.

"Of course," she replied. "To steal more would ensure even more police resources coming after me. And stealing this item—whose ownership is in legal doubt—enhances my reputation rather than making me look greedy. Furthermore, the real target was always you, Von Bork. Now, you must see to it swiftly that the video of this evening's events is edited properly."

It was at this point that Boris Liatoukine entered the proceedings, appearing in the gallery in a leather jacket and jeans with two stakes in his hand, and a bulge in his jacket.

"Ah, Boris!" exclaimed Irma Vep, "I am so glad you are able to join us. Von Bork, you look surprised. I think what happened is that you managed to kill his duplicate—presumably Boris has improved his skills in that area. Boris made contact with Ivan here," she gestured to the vampire guard, "completely unaware that I, who had given Ivan the *dark kiss*, was still alive. Ivan told Boris only what I told him to."

Liatoukine then realized who he was actually dealing with.

"Polly Bird!" he said.

"Yes," she replied.

Her features blurred, and there she was—Polly Bird. They had worked together once. She had later joined forces with Von Bork, and then fallen under his control. She had chafed under him, as had Liatoukine, but he had used that opportunity to consolidate his position within the KGB, whereas she had not. He had not seen her for decades. She had gone missing during World War II. In that chaos, a number of those working for Von Bork had simply disappeared. Most had been destroyed by the Germans or the Allies, but some had simply used the chaos to circumvent the supernatural bonds that had kept them in servitude to Moscow.

"We thought you had been obliterated in the destruction of the Sepulchre," Liatoukine said.

She smiled. "Not at all, my dear Boris. I kept a rather low profile after the war, but I did put about some rumors that I was in hiding there, which of course the Sepulchre denied for the good reason that it wasn't true."

Damn himself for a fool! He and Von Bork had never fully believed that she had perished in the Great Patriotic War. They even had imprisoned those like Ivan, whom she had turned, just to be on the safe side. With the destruction of the Sepulchre, and her subsequent non-appearance, they had assumed she had indeed perished there. They had let Ivan out to serve them in the 1960s, driven by a shortage of supernatural operatives. They had been complacent and careless. He noticed no green tints on the glass exhibit casing – such tints being a giveaway for certain vampires. She clearly had learnt to control that.

Polly Bird changed her features back to Irma Vep's. "I enjoy the lifestyle and fame I have. The Irma Vep guise has done me good. However, with the opportunity to steal from here, I thought of trying to gain control of Von Bork and eliminating you in the bargain. That would end any KGB threat to me. Von Bork, Ivan, please eliminate Boris. And this time, check if he is a duplicate."

Liatoukine reacted quickly. He pulled a gun from his jacket and fired three shots in rapid succession—silver bullets, of course. One hit Ivan in the shoulder, sending him reeling in agony. Von Bork moved fast out of the way of the bullet, adapting to vampire speed very swiftly. Polly Bird just stood there. She caught the silver bullet in her teeth.

"Ow," she said, removing the bullet and tossing it back at Liatoukine before it could burn her.

Liatoukine moved swiftly, running up a wall and firing again, missing both his targets. He flung a stake with inhuman power at Polly Bird. It smashed into her rib cage, causing her pain, but missing the heart. The silver fragments inside it made it more painful. Von Bork bounded to her and pulled out the stake. Now he was armed and prepared to kill the threat to his new master.

"It is time for you to be destroyed, Liatoukine," said the spymaster. "You always were a counter-revolutionary."

Why was Von Bork indulging in political banter? thought Liatoukine. He decided against using his gun again. Best to get close with the stake.

Von Bork clearly thought much the same as he ran up the wall. Liatoukine jumped back onto the ceiling, thinking this would disorientate the newly-made vampire, but Von Bork took this in his stride. Soon, they were lunging at each with their stakes, gravity seemingly meaningless. Now was the time for the gun! Liatoukine got off one shot which went wide. The German grabbed the Russian's wrists and twisted hard. He dropped the gun and it fell to the floor. Von Bork was adjusting to being a vampire far too quickly for the Russian's liking. However, Liatoukine was well aware that he had more combat experience than the German. Centuries more.

He leapt off the ceiling and somersaulted back onto the floor. There were the Tsarist scepters he had seen in the hands of those long-dead monarchs. Scepters which contained some silver...

Von Bork had also come down. "Yes, look around you, Liatoukine. Look at the remnants of your Tsarist masters, the regime you served so faithfully, if for your own ends. And now, I will destroy the last of their ranks. It takes the death of Von Bork to do so--reborn in my new form!"

He came towards Liatoukine. The Russian smashed the cabinet near him and grabbed the scepter inside, dropping his stake. It caused him pain, but he was able to bear it.

Von Bork laughed. He dropped his weapon and gestured towards another exhibit case. "Ah!" he said, "the one once held by Nicholas II. My comrades dealt with him." He smashed the cabinet and grabbed it. And then screamed with pain. He thought he could deal with the pain as Liatoukine had, but he couldn't. He dropped the scepter.

Liatoukine was onto him, smashing his head with the royal artifact. Von Bork reeled and hit the floor. Liatoukine then drove his scepter into Von Bork's heart, pushing down so hard that it went right through the German and onto the floor. Von Bork was clearly in rage and agony.

Liatoukine glared into his eyes. "For Imperial Russia!" he hissed at him in contempt. Then, he started to drain the spymaster of his power. Von Bork disintegrated into bones, with the skull seemingly staring at the Russian, and then, that too turned to dust.

Von Bork was finally dead. Liatoukine was now full of energy. He had handled silver before—painful as it was—and had accumulated a certain tolerance to it for a very short time. Von Bork had not, and had suffered the consequences for his Prussian arrogance. Now for Polly Bird...

She had already regenerated somewhat and was crouching on the floor, aiming his own pistol at him. Out of the corner of his eye, Liatoukine could see Ivan staggering to his feet. He appeared to have dug out the bullet that had gone inside his body. But neither would be able to defeat him. Polly Bird leapt, but not at Liatoukine. She went for the wall, smashing the glass on a fire alarm, which duly went off.

"I suggest a truce, Boris," she said. "This alarm will not go unnoticed, and we can fight until others arrive—or leave. Go now, let Ivan clear up. We have no real argument now."

Liatoukine was not sure about any of that. He thought that Von Bork had cleared the building. Nevertheless, it would be best not to complicate matters with the arrival of any police or even regular KGB agents. He simply nodded and swiftly left. He had achieved much tonight, and had something of a journey ahead of him.

Liatoukine sat at his desk in his Moscow office. He had a decision to make. Things had gone rather well in the months since August. It was now December—and he had taken charge of the Special Logistics Directorate.

The official report by two surviving Spetsnaz operatives stated that the Antonov had suffered a major technical fault. They had been picked up fairly swiftly by the Russian Army. They hadn't seen Liatoukine bailing out after them, but he must have, and it had taken several days for him to heroically walk all the way to Kabul, killing some rebels along the way.

He had been given the Order of Lenin for his remarkable survival and endurance from a plane crash. The Spetsnaz troops were delighted to see him, of course. Liatoukine had to return to Moscow urgently due to Von Bork dying in a botched kidnapping scheme in Southern France.

Liatoukine allowed himself a smile at the story. All nonsense of course. It had been a bit of journey to get to the outskirts of Kabul from Nice, but the authorities had not questioned his survival. The two terrified Spetsnaz survivors had raised no questions. He had assured them of no hard feelings—they had to obey Von Bork, who was now dead. They would be staying in Afghanistan, which they were happy to do, as he was returning to Moscow. If they were not killed there, he would organize something later.

Ivan had cleaned up the situation in Nice. The KGB was told that Von Bork had tried to defect to the West. Liatoukine had investigated the matter personally, and reported that his former superior may have defected but may also have been kidnapped, and that he had learned from their own moles in Germany that, either way, he had died soon afterward. The story was accepted—nobody much cared to look into this too deeply—and the German was posthumously awarded the Order of Lenin too. It was thought best to keep quiet, in case the West produced evidence of his defection. Ivan himself disappeared soon after, no doubt going back to serve Polly Bird, who, as "Irma Vep," had been celebrated for her "liberation" of the Petrovski Cameo, now beyond Soviet reach in America. Liatoukine knew that he would have to deal with her at some point. But for now, let her enjoy her notoriety.

Now he had an important meeting to take. His secretary showed in a party official who worked directly for Andropov. Andropov had convinced the ailing Brezhnev of the need to invade Afghanistan. That was imminent.

The official sat down in front of Liatoukine. "Well, Comrade, what will be the contribution of the Special Logistics Directorate to helping our friends in Kabul?"

Liatoukine was all in favor of empire building and repressing others. He had done much of it himself. However, unlike these communists, he did not look at such matters through Marxist-Leninist eyes. His age gave him a sense of history. He knew how the British had had problems in Afghanistan for decades, leading to them to leave. He knew the power of religion there. And he knew the country was five times the size of Vietnam, where the Americans had failed. He did not want his division sucked into a similar quagmire. But he also knew how invested the KGB were in this operation. He had to play things carefully.

"Comrade," he said, "I propose to send a special team of operatives to assist there. We consider there are few, if any, threats that require our specialist skills. However, we will assist regardless, in whatever ways are required." He did not say that he would be sending those he considered easily expendable or that he wanted to be rid of.

"Merely a team? Von Bork was thinking of the majority of your division going?" asked the official, clearly not impressed, no doubt expecting a much fuller commitment.

"A team which may be increased if the need arises," added Liatoukine, starting to emit a low-level mesmerism. "There are a number of threats that may require out attention in Europe. I have heard of Golem sightings in Prague and an increase in strange incidents reported from here in the Soviet Union. I have also heard that Countess Petrovski may be part of a private network operating in this Directorate's field of interest against us, and that she may have had something to do with Von Bork's disappearance."

"That decadent Countess?" asked the official. Mesmerism was hardly needed. The theft of the Petrovski cameo was a sore point. Liatoukine pushed things home. "And I would certainly like to look into the activities of the criminal Irma Vep. Please, comrade, take this file on the matter. I am sure you will find it most informative."

"I am sure I will," the official said, picking up the file. "These are enemies of the Soviet Union. I am pleased you are taking the matter so seriously. Proceed as you have outlined; I am sure I will be able to confirm matters after I have had read your file and consulted with Comrade Andropov."

He left, clearly satisfied with the way the meeting had gone.

Liatoukine, too, was delighted. He had placed his department in a good position—and himself of course. Von Bork was gone and the rest of his generation was going too. Change could well be on its way. Boris Liatoukine was going to make sure he would be on the right side of whatever the future held.

Ill. by John Gallagher

In his story "The Heart of the Moon," published in Tales *of the* Shadowmen, *Volume 3, Matthew Baugh imagined an assault on the vampire city of Selene, one of Paul Féval's most wondrous creations, led by none other than the mysterious Doctor Omega, ably assisted by the dour, old Puritan, Solomon Kane, the swashbuckling Captain Kronos and his associate, Dr. Grost, the superhumanly strong Maciste, and a young telepath from the future named Telzey Amberdon. John Gallagher (no relation to Brian) has now penned a sequel to that earlier tale, concentrating on the character of Kane...*

John Gallagher: *Princes of the Universe*

Selene, 1790

As Jacob had once wrestled with an angel, so Kane now wrestled with a devil. The difference being, whilst Jacob had been contesting with his opponent for access to Heaven, it would seem that both Kane and his opponent were bound for the pits of Hell. Incalculable forces destabilized by Doctor Omega's removal of the chronon nodal point generator lit the well shaft with lurid flashes like lightning bolts from the abyss whilst Kane and the Vampire Queen Phryne tumbled together down through the void.

Huge wings beat in the air and sharp claws griped Kane tightly. Baroness Phryne was no longer in the form of a beautiful woman, but some hideous harpy from Hell with the face and torso of a woman, but the wings and claws of a gigantic bat. Her long black hair whipped wildly around her furious face and her mouth and fangs elongated as she screeched and snapped at her grimly struggling enemy. Not blood, but glowing ribbons of greenish ectoplasm streamed from the wound between her full naked breasts as her white-haired foe used the point of his cat-headed staff to stab at her again and again with all of his waning strength. As if in response to the furious demonic energy being released by Phryne, Kane's staff also coruscated along its length with answering flashes of brilliant argent energy.

As Kane's mind flashed briefly back to a similar battle he had engaged in many, many years ago with a winged demon high above the African veldt, Phryne lunged forward smashing the Puritan into the wall of the shaft. He replied by striking her on the side of the head with his staff, gripped her neck with one strong hand and plunged the staff once again into her heart, whist she, in turn, tried to tear out his wrinkled bewhiskered throat with her fangs.

Suddenly, something within Phryne finally broke under Kane's persistent assault and there was an explosive detonation during which the Puritan had a brief glimpse of some hideous skeletal creature blackening and bursting apart. A wailing shriek of agony accompanied this blast and then, all light vanished.

Burned and stunned, Kane was falling down and down into pitch darkness, caroming off the stone walls of the shaft before he crashed down onto a dust-covered stone floor with bone crushing finality. Shortly afterwards the ash-like remains of Phryne drifted gently down to settle like snowflakes upon her destroyer's prone body.

For a long time nothing stirred in the darkness, then suddenly Kane gave a loud gasp for air and rolled over.

"It would seem that the Good Lord has not done with me yet!" he murmured as he propped himself up on his elbows, giving a wince of pain as he discovered his right leg had been badly broken.

Kane rummaged through his pockets for his tinderbox and flint and soon got a flame going. By its flickering, equivocal light, he was able to see that he was now in a vast cathedral-like space. But, unlike the sanctified atmosphere of some medieval church, this cavernous space reeked of evil. He found himself in a large, domed circular vault; the shaft he had fallen through was at the very apex of the ceiling. Alcoves carved into the walls presumably provided niches for sleeping vampires. Here, they must have once roosted like bats, sleeping during daylight before flying out at dusk to seek out their prey. But it was obviously that it had long been abandoned.

Kane checked he still had his rapier and dagger with him and examined the scars left by Phryne's talons through the rips and rents in his somber attire. They had stopped bleeding, were healing up and some were already beginning to fade. From past experience, the Puritan knew that the damage to his clothing would be far more permanent than any to his flesh.

Kane waited for several minutes whilst his broken leg re-knitted itself together before arising to more fully explore his surroundings. Several round tunnels were also visible, which presumably allowed the vampires access and egress. Fortunately, a few of these were at ground level. Limping and using his voodoo staff for support, the Puritan approached one and felt a faint breeze on his hand; he detected an even fainter aroma of fresh air. That was enough for him; he crouched down and entered the dark tunnel. As he made his way cautiously along the shaft, his restless mind took to brooding upon the circumstances that had first led him to being cursed with immortality.

England, 1719

One of the most appalling and shameful blights upon early 18th century English society was the rise of the so called "Hellfire clubs," although, in most cases, the claims of devil worship were simply a cover for wealthy and aristocratic hedonists to indulge in drunken debauchery and licentiousness, and the rituals and themes of Satanism mere theater dressing to add piquancy to the proceedings. The first and original Hell-fire Club, founded and presided over by

Lord John Cleverly Cartney, was an entirely different matter. For he and his close associates were no idle rakes, but in truth active Satanists. And one of their most egregious crimes had been the recent kidnapping of the beautiful Rowena Taferal, daughter of Sir Roger Taferal. Rowena had previous spurned the advances of the lustful Cartney, and thus, purely out of vengeful spite; he had selected the virtuous young girl as the ideal victim to be sacrificed during his next Black Mass.

Solomon Kane had known the Taferals for generations; thus, as soon as he heard of this abduction, he had rode to Sir Roger's aid. This was more than a simple mission to rescue a kidnapped girl; to Kane, it was a quest for personal redemption.

The Puritan had recently returned from Europe where he had endured a most soul-shocking experience, one that might well have robbed a lesser man of his sanity. Ever prepared to come to the aid of the weak and helpless, the elderly Kane had embarked upon a quest to rescue several children who had been kidnapped to order by a gang of wealthy and cruel libertines. These human monsters made their lair in the isolated Château de Silling, deep within the Black Forest, which they viewed as an impregnable fortress from inside the stone walls of which they and their acolytes could satisfy to the fullest their degenerate lusts.

Penetrating this grim schloss, Kane came upon the aftermath of a Herod-like massacre of the innocents. Scenes of unbelievable horror and torture that would come to haunt him for the rest of his days. Tragically, he had arrived too late to save any of the young victims from the most grievous suffering and grizzly deaths.

His frustration at the failure of his rescue mission, and his disgust at the cackling lunatics that had perpetrated this unspeakable atrocity, sent him temporally berserk. Kane made a red ruin of the place, and, when he rode away from that grim castle in the forest, he had left not a soul within it alive.

Kane returned to France where, for months afterwards, he behaved like a broken man, denied both sleep and peace of mind, hardly eating and avoiding all but the most necessary contact with his fellow man. But finally, by a ferocious effort of will, he threw off his black depression and decided to return to his boyhood home of Devon in England to try to seek some ease for his driven and tormented soul in a familiar and well-remembered surroundings.

Solomon Kane was finally returning home, as all men sick at heart tend to do... or long to do so.

But the Puritan was destined never to reach Devon, for no sooner had his ship docked in London than news reached him of Rowena's plight. Here, again, was another young innocent facing a similar dreadful fate... and Kane swore to himself and by his God that, this time, he would not be too late.

By then, the Puritan was older than he cared to brood upon. And certainly older than any normal man had any right to be. Although his hair was now grey and his face lined, and he felt certain stiffness in his joints in the cold mornings, he seemed to be suffering no other detrimental effects due to his great age. His strength and ability to wield a deadly sword remained undiminished. His old witch doctor ally and blood-brother N'Longa, who had preserved his own lifespan indefinitely by transferring his spirit to a new body every time the old one was worn out, had speculated that Kane's cat-headed staff might be responsible for this unnatural longevity. That it was somehow sustaining him, feeding him vitality and increasing his lifespan for its own purposes.

Kane's mood darkened every time he considered this. Whatever the real reason, the result was that, like some Old Testament Patriarch, he still trod the Earth nearly two hundred years after his birth.

Eilean Donan Castle, Scottish highlands

In the aftermath of the Jacobite rising of 1715, whilst the English were still engaged in reconsolidating their control over the rebellious Scots, the man who nowadays called himself Adrian Montague had arrived back on these shores aboard a boat full of troops sent by Cardinal Giulio Alberoni, Minister to the Spanish King, as part of an invasion force intended to help bolster the clans and reignite the war to push south and place the Catholic James the Third on the English throne.

Like Kane, Montague was also returning to the land of his birth. And, although he had been instrumental in negotiating this deal along with George Keith, 10th Earl Marischal, the delivery of these foreign solders to the leaders of the rebellion was to be his first and only involvement with the Jacobite Rebellion. For, although in his heart he still held a great deal of sympathy for the Scottish cause, and indeed, in his youth, would have been one of the first to fling himself, claymore in hand, upon the English lines for the glory of Scotland and his clan, now, much older, sadder and wiser, having traveled as far around the world as Kane, if not further, Montague had ambivalent feelings about the whole business.

These days, the descendants of his original clan were, for the most part, government supporters, and he himself no longer felt any real personal investment in the war over the British succession. It honestly mattered not one jot to Montague whether and Catholic or a Protestant King sat upon the English throne. The war he was nowadays engaged in was a very different one, and fought between a select few, particularly gifted men.

And so, as his fellow highlanders partied and caroused below, singing songs of victories yet to come, he found himself walking the battlements of the picturesque old castle alone. Indeed, Montague felt a strong feeling of nostalgia to be back at Eilean Donan again, as he had trod these parapets before, when it had been the ancestral home of his clan, many long years before any of the men below had been born. He also recalled less pleasant memories of being cast out and driven away with an ox yoke about his neck. The chill night air blew his long hair about as his face turned this way and that, gazing over the loch, towards the rugged highlands, almost as if he were listening to some distant and barely audible call.

Montague closed his eyes and focused... Yes! Definitely! Now he was certain he could feel it. Once again, he felt the summoning, drawing him, compelling him to follow wherever it might it lead. And so, prompted by a compulsion he could neither explain nor resist, he found himself gathering his belongings, bidding a hasty farewell to his hosts, and riding off along the castle causeway to he knew not where. The older he became, the more his psychic powers seemed to increase, so he no longer doubted these enigmatic promptings; they had proved to be the correct thing to do so often in the past that, now, he would simply follow it to its source, knowing that there he would discover the answers he sought.

Traveling down from the highlands, he eventually crossed the border into England whilst still being drawn ever further and further south, making his way slowly towards London. Montague was met with continual hostility in every town and village he passed along his way. For, although his once broad Scottish accent had been blunted over the years, as he had learned new tongues and lived new lives, he was still recognizably a Scotsman, and to the prejudiced and suspicious locals, this was all that was needed to instantly mark him out as a Jacobite spy, or at least sympathizer. Thus, despite making every attempt to avoid trouble, he was constantly being challenged to duels by overly patriotic, or overly drunk, Englishmen—although his skill with his ivory-handled katana meant any altercations invariably ended very badly for his foolhardy attackers.

The pull grew much stronger as he approached the estate of Sir Roger Taferal and, when he heard about the kidnapping of his daughter, Montague somehow knew he was approaching both his destination and his destiny. He decided to offer his services to the wealthy landowner to aid in the recovery of his beloved daughter.... for a suitable financial remuneration, of course.

Sir Roger Taferal did not believe for one minute that the tall, grim, old man who had turned up on his doorstep claiming to be Solomon Kane could actually be the same man who had rescued his great, great-aunt from some barbaric Africans over one hundred years ago. But this pallid, elderly gentleman in black insisted on being called by the same name and, in some respects, did resemble the legendary puritan warrior, so Sir Roger decided that, as long as he was willing to risk his life to save his daughter, he could call himself whatever he wished.

Kane himself was well aware of the problems that the continued use of his original name was causing him... but he was far too stubborn and rectitudinous to lie. Sir Roger soon decided that, whoever the newcomer was, he knew what he was doing, as Kane quickly outlined a strategy for recovering Rowena from Lord Cartney's vile clutches. One detail that caused Sir Roger some ironic comfort was that Rowena still had to be a virgin for the ritual to be completed, which would at least prevent the lecherous Lord from having his way with her.

To a veteran of so many similar endeavors like Kane, many aspects of this mission were fairly straightforward. He knew who had kidnapped Rowena and why, and he knew when she was supposedly to be sacrificed; it was to be the night of the summer solstice, some three weeks hence. This gave Kane plenty of time to assemble a fighting force, basically just some able-bodied men gathered from amongst the estate, plus a few ex-soldiers recruited from the surrounding villages, in sufficient numbers to mount a successful rescue raid. Kane also reasoned that, although he had no idea where Rowena might be being held—the villainous Lord Cartney was no doubt crafty enough to have her safely sequestered away—he knew that she had to be returned to Cartney Hall, the Hell-fire Club's meeting den, for the actual ceremony, for it was in the cellars of that grand old house that the Club held it revels and orgies and Cartney had built the satanic temple upon the altar of which the sacrifice was to be made.

Having set spies to watch Cartney's estate and the surrounding roads for any developments, Kane could now concentrate on instilling some combat training into his hastily assembled militia. And in this, he had some help. A few days after Kane's arrival, another swordsman and mercenary, one Adrian Montague, arrived to offer his services. Kane was not such a egotist that he would refuse the assistance of an experienced soldier of fortune in this endeavor; indeed he had partnered up with many such men in the past, But he found a few things very disturbing about his new comrade-in-arms.

For a start, when Kane had first been notified of Montague's arrival, he had hurried to meet the man and make his own assessment as to his suitability. He found the newcomer in the main hall of Taferal Manor, casually examining an old suit of armor whilst he waited. Adrian Montague was striking figure, dressed in expensive, if travel-worn clothing. Of medium height and of a lithe, compact built, he had eyes of cold blue which gazed out levelly from beneath a high brow. His light chestnut hair was long and swept back, uncombed and thick, reaching to his broad shoulders. And he carried a strange curved sword scabbarded at his hip. Kane had seen similar weapons before, amongst the warrior class of far off Japan, and he could not help but wonder how on Earth a Scotsman had come by one.

However what disturbed Kane so much was that the second he set eyes upon Montague, he felt a jolt, as if an invisible charge of energy had passed between them. He mentally likened it to the electric charge crackling between two twin poles. He felt sick and nauseous, and the spacious hall itself seemed to reel around him with flashes like lightning bolts. The only other time Kane had experienced anything similar had been on the few occasions his ju-ju staff had warned him of some dire supernatural threat. He would have passed the whole thing off as some kind of seizure due to his advanced age, but for the way the Scot's mouth had quirked up in a sly, half-smile. Kane was sure that the other man had experienced the same thing. As it was, he was just relieved that there had been no one else present in the hall to observe his brief fit. The Puritan was also troubled by an indefinable feeling that he had met this man before... Although he was sure he had not.

There were other things about Montague that perturbed Kane. For example, over the next few days, as they drew up their plans and discussed various strategies, Montague made several attempts to draw the taciturn Kane into conversation, during which time the Puritan noted that he made occasional casual references to events he had witnessed, or participated in, which, although Kane himself could recall living through them, must have occurred long before Adrian Montague was born. For the fresh-faced Scotsman could not be over thirty summers-old.

Finally, upon the eve of the summer solstice, Kane's spies informed him that, early in the morn, a woman answering Rowena's description had been seen being hurriedly bustled from a carriage into Lord Cartney's mansion. As the day progressed, many more carriages deposited their passengers; the wealthy Hell-fire Club members were arriving, intent upon attending the coming Black Mass. Kane knew that Rowena was to be sacrificed at the stroke of midnight, so he chose late afternoon to launch his attack.

The Puritan decided that the most direct tactic was the one with the best likelihood of success. He and Montague stealthily made their way onto the grounds of Cartney's estate, gliding through the dusk like twin shadows. They successfully approached the house without being seen and quickly dispatched the two footmen who stood in attendance upon either side of the large front door. Kane then signaled the rest of his men who came charging down the broad carriageway which fronted the house and barged straight through into the main hall, shouting, firing off pistols, and generally making a row.

The attending nobles and guests scattered in confusion, but, within seconds, the men encountered armed resistance, for the wily Lord Cartney had kept a large retinue of hired ruffians on hand for his protection. A general melee of sword fighting and hand to hand combated ensued as the two forces clashed.

Kane had designated Montague his second in command and assigned him the job of leading the battle with Cartney's men, thus leaving the Puritan free to attempt the rescue of Rowena. It took Kane only a few seconds to come to the conclusion that he had made the right decision. Montague seemed to be in his element in this savage brawl, and Kane watched his brilliant but reckless swordplay in awe as he cut down one Hell-fire bravo after another. With the support of his men, the highlander seemed more than capable of handling the situation in the main hall, so Kane raced up the grand stairway to the second floor. For he knew that, not only was Rowena being held a prisoner in one of the bedrooms on that wing, but where she was, he would also most likely find Lord Cartney himself, whom Kane had reserved as someone he would deal with personally, deeming him to be the most dangerous of their opponents.

But, as arrogant as he was handsome, and with a pride to match his master Satan, Cartney could not countenance being thus bearded in his own lair and had rushed to confront his intruders. So that, when Kane reached the top of the stairs, he found the Lord already awaiting him on the wide landing, sword in hand. Cartney stood confidently in front of an elaborate and obviously expensive circular stained glass window. It was a masterpiece of painstaking work which depicted a triumphant, muscular Satan arising from a fiery pit. A double blasphemy in Kane's dour opinion, who did not care overmuch for the papists fanciful artistic representations of Christ, his apostles and angels, let alone one dedicated to the glory of the devil.

Cartney looked Kane up and down with undisguised contempt.

"So, I am meant to believe that this is Solomon Kane, am I? This dusty old scarecrow? A dotard too old to wield a blade? For in sooth, you certainly cannot be the legendary warrior of whom the old tales speak. For that one must have passed ages ago. So, if not he, then who are you? Some impostor? A charlatan who thought to assume the mantle and reputation of a dead man? Well, your pathetic charade ends here, my friend. In seconds, you will be dead, and this whole sorry farce concluded!"

Kane remained silent. He had learned long ago that doing so always unnerved the more talkative amongst his opponents. He advanced, grim of face, until he came within sword range; then, galvanized into action, he struck with a cobra-swift thrust of his sword. Cartney sidestepped and parried almost nonchalantly and then move in to counter attack.

Meanwhile, Adrian Montague paused after cutting down the last of Cartney's men to glance up at the two figures furiously battling back and forth on the floor above. It seemed that Kane had found his man. Montague was confident that the grizzled old adventurer was capable of handling Lord Cartney by himself, and indeed may well have resented any interference. He took stock of the situation: most of the Hell-fire Club's men were down, and the balance of the crowd was made up of Cartney's devil-worshiping guests, who might well have souls black with sin, but were all well-bred cowards and fops, with no stomach for a real fight. Montague had his men train their muskets on the few remaining combatants and ordered them to lower their weapons. He allowed himself a tight smile of satisfaction; so far everything seemed to be going well.

But, unknown to the Highlander, on the floor above, Solomon Kane was beginning to get the worse of the encounter. Cartney was an accomplish duelist in the prime of his life and with the reckless courage of one who knows himself to be damned. Kane was unused to fencing for so long against an opponent of equal caliber. Cartney's face split into a triumphant leer as he realized that his older opponent was tiring fast. He pushed forward, backing Kane up against the balustrade which ran around the second story landing. He had his sword poised above Kane's neck, but his foe had managed to bring his own blade up blocking it. Unfortunately for Kane, weight and leverage favored Cartney, and, slowly, the Satanist was managing to push the crossed swords down so that his blade grew nearer to the Puritan's neck.

Kane felt his sinews failing him, and, like the biblical Samson, he called upon his Lord to give him strength. And Kane's God did not forsake him! Whether from some heavenly source or from deep within his own reserves of will power, he felt an upsurge of strength sufficient to thrust his younger opponent back. As Cartney struggled to regain his balance, Kane lunged forward, his body and rapier extending in one straight line, skewering the Lord of the Hellfire Club through his wicked heart. Lord Carney fell dead without a word, a look of astonishment upon his twisted face. Kane stood panting over the body.

A quick search along the corridor disclosed a locked door which yielded to Kane's boot. Inside, he found Rowena bound and gagged upon a bed. Unfortunately, she was not alone... Cartney had left one of his ruffians behind to guard her, and when he saw this gaunt, black figure burst through the door, he raised his musket with a shaking hand and fired. The ball hit Kane square in the chest, penetrated his heart, and emerged from his back to lodge itself in the wooden paneling of the opposite wall.

The Puritan was thrown back by the impact. He glanced down at the slowly spreading crimson bloom upon his breast, then snarled and advanced towards the man, his sword raised, only to stumble to one knee and then collapse to the floor, a widening pool of dark red blood spreading out beneath him.

"Lord into Thy Hands I Commend My Spirit," he murmured in one final prayer as blood welled up into his throat and the darkness took him down.

Kane's return to consciousness was gradual; slowly, he became aware of the rough nap of a blanket under his fingers and of a pillow supporting his head. He was lying on a bed with tight bandages constricting his chest. He was astonished to find himself still alive and breathing, and also somewhat relieved not to find himself in Hell. (Kane was harsh in his self-judgment and deemed that he had many grievous sins, not the least of which several murders, weighting heavily upon his conscience.) He chose to believe that this seemingly miraculous escape from death's clutches was a work of God's Providence, and a sign that he should continue to do the Good Lord's work.

"You might as well open your eyes Solomon Kane. I know you are awake."

Kane recognized the voice of Adrian Montague and, turning his head slightly, he made out the darkened silhouette of the man sitting in a chair in a corner of the dimly-lit room.

"No doubt you are surprised to find yourself still breathing, yes? Well I've got another surprise for you, my friend. You died, shot straight through the heart. When I carried your body out of there, not a flicker of life remained. And yet, only a few hours later, and here you are, well on the road to a full recovery. How do you imagine that happened eh?"

"Witchcraft!" mouthed Kane almost too feebly to be heard.

"Maybe, maybe not." replied Montague.

Kane got the disturbing impression that Montague was reading his mind rather than his lips.

"Maybe it would be best if I told you my story, eh?" the Scotsman said, leaning forward so that Kane could make out his face more clearly. "My true name is Connor MacLeod of the clan MacLeod. I was born in the year 1518 so, age-wise, we're nearly contemporaries. In 1536, I was stabbed through the heart, but I did not die. It was then that I discovered that I was one of a race of immortals. And I knew the second we met that you, Kane, were also a member of that same race. We can recognize one another, we're all connected somehow... and we can feel it."

As if to demonstrate this fact, Montague raised a hand and allowed a brief crackle of electricity to flicker around his fingers. He arose and moved closer to Kane's bed. The Puritan knew every word he was being told was the truth. He didn't know how he knew this; he just did.

"One problem you've got with your condition is how long it took until you finally died." continued MacLeod. "I look and feel the same age now as I did when I first died, and will stay that way until the end of time... or 'til someone takes my head. But you, you were such a tough old skurlie that you managed to survive until your old age before you were actually killed. So, like my friend Ramirez, I'm afraid you're stuck with being an old immortal... Sorry!" He gave a short breathless laugh which Kane was to learn was a persistent mannerism. "Anyway," MacLeod continued, "as soon as you are feeling fit enough, we'd best be on our way. When a member of the English House of Lords gets murdered, however much of a scoundrel he was, there are invariably a lot of questions asked. So we'd best make ourselves, er, unavailable for questioning."

Kane saw no reason either to disagree or remain in bed. He pushed himself up and swung his legs over the side. He felt a little dizzy and weak, but otherwise sound. He was still trying to digest all that MacLeod had just told him. The Highlander went and fetched him his old clothes and Kane began pulling on a much worn-looking shirt and trousers.

"We'll be alright for money for a bit. Extremely grateful Sir Roger was to get his daughter back in one piece," MacLeod said, hefting a small bag of coins in his hand.

Kane scowled at such a mercenary altitude. According to his own stringent ethics, such deeds should be undertaken simple because it was right to do, with no thought to any monetary reward. But he realized that MacLeod was merely being practical. The Highlander drew on his own traveling cloak and began to pack some items into a battered travelling bag.

"We'll ride together for a bit, if you've a mind to... There's still a lot I've got to explain to you... well, as far as I understand any of it myself, that is... I know that we cannot be killed, unless our head is removed... That each time one of us kills another immortal, we grow stronger. And that, sometime in the distant future, the few of us who are left will find ourselves drawn to a distant land to battle to the death, until there is only one left, who will then gain 'The Prize.' But as to what this prize actually is, no one seems any the wiser. So it's sort of like a game, if you like. And you, Solomon Kane, have got to learn the all rules. After all, if you don't know what the rules are, how will you know when to break them?"

MacLeod gave a winning smile. And for the first time Kane got the feeling he could come to like this man.

Epilogue

Kane's reveries ended as he emerged from the tunnel and found himself, blinking and coughing, onto the side of a steep hill. He could see the mist rising above the trees, the birds carelessly singing, and the warm sun beaming down upon his leathery face. Yes, it was a good day! A fresh day. One during which he could gain the rest and recuperation he so sorely needed, to ease the last of the hurt and aches out of his centuries-old body.

It didn't take long for the old scout to locate Kronos' camp. He soon espied the mighty figure of Maciste grooming the horses tethered nearby but Doctor Omega and Telzey Amberdon were nowhere to be seen. He assumed that, having gained his prize, the Doctor and his companion had both departed in his time-traveling vehicle. (More Devil's work in Kane's gloomy opinion.) He could see Kronos sat, smoking one of his hand rolled herbal cigarettes, whilst the hunched figure of Hyeronimus Grost was busy frying a breakfast of bacon and eggs over the camp fire. Which was just as well, as Kane, who usually scorned the needs of his body, had to admit to himself that he was starving.

The sharp-eyed Kronos spotted Kane making his was down the slope and his handsome face split into a broad smile as he arose to hail him. And, as their eyes met, Kane felt once again that sudden electric jot of recognition, of... connectivity... which he had experienced the first time he had met the vampire slayer... The very same sensation that he had felt when he had encountered MacLeod... One that united them all, each recognizing the other as a member of that small elite band of brothers... a fellow immortal. What had MacLeod called it? Ah yes... *The Quickening.*

For several years now, Martin Gately has been building a corpus of stories centered around Gaston Leroux' journalist sleuth, Joseph Rouletabille. Each story can be read independently, but this new tale is an early one in a chronological sequence that includes "Rouletabille Rides the Horror Express" (TOTS 13, 1906), "Leviathan Creek" (TOTS 8, 1916), "Rouletabille and The New World Order" (TOTS 11, 1926), "Rouletabille vs. The Cat" (TOTS 10, ditto), and "Rouletabille on Mysterious Island" (TOTS 12, 1927).

Martin Gately: *Rouletabille at the Old Bailey*

London, 1909

Standing on the pavement opposite, Rouletabille looked up at the grand palace of Judgment that is the Central Criminal Court to see Lady Justice herself appeared to be looking back down at him beneficently from atop her dome. He checked his pocket. Yes, he had his notebook, a couple of pencils and the credentials which identified him as a representative of the French press. This would be his first time covering a case at the Old Bailey, and he felt a frisson of unaccustomed excitement. British justice was swift, and the entire murder case might not take more than a couple of days. And if an appeal was not lodged in a timely way, and there was no intervention from the Home Secretary, then execution by hanging was likely to follow equally swiftly.

The reporter crossed the street and saw for the first time the words engraved on the front of the building's portico: *PROTECT THE CHILDREN OF THE POOR AND PUNISH THE WRONGDOER.* A fine motto, and, to some extent, the very words he lived by. He joined the throng of people seeking admittance to the court building. Once inside, the black uniformed guardians separated journalists and witnesses from the general public. The public were ushered up a staircase towards the public gallery access corridor. Rouletabille and a handful of others—after the most perfunctory of security checks—were directed up a wide, green-flecked marble stairway up towards Court 4. Everything about this place seemed fresh and new, for although it had been built in a splendid and ancient architectural style, the building was actually less than two years old. Like some other courts he had been in, it seemed to combine the hustle and bustle of a railway station with the calm of a cathedral.

Rouletabille strode almost up to the door of Court 4 in order to examine the list sheet tacked to the courtroom notice board, on it; it simply said *Regina Versus Schellenberger - 10:30 a.m.* He removed the pocket watch from his vest to check the time. It was just before ten. There was time to repair to the cafeteria to get a drink, and since he found English tea to be virtually undrinkable, he hoped they served good coffee. The reporter located the cafeteria, got served at the counter, and then grabbed one of the small booths where he lit his pipe and sipped at the sweet strong coffee. Several of the booths and tables were occupied by barristers, unmistakable and resplendent in their powdered white wigs and long black robes, their garb unchanged since the 18th century. Each barrister had a bundle of papers tied with a blue or red ribbon—this was their *brief*—all the information they needed to defend or prosecute a case; officially, their job was to be "Master of their Brief," totally conversant with all of the facts and arguments involved in the matter to be tried. Some of the barristers also had with them huge red-bound volumes of *Archbold,* the criminal barristers' bible of evidence and pleading practice, and just as a devout man might be able to quote a large number of passages from the Bible, so too a senior barrister, or *King's Counsel,* would have committed to memory great swathes of *Archbold.*

Sticking out like a sore thumb in the cafeteria was a boy of about twenty, dressed in a long grey raincoat and sporting a wide-brimmed felt hat. The boy removed from his pocket a meerschaum pipe and chuffed on it studiously. He looked a little nervous, and Rouletabille wondered if he was a witness in a forthcoming trial. He was unlikely to be a defendant since only the most serious criminals were tried at the Old Bailey, and most were not bailed.

The Frenchman had been sent to London to report on the trial of the infamous Gustav Schellenberger, a German immigrant who had murdered his French wife, Antoinette, and also two other people in what had become known as *The Pigeon Loft Murders.* These crimes had taken place in Bethnal Green in the heart of London's East End, a mere stone's throw from Whitechapel where Jack the Ripper had once plied his deadly trade all those years before. Bethnal Green was an area of great deprivation; there, crimes were commonplace and life was cheap. Yet, the people who dwelt in that cultural melting pot had a marvelous resilience, a determination to survive coupled with a desire to assist their friends and neighbors in doing the same. It meant people there had a community spirit, and a sense of collective identity to rival any urban citizenry anywhere in the world.

It was almost half past ten now, so Rouletabille drained his coffee cup and headed back towards Court 4. As he walked out of the cafeteria, he was aware the boy with the meerschaum pipe had gotten up to follow him. His instincts told him this young fellow was a witness in the Schellenberger case; whether that was correct, only time would tell. As the reporter approached, the usher unlocked the door to the courtroom and the interested parties commenced to flow in. There were four barristers, their accompanying solicitors, and a handful of policemen: three uniformed constables and a couple of plainclothes Scotland Yard men. Fellow journalists, all from London's Fleet Street newspapers, numbered about half a dozen; these were easily identifiable in their trademark loud checked suits. Just a handful of witnesses had been warned to attend on this first day of the trial; among them was a tearful and plump middle-aged woman, a man of about sixty who looked to be unaccustomed to wearing a suit, and a girl of about twenty. They all waited on a hard wooden bench directly outside the courtroom.

Once inside, Rouletabille attached himself to the phalanx of Fleet Street journalists and followed them into the press box. The reporter drank in every aspect of the windowless courtroom. Dominating the chamber was the Royal coat of arms—the lion and unicorn device—gilt and almost two meters across; it hung from the wall directly behind the judge's red leather chair. Just in front and to the right of the judge's raised dais was the witness box. Then there were the barristers' benches. The senior barristers were already setting up the little portable lecterns they were entitled to use due to their status as *King's Counsel*. Rouletabille struck up a conversation with Ben Bates of the *London Star*, something of an "Old Bailey Hack."

"That's Sir Wilfrid Robarts, KC, the prosecution leader," said Bates. "He's scarcely lost a case for years. And behind him is his junior, Mr. T. C. Rowley, a bright and shining young star in the legal firmament. Both of them are from the elite and somewhat legendary *Eleven Queen's Bench Walk* chambers. Now, over there we have the Defense: Mr. Edward Leithen, KC, Tory MP, and Mr. Impey Biggs. You'd never know it in here, but all four barristers are actually good friends; they can be seen frequenting the wine bars together and drinking claret. But, in here, they give no quarter and take no prisoners."

From this point, the day moved forward briskly. All rose and bowed to the judge, Mr. Justice Wargrave, upon his arrival. And then the jury was sworn in. Distracted by these formalities, Rouletabille had initially not even noticed the arrival of the defendant, Schellenberger—brought up from the cells far beneath the Old Bailey and up into the dock by bailiffs who now flanked him on either side. The reporter shot a few surreptitious glances at the big German. He was pleased to see he was heavily manacled, rather like a modern day Jacob Marley. Schellenberger was about forty and had a shaven head and a drooping walrus moustache. He was huge, bear-like and savage. There did not seem to be any question that he looked very much like a man capable of eviscerating his wife and cutting up her body in a rooftop pigeon loft.

Moments later, Mr. Justice Wargrave asked Schellenberger to stand, and then the clerk of the court read out the charges on the indictment—three charges of murder. Following this, the German was invited to make his plea. Schellenberger's deep, guttural voice boomed across the courtroom:

"I plead not guilty by reason of insanity."

A murmur rippled across the chamber like the buzzing of bees. Judge Wargrave barked a demand for silence without ever looking like he was going to reach for his oak wood gavel. Then, he addressed the Defense leader.

"Mr. Leithen, will you be calling expert testimony to establish your client's insanity?"

"Yes, M'lud. In due course, you will be hearing from Dr. Rupert Grierson, the Director of Leytonstone House Insane Asylum. Dr. Grierson is a fully qualified independent forensic psychologist," answered Leithen.

"Very well. We will now proceed to hear opening statements. Sir Wilfrid, please commence."

Sir Wilfrid stood up and fixed the jury with his icy blue eyes.

"Members of the jury, you have just heard Gustav Schellenberger plead not guilty to the murder of his wife, Antoinette, Reginald Scott his employer and his acquaintance, Edward Cookson by reason of insanity. The Crown's case is that Schellenberger is as sane as you or I. We will seek to prove his every action was coldly and fully reasoned out. He is cunning, cruel and evil—but he is not mad. The plea of insanity is a cynical ruse, attempted in order to elude the hangman's noose, and live out his life in the comparative comfort of a padded cell," said Sir Wilfrid, his calm and even voice resonating in every corner of the courtroom and up into the public gallery on the level above.

"The defendant, Schellenberger is a brutish and jealous man," he continued. "His motive in this appalling crime was simple. He feared his wife was going to leave him for Edward Cookson. Although he cared little for her, and is known to have struck her on two occasions, he was reliant upon her financially. She had a successful bookkeeping business with a large number of local clients, while he was only ever to gain casual work as a market trader, selling fruit and vegetables. Even in this meager occupation, he was a failure. He had quarreled with Mr. Scott, the manager of a variety of stalls on Bethnal Green High Street, regarding his poor attendance—apparently he would rather sit drinking bottles of beer on Wanstead Flatlands than work—and then, the two men came to blows outside the *Salmon and Ball* Public House, where Schellenberger beat his employer to death in front of witnesses."

Sir Wilfrid paused for a second and consulted a typewritten list on the right hand side of his lectern.

"I call Mavis Blythe," said the prosecution leader.

With swift and practiced efficiency, the usher brought in the plump and tearful middle-aged woman Rouletabille had seen waiting on the bench earlier. Mrs. Blythe, landlady to the Schellenbergers, was led to the witness box and sworn in. The Judge could see the woman was fair shaking with nerves, and he did his best to put her at her ease and invited her to take her time and think hard before each of her answers. Further prompted by Sir Wilfrid, she began to give her *evidence in chief.*

"I had not seen Antoinette, Mrs. Schellenberger that is, for nearly three days when I decided to have a word with Mr. Schellenberger regarding 'er whereabouts. He could be something of a beast, so it was with some hesitance I went up the stairs of our building—Waterlow Buildings on Wilmot Street—to the roof. The roof is a flat one, and Mr. Schellenberger had constructed quite a large wooden loft to keep his pigeons in—these birds were his pride and joy.

And caring for them was the only thing which seemed to even his temper. When I got up there, I saw he was making quite a noise…flattening old bits of metal by hitting them with a hammer. Lord knows why. Anyway, I asked him where his wife was and 'e says she's gone to Hammersmith to look after a sick cousin and won't be back for a week. Even as 'e said it, I didn't believe a word of it. Just as I was going, I looked back at the pigeon loft, and against the white painted wood inside it, I could see a spattering of little red dots. 'E saw where I was looking and shouted that a cat had got in and killed a pigeon before he could shoo it out. Such nonsense I've never heard, but it was time to start cooking my husband's dinner, so I had to go back to my own flat for a while. But I resolved to creep up there and see what was what after the brute went out to the pub."

Mrs. Blythe paused for breath and to take a swig from the glass of water which perched precariously on the edge of the witness box.

"And what did you find when you returned to the roof of Waterlow Buildings later," asked Sir Wilfrid.

"Well, sir, I thought I'd heard him go out, but I still went up careful like. I went towards the pigeon loft because I was worried he'd done her in, and wanted to have a closer look at those little speckles of blood. I was about to step into the loft when I saw the floor was inches deep in birdseed. Every single sack of birdseed had been emptied onto the floor, and there wasn't a single sack in sight. What's more, the birdseed was all stained bright crimson…"

"Stained, Mrs. Blythe?" pressed Sir Wilfrid.

"He'd done her in all right. Chopped her into little pieces and put her in the birdseed sacks," said Mrs. Blythe, suddenly sobbing.

Mr. Leithen, for the Defense, rose slowly to his feet.

"M'lud, if I might be allowed to interject, since the body of Mrs. Schellenberger has never been found, it is not possible to know whether it was, as the witness suggests, cut up and placed in birdseed sacks. It is merely conjecture on the part of Mrs. Blythe. Indeed, the sacks themselves have never been found."

Judge Wargrave aimed a withering glare at the barrister.

"I had understood the prisoner had entered a plea of not guilty by reason of insanity. Are you suggesting Schellenberger is not guilty of the offence at all?" he asked.

"M'lud, my client admits to the murder on the basis of the circumstantial evidence, and the disappearance of his wife—but, very unfortunately, his mental condition means he has no recollection of events around this time. Nevertheless, there would seem to be little purpose in disputing the reality of the murder on the basis that the prosecution cannot prove evidence of a body when multiple witnesses saw my client murder Mr. Cookson and Mr. Scott. And these are murders he can recall."

Leithen sat down on the bench and Sir Wilfrid immediately rose.

"M'lud, the jury will also hear that the blood-soaked mulch of birdseed described by Mrs. Blythe contained fragments of human bone, human brain tissue and also blonde hair."

Rouletabille, unable to converse even at the level of a whisper while the court was in session, wrote a question for Ben Bates to read in his note book.

Why claim to be unable to remember the murder of his wife and yet admit to the murders of the two other men? Does it make any sense?

Bates scribbled his reply.

Who can account for the actions of a lunatic?

Rouletabille then wrote:

There is more to this than meets the eye.

But Bates only shook his head.

After this came the cross-examination of Mrs. Blythe, and while Leithen did his best to confuse the woman, shake her from her account, and generally muddy the waters, she stuck doggedly to her story. After this, Marie St. Claire, Mrs. Schellenberger's cousin from Hammersmith, gave evidence to establish she had not been ill, and had not asked Mrs. Schellenberger to come and look after her.

Next, Sir Wilfrid called someone named Harry Dickson. And Rouletabille was not surprised to see the young man he had spotted earlier in the Old Bailey cafeteria enter the courtroom. Dickson was sworn in by the usher.

Sir Wilfrid commenced questioning for Dickson's *evidence in chief.*

"Mr. Dickson, how did you first make the acquaintance of Mrs. Schellenberger?"

"The lady called at my consulting rooms in Baker Street with some concerns about her husband," said the young American. "I have recently started out in a small way as a detective, and had advertized my services in the East End newspapers with a view to drumming up business. She told me her husband had become progressively violent, abusive and secretive. He was having trouble holding down even the most basic forms of employment and seemed to spend a lot of time wandering on the Wanstead Flatlands. Although she could not be sure of the cause of this abhorrent behavior, she suspected another woman was at the bottom of it. Naturally, she hired me to follow her husband and give a full report."

"So you followed Schellenberger?"

"Yes, at the first opportunity, which was the following Monday. I donned common workman's garb so as to blend in with the populace as best I could. I followed Schellenberger when he left Waterlow Buildings in Bethnal Green and his first call was at an off-license on Cambridge Heath Road, where he bought half a dozen bottles of beer. He then took an omnibus to Wanstead and walked out onto the grassy plain of the flatlands."

"He did not see you?"

"People do not generally see me when I am following them. But in this instance, it was extremely difficult to avoid being spotted. Once past the oak trees that line the main road, I had to crawl through the long grass in the manner of a big cat stalking its prey. After a few hundred yards, he took off his coat and placed it on the grass to sit on, as if he was getting ready for a picnic. And there he stayed, largely immobile. I now saw he also had on him a pair of powerful looking military grade field glasses, and with these, he occasionally scanned the horizon. And sometimes he cupped his ear, as if straining to listen for something in the far distance. After about ninety minutes, I saw what he had been looking and listening for: a delicate bright yellow tri-plane with a droning engine that was little more than the buzz of a wasp. It was quite obviously one of the experimental planes constructed by the nearby A V Roe company."

"And you believed he had gone to Wanstead to observe this plane?"

"I could draw no other conclusion. Moreover, I almost immediately formed the strong suspicion he was a German agent. Aviation is bound to have military applications, and already some political commentators are saying war with Germany is inevitable. Mrs. Schellenberger had informed me during our short interview that her husband had been dishonorably discharged from the German Navy—that sounded to me to be rather a transparent ruse. Schellenberger had been sent to England on a specific mission of espionage. His job was to discover what progress A V Roe's company had made to produce a reliable and maneuverable aircraft. After he had watched the plane for a little while, he put down his field glasses and commenced to make notes and possibly sketches in a little leather-bound book. By this moment, I was already adamant whatever information he had gleaned would not fall into the hands of a foreign government. Mrs. Schellenberger had mentioned to me her husband had the hobby of keeping pigeons, and it seemed to me homing pigeons would be an excellent way of passing information to confederates. Why, from East London, a pigeon could easily fly across the Channel to German agents in Belgium, and there would be no way of stopping it," said the American detective.

"Sir Wilfrid," began the Judge. "The defendant Schellenberger has not been charged with espionage. I therefore have to query how directly relevant the testimony of Mr. Dickson is."

"M'lud, through Mr. Dickson's evidence, the Crown will seek to prove Mr. Schellenberger's apparently aberrant behavior was, in fact, a ruse. His actions are highly rational. It is true that, while there is insufficient evidence to charge him with espionage, his behavior on the Wanstead grasslands is hardly that of a drunken lunatic," said Sir Wilfrid.

The Judge returned to writing notes, and Sir Wilfrid took this as an instruction to recommence Dickson's evidence in chief.

"Mr. Dickson, you had determined you would prevent Schellenberger from passing any information to a foreign power. What action did you take next in this regard?" asked the prosecution barrister.

"I continued to crawl through the long grass towards where he was sitting. My intention was to grab his notebook and run off with it. I thought it might provide sufficient evidence for the police to effect an arrest," said Dickson. "However," he continued, "I had advanced to almost within ten feet when he spotted me. Lying in a prone position, I was now at a considerable disadvantage. I attempted to swiftly get up, but he struck me in the side of the head with one of his unopened bottles of beer, wielding it like a stumpy club. The bottle broke and cut open my scalp. A brief physical altercation ensued, during which I was able to strike him with an uppercut and disarm him of the broken bottle. Nevertheless, due to his great physical strength and fighting prowess, I was soon bested. I ended up back on the grass flat on my back. I made an undertaking to myself that if I survived this encounter, I would devote as much of my time as possible to the study of an oriental martial art, such as *baritsu.*"

"How were you able to escape, Mr. Dickson?" asked Sir Wilfrid.

"At this point, fate intervened. As I lay there in a semi-concussed daze, I saw Schellenberger had removed from his pocket a box of matches, and it seemed he would use them to set fire to the dry grass around me. But the miscreant's plans were spoiled when a dog walker—a retired man—came into view and challenged the German as to what he was up to. At this, he fled, muttering what I took to be curses in German. The retired man, Mr. Newcombe, then half carried me to the nearby infirmary at Whipps Cross, where my wounds were most efficaciously tended. And just as soon as I was patched up, I reported this matter to Scotland Yard. Little did I know then that Schellenberger was about to go on a killing spree," finished the young American detective.

With no further questions from Sir Wilfrid for the prosecution it was time for Dickson to be cross-examined by Mr. Leithen.

"Mr. Dickson, what formal qualifications or experience do you possess to qualify you as a detective?" asked the barrister. "Are you perhaps a former employee of the Pinkerton Detective Agency or an ex-Scotland Yard man?"

"I have no particular qualification or experience of that type, but I have had practical experience of detective work from a young age, doing some spot work for Nick Carter," said Dickson, defending himself as best he could.

"In fact," said Leithen, "you are still enrolled at the University of South Kensington. What is your degree course at the university?"

"English Literature," answered Dickson

"Not Criminology? Nor Chemistry, nor indeed any subject even peripherally associated with the investigation of crime?" asked Leithen.

"No, sir," said Dickson.

"Why did you take rooms in Baker Street? What was the particular attraction?" asked Leithen.

"My student accommodation is shared, and affords little privacy when consulting with clients. I therefore found it necessary to also take rooms off campus," said Dickson.

"It is then, merely a coincidence that all four of London's greatest detectives—Sherlock Holmes, Sexton Blake, Sir Seaton Begg and Victor Drago—all operate out of the exact same street where you just happened to rent a room?"

"It is an extremely convenient location," said Dickson.

"Is it not the case that you are a mere dilettante imitator of the great consulting detectives of our time? A talentless amateur, a dabbler involving yourself in matters far beyond your abilities?"

"It is true my career is at an early stage, but my early successes speak for themselves. And regarding having a Baker Street address—why, it is no different from surgeons congregating in Harley Street, or the accumulation of barristers in Lincoln's Inn. There is room in the market place for the novice in every profession—everyone has to start somewhere. As a novice, my fees are modest, sufficiently modest a respectable East End lady could afford them—and that, sir, is why I am here. I have nothing to apologize for. I am a good detective, and I expect to make my living in this job for many years to come."

Rouletabille smiled inwardly. Leithen had sought to provoke Dickson using his youth and inexperience as levers in order to discredit his evidence and it had backfired spectacularly. The young American had kept his cool. And although originally skeptical, Rouletabille had been won over to his way of thinking. He thought it highly likely Schellenberger was a spy. But questions remained: where was the body of Mrs. Schellenberger? How had the bags which had previously contained just birdseed for the pigeons (and now presumably contained the dismembered Mrs. Schellenberger) been disposed of?

This was the sort of puzzle to which the Frenchman was attracted, like a moth to a flame. The cross-examination of Harry Dickson continued for a little while longer without a great deal of incident, and when it concluded, Dickson went to the public gallery to watch the rest of the proceedings. The Judge directed the reporters not to place into the public domain details of the target of Schellenberger's alleged espionage on the grounds of national security. There then followed several more witnesses recounting the events around the publicly witnessed murders of Cookson and Scott. The first of these was Thomas Dewe, the landlord of the *Salmon and Ball* public house, who had tried to intervene during the fatal assault on Reginald Scott, Schellenberger's employer.

Lunchtime approached, the court would break for an hour shortly. Rouletabille's every instinct was that he would not solve the mysteries of this case while sitting down on a hard wooden bench at the Old Bailey. The answers were out there somewhere... in the alleys and tenements of Bethnal Green, or perhaps in the sparse woodland and grassy expanses of the Wanstead Flatlands, where an experimental airplane was probably even now under testing. Then it struck him. He scarcely knew London at all. It would be an arduous quest indeed to find and gain access to all of the important locations in this case without some sort of guide. Ben Bates was out of the question; his editor would expect him to attend every minute of the trial, whereas Rouletabille could, in theory, operate with rather greater latitude, especially if he was able to locate Mrs. Schellenberger's body, or prove the killer was also a German spy. The only option seemed to be to forge an alliance with Harry Dickson himself. He just hoped the American would agree to it.

When the lunchtime adjournment began, Rouletabille followed Dickson out of the court with a view to making his acquaintance.

Less than ninety minutes later, Rouletabille and the American detective stood on the flat, zinc-covered roof of Waterlow Buildings, close to the pigeon loft. The birds fluttered and cooed, their grayish feathers made iridescent by the bright afternoon sun. Rouletabille moved to the edge of the roof and looked to the east and south. They were adjacent to a primary school, but beyond that were more tenements. In the distance, the Frenchman could see the back of Bethnal Green Police Station, which was only just along from the *Salmon and Ball* public house. Looking to the west, there was a similar three-storey tenement across the street, and although he could not see it from this vantage point, Dickson had told him Weavers Fields—a large open play area, and one of the last expanses of greenery before the City of London proper began—lay on the other side of this neighboring building.

Dickson opened the door into the pigeon loft, and Rouletabille noticed none of the birds took the opportunity to escape. Then, on closer inspection, he saw why. The pigeons had their own exit—a little window opening to the sky, which could be closed if required. However, there were four little lockable nesting boxes in which a pigeon could be placed with just about enough room to turn around.

"These boxes must be where he kept the homing pigeons. The other birds are free to come and go as they please, as you can see," said Dickson.

Rouletabille looked down at the floor. The blood-soaked birdseed had long been cleared away, although some rust-like stains remained. Then his eye was attracted by a loose board in the wall of the loft. He bent down and picked at the edges of the board with his fingertips. After just a few seconds, he was able to tug it from its place. Concealed in the hollow of the wall was a battery, about twenty centimeters long and ten high, two brass terminals on its top.

"Well, the police missed that," said Dickson. "Logically, he must've had a transmitter too. But the police didn't find that either. Crucial evidence in this case just seems to vanish into thin air."

The Frenchman lifted the transmitter battery from its hiding place.

"It's heavy. Much heavier than it looks." He looked around the roof and spotted something that had been placed to the side of one of the building's chimneys—flattened sections of metal.

"The metal Schellenberger was flattening with a hammer. Mrs. Blythe mentioned it in her testimony," said Rouletabille as he picked up the pieces and examined them minutely. He considered every fact he had so far heard about this case, mulling the information over like a wine taster trying to identify a particular vintage.

"We are going to need meteorological reports for the night Mrs. Schellenberger was killed and the following couple of days," said Rouletabille.

Just as Dickson started to nod, a projectile struck the chimney brickwork at high velocity and ricocheted off, spiraling away like an enraged insect. The French Detective's swift eyes were able to see it was some kind of dart, most likely shot from a pneumatic rifle.

"Keep down!" shouted Dickson, and they both rolled for the cover available. It seemed to Dickson the dart must have been fired from the tenement opposite. Ignoring his own advice, the American raised his head above the level of the parapet to see if he could spot their assailant. A small black-clad figure was in the open stairway of the building across the street; a scarf obscured his features and he had a small carbine with a telescopic sight.

No sooner had Dickson seen him than he fired again, this time missing only by inches. The dart zinged off the stone of the parapet balustrade and fell into the street below. In theory, the two detectives were trapped on the roof, but Bethnal Green police station was a matter of only a few hundred yards away, and once the populace realized shots had been fired, the coppers would be summoned. Time was the enemy of the assassin. Rouletabille prepared to hunker down for a long period of concealment when he realized Dickson had armed himself, albeit with one of the smallest firearms the Frenchman had ever seen. It was some kind of Derringer, and Rouletabille suspected it had been concealed in the American's sleeve, like he was some riverboat gambler, though he had not seen him remove it. Dickson rapidly fired off two shots in the direction of the open tenement staircase, and then with practiced dexterity, deftly reloaded the weapon.

Dickson stole a look above the parapet stonework and saw that, although his shots had both missed, the marksman was fleeing the scene, running along Wilmot Street and heading towards an alleyway which ran between the tenement blocks before exiting onto Weavers Fields. Although he had little chance to aim, Dickson discharged an opportunistic round at the running figure; who stumbled momentarily, as if the bullet had just clipped his arm, then continued on his way with short irregular strides suggestive of someone not much given to physical exercise.

"We should get out of here too, my friend," said Dickson. "Technically speaking, I don't actually have a license for this thing."

It was early evening by the time Rouletabille presented himself at the Fleet Street offices of the *London Star,* Harry Dickson having gone back to his Baker Street lodgings. Ben Bates had returned from the Old Bailey and was typing up copy of the day's events at court. Nevertheless, he found five minutes to show the young French journalist down to the newspaper's morgue where he could examine the weather reports from the week when Mrs. Schellenberger was murdered. After, following some improvised calculations, Rouletabille had cause to send telegrams to his own newspaper's office, as well as a journalist colleague in the Netherlands.

Having finished his inquiries for the day, Rouletabille returned to the *Star's* bullpen, and sat with Ben Bates, adding plumes from his own pipe to the bluish grey fog of cigarette smoke which hovered above the desks of the loudly dressed London newsmen.

"So who is on the witness stand tomorrow?" asked the Frenchman, over the general racket from the typewriters.

"It's Dr. Grierson, the head of the Leytonstone Insane Asylum; you'll probably recall him getting a mention this morning. His job is to give a professional forensic opinion on whether or not Schellenberger is really insane. But I've seen Grierson before. He's a nasty piece of work," said Bates.

Rouletabille's puzzlement at the idiom showed on his face.

"An unpleasant, sadistic-looking character. I wouldn't want to be subjected to his tender mercies... electric shock treatment and so forth. He has the look of a villain, bald as an egg and a face like a defrocked priest!" laughed the cockney journalist. "In some ways, it is the most important evidence of the case, because it determines whether or not Schellenberger will hang."

"I do not know if I would want to escape the hangman's noose only to live out my life in some lunatic asylum," considered Rouletabille. "I think I would rather suffer that short drop through the scaffold trapdoor and face my final Judgment than cling so very desperately to this world."

"But Schellenberger is almost certainly some brand of nihilist, and probably an atheist into the bargain. He does not have your sensibilities, nor your moral compass. If he's an atheist, he's putting off the blank emptiness of non-existence; if he has some semblance of religious belief, he's avoiding imminent damnation. Not so very long ago, we hanged people for every conceivable crime in this country—stealing a lamb, or even a handkerchief—right the way up to assault and bestiality. And so I have to wonder just how much of a deterrent capital punishment is. More crucially, you have seen how courts work: some well-educated men ask questions in order to bring out certain points, while other well-educated men do their best to obfuscate and confuse the issues. Following that, twelve good men do what they can to decide the matter. The whole process is too susceptible to human error. No one's life should really be resting on it. In another fifty or sixty years, the whole business of execution will have been reformed. I doubt if they'll be hanging anyone except traitors," said Bates.

"Which brings us back to Schellenberger," said Rouletabille. "I have seen today the strongest evidence he is guilty of espionage, so I have caused inquiries to be made abroad—in both Holland and France, and I expect these investigations to reach fruition some time tomorrow afternoon. I have, as I believe you say in England, 'set the hares running.'"

Bates merely smiled at this and inhaled deeply on the remnants of his cigarette.

"My intention," continued Rouletabille, "in terms of London newspapers, is to give the story to the *Star* as an exclusive in thanks for all the assistance you have given me. Naturally, the story will also run in my own paper."

"You are pretty sure of yourself," laughed Bates.

"I suppose I am. But I should probably say no more at this stage; to some extent, the whole thing is in the lap of the gods, or more properly in the hands of the east wind," said the Frenchman, and although he was thinking about the wind, he could not get out of his mind's eye the image of hares running hell for leather across an open field, as if desperate to evade a monstrous pursuer.

The following morning, all of the main players had returned to Court 4 at the Old Bailey as the court went back into session. Rouletabille was again sitting next to Ben Bates on the hard wooden benches of the press box. Harry Dickson was up in the public gallery, and Dr. Grierson was being sworn in by the usher. Grierson was a gnome-like figure with thick-lensed glasses, small ears and his right arm held in a sling. Suddenly, Rouletabille was aware of Dickson waving to him frenetically from high up in the public gallery—the Frenchman gestured to him to desist. It was not a good idea to draw attention to one's self in the public courtroom, and depending on the mood of the judge, the slightest infraction could result in a charge of contempt of court, or at the very least removal from the courtroom. This was literally the last thing Rouletabille wanted to be party to. Whatever it was, it could wait.

Since Dr. Grierson was technically a Defense witness, the normal pattern of giving evidence was reversed, and Mr. Leithen took the first turn in asking questions in order to elicit the psychiatrist's *evidence in chief.*

"Dr. Grierson," began Leithen, "you have had the opportunity to examine the prisoner, Schellenberger, while he has been in custody?"

"Yes, on several occasions," said the doctor.

"And what is your professional opinion on his state of mind?" asked the Defense barrister.

"In layman's terms, he is morally insane. By which, I mean he is incapable of telling right from wrong. He is a perfect example of what has been described as the *moral imbecile.* It means no more to him to kill his wife than it would to ring the neck of one of his pigeons," explained Grierson.

"What is your opinion of his apparent loss of memory in relation to the murder of his wife? Is he simply feigning amnesia?" asked Leithen.

"He has an extreme personality, and as such he would be highly susceptible to entering fugue states following episodes of excitement, passion or trauma. Put simply, a fugue state is something like a mental fog. It may lift in time, allowing memories to be recovered, or it may stay in place, becoming something like a permanent curtain within the mind. I have questioned him closely regard-

96

ing his memory loss, and I have found his responses to be entirely consistent. Nevertheless, I think it is right Schellenberger has stood a full trial. The reason being it is highly disorientating for a disordered and amnesic mind to find itself suddenly imprisoned; in cases like these, it can actually be therapeutic for the patient to hear his recent story from the witnesses involved," said Grierson.

"You will be aware Mrs. Schellenberger engaged the services of a certain, Harry Dickson—an inexperienced young detective now resident in London. How do you account for the violent encounter which took place between Mr. Dickson and Schellenberger out on the Wanstead Flats?" asked Leithen.

"Through the application of commonsense and reason, it is quite easy to deduce Schellenberger's motivations. Nevertheless, he has confided in me during our sessions, and I can tell you it is no surprise to me that his deviant mind contains a strong attraction towards voyeurism. His sole intention in his pathetic meanderings on the grassland was to observe courting couples committing fornication. And being something of a skilled amateur artist, he drew the things he had seen. After his confrontation with Mr. Dickson, he burned the notebook. However, he was able to recreate some of the drawings for me during his incarceration. It is unusual for someone with homicidal tendencies to have a flair for illustration. Perhaps if this man had been born into a different strata of society he would've made his living as an artist," stated Grierson.

"Will you be placing these drawings into evidence?" asked Leithen.

"Well, I hardly think they represent suitable material to be placed before an English jury. They are, by their very nature, obscene. I would invite the court to simply take my word for it that such images exist," answered Grierson.

The Judge gave a perfunctory nod.

"The crucial thing is," continued Grierson, "that the prisoner's diseased mind certainly had no interest in aeroplanes. If he looked at them through his binoculars, then that is purely coincidental. They would've drawn his attention no more than they would've anyone else who just happened to be walking upon the grasslands."

The *evidence in chief* continued for just a little while longer and then Sir Wildrid Robarts commenced his *cross-examination*. But Grierson proved himself to be adamant and immovable on every conceivable point. No matter where Sir Wilfrid directed the questioning, the psychiatrist remained calm and utterly professional. Perhaps only when he was quizzed on his academic qualifications did the mask drop just a fraction, and Rouletabille saw a man who clearly did not want to be troubled by any of this, a man who regarded himself as superior to all—there was a titanic ego cloistered within his stunted body.

It was almost lunchtime when a messenger boy unobtrusively entered the court and gave a large envelope to Ben Bates. Bates looked momentarily at the writing on the envelope and passed it to Rouletabille unopened. The Frenchman immediately saw it was addressed to him 'care of' Bates in Court 4 of the Old Bailey. Inside was a sheaf of telegrams which Rouletabille commenced to read.

TO ROULETABILLE:
REMNANTS OF DOWNED WEATHER BALLOON DISCOVERED
EAST OF ARNHEM STOP BALLOON WAS CARRYING SMALL SACKS
CONTAINING HUMAN REMAINS AND A RADIO TRANSMITTER IN
WOODEN CASE STOP

Then Rouletabille read the clincher:

SOME BIRDSEED REMAINS IN THE SACKS STOP. EXAMINATION
OF TRANSMITTER UNDERWAY BY EXPERTS STOP.
REGARDS, J FELDHEIM
INTERNATIONAL NEWS SERVICE BUREAU, ROTTERDAM

Rouletabille was jubilant. This was no time for hubris, but it was gratifying to know that even with the most limited of evidence—part of the examination of which took place while under attack—he was still able to reach a correct logical conclusion, one that had eluded the finest minds of Scotland Yard, as well as the promising Harry Dickson.

Rouletabille scribbled in his notebook and showed what he had written to Ben Bates. Bates blanched somewhat as he read it.

"How do I get to be a witness in this case?" was what the Frenchman had scrawled.

After the court had adjourned for lunch, Dickson rushed up to Rouletabille and addressed him in confidential tones while Ben Bates talked urgently with the instructing solicitors for the prosecution, trying to convince them to call Rouletabille as a witness.

"I've got the hunch to end all hunches that it was Grierson who shot at us on the roof of Waterlow Buildings. I'm pretty sure I winged our would-be assassin, and Grierson just happens to have his right arm in a sling," said the American. "His physical shape is also pretty unmistakable."

"Hunches are not evidence, my dear Dickson," responded Rouletabille. "If Grierson is part of a German espionage conspiracy, we are going to need more than a gut feeling to put him behind bars. He is one of the foremost forensic psychiatric practitioners in London."

"But don't you see? There are enormous ramifications if Grierson is one of Schellenberger's confederates. If German agents can be legally judged to be insane and placed in Grierson's custody at Leytonstone Asylum, he might spirit them out of the country after a period of time, and no one would be any the wiser," said Dickson.

Rouletabille's lunchtime was taken up being interviewed by Scotland Yard officers, who swiftly typed up his statement regarding the foreign investigations he had initiated. Naturally, the sheaf of telegrams from the International News Service was officially registered as an exhibit in the case and formally cross-referenced to his sworn statement.

Finally, the court was called back into session, but this time Rouletabille had to wait outside to be called in by the usher. Inside the court, there followed a short legal argument regarding whether evidence from the French journalist could be admissible at this stage. Once the legal wrangling was concluded, Rouletabille was summoned and sworn in. The court looked a very different place from inside the witness box, considerably more intimidating, and he stumbled a little over his oath through sudden and unexpected nerves—it seemed to him that to be a witness in a court is to be a bug under a magnifying glass, just waiting for the sun to emerge from behind a cloud and start the process of incineration. This sensation of scrutiny, combined with imminent doom, was made worse by the fact Schellenberger now had a direct line of sight to him, and was glaring at him like a gorgon. Perhaps even worse, on the fringes of his peripheral vision, he could catch glimpses of Grierson's face frowning down at him from on-high in the public gallery, looking every bit the malignant imp from some fairy tale, or fevered nightmare.

"You are Joseph Josephin, also known as Rouletabille, a French journalist assigned by your newspaper to cover this trial. Further to this, please tell the court the results of the enquiries you have caused to be made abroad," requested Sir Wilfrid Robarts.

"Yes, I am Rouletabille, and on the first day of this trial I heard, as we all did, the evidence of Mrs. Blythe and how she related the conundrum of the disappearance of Mrs. Schellenberger's body, which she suspected had been cut up and placed in small sacks of birdseed. These sacks were never to be seen again, at least not in this jurisdiction. Most crucially, Mrs. Blythe also related how Schellenberger had been bashing bits of metal on the rooftop with a hammer, flattening them. I investigated this and found these metallic fragments. They appeared to me to be broken up pressurized cylinders. More specifically, helium cylinders. The obvious conclusion was that, in dead of night, Schellenberger had released a helium balloon with the dismembered body of his wife as its cargo. I made calculations on how far such a balloon might travel in the prevailing weather conditions. My best estimates suggested it would lose buoyancy and come to earth somewhere in eastern Holland. And such has proved to be the case. Following inquiries, the downed balloon was discovered in a farmer's field outside Arnhem."

"So, did the balloon carry anything other than the human remains?" asked Sir John.

"Yes, sir, a wooden case containing a powerful wireless telegraphy transmitter. Ideal for use by a spy. In addition, a leather-bound notebook filled not with pornographic drawings, but rather with British military secrets gleaned by travels in and around the south east of England."

"I have no further question, M'lud," said Sir Wilfrid, suddenly sitting back down on his bench.

Flustered and somewhat ambushed by this new evidence, Mr. Leithen stood up to cross-examine Rouletabille with some reticence.

"A man might be a spy and also be insane, wouldn't you agree?" he asked. "After all, what sane man chops his wife up into little pieces?"

"Perhaps," admitted Rouletabille. "But he did not merely cut her up, he sent those pieces on a balloon ride. What I did not know when I made my initial calculations was that the helium balloon was fitted with a slow release valve. Schellenberger's intention was for the balloon to come down somewhere in the North Sea. While he had to find a way to dispose of his wife's body, in any event, she conveniently became the ballast to facilitate the permanent concealment of his transmitter. But the valve jammed—it was still jammed when the balloon and its payload were found. This act proves him to be sane. Only a sane man would seek to eliminate the evidence of his espionage in such a subtle and brilliant way."

"Is this not pure conjecture, Monsieur? The prisoner could just as well have used the birdseed as ballast."

"In which case, he would still have the body to dispose of. When the facts of this case are arranged in order, they can be read like a mathematical equation. Only one interpretation makes logical sense, and the level of conjecture is miniscule. Because of the actions of Mr. Dickson, your client was convinced he was being observed when he left his home. He thought the authorities were closing in. His wife must have revealed to him she had engaged the services of a Baker Street detective to investigate his behavior—many of whom have close ties to the government—in doing so she sealed her doom, and he killed her. Since he believed he was now under surveillance, he had to get rid of the body without leaving Waterlow Buildings. Options such as putting the body into a local canal or park were now out of the question. Whether he hit on the idea of using the helium weather balloon he had been issued with by his masters by chance, or whether it was part of a pre-conceived stratagem to put evidence of his espionage out of reach, we may never know," explained Rouletabille, pausing for breath.

"Then with the primary evidence removed from the scene, the pressure eased. Mr. Dickson is recovering from injuries—no longer following Schellenberger—his report of a German spy in the East End initially dismissed by Scotland Yard. Yet Schellenberger knows Mrs. Blythe has already noticed his wife's absence; soon the clients of her bookkeeping business will do the same. He buys himself a week with his lie about the sick cousin in Hammersmith, and uses that week to complete his spying mission; using the carrier pigeons in his loft to report back to his masters. Now what? The fear of arrest hangs over him like the Sword of Damocles, but still arrest does not come. He worries now there are sufficient human remains—fragments of skull, bone and brain mixed in with the bloody birdseed—to secure a murder conviction, but he dare not remove any of it from the roof for fear of being arrested with it on his person. He is merely a man who has murdered his wife, and for that he knows he faces capital punishment. But what if he can cheat the hangman by proving himself to be a lunatic? This he does by committing two appalling murders in public. For him, it is the safest course, much safer than attempting to flee the jurisdiction when for all he knew he might be placed on a watch list as a spy at any moment."

"I put it to you that your so-called evidence is pure froth and nothing of substance, and that you are simply an attention-seeking charlatan," said Leithen.

"No, sir. I am not a neophyte detective whose reputation you can cast doubt on. My work places me in the first rank of those who seek to explain so-called impossible crimes. Modesty normally prevents me from alluding to the fact that I solved the *Mystery of the Yellow Room*—one of the most famous cases in the annals of French crime, yet you force me to make mention of it. As for proof, all of the evidence I have described here this afternoon in relation to the balloon will be the subject of sworn depositions from the witnesses in Holland—they will be sent to the Old Bailey via courier just as soon as they arrive at the Dutch Embassy in the diplomatic bag," said Rouletabille, passionately.

Breaking his silence for the first time during the trial, Schellenberger made a bellow like a beast caught in the jaws of a trap and lunged to get out of the dock. Fortunately, the alert bailiffs were able to restrain him.

"Your client is going to the gallows," observed Rouletabille, somewhat coldly. "I swear it."

Two weeks later, Ben Bates and Rouletabille stood in the public entrance hall of Newgate Prison, shoulder to shoulder with two dozen other reporters. The Frenchman noticed somehow Harry Dickson had blended himself with the mass of journalists, and was trying to look unobtrusive in the corner.

"You owe me ten bob," said Ben Bates cheerily to Rouletabille.

"Eh? Ten bob? What is that?" asked the Frenchman, suitably puzzled.

"Ten shillings. They decide which four journalists will observe the execution by pulling names out of a hat. Let's just say the journalists from *The London Star* and *Le Temps* have their places pre-booked. Such things should not be left to chance," whispered Bates.

"Well, I don't really approve of bribery and corruption, but today I will abandon my principles for the sake of seeing this monstrous brute hang," said Rouletabille.

The Newgate Prison governor literally pulled the names of the journalists out of a hat on slips of paper, and then announced the "winners" to the assemblage. The other two august journals whose representatives would be admitted to the place of execution were: *The Times* and the *Daily Telegraph*.

All four men were led by the governor and the chief warden up a winding stone staircase to the top floor of the prison. On this top landing were dozens of cells, all with their doors looked and closed—all, that is, except one. Since public executions had been discontinued some years ago, this cell had been converted to be an execution chamber. It was next door to the condemned cell, and this was a fact kept secret from those due to be executed, they tended to anticipate a long walk to their final doom when, in truth, it was only a few steps away through a specially constructed adjoining door. The four journalists were guided to their positions opposite the condemned cell doorway. This meant they had to step onto and across the gallows trapdoor and this sent a chill up Rouletabille's spine.

Rouletabille took out his pocket watch. It was almost midday. In less than two minutes, the condemned cell door would swing urgently open and Schellenberger would be brought speedily into this room by the executioner, and before his mind would be able to process events, the noose would be placed around his neck. Even the normally cocky Bates looked nervous, a film of perspiration glistened on his upper lip. Rouletabille looked up at where the rope was attached to the ceiling via brass fixtures. In the small and airless room, the moments accumulated like flies gathering on rotten meat. These were the final seconds of Schellenberger's life before it would be snuffed out. A scintilla of pity started to form in the French journalist's mind, but before the thought could fully take on form, he exiled it to the recesses of his consciousness.

The heavy iron door of the condemned cell swung open as if had been kicked. Schellenberger already had the death hood over his head. The prisoner was propelled, almost carried, by the guards on either side of him who had tight grip of his arms, which were securely strapped behind his back. Very swiftly, the executioner put the noose around Schellenberger's neck, then almost immediately his legs were strapped together at the calves. He was standing on the trapdoor—what was left of the murderer's life would be over in the bat of an eye. As the executioner stepped towards the lever on the wall which controlled the trapdoor, Rouletabille was aware for the first time of the prison chaplain intoning a prayer. The words washed over Rouletabille. They seemed incomprehensible and irrelevant.

The explosion struck like a thunderclap, tearing away the masonry from this corner of Newgate Prison and exposing the noonday sky. A large section of the brickwork from the wall fell away and disappeared into the street. Rouletabille had been struck by flying debris in the chest and legs, yet he was certainly the least badly hurt of the four journalists. Ben Bates was covered with dust and blood. He lay almost immobile, but when the Frenchman crawled nearer to him, he could see he was still breathing. One of the other British journalists had been blown limb from limb, and the other hovered near death in a growing stain of crimson which was spilling from his throat. The guards and the executioner staggered about, as if drunk or blind. The chaplain must've been screaming something, but no words seemed to be issuing from his mouth. It was then Rouletabille realized the blast had rendered him deaf—temporarily, he hoped. All he could he hear was a sound like the roaring of a waterfall magnified a thousand fold.

Of Schellenberger, there was no sign. Then Rouletabille noticed the rope which was hanging from the exposed roof level down into the condemned cell. The murderer was escaping over the roof tops. In the moments after the explosion, someone had entered the cell and freed him. Summoning vitality, he had no right to possess, the Frenchman grabbed onto the mountaineering rope and started to haul himself up onto the roof of Newgate Prison. Immediately, he saw Schellenberger had not been immune to injury from the explosion; limping, he was being helped across the roof by a small figure whose face was obscured by a scarf and a hat with the brimmed pulled down. The disguised man pulled a nickel-plated automatic from under his coat and loosed a round at Rouletabille. The report from the pistol seemed muffled and unreal—yet his hearing was starting to clear. Rouletabille dove for the cover provided by a raised glass skylight. He wished to God that Dickson was up here with him.

Suddenly, it seemed to him someone was calling his name, far off and incredibly distorted—as if heard underwater. Rouletabille crawled to the bomb-damaged parapet and dared to look down. It was Dickson! He was sprinting from the far side of the street in a fashion that reminded the Frenchman of a cricket player—a bowler. When Dickson came to a stop, he hurled something small and silvery up towards the roof. To Rouletabille, it seemed futile; the claws of gravity would soon grab it and pull it back to earth. But on it spun, before clattering to the prison roof just yards away from him. It was Dickson's Derringer. He lunged for it and cocked the hammer. Aiming and firing at the same instant, he missed and struck brickwork near Schellenberger's head. The disguised figure—could it really be Grierson? —tried to urge Schellenberger on to escape, but instead, he wrestled the automatic from the hand of his benefactor and aimed it at Rouletabille. Rouletabille's shot passed directly through the murderer's left eye socket and into his brain. His reprieve from execution had been but a few minutes. Now at the end of his endurance, and with no further ammunition, Rouletabille could only watch as Schellenberger's would-be rescuer made good his escape.

Four days later, Rouletabille was escorting Dickson back to his Baker Street apartments after they had visited Ben Bates in Marylebone Hospital. The cockney journalist was recovering well, and was due to be discharged from the hospital the following week.

"It is my firm belief there is still a German espionage ring operating out of the East End of London. Our work is not yet done. In particular, there is the matter of gathering evidence against the traitor Grierson," said Rouletabille.

"Forgive me," said Dickson, "but I now have cases piling up which need my attention. Give me a couple of weeks to clear my desk, then I can devote myself more properly to the spy ring affair."

"Very well, but it will be difficult without you since I do not know London as you do," said the Frenchman.

A swirl of fog had descended across Baker Street like a physical barrier, and Rouletabille could see a group of partially obscured figures waiting ahead of them. He could not quite make them out or tell them one from the other, but there seemed to be four men—all of them wearing fore and aft caps and mid-length Inverness capes.

"They are outside my door. They must be waiting for *me*. Stay here, my friend. I'll see what the problem is," said the American detective.

Dickson approached the identically dressed men with some trepidation, and then, after a little while, it became apparent he was conversing with them in a good natured fashion, and so Rouletabille relaxed. And after a few moments more, Dickson walked back along the pavement.

"It seems extraordinary, but they have accepted me into their number. They regard me as an official Baker Street consulting detective, due to my recent success," said Dickson.

"That is marvelous news," said Rouletabille.

"It seems there is a short ceremony in a local hostelry, followed by toasting and dinner. Do please join us," implored Dickson.

"I think not, Harry. I would be out of place at such a gathering. This is your moment. Savor and enjoy it. Do not speak to them of our case and I will see you in two weeks."

The two men shook hands, and Dickson broke into a run on his way back to the consulting detectives.

The fog had lifted a little, but even so Rouletabille could not tell Holmes from Blake, Begg or Drago. In some respects they were a single man—the archetype, and those he had inspired. They belonged to London. They belonged to everyone.

Micah Harris already featured the mysterious religious Order of the Barbusquins, created by Raymond De Kremer (1887-1964), better known as Jean Ray, in the classic horror novel Malpertuis *(1943), in his short story "The Goat of Saint Elster" published in our last volume. This tale, also featuring Brom Cromwell of the Barbusquins, takes place well over a century before "Goat"...*

Micah S. Harris: *Beneath the Mount of Divination*

Rome, December 1642

1.

"At least, the woman's voluptuousness will make this prodigious inconvenience somewhat less than a total loss."

A rather inappropriate thought, to be sure, to be had by a priest. But this was the Abbot d'Herblay, as he was now known, and the Abbot d'Herblay had never allowed religious pursuits to interfere with his pursuit of a lovely lady.

The lady in question had no reason to suspect his calling from his appearance. He wore not a priest's cassock, but his old musketeer's uniform, to which he had added a cape. And it was under his old assumed name of Aramis that he had answered the summons to the Vatican hill, which, long ago, had itself had another identity: *Vaticanus Collis*—the mountain of divination.

His business did not bring him to the Vatican palace itself, and certainly not to the Pope, but rather to an old, concealed hunting lodge that the Borgia family once had used for their trysts. Here he had come to rendezvous with Cardinal Mazarin, Italian-born but lately of France, where he had performed a service in the affairs of Christine of Savoy, King Louis XIII's sister. Aramis' presence here was in payment of that particular debt of the Crown.

It was old and dying Cardinal de Richelieu who had recommended him to the king for this task. "For I know of a certainty," Richelieu had said with a grin that could only be described, in Aramis' mind, as "dung-eating," "that there is no man more dedicated to the interests of the throne." The throne Richelieu spoke of was not Louis XIII's, but that of his queen, Anne, who once had an interest in the Duke of Buckingham. Of this affair, Richelieu had known very well, but Aramis and his friends had seen to it that the king would never have knowledge of it—at least, no knowledge that could be proven.

A reuniting with his former companions who had joined him to save Queen Anne from compromise would have been ideal for this current adventure. Alas, at the moment, they were either too far dispersed or retired into a seclusion from

105

which it would be less than timely to extricate them. Thus, his new cohorts in arms.

Of course, it was the woman who had captured his attention first upon entering the lodge. She was blonde, statuesque and superbly proportioned. Even her man's blouse and britches could not conceal the *rondeurs* of her body. She wore leather boots to the knee and on one thigh was strapped a *poignard*. On her other side, her sword was sheathed. Dressed as a man she may have been, but her perfume—orange flowers and vanilla, if he knew his scents—and he did—was a welcome whiff of femininity.

The woman's companion, who had accompanied her from England, was a man who appeared to be approaching middle-age, but still radiated youthful vigor. He retained the trace of a once-Irish accent to judge by such small talk between the two that Aramis had overheard from outside, just before he interrupted the conversation with his entrance.

The man wore a waist-length hooded cloak, the shirt a plowman might wear, tight pants of humble but sturdy material, and tight-fitting boots as well. He was clean-shaven, with a pale face, high forehead, sunken cheeks, and eyes that were a vivid blue.

Before Aramis or either of the couple could initiate an introduction, a fourth man had entered the room from within the lodge and motioned that they should be seated around a long wooden table where the Borgias once had supped with their mistresses. While the Irishman sat close to the lady—to Aramis' great envy—there was great space in the seating between them and Aramis and the man at the head of the table. This was none other than Cardinal Mazarin himself. He had shed his cardinal splendor for rustic clothing to move incognito to and from this meeting.

"Now that we have convened," Mazarin began, "introductions are in order, though whether the names used are truly your own or pseudonyms, it matters not. But you must call yourselves something other than 'hey, you,' must you not? Quick and clear communication will be necessary in the success of this endeavor. It may, in fact, be necessary for you to survive it. So, if we may begin with our latest arrival?"

"I am Aramis," the Abbot d'Herblay said, pushing his chair back to stretch his legs out, leaning back and clasping his hands to his breast. "Formerly a black musketeer serving the throne; currently serving the church as an abbot. I have been recalled by the throne into active service. For this mission only," he said, eyeing Mazarin, "I departed my current situation most reluctantly. But, for king and country, one must be willing to make certain sacrifices I suppose."

"Not only for your country, but for all of Europe," the woman injected.

"Ah, the lady speaks," Mazarin said, templing his fingers and smiling over them. "And when you hear her tale, you will understand her urgency. But first, we have another agent, her traveling escort."

The pale faced man smiled. "I am Brom Cromwell, a monk of the Barbusquin order. I go by Brom."

Aramis suddenly drew himself up to the table and leaned toward Cromwell, his thoughts turned momentarily from the young woman. He felt as though he were looking at a unicorn come to life from a medieval tapestry. "I have heard of your order, but thought it only a legend. Do you truly seek out pagan horrors yet lingering in Christendom and eradicate them?"

"'Tis the express mission of a Barbusquin monk."

"Yet, that one of your order lingers on in the world in the age of the Enlightenment is no less astonishing to me than if you were to produce a basilisk."

"I'm sure you will find my stare much more agreeable," Cromwell said and there was a gleam in his blue eyes and the touch of mirth at the corners of his mouth.

"And, finally, the lady whom Brother Cromwell has escorted from England, who alerted us to this potential catastrophic danger of which there is yet a chance of aborting. This is Mademoiselle Françoise de Bretigny, of the Scurvhamite Puritan sect."

"A puritan? And I, a priest." Aramis said, tweaking his moustache, then resting his chin on his hand and smiling at the young woman. "Strange bedfellows indeed."

Françoise raised her chin and cast a haughty gaze upon Aramis as she spoke. "I am of the court of Charles I, sir, a lady in waiting to *your* king's sister."

"I do not think that Charles would be glad to know the royal bosom harbors a puritan in it," Aramis said and looked her up and down, ostensibly as if he were reconsidering his new partner with respect to her loyalties, but in truth, to review her figure, which he was pleased to find in accord with his initial estimation.

"We are not all followers of Oliver Cromwell, sir," Françoise sniffed. "I love my mistress and would never do her harm. My loyalties to God are not in conflict to with my loyalty to the crown. I am come as a royalist first; a Christian second. I have much inconvenienced myself if I am in a plot to bring hurt to the British throne. I might have worked mischief more effectively at court and kept the comfort of my own bed."

"A much better bed into which to be cast with you than our present one, I am sure," Aramis said and grinned.

Françoise flushed and Cromwell narrowed his eyes at the musketeer.

"And now it seems that I have drawn the ire of her watchdog," Aramis said and resumed his grin.

"Her guardian," Cromwell said. "And well adept at it as there are men on both sides of the channel with at least *one* member no longer to call their own who will tell you. In falsetto."

"Let us not be quick to take offense, Brom," Françoise said and laid her hand on Cromwell's arm. "Perhaps...," she said, "...I am but a maid overly sensitive to sincere but uncouth expressions of admiration, being accustomed to courtly behavior."

Aramis colored. "Mademoiselle, I assure you, my manners would be at home in the highest courts of France."

"But we are not in France, are we?" Françoise said. "And by your Roman air of superiority regarding my own faith, I do not think you believe you owe me no more than the courtesy you would give a scullery maid."

"Aramis?" Mazarin said and raised an eyebrow.

He did not acknowledge Mazarin but locked eyes with Cromwell's. "I can see that I have seriously compromised the *esprit de corps* needed here. Know, sir...," and here he turned to Françoise, "...and mademoiselle, that I have never touched a lady who did not first wish me to do so." He looked back at Cromwell. "And, as you, Frère Brom, are beyond fleshly desires, we should all get along famously. 'All for one and one for all.' That's what I say. My apologies to you both."

"Accepted," Cromwell said, "on my part. Mademoiselle de Bretigny?"

"My dear Brom," she said. "You have, due to your calling, spent so much time among men lately that you have forgotten women do not forgive so readily as your own sex. Monsieur Aramis must henceforth earn *my* regard."

"Ah," Cromwell said and smiled at his charge. "I am not as much a stranger to women as you think, milady. Nor their capacity to harbor resentment once insulted."

"I shall strive to raise your estimation of me, milady," Aramis said with a bow of the head.

"Well, then, now that we are all friends again for the first time," Mazarin said, "let the lady pass on her intelligence."

Françoise began: "The Scurvhamite sect of Protestantism was founded by our leader Robert Scurvham. We hold to predestination..."

"Calvinism," Aramis hissed and studied a splash of mud on his boot.

"Not quite, if monsieur will let me finish before dismissing me. Thank you. Our belief is a merger of Persian dualism, with its coeval powers that oppose each other eternally, and the emerging mechanistic conception of the universe. One half of that machine has been set in motion by God, who governs everything in it, cosmic and microcosmic. That is the Scurvhamite Universe which we committed to Christ inhabit. But the Other... the *Other*...," she closed her eyes and shivered, then began again.

"The *Other* of that anti-Scurvhamite Universe that coexists with ours, visible from our place as paradise was from Hades, but... but... there is no chasm which cannot be crossed, as there was between Dives and Lazarus. That antiuniverse is accessible. And mesmerizing in the fatal implications of its horror which hypnotizes as surely as the serpent does the bird. Thus enthralled, many of our numbers have crossed to the other side and have been lost in the maze of cogs and springs of that machine of the abyss.

"But this opportunity for penetration between the dual cosmoses works both ways. And that nameless horror which has set in motion the anti-Universe has now manifested in our own. This being has many names..." She met eyes with Cromwell: "Chief among them since ancient times is 'Baal.' We know him as 'Trystero'..." and then she turned and looked at Aramis, "...and sometimes by a more obscure variant, 'Simara.' But I will tell you now with all levity: Oliver Cromwell has become a secret follower of Baal."

"What?" Aramis said, slamming his palms down on the table. Only he appeared thus shocked and appalled. Brom apparently had already been privy to this intelligence, as had been, to judge by his demeanor, the silent Mazarin who regarded Aramis coolly.

"Do you see how wrong you were to judge me guilty by association, monsieur?" Françoise said to Aramis. "I am opposed to Oliver Cromwell more than you could have believed possible. He awaits the signal now to overthrow the English monarchy, and from there spread this pernicious belief throughout Europe, where all thrones will be cast down and their people become but mechanisms assimilated into the engine of Baal's anti-universe. They will become simple extensions of his will; their personalities annihilated."

"And what shall this signal be?" asked Aramis.

"*Baal shall be seen on the mount of divination and then shall the end begin.*"

"The Vatican hill!" said Aramis. "That explains our current location. But what are we to do against such a cosmic horror?"

"Where is your faith?" Brom asked calmly. "Jesus Christ is Lord of all, above all principalities and powers, whatever they might be. Angels, demons, creatures of deep time, or a demiurge from someplace other—it is no great matter to Him."

"This power," said Mazarin, "is yet vulnerable in its present form and, if it cannot be destroyed, it may yet be contained."

"Do I understand that it is already here?" Aramis asked.

"Yes."

"And how did it come to be?"

"I brought it here," a new voice announced.

The speaker was a man in shadow who stood behind the seated Mazarin. No one knew how long he had been there. He stepped forward into the light and Aramis gasped.

"The Grey Eminence?" he said. "But... he is dead!"

The old man with bald pate and fringe of a white beard still wore his grey robes of office. Despite the rumors of his death, and his age, there was still much strength apparent in that body. He stood tall and straight, not bent, and whatever reversals he may have suffered of late had done naught to quench his haughtiness. On the left hand of the left finger was his black signet ring, which had been missing when his "body" had been discovered. Unless... was this man an impostor? Or had the real Grey Eminence transferred his support from Richelieu to Mazarin, and faked his death to better facilitate this new alliance? It would fit with his *modus operandi* of operating from the shadows.

"I live, Monsieur d'Herblay," the Grey Eminence said and smiled as though he was something, a were-creature, which had never smiled before and was merely imitating what it had seen. Aramis shivered at hearing his name spoken by the one who had also been known as "Father Joseph" in past days. The man had been deadly then, and best that you were of no importance to him. Now Aramis was important to him.

Father Joseph extended his ring hand. Brom and Françoise made no move. Catholic authority had no claim on her and Brom, though ignorant of the Grey Eminence's past reputation, nevertheless discerned that something wasn't right about this "priest." He noted the sign of the signet, a loop of stars. Why stars? He wondered. And why that formation? He bent forward. He had seen this esoteric sign before in performing his holy tasks. And it was not good.

Mazarin must be completely ignorant of its significance to ally himself thusly, he thought.

He was relieved to see that Aramis refrained from approaching the offered ring. "How do I know it is you?" he asked the old man. "That you are not some impostor? Few are those who ever got a good look at Father Joseph. Fewer still that wished to. You could be anyone to whom I am swearing fidelity in your cause."

The ring was withdrawn, and the old man looked on, impassive, as though his were the face of a stone cliff or some other soulless and indifferent form out of nature.

Seeing that Aramis was having second thoughts about this alliance, Mazarin said, "Do I need to remind you that your service is to your king?"

"No, Monseigneur," Aramis said. "I always keep my vows... to the living."

"It's necromancy then!" Françoise said. "And in league with Baal by his own admission!" Her hand was on the pommel of her sword as she shoved her chair back from the table and stood up. "We are betrayed, Cromwell!" she shouted.

She drew her sword and turned her gaze on Mazarin. "And we have been delivered into his hand by this agent of the Papacy! Well, we shall not sell our lives cheaply, nor hand ourselves over to them for torture."

Brom was already on his feet and his sword out. Aramis had also risen and was backing away from the table. But instead of drawing his sword, he held his palms up. "Please, milady. Do not act hastily and do that which cannot be undone."

Mazarin and Father Joseph had not moved, the former regarding the girl calmly but with obvious annoyance. "I do not practice 'necromancy,' young woman. The Grey Eminence 'died' as a result of a failed assassination attempt by Richelieu. And his bringing of Baal to the Vatican mountain was not with the intention you presume.

"Be seated," the cardinal continued. "Keep your swords drawn—both of you—should it gives you comfort. But give me time for an explanation before you commence hacking."

Françoise looked at Brom who nodded. They sat down again, as did Aramis.

"Thank you," Mazarin said. "Your Eminence?"

The Grey Eminence did not move, but remained standing straight, hands clasped behind his back. "I am not responsible for this being's manifestation in our realm of time and space," he said. "That was the astrologer and mighty wizard Orazio Morandi, whose study of the stars and forbidden astronomical charts gave him knowledge to bring this living horror here. Fortunately, in that day, there was a man named Maciste, who confronted Baal. In their struggle, his mighty thews and massive trunk became bound by Baal's tentacles. He strained with all his considerable power to dislodge it from wherever it was anchored, but failed. It was an impossible task, even for Maciste—and that was a rare event indeed!"

"Wait—*wherever* it was anchored?" Brom said.

"This is a higher dimension entity of which I speak: its full body lies outside human perception."

"Ah, Natvilcius has written of a similar phenomenon in his analysis of angels," Brom said.

"And how did this strong man remedy this dilemma?" Aramis asked.

The Grey Eminence smiled again, as though his mind did not understand how to operate his facial muscles to appear natural. "Amidst his struggle against the ropy, writhing tentacles that grappled with him unceasingly, he was nevertheless able to draw forth his sword. His wrists were bound together by tentacles trying to shake his weapon from his hand, but with only a fumbling grip on his sword, he yet managed to slice the tip off of one tentacle.

"To this creature, so small a wound apparently felt like a hornet's sting. Or perhaps, the creature had never felt pain before? Any pain. Regardless, it immediately withdrew completely into whatever other dimension it inhabited, and has not been seen since, apparently uneager to repeat the experience."

"After such a minor wound?" Aramis asked.

The Grey Eminence turned his head and looked down at Aramis. "Would you return to a hornet's nest and plunge your hand in it after having done it once, musketeer?"

"But if it is gone and has not returned, why do you fear it shall do so now?" Brom asked.

"We fear not its return, but what it left behind, something of itself: that tip of a tentacle that Maciste cut off.

"I was not there that night," the Grey Eminence said, "but passing through the village where the battle occurred, much later, I learned that the locals proudly displayed it as a relic they called the *Devil's foreskin*. They told me the tale of how Satan's circumcision came about. I, of course, could not leave such an artifact behind. You see, it still lived, curling upon itself and writhing in the glass globe that displayed it, a fragile prison that could be shattered at any time and 'twas only a wonder it had not been up to then.

"I was traveling up the Vatican mount to deliver it for a proper exorcism when my horse stumbled. At last, the glass did break. And that still living sliver of Baal escaped into the tall grass."

Mazarin spoke: "Recently, there was rediscovered beneath Mount Vaticanus a lost archive of ancient scrolls from the first century. Based on inscriptions in this library, we learned that among them are stored all the writings of the New Testament in the *original autographs*."

Brom's eyes brightened. "You mean, one might read them in the apostles' own handwriting?"

"One might... except this is where this blasphemy called Baal has been pleased to come to dwell," Mazarin said.

"It is the nature of Evil," the Grey Eminence said, "that it is a parasite of what is holy, and here are the original inspired texts, only one step removed from the hand of God Himself. So, there Baal feeds. And grows. Preparing to rising on the mount and signaling the fall of England, and hence all of Europe. But the last report from one who survived a venture into that crypt was that it was but the size of a large dog. Nevertheless, the creature is lethal. But it is physical; it can be hurt; it can be contained; perhaps it can even be destroyed. In any event, it can, and must, be stopped."

"Amen," said Françoise the Scurvhamite, bowing her head.

"You have my sword," Aramis said.

"And mine," said Brom.

"Then, go," said Mazarin. "On the south slope, among a forest full of sycamores, you will find an area that has been cleared. There is a door in the ground. Steps descend within the earth. Enter, and you will find a door at the end of a corridor in a wall behind which is a massive vaulted crypt. Within dwells this horror. And you must find a way to remove it hence. Go, now. And God go with you." The three agents rose. Only then did they notice the Grey Eminence had departed as he had arrived: without witnesses.

2.

They rode under the distant winter the sun, reining their horses up the mountainside over brown grass.

Three abreast, they headed toward the heavy sycamore forest now visible on the horizon. Aramis shielded his eyes with his hand and looked up. "At least there are still plenty of hours of sunlight yet," he said. "If we maintain our present speed, we should arrive by early afternoon. Which is good. I like not the idea of performing this deed unable to retreat into the light."

Brom turned to Françoise. "Mademoiselle de Bretigny, you gave another name for Baal during our conference that you have never shared with me during all our time together. Samras, wasn't it?"

She waved him off and glanced at Aramis whose eyes were trained ahead. Then she nodded at Brom that they should drop back a pace or two. When they had withdrawn, she said:

"Do not even try to speak that name."

"Was that not it?"

"No. But it is good that you do not recall how to say it. Do not even try, lest you strike upon the correct pronunciation by chance and risk making it aware of us."

"Did you not speak it yourself less than an hour ago?"

"You remember I hesitated. And I took care to put the emphasis on the wrong syllable. But recall that I..."

"What do you two conspire together about back there?"

Aramis had paused and was turned around on his horse, having realized he was alone. Françoise nodded at Brom; they kicked their horses' sides and galloped up to the former musketeer, now an Abbé.

"Merely some finer points of Scurvhamite doctrine," Françoise said and smiled, her full lips parting to reveal white, even teeth. Aramis was so pleased to have the lady's smile for the first time that he immediately forgot his suspicious sense of being excluded for some reason. "I seek to convert Brother Brom."

"I cannot imagine a more charming evangelist," Aramis said, his vision level with her breasts.

"Abbot," Brom said, "might I turn your thoughts from higher things for a moment?"

"Yes, *mon frère?*" Aramis said.

"Did you have any knowledge of this 'Grey Eminence' in France?"

"Only by reputation."

"Which was?"

"Dangerous. He was a man to be feared."

"And now that you have met him face to face?"

"He seemed most... unnatural."

"My estimation exactly."

"His arrival in France was preceded by an infestation of rats in Paris which brought a plague with them. A bad omen. Or, perhaps, his harbingers."

"Are you familiar with his signet ring?"

"Ah, it is a constellation: the noose of the Hyenaes."

Cromwell looked ahead as he remembered. "The Cendrée Sign."

"What was that?"

"A cult sigil I have encountered in my conflicts with, as you said, those pagan creatures which linger on in Christiandom."

"Things which do not die as men, do?"

"Oftentimes."

"Then perhaps that would explain his 'resurrection.' But, no, it must be as Mazarin said. He simply faked his death four years ago. The man has a brother who oversees the Bastille; he is human."

"Relationships can be as false as identities," Brom said. "Whatever his appearance, he is not human. My guess is that he was Richelieu's familiar and now 'twould seem he has abandoned his former master for a new one. Or Mazarin found a way to sway him under his power."

"You did not know Richelieu as I did," said Aramis. "He was devil enough. He had no need of assistance from hell."

"Nevertheless, I do not like finding myself suddenly in this Grey Eminence's service. Françoise? Your thoughts?"

"You see, monsieur Aramis, how Brom Cromwell pays respect to a woman's brain as well as her bosom?"

"To be fair to the abbot, I have always found the idea that the admiration of one of a necessity excludes an appreciation of the other to be a false dichotomy, milady," Brom said.

"So, you are no gelding after all," Aramis said.

"My order allows us, as children of the present age, to marry and give in marriage."

"My thoughts on the Grey Eminence, Brom, do bear hearing," Françoise said. "I am not one unfamiliar with the occult. Once, long ago, after I had betrayed a royal lover, I had to make expiation by infiltrating the ranks of those conversant with the dark arts, to play Delilah as it were, to learn of their doings and goings within France so that they might be destroyed by the High Inquisitor." She smiled at this memory, and it was a bitter grin indeed.

"I learned much of sorcerers in those days. I was sent in with nothing but my beauty as my weapon. My softness and allure, which had been enough to bring one such wizard down, were nothing when it turned out that death could not hold him, so, consequently, I almost felt its embrace before he was done with me in his quest for revenge.

"Fortunately, I had rescuers. One of whom was a woman, as good with the sword as any man. Dark Agnes, they called her. When she and her cohort returned me to my home, naked and quivering with fear for what had happened and what yet may come in the execution of my future duties, I persuaded her to stay and teach me to be as she was: a swordswoman.

"Only thus did I survive my penance. By the time I had returned to court, though, I had knowledge of sorcerers indeed. And I can tell you, this Grey Eminence seems sorcerer enough to me… and mayhap more. I almost wish that I had not listened to Mazarin and put the sword to this 'Father Joseph' where he stood while I still could."

"Ho! It is a brazen wench with which we find ourselves aligned, Frère Brom," Aramis said. "And so much the better. We shall benefit from such fearlessness when we face this Baal. As well, I wager, as from her hard-earned knowledge of those netherrealms hence this horror proceeds."

Françoise smiled at this acknowledgment, then spurred her horse's side to send it galloping forward. "Then let us make haste, men, to do God's work."

She rose in her saddle, providing a choice view for both Aramis and Brom in her tight riding britches of her perfectly rounded behind. Brom, it was apparent to Aramis, was as charmed with his charge as he.

The men kicked their horses' sides to catch up with her. But Aramis also was thinking: *The girl is barely more than twenty. I was a court confessor—and lover—to many ladies not so long ago, but I have no knowledge of a Lady de Bretigny, and her, I would have certainly remembered. Yes, and I would have known a royal's mistress in Louis's court, even if by reputation only. And clearly, it is the court of France of which she speaks. Yet, I know her not! How is such a thing possible?* He sighed. *If only a gentleman were not to ask such things of a lady he has just met.*

3.

They rode into the forest, a land of twilight in the afternoon under its high boughs. Here, the birds did not sing. Was it because of the comparative darkness? Or simply because they had departed for the winter? Or had they fled the presence of something darker than the perpetual shadow? From time to time, they all found it a relief to look up for the glimpse of distant grey sky afforded by where the tightly interlaced branches high above opened to allow a bit of dappled light upon the forest floor.

Then they saw the clearing ahead, where the trees had been razed after the crypt had been discovered. This man-made meadow riddled with stumps was an oasis of light in the forest, and it was here that the deepest dark had made its home.

They tied their horses among the trees that made the edge of the woods. Muskets were left in the saddle bags, for the enclosed space of the archive meant risking one of them being wounded by a ricochet if a ball were fired. Armed only with blades, and carrying unlit torches, they proceeded into the clearing.

The dinted metal door in the ground, with a ring set in the middle, was unhidden, with neither lock, nor guard, to protect its precious contents. There was no need for either. The reputation of what lurked within kept the precious scrolls safe. And, if one ventured in ignorantly, one tended not to venture out.

The door was heavy, though. Both Aramis and Brom had to put their entire upper body strength into opening it. Immediately, sunlight filled the interior, illuminating suddenly disturbed swirling dust and revealing stone steps that terminated on a paved floor and hallway.

The trio descended the steps. At the bottom of the stairs, where there was still much light, they struck the flint, lit one torch, then passed the flame from it to the other two. Then they began moving forward.

The stone hallway was wide enough for the three to easily pass. The air here was cool, but stale. Again, Aramis found the whiff of Françoise's perfume a welcome relief. The opportunity to press close to her came as the hallway became darker. Aramis bent his head to Françoise's ear.

"Mademoiselle?"

"Yes?"

"Your earlier story of your misadventures at court has intrigued me. You see, I was still about the court not so long ago. You are still young, so our time in and about Louis XIII's circle must have coincided... Mademoiselle... Françoise... you are a striking woman, and I would certainly have remembered you."

"Louis XIII's circle, you say?"

"Yes."

"Ah. Then the mystery is solved: *my* royal circle was that of Savoy."

"Ah." Seeing that she remained taciturn after this brief explanation, Aramis did not pursue it further, but he began sorting it out with such information as he already possessed.

Savoy. Louis XIII's sister, Christine, had married the Duke of Savoy in 1619. Before this, she had been *Madame Royale* of her brother's court for four years, Françoise would have become mistress material as a young woman in her teens. If she had been, say, eighteen toward the end of Christine of Savoy's reign as Madame Royale, then today she would be almost forty—but she appeared twenty years younger.

What made more sense of her age was the court of which she had spoken was that of Savoy itself after Christine had become regent, a hotly resisted ascension which Mazarin had been invaluable in securing—the very debt the throne of France owed the cardinal which Aramis now find himself paying.

Christine's reign had lasted only from 1630-1637, ending only five years ago. Françoise would have then transferred into the service of Christine's sister, Queen Henrietta Maria of England. Consequently, she must have become embroiled in the brewing Puritan conflict, which, in turn, had led her to this mission. But her earlier account indicated that her royal lover belonged to the French court, not that of Savoy... Aramis looked at the beauty and knitted his brow.

Now they had come to the iron door that opened into the archive. Brom thought of the scriptures that lay just a few feet from him now, the original autographs that no Christian had been privileged to see since perhaps the first century. Yet, a cosmic obscenity, in opposition to all the holy writ, dwelt alongside them.

Two of the torches were placed in sconces in the two upper corners of the outer doorway. Brom held the third one in one hand, his sword in the other. Aramis and Françoise's swords were also drawn and at the ready. Aramis pushed on the heavy door, which barely bulged. He called for Brom's help. The Irishman passed the torch to Françoise and put his shoulder into it. The door moved, resisted, but then, with a tortured grating, began to push inward.

Françoise, still brandishing the torch, quickly stepped through the now-open doorway, moving beyond the men with no sign of stopping.

"Françoise! Have a care!" Brom said.

The light of her torch, combined with that of those that still shone from outside, revealed a dim archive of ascending shelves, stacked with scrolls, as high as the ceiling. The air was full of motes of dust milling in the air, and the scent of earth was oppressive. Dirt littered the floor and the ceiling was revealed to be not stone, as were the walls and the floor, but of the earth, supported by wooden cross beams. The weight of the ground above, from long bearing down on them, was causing some of the beams to sag.

One of the wide, wall-high ladder of shelves had overturned, dislodging its many scrolls into a massive heap on the floor. But of any obscene cosmic horror, there was no indication.

Françoise's bosom began to rise and fall, her eyes wide. "We are too late," she said. "This creature has already escaped this chamber, perhaps already burrowing upward to appear on the mountain side?"

"Do not leap to conclusions so quickly, girl," Brom said. "We have yet to investigate this chamber properly."

Now their eyes were growing accustomed to the gloom. Aramis' adjusted first. He leaned forward, then pointed. "Is that mound of scrolls *breathing*?"

Brom and Françoise trained their eyes where he pointed. There! It was barely perceptible... or was it merely the suggestion of Aramis that had caused them to see it now?

Françoise passed her torch to Brom. The three together, swords drawn, moved in tentative steps toward that mound. One scroll dislodged from the others and tumbled down the heap, bringing them to a unified halt.

Now other scrolls were rolling away from the massive pile, and it became clear that the heap of scrolls covered something else—something *large*. More scrolls were dislodged, enough to reveal glimpses here and there of some grey and pink mottled colors of what was *living tissue* beneath.

As the remaining scrolls dropped away, a large form curled upward like a tentacle, revealing a protoplasmic amoebic thing that tapered to a tip. It rose to full height, revealing rows of pulsating suckers on its underside. Evenly spaced along each side were organic stubs that resembled twitching vestigial serpent's legs. It collapsed onto the stone floor, wobbling on impact on its stubs that held it just above the ground.

Mute and eyeless, it honed in on the three as if it had been born to blindness, like a subterranean fish.

A shiver passed through Françoise. "The demiurge of the anti-universe," she said quietly.

Brom noted the awe in her voice, and how she stood planted. Many of her fellow Scurvhamites had been doomed by contemplation of the clockwork abyss. Now, she faced, as it were, "the hind parts" of the clockmaker itself— alive.

"Françoise!" he shouted.

Her arms hung at her side; her sword slipped from her numb fingers, as she watched the creature; her eyes had grown wide, like the mesmerized bird of which she had spoken.

"Aramis, keep your eye on that thing!" Brom shouted and darted toward his charge. He immediately shoved the flame of the torch against Françoise's upper back.

She cried out, back arching at the contact as she sprang away.

"Are you mad?" Aramis said, turning his eyes from the creature at Françoise's wail.

In the moment of distraction, the bloated tentacle of Baal lurched upon them.

Immediately after touching his torch to Françoise, and shocking her mind from its state of stupor, Brom shoved her out of the path of the oncoming monster. He whirled back around with his broad sword, slashing Baal while thrusting the torch against it.

Aramis, having grasped the method to Brom's apparent madness in putting the flame to Françoise, turned to find the pulsing body of the creature was upon him. With a shout, he thrust his rapier into the creature simultaneously with Brom's slashing and burning. The monster screeched and recoiled as both men bounded back from it.

With a battle wail, Françoise, her sword drawn, lunged forward across the open space between them and Baal, which the two men had gained by wounding the abomination. Aramis and Brom followed, weapons raised.

Françoise lanced the monster with her rapier, and its screech was like fingernails drug over slate. The creature's wail set her teeth on edge, but as uncomfortable as it was to hear, she immediately plunged her sword into it. Again and again.

Brom and Aramis joined in, hacking and stabbing, Brom also putting the flame again to the creature, its flesh bubbling and sizzling with the contact. It quivered and screeched with each assault.

The trio's blades opened gaping wounds in its body—but, all too quickly, the wounds closed and the blistering from the fire was absorbed in accordance with whatever strange laws governed the otherworldly substance that composed Baal. While able to deal the monster pain, the warriors found it almost immediately healed itself.

The tentacle-like body of the monster rose again, curling back upon itself, then lashing out powerfully. Its strike sent the trio reeling back. Aramis tripped and hit the stone floor. Baal's tentacle hooked him by the ankle as it withdrew, wrapped and tightened on his boot, and began to pull him to itself.

Out slashed Aramis' sword, severing the portion that clutched him from Baal's body. The part of the creature that remained about his boot detached and flowed like a fleeing snake back across the floor to rejoin the main body. Brom ran forward to Aramis' side, gave him his arm and drew his comrade back to his feet. They rejoined Françoise.

Wiping the perspiration that matted their hair from their eyes, the three regarded the creature across the room, either side waiting for the other to make the next move. But Baal had not merely retreated; it was studying them with weird senses beyond human ken.

"Let us take council," Brom said, his eyes searching the chamber. He took note again of where the wooden beams sagged from the earth weighing heavily upon them. "We have seen this thing so quickly reconstitutes itself that killing it, as we have been attempting to do so far, will not work. It must be dealt a blow at once so catastrophic that it is destroyed immediately. If we could but bring the ground above down upon the thing..."

"And bury ourselves in the process?" Aramis said. "There is no way we can dislodge those beams and escape with our lives."

"Only one of us need make the effort," Brom said. "I can climb the shelves and, from there, easily reach the beams. If the two of you can maintain that thing's attention, I will do the work above. I will signal you when all hangs by a hair and allow you time to flee the crypt before I deliver the final cut."

"Brom, no!" Françoise said, grasping his forearm. "I will not allow it!"

He raised her hand to his lips and kissed it. "Milady, the longer we battle, the longer you are at risk. Of us three, your life is the dearest."

"This is no time for gallantry, Brom. We are all equals here."

"Hear, hear!" Aramis said.

"Forgive me, Françoise, but we are not. You are the agent who was sent to see this mission accomplished. It is you who are answerable for the details of its success to your superiors. Would your fellow Scurvhamites trust either my or Aramis' report that Baal is no longer a threat? With Aramis being a catholic, and my order likewise?"

"But the effect of your sacrifice remains too uncertain as to effectively achieve the desired outcome," Françoise said. "You know not that this creature will perish, and, with time, it might yet burrow out from under the earth to appear upon the mountain and fulfill the prophecy. All your efforts may be but an exercise in futility."

"Is this not *all* an exercise in futility, according to your Scurvhamite doctrine?" Aramis said. "If every atom has been set in motion by this anti-god from the creation of the universe, what is the avail of our struggles against it?"

"Has she made a convert of you, Aramis?" Brom said. "This doctrine is false!"

"The doctrine is *not* false!" Françoise said. "Remember, there is another will that opposes Baal's own, also from the setting in motion of every atom. This is that good and right will that will allow for no tipping of the balance with its coeval power."

"I like not this doctrine, milady, as I have told you, and its predetermined universe. There is too much of Calvin in it," said Brom.

"I like it not because there is too little of Aramis in it!" said Aramis.

"But in that universe I am, and whoever loves me..." and here she thrust her arms around Brom's neck and pressed her mouth to his "—there you will find me!"

Then, pushing Brom away, she grabbed Aramis and kissed him the same. "*Whoever* loves me!" she said, grasping her sword and charging again the beast.

She swung it, carving a groove into Baal that its substance immediately filled in her blade's wake. Françoise drew back her sword again as the agitated tentacle surged forward and brought her shoulder in contact with its substance. Immediately, its many-suckered underside adhered to her. Such was the twist of her waist and turn of her arms that she could not bring the sword back around in her defense.

By the time she cried out, Aramis was already running to her, Brom following. "Drop your sword!" Aramis cried out, and then he was upon her from behind, hooking his hands into the back of her blouse's neck and tearing it in half all the way down, revealing a corset's lacing. Reaching beneath her shirt, and locking his arms around her waist, he pulled, ripping her free of the blouse.

As Brom hacked at Baal with his broadsword to hold it at bay, Aramis and Françoise stumbled backwards, clear of the creature. Françoise landed on her back on top of the former musketeer. Aramis grunted with the impact.

"Happy to be of service, milady," he said, running a fingertip along the corset's lacing and contemplating the undergarment. "I've never seen one of these in this fashion. How do you *ever* have the mobility to handle a sword in this thing?"

She leapt to her feet. "I made some modifications of my own," she said, extending her hand to him. Aramis grasped her wrist firmly, and allowed her to help raise him to his feet. "And while I am grateful, and I realize you had no choice but to tear off my blouse, you do *not* have to so obviously enjoy having done it. A gentleman would have offered me his cape by now."

Brom ran up to them as Aramis was attentively wrapping his cloak about Françoise. "If this is an exercise in futility," he said, "it is only because we have not taken the nature of evil into account. The right one pains me..."

"*What* man?" Aramis said. "Get on with it!"

Brom gave a heavy sigh. "We have to burn the scriptures in their original autographs."

"Create a conflagration?" Aramis said. "That thing isn't vulnerable to fire."

"No, but the holy scrolls are. In this, the Grey Eminence spoke true: evil is a parasite of good. Baal is drawing its strength and massiveness from these scrolls. It is why it sought out this cache in the first place, I am certain."

"At least, there is no longer need that we should lose you," Françoise said and laid her small hand on Brom's arm. Aramis' eye was drawn to this gesture of her regard.

"We still have fire. Who shall distract the thing, and who shall set the scrolls to fire?" Aramis asked.

"I am without a sword," Françoise said. "I will take the torch."

Aramis and Brom charged the creature, herding it to one side of the room as it dodged their strikes. The moment she was clear of the tentacle-like thing lashing out, Françoise ran for the scrolls and put the torch to them.

In a moment, the flame was spreading through the ancient paper, climbing the shelves and into the timbers holding up the ground above it.

And Baal shrieked.

"Run!" Aramis shouted. But Françoise lingered, staring at the writhing demiurge of her faith's anti-universe. Brom feared she had once more come under the creature's thrall and that it would yet drag her after it into the abyss.

He hefted her up into his arms, startling Françoise from her obsession.

Smoke was rising in columns among the scrolls, and oxygen would soon be gone from the enclosed chamber.

They fled. But having reached the door into the archives, all three could not help but turn to see what was happening to the creature.

Writhing, thrashing, Baal was dwindling and dwindlingfast, already reduced to the size of a large dog.

"Stop!" Françoise said. "Put me down! I can run on my own!"

And she did. Throwing Aramis's cape over her head, and bent at the waist, she ran *back*—into the smoke and flames.

Taken by surprise at a turn they both felt foolish for not anticipating, Brom and Aramis stared aghast after her in her mad suicide dash.

Then they were running to overtake her, but a barrier of heat repelled them, the heavy hanging grey smoke making it impossible to see…

Suddenly, Françoise charged by them, emerging from the boiling cloud, cloak still cast over her. "Why are you still here, you fools?" she shouted in the passing.

They ran into the hallway that was already filling with smoke. The sky was still just ahead from the open door above them. They were able to climb the stairway, clear the doorway in the ground, and thrust themselves out onto the withered grass, choking for breaths to assuage their broiled lungs with the clean winter air.

A column of thick, grey smoke, swarming with cinders, erupted out of the opening in the ground as though Hell were enlarging itself.

The three scrambled to their feet, running away from the sudden rush of heat to regain fresh air. They reached the spot where they had left the horses when the terrain behind them trembled, and then the earth itself began to thunder. Their horses, still tied, reared, eyes bulging to burst free of their sockets. Aramis cut through the rope that held his and it darted. He followed, Françoise already having absconded.

Now the cleared forest floor that had made the roof of the archive, as the rafters beneath burned beyond enduring their burden, buckled and the topside earth collapsed and rushed into thestone vault beneath.

Brom, recalling Françoise had lost her sword, sliced the rope that held her horse, but then there was no time to save his own. He turned and ran after his comrades, the opening in the ground pursuing them.

Brom's horse reared, forelegs beating at the air, hind hooves stomping the ground, and then that ground did not exist, and the animal was snatched away with the collapsing earth forever.

Aramis and Françoise had managed to recapture their horses and restrain them by their bridles. Brom caught up with them, then turned and joined their gazing at the pit they had narrowly escaped. Heavy veils of dust hung in the air over it.

"That was almost the end of us all!" Aramis shouted at Françoise. "And needlessly so! Woman, what possessed you to run back into that fire?"

"This," she said, and produced from her pants pocket a small, clear-glass container. Visible inside it was Baal, or the tip of its tentacle, curling and twisting itself about, restored to its original size.

"You saved what we came so far to destroy?" Brom said.

"How could we be certain that it would not yet survive to escape? Perhaps burrow into the earth through a crevice or some such," Françoise said. "Now it can be contained forever."

"And who shall be its warden?" Aramis asked.

"'Tis best to pass it on to Mazarin," Françoise said. "My sect is too fascinated with this horror. It would charm them to its will and escape again. I trust the cardinal will pass it on to those who will bury it so deep in the Vatican that it will never escape."

Brom stepped forward for a closer look at the slug-like thing in the glass. "There is a mark on the creature that was not noticeable until it contracted to its original size. I have seen it before. We *all* have seen it."

"Yes, well," Françoise said as she shoved the glass into her pants' pocket. "There will be time to examine it when we have brought it to Mazarin."

"You wish to take it to Mazarin?" Brom asked.

"Yes," she said, mounting her now-calmed horse and smiling down at him. "To Mazarin. I've already said so. Do you think to take it elsewhere?"

"Perhaps, mademoiselle," Aramis said, "he merely thinks you are not the best choice to bear the creature, given the mesmerism of your will by Baal that we witnessed twice earlier."

"*I* am not fit? Think so, do you Aramis?" she said. "Or should I say, *Simara*?"

"What the devil are you talking about, girl? My name is not Simara!"

"No," Brom said. "She said it was one of the names by which her sect knew the god of the anti-universe." He turned to the musketeer. "Simara—that is an anagram; your name backwards, to be precise, Aramis."

"What? Why, that is just a coincidence!" He looked up at Françoise. "And if you suspected I was in league or even some manifestation of your sect's arch-fiend, why did you not mention it before now?"

"I did. Directly, no. But when we were sitting at the table in the hunting lodge, when I gave Simara as one of the names of Baal, I intentionally turned my eyes on you, hoping to draw Brom's attention."

"I recall now that you made a point of it," Brom said.

"This is madness," Aramis said. "What? Am I supposed to be a secret follower of this monster now? Yet you trusted me to help you destroy my own deity? I saved *you* from it, woman!"

"Saved me for yourself! 'Tis been obvious from the first that you want me. Do you deny it?"

Brom, flushed, turned to Aramis.

"Deny my lust? No! That is a well-established fact, as many ladies of the court can tell you. But that is no evidence that I am in league with what I just battled to destroy."

"Mayhap you have turned upon your deity and wish to enslave it to your will by performing black rites for which you need my young body!"

Brom drew his sword.

Aramis stepped back. "Are you going to strike me down out of sexual jealousy, Frère Brom?" he said. "It was obvious from the start that you are in love with her!"

Brom paused. He took a breath, then sheathed his sword. "There is something else at work here, I sense." He looked up at Françoise. "You are under Baal's influence again, lass. He is manipulating you to set us against one another so that it may yet escape." He held up his hand. "Françoise, I want you to give me that glass. You are not fit for that burden."

"And are you, Brom *Crom*well? Why, there is a pagan deity right in the middle of your name!"

Brom's eyes narrowed. "My name has been the same from the start, and you have trusted me completely for over a month. Whence comes this?"

"It comes from the same Cannanite pantheon as Baal, you lustful monk! *Crom* is but the Celtic name for Moloch of the east, the god of child sacrifice. You worship at the same pagan altar as Aramis!"

Aramis looked at Brom. "I do not worship—wait." He turned back to Françoise. "You said 'lustful,' child? What have you known of his lust?"

"He did not know I saw him watching me in the dark when he thought I slept."

"I could hardly see through walls, woman! I either guarded your door from the outside or slept in the room next to yours."

She lifted her chin and looked down upon him. "But then you came into mine."

With a hissing rasp, Aramis' rapier came out of it sheath. Brom leaped back and drew again his sword.

"Aramis!" Brom said. "Do you take her at her word *now*, who moments ago you did not believe?"

"I do not have to believe her; I have seen that lust in your eyes with my own!"

The men faced each other, eyes locked, raised swords trembling in their hands.

Then Aramis' nostrils flared but not with passion.

"Gun powder?" he said and turned his head—

The air cracked and Aramis' horse shrieked and collapsed dead as both men fell back and looked up, chalk-faced, at the smiling woman who held the still-smoking musket aimed in the direction of the dead animal.

"It was most fortunate that the opening ground took your horse, Brom," she said. "It solved my problem of having to disable *two* mounts."

"You *did* set us against one another to distract us," Aramis said.

Françoise patted the pocket that contained the bottle, shook her head and clucked her tongue. "You were concerned about my coming under Baal's influence, messieurs, but you should have been wary of his possessing you."

"We are not morbidly obsessed Scurvhamites!" Aramis said.

"No. You are typically sex-obsessed males. And Baal is a creature of lust who was able to excite yours and bring you under his power."

Brom cocked his head. "And who compels you, Françoise? It has never been Robert Scurvham. Nor, do I suspect, that it is Mazarin. "

"I serve myself," she said haughtily.

"And another," Brom said calmly.

The girl frowned down at him for a moment, then turned to Aramis. "Sir, I suppose I should tell you, that what I said about your name spelled backwards being another name of Baal…"

"You made up on the spot, looking ahead to the moment when you would use it to turn Cromwell and me against one another. Sorry if I am spoiling your chance to gloat."

The girl's lower lip jutted. "I thought I was rather quick and clever. Crom, on the other hand," she looked again down at the monk and smiled, "was all too easy."

"In every sense, eh?" said Brom. "You should not be so arrogant regarding your power over men, girl. Your body cannot defy age forever..." he pointed at her, "...nor gravity, as that corset, I think, testifies."

She quickly drew the cloak around her that she had allowed to uncover her in her abandon and curled her upper lip at Brom. "I shall maintain my looks much longer than you could imagine, Brom. In fact, I already have."

She turned to Aramis. "You were, right, monsieur, to puzzle over my age. The court of Savoy of which I was a part was not that of Louis's sister, but that of that Louise of Savoy who was the mother of King François 1er. It was François whose mistress I was, but Louise I betrayed, who then sent me from the court to move among France's occult world, hoping, no doubt, I would come to a bad end for which she could not directly be blamed by her son."

Aramis narrowed his eyes at her as though seeing her for the first time, and shook his head. "You are insane! Louise of Savoy died almost a century ago!"

"One does not consort with wizards without learning a few things—and incurring a debt or two. One of which now I shall pay. Enjoy the countryside, messieurs. Exercise will be good to release the tension you both no doubt feel mounting."

With that, she kicked the horse's sides, reeled it about, and drove hard, the hooves kicking up clods of earth from which Brom and Aramis were obliged to duck and throw up their arms to shield themselves.

Silently they watched together her disappearance into the distance. Then they looked at each other. Aramis motioned with his hand for Brom to take the lead.

"No, by all means, after *you*," the monk said.

4.

They trudged along in silence for a while. Then Aramis spoke: "You know my greatest regret in this debacle?"

"That you did not get to bed the wench."

"That I did not get to bed the wench. Despite your own ardor, I am going to guess that yours was the loss of the original autographs of the New Testament."

"Yes. It is most unfortunate, but it does not especially trouble me as you might think."

"But now, however shall we know what the New Testament authors truly wrote?"

"We have copies. And copies of copies of copies."

"But surely errors have inevitably crept in with all that copying and passing of manuscripts about. And men, being men, are certain to have altered the apostles' words to suit their own purposes. How can we know it is not otherwise?"

"Because we have copies of copies of copies."

"I do not follow you. The multitude of variants…"

"Would you prefer no variants?"

"Who would not? For, with all the variants in the copied texts, there is no way to know what the New Testament writers actually wrote."

"Not so."

"By what standard, then, can one hope to judge veracity?"

"First, consider the standard by which you have dismissed the texts of the original autographs of Biblical manuscripts as hopelessly lost. If we are consistent and apply that same rule to the classical texts, we must acknowledge that we are equally agnostic regarding the validity of what *every* major author of antiquity wrote. All we have of the words of Caesar, Plato, Aristotle, Tacitus—any important writer from the ancient world—have come down to us only by copies. No original autographs exist. Why should those manuscripts, then, be accepted as more certain than those of the New Testament?"

"Well, if the rules of scholarship are applied without bias to these secular texts as well as the scriptures, one must conclude what *their* authors wrote down is equally unknowable."

"Ah, but the original autographs are not the only option that historians have by which to authenticate the text of a copied manuscript. Multiple copies with variants in place of the original is far from an insurmountable problem in determining with a great deal of certainty the wording of that original. In fact, it is desirable."

"Are you saying the discrepancies in the copies we have actually *increase* the certainty?"

"I am. Suppose we had had the opportunity to make one perfect copy of those original New Testament manuscripts before they were lost to the fire. Would the texts be better authenticated if, in place of the copies with variants from different lines of transmission that we do have, every copy of our perfect copy were exactly the same as what would be the world's *single source* to be had?"

"Of course they would."

"Why so?"

"There would be zero variants."

"Which would actually *increase* the unlikelihood that those generations who followed us could ever be certain of what the originals said. Would it not seem suspicious that we claimed we made one perfect copy each of the New Testament books, then *burned* what we claimed to have perfectly copied?"

"A critical mind could not help but find it questionable."

"Because then one might truly worry that things had been changed in what, by our word alone, we claimed to have copied verbatim. For then there would be no possibility of either corroboration or contradiction. Thus, the bountiful amount of ancient copies of the New Testament from various independent sources that we have, copies distinguished as such by variants, make it possible to deduce with confidence the vast majority of the words of the original texts."

"I understand you. A lone witness in a court case is not desirable. He could say *anything* and who would know? The more witnesses one has, the better the chance of getting to the truth. In fact, that there should be variations is to be desired. For if all the witnesses agreed precisely..."

"...then it begins to look like they are participants in a conspiracy. So it is with the Holy Word: if there were no variations in the copies of the biblical manuscripts that have come down to us, the veracity of the texts would truly be questionable because it would strongly indicate somewhere in the transmission of the originals, a group of individuals had gotten together and agreed exactly on *what* would be copied and preserved—and what would *not*.

"In truth, a very large portion of the variants of our scriptural manuscripts are merely spelling errors. And many errors are so obvious, they are easily corrected. I have seen one manuscript that reads, *Thou shalt commit adultery.*"

"Ah, such a text would bring more people to church," said Aramis.

"Such a text is one where someone simply left the *not* out. It is an easily corrected scribal error that the vast majority of other manuscripts testify against, as well as a command contradicted elsewhere by the total tenet of scripture. And then there are obvious nonsense errors. Did you know..."

"Why are you smiling?"

"Because that scripture where John the Baptist says to those gathered at the Jordan river, *After me comes a man...* has also has been translated as *After me comes wind...*"

The two men broke into laughter so hard they were compelled to stop walking. Aramis had to clasp his hand onto Brom's shoulder to steady himself.

"I tell you, Frère Brom," Aramis managed to get out after a few minutes, "that text can easily be determined to be the wrong one. For who in a crowd, in the whole of human history, has ever silently broken wind and then announced to the others his oncoming scent so as to remove all doubt of its source?"

"And," Brom said, "preserved the account of his posterior for posterity?"

The men fell into each other in their paroxysms of mirth.

After a few minutes of collecting themselves, they began to walk again, still wiping tears from their eyes.

"I begin to like you, Frère Brom," Aramis said.

"And I you, Abbé... now that there is no longer a woman between us."

"And what a woman, eh? We are both better off shed of her."

"There is no chance, of course, that she will still be around when we reach the Vatican mount."

"Of course not. I am hardly disappointed."

"And what shall you do, then, when we arrive?"

"Do? Why, I shall strangle Mazarin. Immediately."

"Of course."

"Of course!" Aramis said, slapped Brom's back, and laughing together again, they proceeded to walk all night.

Aramis' joviality, at least, did not last. Upon attempting to contact Mazarin, he was told the Cardinal had "suddenly" left Italy. He had been, in fact, called back to France. Richelieu was finally dead. Mazarin was to replace him.

"It is perhaps best, after all, that you are unable to carry out your intention to assassinate a Cardinal," Brom said.

"Aye, my blood may have cooled, but when I return to France, Mazarin shall have no love from me. If opportunity shall arise for me to work against whatever intrigues in which he conspires, I will seize it with alacrity. And you, Frère Brom? What shall follow for you, now that your charge has abandoned you?"

"Have you seen the Cendrée Sign?"

Aramis looked at him silently for a long moment, then shook his head slowly from side to side. He then clasped Brom's shoulder and said:

"You are a far braver man than I, Brom Cromwell. Or far more of a fool."

"I do not see that either possibility of a necessity precludes the other," Brom said, and there was mirth in his blue eyes and in the upturned corners of his mouth.

The Borgia hunting lodge set silent now among the trees whose dead branches above him creaked in the wind. An owl called out in daylight. Brom paused, looked up at the sound, but saw nothing. Then he continued his approach to the lodge.

He pushed the door inward with no regard for stealth. The inside, where he had conspired with Mazarin, Aramis, and Françoise, was empty, and he was alone now...

Except for one other.

He walked past where Mazarin had sat at the head of the table, where was the chair behind which the Grey Eminence had appeared from nowhere, and then seemed to have returned there with no notice of those others gathered in the room. Brom approached the wall behind that chair.

He discovered what he had suspected: the wall was a false one. With time to examine it, he quickly found the panel that opened into the space behind, pushed it open, and let in the light from the lodge's windows.

Brom entered what was a comfortably wide passage. The rasp and ring of his sword drawn from its sheath was loud in the silence there. The passage became dimmer the further he went. Then he saw in the gloom a familiar robed figure, its back to him, making its way on quick but silent, slippered feet.

"Halt, *Eminence Grise!*"

The figure went stock still. "Who so dares command?"

"One who has seen the Cendrée Sign—which you bare upon your finger."

"How know you this? You are not of the seed of Abhoth."

"Most certainly, I am *not*. But I am acquainted with Abhoth's children. And am known of them. In Hell they remember me still."

"And why do you accost *me*, sir monk?"

"I do not relish having been pressed into the service of mine enemies. Why did you have Françoise lead Aramis and me to destroy that part of Baal which remains on the earth—though, you instructed her, if possible, that we should subdue and claim it for you instead? In what evil mischief have you involved me, Grey Eminence?"

"Why should you connect the wench with me? She served Mazarin..."

"'Twas not Mazarin's signet ring whose impression could be seen to mark that bit of the tentacle of Baal when it was returned to its original size; rather, it was the sign of the noose of the Hyanaes upon your own. You impressed your sigil into Baal's flesh to bring this splinter entity of the creature under your authority. But that bit of him escaped you.

"Somehow you learned where it had sought sanctuary to survive, but when you went to claim this creature as the slave of your will, you found it had grown too powerful from the holy scrolls. You found, instead of a familiar, that a rival had been created."

At that, the Grey Eminence, his back still to Brom, chuckled, and the sound was like the creaking from the dead branches in the wind outside.

"Listen, and I shall school you in familiars, Brom Cromwell," he said. "That tip of the tentacle of Baal did not find its way by chance to that vault of holy scripture on which to feed. No, long, long ago, *I* placed it on one of the scrolls, as though it were a seal of wax, to hold the roll together. I impressed it with my signet ring—for in those days, the significance of the noose of the Hyanaes was not yet known in Christiandom—so that I might indeed keep it under my subjection when it had grown in power.

"My intent had been to monitor that growth. But I was forced to leave that bit of Baal behind when my cult was exposed here at the gate of the Vatican itself. Much time passed before I could return, my last obstacle being Richelieu. I came back to find that Baal had fed well—*too* well. So much of that holy virtue had it drawn and corrupted into its own strength that now its power dwarfed my own. My familiar was now an autonomous entity that did resist me most robustly.

"Baal had to be, shall we say, whittled down to size. I hinted to you what the key to victory would be the destruction of the holy scrolls. I understand you took that hint, and, so you thought, the initiative. A false sense that you were in control of your own destiny still was preferable at that moment, but Françoise had been instructed to set fire to the scrolls, as though by accident, if you did not. But you did. And now, at last, Baal has been put in his place."

The Grey Eminence began to turn his head over his shoulder. Brom stepped back, sword raised…

The old man opened his mouth wide…

…and out slithered, to droop onto his lower lip, the tip of the tentacle of Baal.

Wide-eyed, Brom, who had been set to charge, instead took another step back.

The tip of the tentacle withdrew back inside the Grey Eminence, his jaws snapped shut, and then his lips formed a smile.

"Goodbye, Brom Cromwell," he said. "You have done the children of Abhoth much harm, and for that, I suppose, I should strike you down. But you have served me well, and who knows if you may not prove useful yet again? For even such as I cannot see the future. After all, what are the lives of those fool enough to worship him to Abhoth? Until, then, that I have need of you again…"

Brom rushed forward, sword raised, but when he swung it, it only met air. This time, no secret passage was found, and he was truly alone. With a sigh, he sheathed his weapon and began making his way back through the passage. From the lodge, then, into the surrounding woods, where the distant sun still shone, brightening brown leaves and dead grass, and, from there, once more into the world beyond, to seek out the shadow, wherever it may be cast.

Travis Hiltz introduced us to the world's most unusual detective agency in "The Case of the Curious Cadaver" published in our Volume 12. Its members are Etienne Camparol and Spiridon, the giant intelligent ant from André Laurie's eponymous 1907 novel (available from Black Coat Press, ISBN 978-1-934543-61-3), and the selenite female Stella Astarte from Alfred Drious's 1856 novel The Adventures of a Parisian Aeronaut *(Black Coat Press ISBN 978-1-61227-067-8), in which the Moon is reached via hot air balloon...*

Travis Hiltz: *The Case of the Remains to be seen*

Paris, 1910

The manor house loomed over the gravel driveway, not in an imposing or haunted way, but rather stern and faintly disapproving. It was all sharp corners, tall, narrow windows, gaunt chimneys and turrets. Whatever color or cheer it had once held had long since been worn away by time and the elements, leaving only drab, grey stone.

The black touring car slowly rolled to a halt, and three figures bundled out, their footsteps crunching the gravel as they approached the young police constable standing sentry at the front door.

In the lead was a man in his early 30s. His suit and overcoat were neat but obviously had seen better times. He took off his hat as he peered up at the manor and the grey clouds that lurked above it.

"It makes you feel sad just to look at it," his companion commented quietly.

She was tall and stately-looking, her skin like ivory, and her hair black as starless midnight. Her white ensemble was pristine and fashionable. She moved with a graceful economy of motion, so in moments of stillness, she could easily have been mistaken for a statue.

"Well, it's not intended as a holiday retreat," the man shrugged, replacing his hat and thoughtfully stroking his thin mustache. "You come here for solitude in order to think deep thoughts and meddle in god's domain."

With that pronouncement, they both glanced behind them at the third member of their party.

He was short, his posture hunched, his over-sized overcoat and homburg hat adding to that appearance. His sleeves hung down, concealing his hands. His Asian features appeared swollen and exaggerated.

"Help the doctor along will you?" the detective asked, as he headed up the steps.

The young policeman gave him a brief salute.

131

"Who might you be, Monsieur?" he inquired.

"My name is Etienne Camparol," the man replied. "Inspector Juve asked me to consult on this matter. These are my associates, Mademoiselle Stella Astarte and… um… the Doctor…"

The policeman nodded and handed over a small, much abused-looking notebook.

"Third floor, just follow the stairs. The Inspector was called back to Paris. He should return tomorrow afternoon. He wanted you to have his notes."

The detective nodded, flipping through the notebook as he entered the large, shadow-draped foyer.

A butler stood to one side of the door—whether lurking or merely being discreet was hard to say. He had a foreign appearance, though Camparol couldn't place his nationality at a glance. There was something off putting about him. Never having lived at a social level where servants were about, Camparol might have be projecting his own prejudices upon the man, who was likely just naturally sullen or disturbed because a crime had occurred in his employer's home. The detective nodded in greeting.

"Will you be able to see yourselves up?" the butler asked, in accented tones. "I am still seeing to your rooms…"

"Of course," the detective said. "We'll find our way."

The butler gave a faint bow and drifted off.

"Whom are you talking to?" the tall young woman asked, glancing about thoughtfully. She was carrying a small suitcase and had a small equipment case tucked under her other arm. The diminutive Doctor was behind her, clutching a carpetbag in his arms, his hands still tucked into the voluminous sleeves of his overcoat.

"Butler," Camparol shrugged, taking the suitcase from her, as he headed up the wide main staircase. As he walked, he glanced over Juve's scribbled notes.

"What are we dealing with?" his statuesque assistant asked.

"Missing scientist," Camparol muttered absently in reply. "Possible murder… all having occurred in… a locked room…"

He sighed and shook his head.

"Interesting," she nodded.

They trudged to the top floor, passing several landings and encountering eccentric individuals as they went; on the second floor, the gentleman Camparol tried to question turned out to be stone deaf, as well as being convinced the detective was asking after a missing goat.

Both he and Stella raised an eyebrow when they recognized the infamous Doctor Ox go ambling past them, muttering to himself while fiddling with a twisted bit of pipe.

They reached the third floor. Down a narrow side hall with several doors, a door hung open at the far end.

Camparol peered in. It was one large room, a collection of work benches, containers of exotic-looking chemicals and a pair of mismatched, ancient sofas, all within four dark, oak walls. There was just the one door and it was a solidly intended to keep the rest of the world out. Camparol held the door open for his companions, and then paused for a moment to study the lock. Aside from where the police had had to force their way in, it was untampered with and looked sturdy enough to resist most attempts.

Once all three were in the room, Camparol eased the door closed and shrugged out of his topcoat, draping it over the back of one of the sagging sofas. He placed his hat on top of it.

"You'll know best about what Brainard was working on," he instructed his tall, female associate. "I'll see about the walls... Doctor, don't touch anything!"

The diminutive member of the team hunched his shoulders sullenly.

Camparol paced the room, studying the walls and floor, occasionally pausing to tap the dark oak.

"Professor Brainard must have been quite an accomplished chemist," Astarte mused, gazing over one of the workbenches.

"Yes?" Camparol nodded, pausing to further flip through Juve's notebook. "Yes, the whole family is, both this branch and the American cousins as well... The family converted the ancestral home into a sort of... commune for the scientifically-minded... or at least, that's how they refer to those wandering lunatics."

"So, what happened here?" she asked.

"Professor Brainard came up to work, early yesterday... The butler followed him up, left his lunch... He did that regularly, because Brainard tended to spend hours up here and lose track of time, which is why it was hours before anyone noticed him missing... Several of his fellow savants became concerned and it was the gardener that eventually forced the lock, to find no sign of Brainard... Very odd—these walls are solid as my grandmother's corset, but I can feel a slight draft...?"

Stella reached out and touched Camparol's arm as he paced past her. Once she had his attention, she pointed upwards.

Camparol glanced up, following her gesture and felt like an idiot when he spotted the skylight. It was small, though a body would have easily fit through it, but it would have been tricky.

"Odd," Camparol muttered, stroking his chin in thought as he peered upwards. "It wasn't opened, yet the glass is broken... You can still see shards attached to the frame..."

"So, whoever attacked or kidnapped the Professor came in through the skylight?" Stella asked.

"Then where did all the glass go?" Camparol asked. "If the attacker broke in, there should be glass all over the floor; if the attacker broke the skylight to get Brainard out, then how did he get in to the room...?"

The detective paced around the area below the skylight, peering from the ceiling to the floor.

"Blood...?" he muttered, kneeling down.

Stella came and stood behind him, peering over him at the droplets of dried blood on the wooden floor.

"He was hurt during... whatever happened?" she added.

"Looks that way," Camparol nodded.

The Doctor ambled over. As he did, he reached up and removed first his homburg and then, more surprisingly, his face.

He was in fact, not a diminutive Asian physician, but was instead an enormous ant! Still a brilliant medical practitioner, the ant, called Spiridon, had been the toast of the French scientific community several years back, until the jealousy of his human rivals and his own amoral attitude towards his patients had led to him retiring into seclusion and Camparol's care.

Using a claw to scrape up some dried blood, he sniffed them before transferring the blood flakes to a small test tube.

"Doctor Spiridon has found something," Stella said.

"Where'd the glass go...?" Camparol muttered to himself.

He turned to face his statuesque partner.

"Keep an eye on the good doctor," he advised. "I'm going to see if I can have a look at the roof."

Camparol was only a few paces down the corridor when he encountered the butler coming out of a linen closet.

"Can I help you, Monsieur?"

"Is there any way I can get up onto the roof?"

"The roof, Monsieur?"

"Yes, the roof."

"End of the corridor," the butler instructed, obviously curious but too well-mannered to show more than a slightly raised eyebrow and a guarded tone. "The door has a tendency to stick, but it is not kept locked. Anything else?"

Camparol shook his head and made his way along the hallway. He only became aware of how many doors there were after the butler had gone out of earshot.

Camparol sighed in annoyance, and decided to just try doors until he found the right one.

Behind the first, he again encountered the little deaf savant, who, no matter what Camparol said, kept explaining to him that there were no goats on the property. Behind the second door, a man sporting an obviously fake mustache lectured Camparol on how his recently discovered radioactive element had uses as both a medical aid and a devastating weapon.

Much to his relief, the third door, which did stick, lead to a narrow flight of stairs. The detective wound his way through a cluttered attic before spotting a trap door that opened up onto the roof.

It was steep and uneven going, but he eventually made his way across the slate tiles until he reached the skylight. The metal frame was bent in several places and the roof was littered with shards of glass.

Camparol skidded along, kneeling down to study the skylight.

"What did you find?" Stella called up, as soon as she spotted him.

"The glass blew outwards," he replied, thoughtfully.

"So, they broke it to take Professor Brainard away?" she asked. "Kidnapping?"

"We are still left with how they got in the laboratory in the first place," he shouted. "And if they could sneak in without being seen, why not take him out the same way? They shattered the glass... whoever they are... Did they shoot him out of a canon...?"

"This is quite awkward," she said, looking upwards and having to keep one hand on her head so her hat wouldn't fall off. "Should I come up?"

"No," Camparol grumbled, getting to his feet and dusting off his hands. "I'll be right down."

Back in the missing scientist's laboratory, Camparol pulled off his gloves and perched on a stool next to the workbench where Spiridon was testing the dried blood.

"I can see why Inspector Juve would prefer to return to Paris and tangle with Fantômas... This is a... jumble." Camparol sighed, rubbing his jaw in thought. "We have so little solid information to work with. Are we looking for a murderer or a kidnapper?"

"Good question," Stella mused. "Could it have started as a kidnapping attempt that then went wrong?"

Camparol shrugged and opened his mouth to speak. But he was distracted by Spiridon tapping against the workbench. While a genius when it came to the physical sciences, the enormous ant was incapable of human speech.

Once he had his associates' attention, he held out a small test tube with a faint, opaque residue in the bottom. He tapped further, explaining his discovery using a makeshift Morse code that the trio had established in order to communicate.

"So, you found traces of chemicals mixed in with the blood?" Camparol shrugged. "He's a chemist, this is his work room, isn't that to be expected?"

The ant shook his head and held the test tube towards the detective. Camparol reached for it. Just before he took hold of the test tube, Spiridon let go of it. Rather than falling, the test tube floated several inches above the workbench.

Camparol pulled his hand back, and Stella gave a faint gasp.

The test tube continued to float above the table, while the three detectives watched it with various expressions of surprise and curiosity.

"Cavorite!" Stella breathed. "That's... that's not possible!"

"What?" Camparol asked, glancing over at his partner.

"My people are able to travel between worlds due to a chemical formula that allows our conveyances to counteract gravity. There are many variations on this substance, and as many names for them. On Earth, the most common is *Cavorite*, named for the professor behind the most successful attempt to re-create it."

When introductions were required, Camparol referred to Stella Astarte as a foreign student who had become his assistant shortly after her arrival in Paris. He generally neglected to mention her home was a city on the Moon, inhabited by immortal beings that claimed to be angels.

"So, this... Cavorite... um... cancels out gravity?" Camparol said, thoughtfully, while peering up at the broken skylight. "How much would you need...?"

"One of the reasons my people keep an eye on any Earth scientists dabbling with it," Stella said, recovering her usual composure, "is that it can be a volatile substance. Cavorite is a quite potent variation. It needs to be strictly measured, stored and applied."

"So, if, say, someone were to have cooked up a batch and then spilled it, while standing under a skylight...?"

All three investigators looked upwards.

Camparol then stood up and begun shrugging into his overcoat.

"Be tricky for Juve to recover the body, but I think we can file this under 'scientific misadventure'..."

"No," Stella said, firmly. "We are still looking at an attempted kidnapping or robbery, if not premeditated murder."

"What?" Camparol asked, pausing with his overcoat half on. "What am I missing? Seems fairly obvious Brainard spilled his version of Cavorite on himself and was sent shooting into orbit."

Stella sighed, looking thoughtful, yet slightly conflicted.

"Because, my people... monitor certain sciences, here on Earth. You are an immature species and access to certain devices or substances would be most detrimental."

"You aren't just here to learn about Earth civilization, but to also spy on... I mean, 'monitor our progress'?" Camparol said, archly, pulling on his coat and looking around for where he left his gloves.

"Any reasonable adult understands that it's not 'spying,' but common sense to keep the child away from the bottle marked 'poison.' The point being," Stella continued, frowning at her fellow investigator, "that Professor Brainard was not being observed. The American branch of the family, we believe, within a generation may decipher a working formula, but not here."

"You missed one," Camparol shrugged, before looking at the tall woman in surprised understanding. "Nobody's perfect, except your people supposedly are!"

"Supposedly?" Stella muttered, frowning.

"How did you miss what he was working on?" Camparol said, beginning to pace again. "Especially here, a retreat for savants, the Lunar Angels had to have a spyglass trained on a house full of scientists!"

He turned, glancing a question at Stella.

"Someone has been deliberately shielding Professor Brainard and his studies from us," she nodded. "I think what happened is, that same someone, aware they couldn't keep his discovery hidden for long, tried to abduct the professor, or steal his formula..."

"...And broke a container or accidently killed him," Camparol continued. "And whoever they are realized they had in their possession a rather unique way to dispose of a body. We are still left with the question of 'who' and 'how'."

He began to prowl the lab again, peering accusingly at the oaken walls and floorboards.

"Anyone who had knowledge of Cavorite," said Stella, "as well my people's interest, would most likely have access to such powers or technology that this room would be no more than an inconvenience."

"No," Camparol said, shaking his head, while he continued to pace. "If our culprit had magical, otherworldly abilities, then why shatter the skylight? Forget strange formulas and just see the crime. This was rushed. Something went wrong. That explains where Professor Brainard went, but not how the culprit got in and out... There's that gap between when the butler brought him his lunch and the breaking glass..."

The French detective stopped, glanced up at the skylight, then over to the door. He paced back between the two, silently measuring the distance. He stopped and peered intently at the stain on the floor, pulling at his lip in thought.

The woman from the Moon and the enormous ant waited patiently, knowing from past experience that their mundane chaperone had abilities of his own.

"Maybe...?" he muttered to himself. "It could be...!"

Stella came and stood at his shoulder. Camparol looked over, as if just noticing her.

"I think I know how it was done," he said, the corner of his mouth going up in a brief, self-satisfied smile.

"Before you make any announcements," she said, very quietly, "you might want to know that someone is lurking on the other side of the door and has been there for several minutes."

Camparol started to ask how she knew, but realized she would only reel off a list of how her people were superior to mere earthly mortals, and her senses were refined to a level a poor souls like himself could never reach, and instead decided he'd rather wrestle with a desperate murderer.

He snapped his finger to get Spiridon's attention and, gesturing, directed the ant to stand by the door. Moving stealthily, Camparol went and stood on the other side. When he nodded, Spiridon pulled the door open, and the detective reached out and yanked the lurker into the room.

The butler went wide-eyed, sputtered in protest and then reached frantically into his coat.

Stella was immediately at their side and caught his wrist in a grip of iron. She pulled his hand out and then wrenched a thin-barreled shiny pistol, tossing it onto the nearest workbench.

The lady detective and the furtive domestic locked gazes. Stella muttered something under her breath in the language of her angelic people.

"Much as I am pleased to find my theory concerning the culprit was correct," Camparol said as the trio forced the butler over to one of the dilapidated sofas and pushed him down onto it, "I get the feeling you know a bit more about what has occurred here. What was it?"

"Our new acquaintance is a Radar Man," Stella said, crossing her arms, and sternly peering down at the butler. "My people share the Moon with several other races. The enclave of the Radar Men is our most bothersome neighbor."

The butler glared at them sullenly.

"While their science is far beyond that of Earth's, their constant state of warfare and limited resources have kept them from ever being more than troublesome. To have transported an agent to Earth and erected some kind of energy field to shield them from the Lunar immortals, I would guess, is not only a gross violation of our treaty, but must have been a major undertaking for them."

"So, we were both right in our theories about what happened," Camparol said. "Otherworldly agents and a rushed kidnapping attempt: the butler, using the cover of bringing up lunch, attempts to get a hold of Professor Brainard or his formula at gunpoint, things go wrong, and he fires..."

"The gun fires a narrow beam of concentrated energy," Stella prompted.

Camparol raised his eyebrows at her informative interruption and continued.

"The shot shatters the container, and the professor is doused and promptly shot into the heavens. We are going to have to be creative when we explain this to Inspector Juve. He'll accept 'foreign operative,' but we can't produce Brainard's body, can we?"

"Possibly," Stella said, giving a faint shrug. "Depending on how much he was splashed with, he might come back down, but taking into account the Earth's rotation..."

Camparol waved away any further calculation, and returned his attention to the Lunar villain slumped on the sofa.

"He looks human," he mused, thoughtfully. "And he's been able to fool this house full of absent-minded savants, but will he hold up to intense scrutiny?"

"I can send a message to my father," Stella said. "He will need to be informed about this incident. I think he will want to send a delegation to investigate all this. The looking devices on the Moon should be able to find Professor Brainard's body if he reached orbit."

"And take him off our hands?" Camparol asked, gesturing toward the glowering Radar Man.

"Oh, yes, we can't have extra-planetary powers interfering in the scientific progress of the Earth," Stella said.

Camparol glanced over at his partner, realized she wasn't being the least bit ironic, and returned his attention to their captive.

The lunar agent provocateur glared at Stella as she drew a tiny-looking glass set on a long ivory stem and moved away to study it. She appeared to be speaking to the mirror.

Camparol and Spiridon stood guard over the Radar Man, the enormous ant taking a professional interest in the extra-terrestrial, intently studying him.

"It's rude to stare," Camparol chided his associate.

Spiridon glared at the detective and moved away, perching on the far arm of the sofa, but still unabashedly studying the lunar criminal like a sample in a test tube.

Camparol glanced over at Stella. He knew her long-stemmed looking glass was a device that bordered on magic, and impossible as it sounded, could be used to communicate with her Father, who dwelled in a city on the Moon.

With the assistance of Stella's people, they would be able to resolve this case and hopefully keep the Earth safe from further interference from the Radar Men's machinations.

It was fascinating and a daunting for a humble ex-police detective from Paris to be involved.

At the same time, so many of his recent cases, since taking on his two extraordinary charges, had been amazing and other-worldly.

He perched on a stool, sighed and found himself almost longing for the days when his investigations concerned mundane murderers, thievery and corruption.

As always, Paul Hugli's new tale is steeped in Egyptian myth and esoteric knowledge, but this time, it is G.G. Fickling's Honey West, and Harry Dickson's former protégé Tom Wills, who tackle new threats under the Californian sun of the early 1960s...

Paul Hugli: *The Night of the Dazzling Sun*

"Great Scott! Creatures from Outer Space!
Here on Earth, in Ancient Egypt!"
Rip Hunter, Time Master! (*Showcase* #26; June 1960)

Bellflower, California, November 1941

Bellflower was a sleepy little cow-and-dairy town, just North of Long Beach, where nothing really exciting ever happened. And little was different on this surprising warm winter morning. But this didn't deter a certain precocious, azure-eyed towhead girl from holding court, with a sense of innocence mixed with a dab of Machiavellian craftiness. Though neither of these traits was needed on this particular day: *The Every Other Sunday Save for July Tea Party, sans* Dormouse, Turtledove, Mad Hatter and the Tweedles. In their place were the usual suspects: Winnie-the-Pooh, Shirley Temple, Charlie McCarthy, Mickey Mouse, Raggedly Ann (*sans* Andy), and The Bat-Man (actually a Buster Brown doll with a black cape-and-cowl her Aunt Meg had sewn together). Yet one guest was missing. Conspicuously so. *Now we are seven*, the towhead thought with a sigh.

Yet, this eleven year-old wouldn't—couldn't!—allow absent friends to deter her from her hosting duties, precise and unforgiving; her perfectly pressed blue sundress with a white apron design, and spit-polished black shoes with buckles were *oh-so* correct. Leaning forward—most lady-like, of course—she performed her societal responsibilities as dictated by her station in life, hosting the *Every Other Sunday*....

After three choruses of "*Hip-Hip-Pooh-Rah!*" the hostess began serving tea (*Coca Cola®*) from a pink Bakelite tea-pot, and passed around scones (*Oreo®*). Still as much as she tried to be prim and proper, she remained in a diz: *a friend was missing*. Yet, none of her guests asked about the absent friend; it wasn't proper.

A disembodied voice interrupted the non-festive festival:

"Honey! Honey-Child! Mister Ryder, the mailman, brought you a package."

Without diverting her eyes from her guests the girl—Honey—replied: "Bring it out here, Auntie."

Aunt Meg has been little Honey's mother since her own mother had died giving birth to her; actually, realistically, Aunt Meg has been the only "mother" she had ever known.

Auntie set the small, brown-papered package on the table before her niece. Honey studied it, tilting her head this way and that, her white silk-gloved fingers opening and closing, pondering the wonders the box might contain.

"My, oh my, I wonder what's inside," she said, clapping her gloved palms together. "It becomes curiouser and curiouser."

"Maybe, Honey-Child," Aunt Meg suggested, "you should open it."

"Yes, yes , a splendid idea," Honey giggled, clapping her hands together. "Yes, yes... *off with its lid!*"

The string and wrapping paper disappeared in a flurry of dexterous frenzy, revealing a small cardboard box, with a note on the lid, in bold black ink: *This Happens When Demands Are Not Met!!!*

Huh? Honey thought as she lifted the lid, pushing back the tissue paper. She bolted up right, knocking over her chair, fainting dead away.

Nested in the tissue was the head of her Tea Party's "absent friend," that of her Superman puppet. The Champion of the Oppressed has been silenced, when he would soon be most needed. This was Honey West's "Day of Infamy"— FDR's own was but a week away, with the bombing of Pearl Harbor, threatening, testing: *Truth... Justice... and the American Way!*

With Superman decapitated, the only Man of Steel left was Joseph Stalin!

Mojave Desert, California, May 1960

It was a dark, rainy night.

Actually, at this precise moment, I had no idea what the weather was like as I was trapped in an underground chamber, my back to a magnetically-locked steel door, but considering it was May, in the Mojave Desert, the sky was no doubt dark, but starry; yet I doubted it was rainy.

I was like Alice down the Rabbit Hole, and as Lt. Mark Storm would say: "You're... destructible... Infallible... Insatiable... and, as usual, In-Trouble!"

He had never been so right as at this moment; the *plink-plink-plink* of dripping water echoing though the dimly red-lit dampness of the chamber... A Hellhole! And then came the mumbling, low groans and rumbles from the belly of the earth.

What could I do, dressed in a skimpy white gown, with my trusty .22 elsewhere. Nor was my partner-in-crime-prevention, dressed in a light-blue jumpsuit, in much better shape.

But I wasn't ready for the Big Sleep, not in this *Poisonville* that Osiris Prime considered his dream society. But this wasn't what dreams were made of... well, at least, not mine. "It's a nightmare!"

"Huh?" my partner said.

"I said, this is a nightmare!"

"Quite right, Miss West... A bloody nightmare!"

How does a nightmare begin—bloody, or otherwise? For a private eye returning from a case at just a little past 4:00 a.m, it had been looking for a short-cut she'd never found.

It had all begun: at Angel Flight's Tram Landing, on Hill and Olive Streets, in L.A., with a P.I. lost and too long without sleep to really care about the gum on her shoe.

It had all begun: with a rip in her very best black nylons—$2.00 at Penney's.

But she'd finally made it to her office, on the 2nd Floor of the Wilkes Building on Anaheim Stree, in Long Beach, and crashed on the threadbare sofa, passing out from exhaustion, only to be awoken a few hours later by the rapping on her office door that read: *H. West - Personal Investigations*.

Oh, by the way, that weary P.I. is me. My name is Honey West, private eye of the female species: *Honey sapiens*.

Who'd be rapping on my office door this early in the morning? I asked myself, glancing at the wall clock. It read: 10:00, and a glance out of the window told me it was a.m.; so, I guess it wasn't *that* early. I rubbed the redness from my eyes as the raps continued on the door, and mumbled: "Hold your horses, I'm coming."

I was just about to open the door when I realized I was completely nude after the shower I'd taken to wipe the grim from my 38-26-36 torso, and crashing on the sofa. I tossed on the baby-blue terry-cloth robe that matched my eyes, which just barely managed to cover my naughty bits, and wrapped my loose, sleep-mussed-up taffy-blond hair in a towel, like Lana Turner in *The Postman Always Rings Twice*—though I doubted if it was the postman ringing, er, knocking twice or otherwise.

Unlatching the door I opened it, and the man in the hall said, "Miss West?"

"Yes, sir, Honey in the Flesh, so-to-speak," I answered with a smile, as I gave the man the once-over.

He was a well-kept man, in his late forties, clean-shaven with a slightly chubby, jolly face, more interesting than handsome. He was dressed in a three-piece tweed suit, complete with watch-bob hanging from his green vest-pocket, with a brown derby covering his sandy-brown hair. He looked like he'd just stepped out of a Sherlock Holmes novel, and when he spoke, I was sure of it.

"Hullo, Luv," he said, proffering his hand, "my name is Thomas Wills."

"Come in and tell me how I might assist you," I said, ushering him into the office, offering him the chair before my desk as I managed to sit in mine behind it, shoving my copy of *Tom Jones* into the top drawer, atop *Lolita*, whether she liked it or not.

"The Sheriff's Department—Lt. Storm—referred me to you, Luv."

"Whoa! Are we talking about the same Lieutenant Storm: six-five, 240, body of an Olympic god?"

"Quite."

"Why, that...," I began, but let it trail off.

Well, well, Honey Girl, since when does the hard-nose, straight-shooter, often Honey-badger and protector, Mark Storm, toss possibly dangerous business your way? He was full of old chestnuts; in fact, he was a walking chestnut!

Early the previous day, I'd turned down his 10,000[th] marriage proposal, before he was off to NYC to visit his cousins, Johnny & Sue, and just as many times his pleas for me to get outta this business, get married, and raise a parcel of younguns. He treated me like I was some kinda *Carnal Kewpie Doll* to be won at the wedding-ring toss at the Pike Amusement Park. But I wasn't ready to be a housewife; stuck in the *Iron* Age.

"Again, Mr. Wills, what can I do for you?" I inquired.

"Miss West," he said, taking off his bowler, fingering it, "what do you know about UFOs?"

"Just what I read in the papers and see in the movies."

"Ever see one?

"No."

Technically that was true. I had been in Washington, D.C., during the July 1952, "Flying Saucer Flap," when scores of ordinary people, military and civilian pilots had reported a "V-shaped formation" of saucers buzzing over the Capitol Building, and they even had been picked up on radar. Daddy and me had been aboard a plane at Washington National, for our return trip to Long Beach; I hadn't even known about the Saucers until I'd read about them in the next day's *Press Telegram*.

I had come to see the sights when Daddy had had to go to D.C. to testify behind closed Senate doors. I assumed at the time he'd been testifying about Joseph McCarthy and the "Commies in Hollywood." He never told me what it had all been about—client confidentially and all that jazz. When he'd died—had been butchered!—I'd inherited the business and his files. I then found that all events surrounding that visit to D.C. had been purged from his files, as if wiped clean by a pro. Though I'd have bet my by life—often!—that these same events had dovetailed into what had led directly to his slaughter in the alley behind the Paramount Theatre!

All that had led me on my quest to find *and* punish his killer... or killers. Thus I'd become a girl on the prowl, with a kiss for the killer... from my trusty pearl-handled .22.

"No," I repeated, torching the end of a Chesterfield, puffing it into fiery existence. I offered the deck to my potential client, but he waved it off. "Suit yourself—what about you? Have you even seen a Flying Saucer?"

"As a detective, I have seen many things," Wills said with a complacent shrug.

"I understand," I said in agreement. As a P.I., I'd seen many things, but never Little Green Men, or even, a One-Eyed, One-Horned, Flying Purple People Eater... *purple people*? Then it hit me, so tangential I almost forgot. "Oh, yeah, I almost forgot, I saw a Venusian once."

"Great Saturn's Rings, Luv," Tom Wills gasped, almost dropping his bowler. "What? Where? When?"

"You forgot 'Why' and 'How'," I smiled, torching another Chesterfield with my Durrell lighter, sensing he was lost.

"You were saying... about the Venusians...?"

"I was on a kidnapping case that brought me to the Mojave Desert. Between Yucca Tree and Joshua Tree..."

"Near Great Rock?"

"Yes, near Monolith, off Highway 456, near the L.A. Aqueduct," I continued, tilting my head, allowing a stream of blue-gray smoke to escape from my full-red lips, where it leisurely drifted to the ceiling. "Why?"

"Please, Miss West, continue," he said with a flick of his wrist.

"It was really nothing. No more than a nutso wandering in the night. An old drunken professor who thought I had a Venusian Landing Device under my skirt. Well, at least, that was an original approach. Any who, I told him I was not from Venus, that I did not come *twenty million miles to Earth* to attend the Giant Rock Spaceship Convention, or whatever they call their hoe-down. Anyhow, the prof thought that because I was blonde and buxom, I was an alien. So I ended up given him my name, rank and Venusian number."

"The Giant Rock Interplanetary Spacecraft Convention," he corrected me, then added: "And that's why I am here."

"To report an UFO?"

"Jolly Good, Miss West," Wills laughed, slapping his knee. "Jolly good!"

He dug a pipe from his jacket pocket and held it up; I waved my hand it was okay. He began the ritual of packing the bowl, tapping it down, lighting it, taking a couple test puffs, before he was satisfied. Lighting a cigarette, which I did, was much easier.

"The First Giant Rock Interplanetary Spacecraft Convention," he continued between relaxing puffs, "was held in May 1954, and since then, it has become the center, the nexus of the Flying Saucer contactee movement." He saw the confusion on my face and added: "*Tête à tête*, face-to-face with the Spacemen. Over the years, Giant Rock has attracted the *Who's-Who* of contactees: Orleo Angelucci, Truman Berthurum, George Hunt Williamson, Giant Rock's host,

George Van Tassel, and, in the early years, the stellar star of the contactees: George Adamski."

"By George," I said, with a smile, "that's a lot of Georges."

"Quite. In the vernacular, these contactees are referred to as *Saucerians*, those individuals claiming physical or mental contact with alleged Space Brothers. And, in many ways, these annual desert conventions remind one of your country's old-fashion religious revival meetings of the 20s and 30s. In fact, my mentor, Harry Dickson, traced the present flying saucer contactee movement to a space-based religious cult, *I Am*, from some twenty-five years ago."

"Never cared for that 'Old Time Religion'," I two-cented. "I'm afraid they'll say: 'there's no blondes in Heaven'."

"Quite so. Opposing the Saucerians are the 'hardware' or 'serious' *Ufologists*, who believe the Saucerians—and the contactees—are an annoyance, a hindrance, a risk to serious research into the nature, the mysteries of *Unidentified Flying Objects*. These UFOlogists are more interest in the 'nuts-and-bolts' of the phenomena, then in visitor from space."

"Whoa," I said, crushing the smoking butt in the overflowing ash tray, "these UFOlogists believe flying saucers are probably from outer space, yet they shy away from saying spacemen are piloting them?"

"Quite. Men like Donald Keyhoe, Morris K. Jessup, Jim and Carol Lorezen, and the various UFO associations reject all the peace-and-love soliloquy of the Saucerian's Space Brothers, and that the UFOs might actually be a *threat* to Earth."

I turned in my chair to a cooler on the floor. I popped the lid; brown bottles were floating in the melted ice, and asked: "You want a beer?"

"Do you have...?"

"It's Hamms or nothing," I said, cutting him off.

"That will suit me."

I brought up two relatively cool bottles of *the beer that refreshes*, holding them by their necks, popping the caps via a church-key, with such deftness that only few droplets of suds escaped. I handed one across to Wills and we each took a slug.

"And, I guess, all this leads us back to Giant Rock?"

"Quite so," Wills replied, reaching into his inner pocket. "One of the guest speakers at this year's Giant Rock represents the *International Society of Interplanetary Studies* or *I.S.I.S.* This UFO-cult seemingly sprang up out of nowhere. There are rather secretive, erecting a faux Egyptian temple headquarters near Black Rock, in the Mojave Desert. The Founder and Spiritual Leader is called Osiris Prime. A real oddball, that one."

"Like a person who *doesn't* eat the ears first on a chocolate Easter Bunny?"

"Indeed. The *Committee of Information and Defense* knows nothing about him, or his past. He and *ISIS* just popped up a couple years back, with his peace-and-love Space Brother diatribe. He does appear to have very deep pockets, as you Yanks might say. There have been some reports of disappearances connected to the cult, but nothing has come of the investigations. Probably, just the disenchanted, rebelling teenagers, and adults wanting to drop off the social radar, for one reason or another."

From his inner jacket pocket, he produced a folded 8x10" glossy, sliding it across the desk. "Here is a photograph of Osiris Prime, from an image from the back of the *ISIS* brochure: *Osiris Rising*."

I unfolded the full-color photo and my baby-blues dilated. *Yummie, Honey Girl, here's an Adonis to moan for... yuhmmmmm.* In the three-quarter shot, Osiris Prime seems to be six-foot, with bulging biceps straining the fabric of his short-sleeved golden tunic, which extended to mid-thighs, as tanned and as muscular as his arms. His shoulder-length, beach-bum blonde hair was paired neatly down the middle, framed his oval face... deep-blue eyes, full lips, Roman nose.

"So," I said, looking up from the photo. "OK. What's your game? Why do you need of my services?"

"My superiors at the *C.I.D.* believe *ISIS* might be equivalent to George Lincoln Rockwell's *Union of Free Enterprise National Socialists*, but with the patina of a flying saucer cult. They instructed me to investigate, to acquire an appropriate assistant."

"Appropriate? Me? Space Nazis?"

"Quite so, Miss West," Wills said, setting his bottle of beer on my desktop. "Osiris Prime will be speaking at the Seventh Annual Giant Rock Interplanetary Spacecraft Convention, and we believe he will be recruiting new members for his cult."

"And you want us to be invited to a hoe-down at his desert resort, to scope it out. To get the lowdown on his operation. See what's going on."

"Yes. And you are ideal for the assignment."

"How's that?" I was getting a tingling in my tummy.

"Blonde, blue-eyed, and... er, shapely. The ideal Aryan archetype... Hitler's stereotypic Nazi."

"Why did it have to be Nazis? I hate Nazis."

"Then let us do something about them."

"Let me check my daily planner," I said, picking up my Magic 8-Ball, shaking it, then turning it over, reading my future: *Outlook: Not So Good!*

"Problem, Miss West?"

"No, the Ball is broken, it always says that. Yet it always seems to be an accurate prediction." I shrugged. "Well, I'm so much in debt I have to get a co-signer to play Monopoly. So, sure, this girl is for hire."

"Smashing," he exclaimed.

Smashing? At least he didn't say...

"Jolly Good. Miss West."

...too late.

He left some pamphlets from various speakers at the com-fab. A weirder lot you'd never seen. And with nothing better to do for a couple days, I hit Acres of Books and loaded up on some UFOnuts' books, then caught the new release, *The Time Machine*, at the Strand Theatre.

Three days later, outside Riverside, we stopped in Perris for breakfast, where the coffee burned all the way down: Sheer Heaven! Of course, we got the gamut of strange looks, and that was not surprising. We were kitted out, er, dressed in costumed I'd acquired from MGM costume department, the famed movie studio I had done a few job for. I was dressed in a golden gossamer-silk, mid-thigh-length, with a deep scoop in front and back, tan nylons, white low-heeled boots. Tom Wills was outfitted in an elaborated blue jumpsuit. Both were from *The Forbidden Planet*; though I had to let mine out a bit in the chest region. I was still peeved there were no diamonds or emeralds, let alone star sapphires!

While eating and before motoring, er, driving the rest of the way to Giant Rock, I gave Wills a crash-course on American-English: Mister or Miss, not Guv or Luv; no Jolly Good or By George; drop the "U" from colour, humour, harbour, but not ours and yours; it's a hood not a bonnet; a trunk, not a boot; tire not tyre; a car not an auto, which runs on gas or gasoline, not petro; though using *wanker* was okay.

A while later, we were barreling down Highway 247 in Yucca Valley, with Wills piloting a rented red-and-white Chevy Bel-Air, when he informed me of the "mental contactees" who communicated with the aliens via *clairaudience* or "audio" contact; though most did so via *channeling*—automatic writing, Ouija Boards, visions, astral travel or disembodied entities. Both types of contact involved information exchange, with little or no physical or technical details to bother with—similar to the ancient priests who consulted oracles to receive guidance from the gods in the sky.

In contrast, the other group of Saucerians claimed actual *physical* contact with Space Men. But no matter which group you fell in, to them, there were no *Unidentified* Flying Saucers. Because, to them, they were *not* unidentified and their purpose was known: they were messengers of Our Cosmic Destiny, sent to prepare humans for the Coming Change, whether via nuclear proliferation, geological upheaval, polar shift, or a dozen of other global events. And some "Galactic Brotherhood" or other such entities had come to Earth on an errand of mercy to offer us Salvation. In fact, it sounded not unlike *The Day the Earth Stood Still*, but without the threat of blowing up the Earth if we didn't comply.

They were like a popular religious movement seeking some sort of universality, and all these various UFO-gurus represented a densely populated universe, with many advance races forming a Universal Space Brotherhood or Celestial United Nations. And as in analogy to our own U.N., there were a minority group of "evil" aliens, opposing the benevolent ones who would become the saviors of Earth. Those Saviors tended to be human in appearance; most often prime specimens, blonde and Aryan-looking.

Wills had stopped at a crossroad, to check his map for directions. I glanced at the crossroad sign: Bellflower Road. *Bellflower, Honey Girl, out here in the middle of the desert?* And the memories began to flood my brain...

I didn't really want to go down this road; remembering the times of yesterday, when life was an easier game to play... It was the best of times: of Freddy the Bully at Lincoln Elementary, whom I'd sent home crying to his mommy, when I had karate-chopped him [*thanks, Daddy*]... Of playing Alice hosting her Tea Party [save for that faithful day in November, and the decapitated Superman puppet—I'd never discovered who'd sent it; and Daddy had told me to forget about it; *yeah, sure*]... Of trading comic books... Of Daddy reading the pulps to me: *The Shadow, The Spider, The Nyctalope, The Phantom Detective*... Of radio: *Jack Armstrong, Lights Out, Inner Sanctum, The Shadow again*... "The weed of crime bears bitter fruit; crime does not pay!" Actually, it seemed to pay a lot better than crime-fighting of the P.I. kind... Of skipping rope: K-I-S-S-I-N-G... *Honey and Sammy sitting in a tree*... Of my first job slinging hash at Bertha's Grill, on the corner of Compton and Clark... and my time at Long Beach Jay-Cee... Of the Pep Squad [no *Hangman, Shield* or *Comet*, but lots of *Bettys and Veronicas*]... Of the English prof nicknamed "David Cop-*a*-feel"... Of necking in the Drive-In ozoners...

...Of the West Family Tree: Other than a few actresses [like Auntie Mae] and "dancers" [like my mother and Aunt Evelyn], the most *outré*, eccentric member of the West family was my Grand-Uncle Herbert West, who was rumored to have perfected a method of *reanimation* of the dead. Others have said it was all "smoke and mirrors"—more Houdini than science. Yet, if true, I could have reanimated my Superman puppet, my daddy, and my mommy, who had died giving to me... I loved Aunt Meg dearly, but no amount of her love and caring and doting could have replaced a mother's love, or relieved me of my "survivor guilt."

Including myself and my dad, the West Family Tree was littered with members of law-enforcement, in one form or another. My uncle, Captain Robert West, of the Military Intelligence Department, had told of some amazing stories dealing with a Dr. Alex Zorka; of giant robots, invisibility rays from meteorites, and of spies.

Yet, he couldn't hold a candle to my great-great-grand uncle, James T. West, an agent of the U.S. Secret Service under President Grant. Legends of his exploits had been passed down through the generations, but most of the concrete facts were contained in his partner's, Artemus Gordon, diaries, whose Aunt Maude had willed to the family after Gordon had died childless.

If Gordon had been truthful, and not embellishing, then their bordered on *The Twilight Zone* or *One Step Beyond*! There were tales of a deadly toxin called *Franconium*, plastic surgery, noble *and* savage Indians, gypsies, various smuggling rings, Mexican dictators, an assortment of assassination attempts on governmental personnel and foreign dignitaries, a living-size puppet and haunted houses. The most fantastical of James West's foes was one Doctor Miguelito Quixote Loveless, who—if we are to believe Gordon's journal—invented the TV cathode-ray tube, airships, a LSD-type hallucinogen, a mechanical man, the ability to shrink people, and a method to enter framed paintings—though the latter two events may have been more hallucinogenic than actual; some way-out, mind-bending dope that any hophead would sell his soul for...,

And, of course, as in Dickens' novel, there had been the worst of times. No more so than the party my Aunt Meg had organized for my graduation from Long Beach Jay Cee. Everyone had been there, including family friend, Fred Simms of the *Press Telegram*. We had been waiting for my father. A knock had come to the door and I opened it. There stood a handsome, six-foot-four Patrolman; the first time I'd met Mark Storm, eight years ago. For a while, I had hated his guts, because he had been the one given the unpleasant, uneasy task of informing us that my father had died.

My father had been found face down in the mud behind the Paramount Theater. His funeral was closed-casket. And reality had crashed down on me. I had to pick myself up by my bra-straps and dust myself off... It was time to grow up. And I had. I had taken over my father's detective agency, with the expressed purpose of finding his slayer. Then I could retire... rest... marry... raise a family...

Bellflower? Well, one can't go home again; Alice doesn't live there anymore.

"Miss West... Miss West... Miss West," Wills repeated before he shook me, snapping me from my remembrances. He asked: "Are you well, Miss West?"

"Sure, fine and dandy," I said, wiping a tear from my eye.

Tom Wills didn't press me, and I appreciated that. He let up the clutch and drove down Bellflower Road, until the pavement ended in Landers, and there he stopped the Chevy, pointing off to the left. *"The Integratron.* The Great Experiment."

The circular structure was surrounded by Yucca Trees, sand—lotsa it—and sage brush—though I doubted if it was all that wise. According to Wills, it was some 30-feet high and 50-feet in diameter, with 16-sided non-metallic dome, constructed of wood and concrete.

I said: "Impressive. But what exactly in this overgrown Tinker-Toy?"

"It is the ongoing project of George Van Tassel, organizer of the Giant Rock Convention. He was an airline inspector for Hughes' Lockheed factory. Then, as reported in his book, *I Rode in a Flying Saucer*, he quit his job and purchased the land around Giant Rock, and leased the Giant Rock Airport from your Federal Government, planning to open a, er, I think you call it, a Dude Ranch."

I nodded that he was correct. He continued:

"To entertain stop-overs of week-end pilots. Yet, in 1952, his life changed when he began receiving psychic messages from an alien space ship, and a year later, he was invited aboard a Flying Saucer by some being named *Solganda*. Since then, he has been conducting channeling sessions from his underground home, hollowed out of the Giant Rock, itself."

"Okay, nothing weird about that," I managed to say with a semi-straight face. "And the *Integratron*?"

"With the 'Space Brother's' channeled instructions, combined with theorems developed by Nikola Tesla, Van Tassel built this structure, on this site," he continued with a sweep of his hand, "via a complex formula involving the Earth's magnetic field, the Great Pyramid of Egypt, and the world's largest free-standing boulder, vis-à-vis Giant Rock.

"Once completed, with a gigantic Tesla coil in its center, this structure—or 'machine'—will recharge, rejuvenate living cells' *plastic memory*, via a collection of static energy from the air, hence electrostatically recharging the human body, allowing a person to live up to 200 years, by preventing the body from deforming and disassembling over time."

"Sounds like that wacko I read about in the gossip rags," I said. "Wilhelm Reich."

"Quite. I mean, yes," Wills said after a moment's thought, and gave me a capsule version of Reich: "When you look up 'Mad Scientist' in the encyclopedia, you'll probably find Nikola Tesla listed first, then Wilhelm Reich. He had the distinction of being dismissed by the three greatest thinkers of his age: Karl Marx, Sigmund Freud and Albert Einstein! After fleeing the Nazis and being kicked out of Norway, this excommunicated disciple of Freud arrived here, in the Good Ol' U.S. of A. Here, he believed he had discovered the elemental form of life: *the bion*. From this discovery came his theory of *orgone energy*. That this energy is in everything blue, such as the sky, and *all* living things; in all organic matter until it dies.

"By 1939, he'd built his *Orgone Energy Accumulator*, a cabinet, not unlike a telephone booth, lined with alternating layers of organic and inorganic material, attuned to be charged with energy, to restore tissues, as a cure for cancer, obesity, alcoholism and, I imagine, the common cold. So, I guess, you go into that 'phone booth' as mild-mannered Clark Kent and come out as Superman. In any case, his *Organization of Orgonomy* did a brisk business selling both large and small accumulators.

"Then, in 1954, the FDA—his 'kryptonite'—who Reich referred to as 'Hoodlums in the Government'—took an interest in him, forbidding the sales of his Orgone Boxes. His books were banned, burned. He died in Lewisburg Prison in 1957, a broken, discredited and disgraced man.

"But did you know there was a Flying Saucer angle to Reich?" Wills concluded.

"I'm not surprised. But *Confidential, Hush Hush* and *On the QT* tend to lean more towards sex and scandals than little green men from Mars. And Reich was deep in the first two, so, I guess, the third wasn't far behind?"

"In his belief in Cosmic Duality," Wills said, navigating the car down a packed-dirt road, passing one giant boulder after another, "Reich discovered an anti-*bion*, which countered the benevolent *Orgone Energy*, responsible for all human malaises, which he termed *Deadly Orgone Energy* or *DOR*. To battle this deadly energy he constructed the *Cloudbuster*, consisting of a series of 'accumulating' pipes, connected to an 'earthly' water source.

"Pointed skyward, this 'buster' could, allegedly, disperse clouds, scattering the ominous haze of *DOR*. He believed that Flying Saucers were space-crafts powered by *DOR*. Thus his 'Cloudbuster' was a weapon against these hostile spacecrafts, which Reich believed were deliberately disrupting the Earth's fragile atmosphere, seeding it with corrupting *DOR*. Plus, he planned to use the benevolent *OE* to reforest parts of the Arizona Desert."

"This whole theory," I opined, "seems as wacky as a banjo."

"Yes, Miss West," Wills said as the car rounded a scattering of lesser boulders.

"*Woooooow....*," I gasped. It was...

...GIANT ROCK...

...the Seventh Annual Flying Saucer Convention, the public arena for Flying Saucerists and UFOnuts. A masterwork of organized chaos, not unlike the Flying Saucer mythos themselves.

Giant Rock, the largest free-standing boulder in the world, stood seven-stories high and covered 5,800 square feet. It was indeed impressive, definitely worth a *Wow*. But my '*Wow*' was not just for the Rock, itself, but also for the seemingly endless "parking lot," an assortment of cars and trucks, crammed together like so many sardines: Nashs, DeSotos, Fords, Chevys, Studebakers, Impalas, Oldsmobiles, VW bugs and Barndoor buses; plus a scattering of Tear Drop trailers and Ford Woodies, even an Oliver farm tractor. A couple of tailgaters were firing up for a *Beer-B-Q*. All were packed together like a bunch of sausages in a German meat market.

Teenagers were tossing around football, baseballs, Pluto Platters and Frisbees. Still others were setting up telescopes to watch the skies, hoping for some sign or visitation from the stars

Beyond the "parking lot" was row-after-row of hucksters, hawking and hustling heavenly heirlooms of the mysterious visitors of other worlds. All trying to grab a piece of the Spacemen's action. Mobs of guests milled around, checking out the various offerings. It had a bread and circus atmosphere to it.

"Impressive, Miss West?" Wills asked with a sweep of his hand over the spectacle. "An estimated 11,000 Saucerians, contactees, occult tourists, and just the plain curious will convene here. Some are here to channel Our Space Brothers; others hoping for an actual saucer landing."

"And for the hucksters to sell their wares to the True Believers. Thus justifying the 'con' in *con*tactee. A sham. In my 'Uncle' Artemus's diary, he'd written that, while he and James West were protecting a gold shipment through the Arizona Territory, they had come upon two green-skinned women, claiming they were stranded on Earth, and that their spaceship—Artemus called it a 'Flying Pie Pan'—needed gold for fuel, for which they were willing to trade 'worthless' gems such as diamonds. It was all a very terrestrial con... just another scam."

We found a parking place between a VW van and a '57 Caddy and got out. I smoothed down my shirt; checked my make-up. Wills pointed to Giant Rock. A metal stairway led half-way up the rock face, to a platform with a microphone stand. "That where the famous and lesser known espoused the Wisdom of Universal Love, of either ethereal or physical beings, or, often, both. They are all here to spread the Word: the Message of their Enlightened Brothers."

"From the pamphlets you left me," I said as we began weaving our way through the parked cars, "except for the Universal Peace message and such, none of these contactees seem to agree about whom, or even, what inhabits the various planets and moons of the Solar System. Through it appears all the Nordic beautiful women are from Venus, and the less attractive Spacemen are from Mars."

"Deduce anything else, Miss West?"

"That, perhaps, there is mutual, unwritten law or agreement, not to knock someone else's book, so they won't knock yours. So they pretend to 'believe' each other's story. You know: not to cut into each other's book sales. Like they say, each wants to be the bride at every wedding, the corpse at every funeral."

"You don't have to be Harry Dickson to deduce that elementary fact. In fact, this entire Giant Rock Convention reminds me of Eric the Red's discovery of a new land covered in eternal ice and snow. To encourage his fellow Norsemen to migrate there, Eric dubbed the place: Greenland. Shortly, thereafter, 25 ships arrived with eager settlers."

"That seems to sum it up, Wills," I said as I glanced around.

We exited the "parking lot." Only a score or three out of thousands of our fellow travelers were dressed in "costumes" like us. Most of the men were dressed in jeans, short-sleeves or tee-shirts, boots or sneakers; the women in an assortment of sun-dresses or shorts or slacks. Many wore Panama hats and shades, toting binoculars and/or cameras: hoping to capture any Space Visitor for posterity or, more likely, to line their pockets by selling the pics to the newspapers and tabloids.

There was even a clique of beatniks or, at least, *beatnoids*: beaded, turtle-necked, wearing berets; and unsmiling beat-chicks wearing sandals, black leotards. They were all the way-out and still climbing, and probably could pop the cork on any intoximeter as they stood aloof of the Cubes, Nerds and the Squares from Nowheresville.

Standing there, still taking it all in, I felt an itching on my leg, and I reached down to scratch it, and came up with a snake. I tried not to shriek; but it was no use. I tossed the slimy serpent.

Wills laughed. "It's only a garter snake. Quite harmless. It was just seeking ants."

"I'm nobody's aunt! And I prefer my garters silk and blue. Ideally with my pearl-handled .22 safely tucked inside," I said. Then, swirling around before patting my shoulder purse, I added: "But as you can clearly see, I could hardly hide it in this skimpy get-up. Fortunately, there's room in my purse for Miss .22."

There were a few other kooks dressed similar to Tom Wills and me, in tunic and boots, milling around a hunk of a man, a regular *Don Juan-abee*: six-foot tall, broad-shoulders tapering to a slim waist; shoulder-length golden-hair, parted down the middle, with sparkling azure eyes, and muscular arms stretching the fabric of his golden jumpsuit.

Osiris Prime...in the flesh!

After I stopped drooling, I spotted behind the *I.S.I.S.* booth three tall men with olive skin, dressed in black suits and snap-brim fedoras, leaning against a 1955 Rolls-Royce Silver Cloud, its grill topped with a *Spirit of Ecstasy* figurine. *Wow, Honey Girl, this Space-Guru gig must pay well!*

"He's wearing elevator shoes," Wills said, indicating Osiris Prime.

"So? He's gorgeous. But I will make a note: Beware of *Geeks* wearing lifts."

Along with a newsletter, *Universal Wisdom*, Wills picked up a program from the table of the host, George Van Tassel. Flipping through it, he noted: "First, there's a Keynote Speech by Van Tassel..."

"You mean Key*hole*," I two-cented.

Wills ignored me and continued: "Next, Steve Victor, director of *DISC*, will speak on military cover-ups of UFOs at the Nevada Test Training Range, the so-called 'Area 51.' Then, the former recording artist, Bobby Rose will discuss his book, *To Uranus and Back*. Then, there's a guy named Melmac, claiming to represent beings from the Xoth star system. And, then: *I.S.I.S. Speaks*— that's our man."

"Greetings all," a deep voice crackled over the loud speakers. He paused allowing the multitude to turn their attention to the platform attached to Giant Rock. Then he opened this year's festivities: "I am: Knut. I bring you love. Ashtar, Supreme Director in Charge of All the Spiritual Programs on Earth, welcomes you one and all, to have fun, to educate yourselves, and to remind you that a select few of you will be invited to tonight's channeling session. Enjoy the Brotherhood of Love, of Sweetness and Harmony..."

Van Tassel climbed down from the platform, shaking hands with the next speaker, Steve Victor, then wandered off with his followers. *Literally!*

While waiting for Osiris Prime, we did some "window shopping," browsing the various booths and tables offering an eclectic mixture of merchandize, including the expected Flying Saucer-related items: books, magazines, UFO-detectors, photos, post-cards, medallions, View-Master 3D slides; plus ever sector of the occult fringes: palmistry, astrology, numerology, crystal-power, Atlantis and Lemuria, and what-have-you. *One wrackadoole after another, huh, Honey Girl?*

"I read this one," I said, picking up a copy of Frank Scully's *Behind the Saucers.* "He wrote about a saucer that crashed in Aztec, New Mexico, and the Army's capture of the alien pilots. But you can take that with a grain of salt. Scully is a newspaper humorist, so you can't take everything he says, er, writes literally." Then I glanced around at the vendors and weirdoes. "Ah, you know what I mean."

"Quite. Takes one to know one."

Another table was stacked high with books from both camps of UFOlogy. The "serious/nuts-and-bolters": Jessup, Ruppelt, the Lorenzens, Aimé Michel, Keyhole, Wilkins, Gary Barker... And the Saucerians: Van Tassel, Angeluces, a slews by George Adamski and George Hunt Williamson, Bethurum, Fry, the Reeves, Dana Howard, and others telling of their contactee story, from *I Rode in a Flying Saucer* to *My Trip to Mars* to *My Saucerian Lover.*

Passing by a copy of *Wall of Light: Nikola Tesla and the Alien Space Ship* by Margret Storm [*any relation to Lt. Mark Storm, Honey Girl?*], I picked up a copy of *Why We Are Here by J.W., a Being from Jupiter, Through the Instrumentation of Gloria Lee.* Flipping it over, I read the back cover blurb. "Hmmm, thought so. Miss Lee had some bit parts in the early talkies. My mother and Gloria were bathing suit extras in *Run, Girl, Run* and my step-aunt, Mae, got them a part." I saw Wills eyes questioning me. "My mother was a dancer at the Casino on Catalina Island."

"A dancer?"

"A dancer!" I repeated, with more force than needed to make my point; and Wills smiled and dropped the subject.

At one table, I spotted a chart of various types of UFO: saucer-shaped, bell, dome, light source, the cigar-shaped "mother ship."

"Didn't think I'd find one of these gems here," Tom Wills said, "a 'Vero Edition' of Morris K. Jessup's *The Case for the U.F.O.*"

"What's so, er, unique about it?" I asked, turning away from the chart.

"An annotated copy of this book was sent anonymously to your U.S. Navy. Three different hands had annotated the margins, discussing the author's various theories on teleportation and experiments in invisibility, amongst other top-secret scientific projects. Your Navy only printed a handful of copies, by Vero Press, for in-house distribution. Yet, a few managed to reach private hands. This is one."

"Thus the hundred-smackaroos price tag?" I ten-thousand-cented.

The next booth had an equally eclectic assortment of periodicals and news-letters: *True, Saucer Scoop, Saucer Smear, Saucer News, Nexus,* and *NICAP*

Bulletin, A.R.E. Newsletter, Science of the Mind, Science and Health... Across the aisle was an array of pulps and digests: *Spaceworld, Fate, Mystic,* and *Fantastic Universe, Other Worlds,* dozens of different issues of *Amazing Stories,* plus a smattering of funny books: *Weird Science-Fantasy* ("EC's Special Report on Flying Saucers!"), *Batman* and *Detective* (filled with tales of space aliens and strange transformations), and other, including some *Supermans*—an *actual* alien from space. There was even a couple of *Crime Smashers* starring *Sally the Sleuth*; whom Lt. Storm said I based my life on, because she was blonde and had the tendency to lose her clothes. I spotted a copy of *Superman* #60, featuring Orson Welles on the cover, trying to warn of an invasion from Mars.

Though I was only eight at the time I remember the so-called "Panic Broadcast of Halloween, 1938," when *Mercury Theatre on the Air* did their version of *The War of the Worlds.* I'd heard that over 20% of the 6 million listeners had believed we were *actually* being invaded by Martians! That was because they came in late to the broadcast, after listening to Edgar Berger and Charlie McCarthy on the *Sanborn Hour.* Actually, no wonder, they'd believed in a Martian Invasion; after all, they'd just been listening to a *VENTRILOQUIST* on the radio! *I heard your lips move?*

About a decade later, another dummy also named McCarthy—Joseph, in this case—would be waving a list, claiming the government was infiltrated with Reds, of the communist type, this time. Then there was Kevin McCarthy, of the Red-baiting flick, *Invasion of the Body Snatchers.*

Everything considered, we'd been fighting the "Reds" since our nation was founded: Red Coats, Red Indians, Red Commies, so I guessed the Red Planet Mars might just be next.

Wills was flipping through a copy of *Amazing Stories,* the cover blurting something about *The Shaver Mystery.* I asked: "Is that about that barber who wears aluminum foil on his head to communicate with Space Men?"

"No," Wills said, "this Richard Shaver claimed a 'racial memory' of the lost land of Lemuria and it was published in *Amazing Stories,* in 1945, as *I Remember Lemuria.* The editor received a flood of letter from readers, and the editors formed the Shaver Mystery Club, and opened the pulp up for 'factual' material, plus out-right fiction based on this 'mystery'."

"That's fine and dandy, but what is the mystery?"

"Basically, two elder races of Atlans or Atlantis, and Titans or Lemuria, populated the Earth, each with fantastic technology and weapons, with long life spans, due to the positive *Integrative Energy* of the Sun; but the Sun changed, somehow, some 3,000 years ago, now radiating *Detrimental Energy,* which affected their mortality, forcing them underground, into an immense series of tunnels, to escape the Sun's now harmful rays."

"Hmmmm," I hummed, "it sounds like Reich and his *Orgone Energy* and *Deadly Orgone Energy?*"

"Now that you mention it, you're quite right, Miss West," Wills said before continuing his tale: "Somehow, that cavern life 'devolved' them into hideously deformed *Detrimental Robots* or *Deros*: sadistic cannibals who torment the surface people with their advance technology, and kidnap surface women for torture and debauchery. And, in this case, 'robot' refers to being controlled by the Sun's 'negative rays, not as automatons, mechanical men."

"Ooookay."

"The editor of *Amazing Stories* was Ray Palmer, a four-foot tall man, slightly hunchbacked due to a childhood malady, had overcome his disability by becoming an avid story-teller, editor and self-promoter. He helped found many magazine and digests, like *Fate, Mystic, Other Worlds, Search, Flying Saucer...* He also was the promoter of Kenneth Arnold, the man credited with the first Flying Saucer sighting in 1947. Palmer was the ultimate promoter, and some critics credit him with the creation of the *whole* Flying Saucer pandemic. His mantle was picked up by the publisher of *The Saucerian*, Gary Barker."

"Wow, what a perfect name," I said with a giggle. "Like a 'barker' at a circus! 'Come one, Come all! Come see the Saucers! Come see the Contactees! Come let us pick your pockets! Come see the Private Detectives dressed like a castaways from *The Forbidden Planet*! Come one, Come all!'" Then I waved my hand at the crowd: "And so they have!"

It was then I spotted someone I knew, a big, stocky man, yakking with a middle-aged, balding man, with a slightly bulbous nose. I yelled out to the stocky man: "Hey, Gene!"

The man turned around, shading his eyes with his hand; at first, not recognizing me; then, when he did, he scooped me up in a bear-like hug.

"Honey, I haven't seen you since..."

"That's okay, Gene," I said as he sat me down. I introduced him to Tom Wills—as a client.

"Why are you dressed up in that get-up? A case?"

"Uh-huh. But it's hush-hush, confidential, on the Q.T."

"My lips are sealed."

I'd known Gene Roddenberry since 1949, when he'd pulled me over for a traffic violation. He knew my father and had let me slide. Since then, he'd been a member of LAPD's "Public Information Division," and written for *Mister D.A, Highway Patrol*, as well as a raft of Westerns, after retiring from Law Enforcement.

"What you working on now, Gene?"

He told me. With all the interest is Space since *Sputnik*, he thought it was time for a new science fiction TV show; but not just another *Rocky Jones* or *Tom Corbett, Space Cadet*— which were just disguised: shoot-em-ups—Space Opera instead of Horse Opera. He wanted something more sophisticated, along the lines of the more sophisticated TV westerns. I Suggested *Have Space Ship, Will Travel*. He laughed and said he wanted something more like a "*Wagon*

Train to the Stars." Since me and Tom were outfitted in wardrobe from *The Forbidden Planet*, I suggested that to Gene. He *hmmmmed*. He was thinking of calling his idea something like *Space Voyager*; I countered that, since he wanted it to be a "*Wagon Trail* to the Stars," it should have "Star" or "Stars" in the title, like *Star Journey*. He *hmmmmed* again.

Then Gene introduced us to his friend; handshakes all around. "Honey, you used to like funny books; this man creates them. This is Julius Schwartz, editor at National comics. I met him when he was out here on the Coast, visiting the *Superman* TV set, and I was doing my LAPD Public Relations bit."

That was another *Superman*, George Reeves, who had died in his prime, whether by suicide—the official report—or murder—as his mother and others believe. Though, I was pretty sure that *my* Superman puppet hadn't committed suicide—not with his head cut off!

"You work at National," I said to Julie, as he asked to be addressed, "could you get Batman back to being a detective, and away from all those space aliens and weird transformations?"

Julie laughed, then said: "The science fiction elements—after *Sputnik*—where dictated by the Powers-That-Be; we lowly editors could only follow orders. As for Batman, he's outside my editorship, but if I am even in the position to control his fate, I will keep in mind what you said.

"Presently, we are revamping our old characters; updating them, giving them a greater scientific motifs—as we have, so far, done with *The Flash* and the *Green Lantern*. Next will be *The Atom*—a man who can shrink to six-inches. We still haven't decided on a secret identity. But..." he stopped in mid-sentence, looking at the copy of *Amazing Stories* in Wills' hand. "Of course, perfect, my old friend and client when I ran the Solar Sales literary agency: Ray Palmer! Perfect!"

We yakked some more, and said, "Well, Gene, I'll see ya on the flip-flop. 'Til then, don't get lost in space!"

"*Lost in space?*" Roddenberry pondered as we parted company.

"Greetings," a baritone voice boomed and crackled through the loud-speakers, grabbing the attention of the rambling rabble.

On the platform attached to Giant Rock, Osiris Prime allowed himself a slight bow, then a sweep of hand toward the white-toga'ed, blonde, blue-eyed woman—eighteen, if that—by his side.

"I am Osiris Prime , and this is my spiritual mate, Hathor. We, of *I.S.I.S.,* have come here, today, through the assistance of the Great Angelic Brotherhood, which was formed after a neutron bomb destroyed their planet, creating the asteroid belt between Mars and Jupiter. The Brotherhood managed to survive in pre-constructed spacecraft, taking residence inside the artificial moons of Mars, and here on Earth.

"These Space Brothers have often visited Earth, in your past. They are the source of your myths and legends of gods and goddesses. They have appeared in your Bible as angels arriving in 'chariots of fire'—as the Star of Bethlehem. Throughout history, these Sky People have accounted for stories of glowing globes, phantom lights, burning shields in our skies. They are the Sanskrit's *vimanas*, or 'celestial chariots.' These Sky People—our Space Brothers—are masters of matter, time, space and mind. To them yesterday is tomorrow, and tomorrow is yesterday."

Osiris Prime paused, taking a canteen from the blonde devotee, gauging his audience as he sipped, and seemed satisfied that he had captured a sizable portion of the audience. No doubt, mostly Saucerians—and two P.I.s. He continued:

"These Space Brothers are the Elder Races of Atlantis and Lemuria, and are still with us today. They have contacted me, electing me as their Agent on Earth. I did not seek out this honor and responsibility, nor did I shy from it. I just accept it as my *Calling*. And to further their message, we established *I.S.I.S.* to spread the *Word*." He raised his hands and "V-ed" his middle and forefingers, just like Churchill, and bowed his head slightly. "Vee for the Visitors from the Brotherhood...Vee for the Veil of Isis..."

With his hands back on the podium he continued:

"Through the ages, the Brotherhood has been watching us—the Earth— guarding its Wisdom of the Ages for over 25,000 years. Their knowledge and achievements have been recorded on crystalline discs, buried deep in the bowels of the Great Sphinx, on the Gizeh Plateau in Egypt, and via these discs, the Truth of the Great Angelic Brotherhood has been revealed to a selective few. In Egypt's Eighteenth Dynasty, at the feet of the Great Sphinx, these Revelations were imparted on future pharaoh Thutmoses III. Seventy-five years later, his descendent, Amenhotep IV—whom history knows as Akhenaten—became the *Keeper of Secrets,* launching Earth's first monotheistic religion, based on the Ancient Secrets of our Space Brothers, and he designed his own Pharaonic symbols: the *Rose* and the *Cross*. Yet, Akhenaton was called Heretic! His *City of Light* was razed, his beliefs—those of our Space Brothers—were forbidden, then forgotten, until those claiming *Enlightenment*. Yet, they did not possess the Wisdom of the Space Brothers, as I have been blessed with. With the guidance of the Space Brothers—through me—you, too, can gain *Enlightenment*..."

I had no idea what this guy was rambling on about, though a good chunk of the conventioneers seemed enraptured by this, admittedly, charismatic contactee con-man's velvety baritone voice... forceful, yet soothing. Then I saw Tom Wills shaking his head. "What's wrong?" I asked.

"This Osiris chap is spouting a tired mixture of various esoteric rot, heavily slanted towards Madame Blavatsky's *The Secret Doctrine*, her Theosophy movement and 'Root Races,' mixed with heavy doses of the Rosicrucian's *Great White Brotherhood.* And..."

"The Great White Brotherhood," I said, "That sounds like the Klan or the Nazis."

"Only to a degree—yet, it could be interpreted as such. Still, the *GWB* of the Rosicrucian's has more to do with 'White Magic'—the reflection in light, of Knowledge, of Enlightenment, opposing 'Black Magic', which is the collection of All Knowledge, yet *without* Enlightenment. It has nothing directly to do with racial ethnicity. As for the Egyptian connection, well, nothing is written in stone."

"Actually, quite a bit was written in stone by the Ancient Egyptians."

"*Touché*, Miss West." Wills said. "What else do you know about Egypt?"

"Other than the Pyramid I was always atop of, shaking my pom-poms for the Pep Squad, I know of this Akhenaten, his wife/queen Nefertiti, and his arch-foe Horemheb."

"Impressive."

"Not really. I saw *The Egyptian* with Michael Wilding as Akhenaten, and Gene Turney as Nefertiti, Victor Mature as hunky Horemheb, and the god-awful Bella Davi as Nefer-Nefer. He worshipped the Sun as the Sole God, or some such." I paused before adding: "You know, Wilding's ex-wife, Liz Taylor, would make a great Cleopatra."

"Perhaps."

"You still think that this *I.S.I.S.* is a Neo-Nazi cult? Because of their Aryan, er, Nordic looks?"

"Tangentially. The blonde, blue-eyed Nordic look is rather common in the contactees' descriptions of the Space Men and Women; typified by the 'Super-Star' of the Movement, George Adamski." From a huckster table he plucked up a copy of Adamski's *The Flying Saucers Have Landed*, flipping to the photo-section in the middle, and pointing out an artist rendering of Orthon of Venus: shoulder-length blond hair parted down the middle, handsome, tall, decked out in a belted orange jump-suit.

"He looks just like Osiris Prime," I opined.

"Quite. This Adamski, King of the Contactees..."

"Or Court Jester," I two-cented.

"Indeed. Nevertheless, he is the star of lectures, on the wireless and the telly, and is presently touring the world, supposedly having audiences with various royals and heads-of-states in New Zealand, Australia, and throughout Europe."

"Hey, I remember him. He had a radio show in Long Beach. Something like *Royal Order of Tibet*, channeling Tibetan Lamas from Mount Palomar, I believe. I guess Flying Saucers pay better."

We turned our attention back towards the Giant Rock platform as Osiris Prime began wrapping up his indoctrination lecture, er, speech:

"....as Our Space Brothers and Sisters *above*, so shall we *below* on Earth." He again held up his hands in Churchill "Vees" and finished: "Life, Health, prosperity. May you live a Thousand Thousand Years!"

"Oh, great," Wills sighed. "Now he is quoting Freemasonry!"

"Excuse me?" I said.

"Long story."

"Gotcha."

Osiris Prime and his golden-haired discipline, Hathor, descended from the platform, weaving their way through a small crush of admirers, some who appeared to me as, marveled zombies, as if hypnotized without a thought of their own, walking towards the *I.S.I.S.* booth. Behind the booth, the three olive-skinned men in black suits, fedoras and shades, stood erect against the Rolls-Royce Silver Cloud, their beefy arms folded across their massive chests.

A short line of conventioneers gathered before the booth, eager to hob-nob and chat with a *Friend of the Space Brothers*, to scoop up some *I.S.I.S.* literature, or to obtain and cherish a personally autographed copy of *Osiris Rising* (only $6.00, tax included).

"Tom," I whispered, nudging him in the side, "let's get in line and find out his *Plan Nine from Outer Space*."

Osiris Prime was cordial, gracing each person with witty small talk, passing out newsletters and membership forms, cautioning the faithful and occult tourist, alike: "The Space Brothers and Sisters determines the selection of new members, and only a select few are chosen during any recruitment period."

This announcement sent mumblings of discontent amongst the wishful, but Osiris silenced them with a raised hand. "Certain *Enlightenment* must color your aura, and that can only come with the Teachings of I.S.I.S., which you can purchase here to study and await the next recruitment period. All who wish... who *desire*... shall be shown the Light...in time. We are akin to Step-Children of Plato, offering a new Way of Life: Health, Wisdom, Peace, and complete *Enlightenment*..."

Finally we made it to the head of the table, and got a better look at Osiris Prime. Up close, his skin seemed rather pasty; though even with that, and the lifts, he was all man!

"Life, Health, Prosperity," Osiris addressed me. "And what is your name, Child?"

"Salome... wants to see me dance?" My quip flew over his head, so I "Veed" my fingers, moistened my lips, smiled innocently and said: "Actually, it's Hon..., er, Alteria."

"No, no, my Dear," he said, almost tsk-tsking me. "You must use your *birth* name, the one bestowed upon you by our Celestial Brothers, centuries in the past. Your Osiris-Isis name from the *Zee-Tepi*—The First Time—when the Space Gods came to Earth and established the Atlantean, Lemurian and Egyptian Kingdoms, all Followers of the Star-Child, Horus." Then Osiris face went blank, his eyes clouding, as if in a trance. After a few beats, he mumbled: "Yes... yes.... of course..." Then he snapped out of his trance and checked out my body before beaming: "The Celestial Brotherhood have answered my summons. They have informed by that you birth name is: *Nekhakha-t*."

160

I turned slightly around, but enough to catch a combo of amusement and confusion on Tom Wills' face. I mouthed: "What?" And answered, also sotto, "Later."

My attention was yanked back to Osiris as he said: "There is an Initiation Ritual at the Temple, tonight. The Space Brothers and I believe you will want to attend." He stretched his hand over his shoulder and, as if by magic, a sheet of paper appeared in his hand, which he proffered to me. "Here are the directions. Come and see what we have to offer. And what *you* might have to offer *us*. Come and bathe in the *Aura of Cosmic Love...*"

"Oh, that sounds so cool," I said, cooing like a teenager telling her girl-friend about some hep-cat she'd just met. Waving a hand at Wills, I asked: "Can my older brother, er, Morbius, join us?"

Osiris Prime looked Tom Wills up-and-down, who gave the Saucerian guru "reverse V-sign"—which I believe is Brit for "Fuc...er, shove it"—but Osiris didn't react. I reckoned that Wills looked Aryan enough, if not a tad too old. With a knowing grin, Osiris returned to his trance state, mumbling: "I am receiving a clairaudient message from *their* Mother Ship, orbiting the moon... yes... yes! Wise choice." And just as quickly Osiris was back to his conscious state, proclaiming to Wills: "You have been christened: *Seth*."

Me and Tom Wills left the *I.S.I.S.* with a stack of literature and auto-graphed copies of *Osiris Rising* (*gratis*, I might add); sweating the rest of the day in the hot, dry California sun, yakking it up with various vendors and at-tendees.

I found one of those new, very shapely *Barbie* dolls, decked out in a gold-en outfit, similar to my own; and one dressed in a zebra one-piece swimsuit: talk about a *Zee*-bra! I turned to show it to Wills, but noticed his face etched with concern and worry. "Okay, Tom, out with it. Why the bummer?"

"I believe Osiris Prime is onto us, or, at the outside, very suspicious. Do you know the myth of Osiris and Isis?"

"Ah, sorta," I lied. *As far as you know, Honey Girl, they never made a movie of them.*

"Osiris and Isis, brother and sister, were the wise rulers of pre-Dynastic Egypt. Their brother, Seth, became jealous of them, of the love the people, their subjects, had for the Royal Couple. Seth cut Osiris into little pieces, scattering the parts about the land. Isis found the pieces, minus, er, Osiris' phallus."

"Ouch!" I two-cented.

"Quite, Miss West," he said, with a smile. "Even with this, er, handicap, Isis mated with the re-animated Osiris..."

"Necrophilia, too. Those Egyptians were way-out. You dig?"

"Dug? Nevertheless, this union produced Horus. Horus grew into a man, and waged war against Seth, for rule of Egypt and to avenge his father's death."

"Oh, I get it. He's Osiris and he dubbed you Seth—because he sees you as his mortal enemy? His *Joker* or *Lex Luthor*?"

"Yes," Wills said with a sigh.

Near dusk, the sun had beaten the landscape into multitudes of shades, of crimsons, blues and gold. The road was saddled by patches of yucca trees, cacti, rolling sage brush, and crickets' legs scratching their repetitious song. And soon, the silvery moon filled the sky, while surrounded by countless sparkling points of lights.

As we headed East, across the Mojave Desert, into Death Valley, we discussed the case—what Osiris Prime was rambling on about: space aliens visiting Earth in our remote past. And Wills rattled off something about the Extraterrestrialism theory, about Morris K. Jessup's *The UFOs and Bible,* and Harry Downing's *The Bible and Flying Saucers.*

I suggested, considering the newly formed NASA, that perhaps the Spacemen from the Past might be dubbed Ancient Astronauts; and if from the Angry Red Planet Mars, Ancient Cosmonauts. He thought that was spot-on. And he thought I might like to join the *Fellow Lady Astronaut Trainees*. But, I'd never join a group called *FLATS*; just like I never went into acting. Who wants a *SAG* card?

Then he rambled on about psychologist Carl Jung's book on flying saucers, and how they were archetypes for something or some sort. After that, he was off on Freud's Superego, Ego & Id, and all I knew about it was the Monster of the Id from *The Forbidden Planet*; and that sometimes a cigar-shaped mother-ship is just a cigar-shaped mother-ship. Next, he yakked up some of contactee stories, such as the Brazilian farmer, Antonia Villas Boas, who was plowing his field when some humanoid aliens "induced" him into mating with a full-breasted, naked woman, without any kissing or foreplay.

"Wham-bam-thank-you, Space-Mam," I laughed.

"And for the most part, unlike in the motion pictures, they have been no reports of *forceful* abductions or experimenting on humans."

"Mars *doesn't* need women?" I quipped.

"Are you ever serious, Miss West?"

"Not if I can help it. In my business—*our* business—it gets way too serious, way too often!"

"Quite so."

It was then that we came upon a huge black rock reflecting the full-moon's light, almost glowing. No Giant Rock, but still impressive. I was just about to remark that this must be the place, when the Bel-Air rounded the boulder and we spotted the *I.S.I.S.* edifice: plane sandstone block walls, in the ancient Egyptian style of alternating rows of stretchers and header bricks, some 500 feet on a side, and 15-foot high, all done in white-wash glittering in the moonlight. At the rear of the building was a soaring dome, not unlike the observatory at Griffith Park, near where Dodger Stadium was being constructed.

162

Yet, I was somewhat disappointed: there were no pylons or decorative pictographs or sphinx-lined promenade like in *The Ten Commandments*. There was only a gravel road leading to the entrance, with a winged solar disk etched in the stone above the door.

As Tom Wills parked, I didn't see Osiris Prime's 1955 Silver Cloud, only a VW bus, an old Chevy pick-up, a Nash Rambler and a Studebaker, with a teardrop trailer attached. All I could think: *Honey Girl, hope this is the way to Eden, and not some bad day... er, night at Black Rock!*

"*Wide is the gate and broad is the road that leads to destruction*," Wills quoted from Matthew.

I gulped, and suddenly Rod Serling's voice filled my head: "*Picture this: two hard- working, honest detectives, just trying to make a living, having had their minds filled with talk of spacemen from a group of UFOnuts, end up here, in the middle of the desert. The lights are out as they approach the Inner Sanctum of Osiris Prime. It's after hours as they take one step beyond, into...*The Twilight Zone.

The only entrance to the building appeared to be a single opened doorway. We stepped into a small stone antechamber. A voice echoed: "State your name and purpose."

"Friendly cult, huh?" I whispered to Wills. Then aloud: "Nekhakha-t and Seth. We were invited by Osiris Prime."

After a few moments a door *irised* open, and in stepped the main dude, himself, Osiris Prime. Alone, for once. He smiled: flashing pearly white, gleaming teeth. "I am pleased that you have come, my children. Now follow me and witness wonders which have not been seen on Earth since it was new." He swept his hand towards a door, and with a slight bow, added: "Yes, allow my humble self to demonstrate the wondrous accomplishments of *I.S.I.S.*"

Following Osiris, we stepped through iris-door and we did, indeed, see wondrous sights! Stretching the length and width of the temple was a virtual Victory Garden, lush and flourishing: vegetables, fruit trees, corn, squash, beans, apples, oranges, sunflowers, roses, and scores of others. All here in the middle of the Mojave Desert in near Summer!

Overhead were massive interlocking panels of glass, providing a magnificent view of the starry Milky Way in the clear desert sky, only partly dimmed by ceiling halogen lamps. Some twenty blonde and blue-eyed cult members, both male and female, dressed in white tunics and sandals, were tending the garden, raking, hoeing, watering.

"This is amazing!" I honestly uttered; yet I couldn't help not think: *Look at them... children of the night. What music they make...*

"Mere child's play for Our Space Brothers," Osiris said with another sweep of his hand, and more pride than warranted by *others*' achievements. "What the desert took millions of years to claim, I... ahem... the Space Brothers reclaimed within a week."

163

"You went from desert to Eden," I asked, "or, at least, just this side of Paradise, in the middle of one on the driest places on Earth—in a week?"

"Yes, once the matrixes were laid down." He pointed to the glass ceiling. "Actually, that is not standard glass, but helio-generating panels, which collect, store and distribute the energy of Ra, the Sun."

"Interesting," Wills said, "but we would like to know about the Space Brothers."

"Later," Osiris said, with yet another wave of his hand. "You have arrived in time for the *Lifting of the Veil of Isis* ceremony."

"The what?" I questioned. Though that was *exactly* the reason we were here: to lift the veil which shrouded this *I.S.I.S.* cult and expose its true nature.

"You shall see," Osiris Prime answered. "Follow me."

We followed the Leader along the garden for a bit before turning into a narrow corridor of cinder-block walls, into a large room, dominated in the center by a 10-foot by 3-foot, highly polished granite altar, raised some three-feet off the concrete floor. *At least, it ain't a sarcophagus; huh, Honey Girl, you left your Tanis Leaves at home!*

Osiris vanished and we were led further into the chamber by a male and female acolytes, to a stone bench before the altar, ablaze with scented candles and smothering pots of smelly incense. *Honey Girl, someone finally got you to the altar; and you thought it'd be in the City of Lost Wages, and with a different Agent of the Law!*

Sitting down, I recognized another three man and three women—all blonde and blue-eyed—from the Giant Rock queue lined up to greet Osiris Prime after his diatribe, er, speech. *Curiouser and curiouser.* We all nodded "hello" to each other. Then: *show time, Honey Girl!*

A male and female cultists, who I believe I'd seen in the garden, silently entered the room, joining the two who had ushered us in. The Saucerians all faced the wall opposite us, on the other side of the altar: the *Seekers of Truth.*

Suddenly, but slowly, the wall slid apart, revealing a mural in bright primary colors: a six-foot high rendering by a Master's hand of *Isis Lactans*—Mother Isis breast-feeding her son, Horus, similar to *Marie Lactans:* Mary nursing baby Jesus. I didn't know this at the time; Tom Wills told me later. The seated Isis was decked out in a similar gown as the cultists, her long flowing hair was blond, her eyes bright, radiant blue.

In unison the cultists placed their hands back-to-back, then spread them out until they were perpendicular to their sides, forming the "T" of the Cross with their bodies, or an Egyptian *ankh,* if you considered their heads as loops; all the while intoning, rather monotonically, almost *metallic*: "You are all that hath been, and is, and always shall be, and no mortal hath raised your *Veil*..." Then they brought their hands together, completing the incantation: "...until now."

On cue, Osiris Prime entered the fray, Hathor by his side, still dressed in a white tunic, now trimmed in gold. Facing the mural, he peaked his index fingers and incanted: "Isis... Victorix... Resurrector of the Dead... Regina... Queen of the Universe... the Embodiment of Cosmic Order... *Una quae Omnis... The One Who is All...* Through You and Your Space Brothers and Sisters... The Mysteries of Nature are revealed to us..."

And with that, Osiris Prime and his apostles again "T'ed" their arms and bodies, intoning: *ohhhhhmmm... atooooon* before bringing their hands down and back together, effectively, I guess, *Closing the Veil of Isis*, whatever that meant. Then Osiris turned to his collective audience:

"We have communicated with my Space Sister-Wife, Isis, presently in orbit above the Earth, in her Command Ship, 125,000 miles out. She has blessed you, one and all, with the Enlightenment on how to stop the plagues inflicting Mankind. From the Chaos which now strangles our Planet... The Evil Entities which hampers Humans, who believe themselves gods... Yet, they have their limitations... They do not understand... the ineffable God of Light... which governs the Our Space Brothers and Sisters... as well as ourselves."

Again Osiris Prime spread his arms, "V-ed" his fingers: "Welcome, one and all. Life, Health, Prosperity, for a Thousand Thousand Years. Let my Space Brothers and Sisters assist you in your indoc... er, in your preparation for the *Hierogramous...* to make you *One with Isis...* to set you free..."

With that, Osiris Prime bowed, then left. We four women "applicants" followed a cultist woman called Nun, while Wills and the other three men fell in step behind a man called Geb. We girls were ushered into a room dominated by a large sunk-in bath/pool, littered with lotus blossoms floating lazily on the surface. The air was scented with varied fragrances: mint, spearmint, and more than a strong dose of incenses. Apostle Nun spoke for the first time since escorting us here, and once again I noticed that, like the other female cultists, she had a rather deep voice with a haltering speech pattern, as if she was translating from her native tongue into English.

"Please, Ladies, disrobe. Relax in the bath. Afterwards, I shall anoint your bodies with an exotic assortment of herbal unguents and soothing oils. To prepare you for Being at One with the Space Brotherhood of Love."

Honey Girl, you could use more answers, less love. As I let the Nun help me out of my gown, I quipped: "Lifting the Veil of Isis, huh?"

She didn't bat an eye at my quip. *Tough crowd, Honey Girl.* As she slipped my gown off, she intoned, "Ladies, reveal yourself..."

Ladies, Honey Girls? Ladies? They have never been called that before; sure, my Bosom Buddies, who have gotten me into *and* out of trouble, on countless occasions. But, Ladies? Then I realized Nun was addressing our entire groups of "Ladies," asking us to disrobe.

So we did.

Us four "Initiates" slipped nakedly into the soothing pool, *aaaahhhing* relief in the coolness and cleansing after a long day in the hot and dusty environment of Giant Rock. As a private detective, I noted the other three women were, indeed, true blondes; in fact, blonder than me!

Glancing from the pool, I studied the cultist, Nun, who almost mechanically went about her business, preparing the oils and lotions, adjusting the massage table, arranging towels. I turned back to the other three women, yakking in between splashing one another, excited at becoming One with the Space Brothers and Sisters. As for myself, I definitely *wasn't* on the same wavelength; and, perhaps, not even the same planet!

Now was the time to make my move. I stepped from the pool and snagged a Turkish towel, wrapping it around my torso, all without the other splashing blondes noticing that I was inching towards the door, planning to snoop about the Osiris Complex.

Just at that moment, Nun turned, blankly intoning: "Ladies, please reveal yourselves…"

"Huh?" I mumbled to myself as Nun approached me, grabbing my arm. *"Ouch!"* It felt like a vice-grip. I shoved her backwards; she tumbled into her the massage table, which crashed into a shelve of oils and ointments, splattering their odorous on her. She smelled like a French whorehouse; or, what I imagined one would smell like. Then, almost faster than my baby-blues could follow, Nun bolted to her feet, and very un-Space Brotherly, er, Sisterly, hissed: "You *biiiiiitch!*"

So I bitch-slapped her, and then, shaking my stinging hand, yelled: "Ouuuch!" *Honey Girl, what is this bitch made of?*

For the first time, the cultist smiled and launched herself into me, ripping my towel away, crashing, and slamming us onto the cold, wet stone floor.

So much for the peaceful Space Girl ruse, huh, Honey Girl? I said to myself as we wrestled on the stone floor, rolling around like a pair of dice on a Vegas craps table. Nun was tearing at my hair, but thanks to her oil-splattered body, I managed to gain some leverage and bring my bare feet in contact with her stomach; then, I shoved hard.

The cultist was propelled through the air, heavily plopping into the pool with a mushroom cloud of water. Fortunately, it had emptied by this time. The three wannabe disciples had vamoosed, scrambling out of the room, *sans* clothing! Crouching by the pool, I had my left arm across my chest, my right arm upright, perpendicular to my body, in a classic Karate pose, preparing for the next round. But it never came. Nun was floating face-down in the pool, arms at half-mast, the water bubbling around, misty steam rising, hissing.

Cautiously, I leaned forward, flipping her over, and then gasped! Nun's neck was broken, snapped, the flesh ripped away, exposing crackling, smoldering wires, switches, and stuff I couldn't identify, dangling in some kind of gooey liquid seeping from the "wound," beading in the water, her electronic voice intoning: *"Pleeeeeese, Laaaaadies… reveal… yourseeeeeeelf…"*

"A damn robot!" I exclaimed, having an *Eureka*! moment at seeing the floating ex-cultist. "And not even Robbie, at that!"

"Wrestling in oils?" a voice from the door came. "What next? Mud, Honey? That is, if you are not mysophobic."

I whirled, pivoting on my bare heels, ready in a judo stance, only to relax when I saw it was Tom Wills, dressed in his jumpsuit, tugging on his left boot. I then realized I was as naked as a jaybird and quipped: "Remember what happened the last time a Tom peeked at a Go-Go-Diva?"

"I will only look until I need glasses," he smirked.

"Now, you're getting a sense of *humour*?" I asked, looking at him, then at the smothering Nun in the pool, then back to Wills. "She... ah, is, it... was a robot!"

"Technically, an android," Wills stated matter-of-factly. "Geb was also an android, Miss West. He accidently cut his arm, exposing his circuitry. I knew the ruse was up, so I bashed him—it?—over the head with a metal stool. He went down, and I got the other threes gents out. Then I came looking for you."

"We have to get outta here," I said. I found my gown and shimmered into it; I hated to lose my deposit from the MGM Props Department. "We don't know what this loony-tunes Osiris has planned for us. Probably no merry melodies! And I don't want to stand around and find out!"

We looked up and down the corridor before creeping out the door, wondering what would befall us next. Surely, soon, Osiris will be alerted to the naked men and women invitees fleeing the compound, and his three goons would come hunting us. We had to make a quick egress... *But, where*? Which way?

Creeping, inching down the corridor, I longed for my pearl-handled .22, but, alas, I'd left in behind, in my purse, in the Chevy. The damn thing is never around when you need it! We turned a corridor and heard music coming from beyond an ajar door. Nearing it, we heard singing, and I took a peek inside.

The décor was right out of the Victorian whorehouse chic: crimson overstuffed velvet futon, red velvet wallpaper, vermillion drapes with gold trim and tassels, Persian rugs, brass lamps with green glass shades. Dominating the room was an antique harpsichord. At the keyboard was cultist Hathor, her soprano voice singing something in Italian. Osiris Prime stood beside the harpsichord, his tenor voice delightfully alluring.

Then something that had been nagging at my brain for some time surfaced: Hathor, who seemed almost attached to Osiris' hip, was somehow different from the other cultists. Sure, she was blonde and blue-eyed like the others, but plumper and a tad-shorter than the other girls I'd seen. *Hmmmmm...*

My thoughts were side-tracked by Wills whispering: "Osiris is singing *Celeste Aida* and Hathor is answering: 'O thou whom Osiris are...'"

"Later," I whispered back, cutting him off and sneaking pass the half-opened door, Wills hot on my bare heels. We heard heavy footsteps coming up the hallway. No doubt Osiris' three hulky men in the black suits. So, we ducked into the first opened door, silently shutting it behind us. Wills flipped the light switch and we were amazed!

It was a large library, with ceiling-high bookshelves blanketing the walls, crammed with volumes of every size, color and binding. Edison, Darwin, Mendel, Tesla... Genetics, physics, biology, astronomy, philosophy, theology... Scientific journals: *Scientific American, Nature, Science, Applied Physics, Electrical Engineer,* scores of others... Sprinkled about other shelves were tattered old science fiction pulps: *Amazing Stories, Astonishing, Astounding, Galaxy, Fantastic, Marvel Science Stories,* and a dozen others. On a lower shelf were a slew of Tom Swift novels... On a fourth wall was a series of framed photographs and old newspaper broadsides, many with artistic renderings of Airships; one from a 1896 *San Francisco Chronicles* depicted a large, 30-foot elongated, cigar-shaped flying craft, a pair of side-wheels like a Mississippi riverboat, and an under-slung gondola, along with a glowing, flashing bright searchlight lighting up the countryside.

The rest of the room was standard library, complete with a sliding ladder to reach the higher shelves, desk, reading lamp, chairs. *But, Honey Girl, something is really weird here... Everything seemed to have been scaled down... as if for a child. Are there children amongst these wrackadoodles?*

"I have a hunch," Tom finally said.

"So did *Quasimodo*. Does he ring a bell?"

"*The Tempest,*" he said, derailing my train of thought.

"Excuse me," I said, still trying to readjust my outfit. The only Tempest I knew was Tempest "in a D-Cup" Storm" and, according to Lt. Mark Storm, no relation. And I'm not related to Evelyn "Treasure Chest" West. Right...

"No, the Shakespearean play... This whole Osirian compound reminds me of that play." He looked at me, saw the confusion on my face, and smiled. "Don't tell me: your school did not have a copy of the *Classic Illustrated* version?"

"Not while I was in school," I said.

"The short version is this: the rightful Duke of Milan, Prospero, is banished to a desolate island by his ambitious brother, Antonio, along with his infant daughter, Miranda, who had never seen a *normal* man other than her father. Prospero rules this island, surrounded by his immense collection of books. His servants include Caliban, the misshapen progeny of a witch, and Ariel, a magical spirit whom Prospero sends as a ghost to haunt intruders to his island! Yet, the king of Naples' son, Ferdinand, washes ashore as a result of one of Prospero's conjured storms, and the prince falls in love with the now grown Miranda..."

"I get it," I said, "Osiris Prime is Prospero, and these are his books. Hathor is Miranda. This isolated spot in the desert is his island. His burly guards... hey, wait a minute... This all sounds like *Forbidden Planet*, and this Ariel spirit is the Monster from the Id, frightening people from his island—planet."

"Quite so," Wills confirmed.

"We are such stuff dreams are made on, and our little life is rounded with sleep," a baritone voice said from the door. "To quote Prospero."

We quickly turned, and found Osiris Prime and his three bruisers standing in the library's doorway, aiming 9mm Lugers at us.

"Well, well, if it isn't O.P. and his Three Stooges," I quipped. "Or space-men—what, no ray guns?"

Flanked by his three goons, Osiris oozed into the room. "I observed you were admiring my *Tom Swift* collection. Truth be known, I penned them under the house-name of Victor Appleton. Alas, most believe they were penned by Howard R. Garis. Ha! He never got past his *Uncle Wiggy* fantasies. Frankly, he did not have the scientific acumen that I possess. In fact, no one has! No one ever has! And all of Tom Swift's marvelous inventions, I once toyed with, and tossed away as mere toys."

"Hold the phone!" I exclaimed. "Those were written over forty years ago."

"Correct," Osiris said, then pointing at the framed broadsheet of the Airship. "I constructed that. Flew it. Though they never managed an accurate depiction of my *Antoinette*. A shame. "We enjoyed a wonderful year, 1896, soaring above the Pacific Ocean... San Francisco to San Jose, across to Oakland, then down to Los Angeles," he said with a laugh. "We scared the bejeesus out of the seals bathing in the Bay. Then we sailed on, buzzing and beaming our search-light throughout Nevada, Kansas, Arkansas, Texas... then...," he said, his face going blank for a second, mumbling more to himself than to us, "...outside Fort Worth, the damn thing crashed, leaving me unconscious in the wreck, and the ignorance idiots of the town thought I was some kind of space alien, because of my size. They thought I was dead and buried me. Fortunately..."

"Wait!" I interrupted, snapping Osiris off in mid-sentence. "Now, you're dating yourself back sixty years. Yet, you don't appears a day over thirty... thirty-five!"

"Better living through chemistry," Osiris offered.

"Huh?"

"Never mind, Miss West," Osiris said. "You are as stupid as your ancestor, though like him, you have managed to destroy a couple of my toys."

"Your toys? My ancestor? How do you know who I really am? Hell, forget that, who *are* you?"

"I am simply Osiris Prime. My Space Brothers have enlightened me as to your true identities and that of your partner: Thomas Wills, lackey of the self-dubbed *American Sherlock Holmes*, Harry Dickson."

"And you are masquerading as a risen god," Wills snapped back; no doubt not accustomed to be called a 'lackey.'

"Not Jesus the Christ, for sure. I have never claimed to be anything other than a super-genius."

"Yeah, sure," I snapped, "you, Lex Luthor and Wiley E. Coyote!"

"My dear Miss West, you are as irrelevant as your ancestor."

"Again, with my ancestor. Who are you talking about?"

"Do you know this man?" Will asked me.

"I have no idea who he is—other than someone who thinks he's very important."

"Let us all be nice," Osiris Prime said with a sweep of his hand down the corridor, "and proceed this way."

Tom Wills and I did as instructed, with the three goons guns trained on our backs, and the Big Bopper bringing up the rear. The goons gave me the heebie-jeebies and I did something about it. Stumbling forward, I hit the wall, pushed off it and crashed myself backwards into them, propelling them into Osiris Prime, smashing him hard into the stone.

I was in the process of yelling for Tom to run, when I heard Osiris calmly said: "Not so fast, Miss West."

It was then that I saw two huge machine-guns descend from the ceiling, swirling towards me and Tom, rotating their barrels, ready for action.

My attack had barely bulged the goons, but Osiris Prime had been smashed into the wall and had crumbled into a heap on the floor, appearing broken in half, split open, revealing mechanical pumps, gauges, levers, all controlled, I think, by activators, which turned energy in to robotic motion. *Honey Girl, another damned robot. But wait...*

From the wreckage, oozing vicious slime, a man arose, not unlike the popping of the Seed Pods from *The Invasion of the Body Snatchers*. He cleaned himself off with a rag provided to him by Moe (or was it Larry?). He was no taller than four-foot or so, and his *passé* Victorian dark suit, no doubt once hailed from one of Paris' finest tailors.

"We're not in Kansas anymore, Tom-Tom," I informed my partner.

"More of your droll wit, Miss West," Osiris said, "and not at all humorous. I was up for the cushy role of the Wicked Witch of the East's son, Bulbo, but they scraped the scene. And I ended up just another among the twenty-nine nameless background Munchkins, and because of my baritone voice, I was axed from the Lollipop Guild and the Lullaby League." Then he smiled. "The only plus was looking up Judy Garland's skirt."

"Who is this madman?" Tom Wills asked again.

"It's hard to believe," I said, this time having the answer to his question, "but he'd be, what, 120 years-old."

"One-hundred-and-twenty-five, to be exact," the former Osiris Prime corrected, with a maddening smile, having finished toweling himself off.

"Who is he?" Wills demanded again.

"A mini-menace, who believes the sun comes up to just to hear him crow," I said to Wills. Then to Osiris, I stated: "Doctor Miguelito Quixote Loveless, I presume? Everyone thought you were dead, as did your son, Michelito."

"The rumors of my death have been greatly exaggerated," Loveless said, peeling off the rest of his electro-plastic mask. "And I have *no* son. That fool was an impostor, trading on my genius. And they thought me mad!"

"You mean you're not?"

"Miss West!"

"I've read of your exploits in Uncle Artemus' journals. I don't think I believe half of what he wrote. It all seemed, oh, so impossible. The only thing I believe is that you had—have?—a giant-size anger at the world which you believed had mistreated you, and at James West for being James West!"

"But, Miss West, you can believe *everything* Gordon wrote," Loveless said, grinning like the Cheshire Cat. "To quote Napoleon: 'The word impossible is not in my dictionary'."

Honey Girl, this guy could use some Preparation-H *to reduce the swell of his inflated ego!* But I said: "Considering your size, you could be aptly called the 'Napoleon of Crime'."

"Actually," Wills began in his lecture mode, "Napoleon was of average height for Frenchmen of his era. You see, the mistake of his stature was due…" I gave him a steamy look and he finished: "Sorry, Miss West. Yet, if you want an analogy of historic men under four-foot, well, there's Attila the Hun, Pliny the Short, Aesop…"

"Aesop, of course!" I exclaimed, cutting Wills off, turning to Loveless. "I'm sure you have a fable to tell us, some grandiose plan. It can't be the Fourth Reich; you're not quite the Aryan type. Then again, I could be wrong; Hitler wasn't exactly blond and blue-eyed, either. So, Aesop what is your moral? 'Slow and Steady wins the game,' like with the Tortoise and the Hare? You've already did the 'wolf in sheep's clothing.' Thus, I guess, we are left with the 'sour grapes' of the wolf."

"Ignoring your attempts at levity with this Aesop nonsense," Loveless said, "your observations are basically correct. The Nazis did not tolerate *anyone* who were not of their Aryan ideal, even though, as you pointed out Miss West, their leadership was rarely of the blond hair, blue-eyed stock of the *ubermensch*. And, yet, this fact did not deter them from eliminating many who looked just like them, but were classified as *undersarrge—the different ones*—the sub-humans: Jews, gypsies, homosexuals, Jehovah's Witnesses… midgets and dwarfs."

"Then, why," I asked with a sweep of my hand, indicating the *I.S.I.S.* complex, "all this? Some new Machiavellian scheme?"

"It is a front, an illusion. To entice gullible Aryan types," he laughed with a slight giggle. "And the most gullible of all are those who believe in Flying Saucers from Space and their Aryan Brotherhood, to the point of turning it into a quasi-religion. All because, in the end, it's easier to join a cult than face reality. It was no different with the Nazis… Using ancient mythology and grafting it onto various occult beliefs: Theosophy, *The Elders of Zion*, Thor, Odin and the other Norse gods... almost anything which was not nailed down... all to justify their ideal..."

"OK, OK," I interrupted the lunatic. "I get it, I get it! The difference between a $1,000-an-hour call girl and a $20 hooker is $980. A difference that makes no difference is no difference. So, get on with it, Loveless, and tell us why... What this is all about, what you want with us..."

"Oh, pardon my mismanners," Loveless said with a mocking bow, "the two of you are here to undergo readjustment."

"Readjustment?" I echoed. "I don't think I like the sound of that!"

"I know I do not!" Wills concurred. "What do you mean?"

"You will soon find out, Mr. Wills," Loveless promised, now taking the lead down a long corridor, me and Wills in the middle, and the three armed goons bringing up the rear. I kept waiting for them to *o-ee-ooing* like the Evil Witch's Winkie Guards, but my thoughts were interrupted by evil genius' next revelation:

"The two of you managed to 'kill' two of my Gamma Androids. Fortunately, I have my three more durable Betas, to protect me, which are an improvement over my old Alpha, steam-powered mechanical man. Hence the Betas are for my security and protection, which I refer to as *Mechanical Integrated Bions*, which are constructed of sturdier material than the more humanoid Gammas; though less human in appearance and quite mute."

"And they obviously have never heard of Asimov's *Three Laws of Robotics*," I quipped.

"Why, Miss West, do you suffer from *automatonophobia*?"

"Huh?"

"Fear of robots," Will translated, stopping, only to be poked in the back to move-along by one of the robo-goon's .9mm.

"You listen to too much Connie Francis, Loveless," I said to his back as he waddled down the corridor. "You know: *a robot to hold me... impossible to speak...*"

"More irreverence, my dear Miss West!"

"Whatever your villainous scheme is," I interrupted, "what makes you believe you can possibly succeed? Even with your psycho-cybernetic henchmen? You never could get the best of James West, and I doubt..."

"Need I remind you, Miss West," Loveless cut me off, this time, "that I am still among the living. I placed flowers and candy on James West's grave." Then after a sigh, added: "As will I on yours, when the time comes. That is a promise."

"Thanks, but I plan to be cremated," I quipped as we were led into the observatory, though a vastly different one than the one in Griffith Park. Similar to other garden-variety observatories, the space was large, circular, with a slit in the revolving dome, usually with a reflector telescope poking through. Yet, here, poking through the slit was no ordinary telescope; in fact, not a real telescope *per se,* but a thirty-foot long thing with a centrally mounted, three-inch diameter copper tube, with a series of thinner, shorter spider-webbing tubing and wiring crisscrossing the longer central tube, wiring snaking off to a bank of blinking electronic panels, and a coated cable grounded in a pool of still water.

"A Cloud-Buster," Tom Wills stated matter-of-factly.

"Indeed," Loveless said, "perhaps you are not a *complete* idiot after all, Mr. Wills." Before the Englishman could reply, the evil genius raised his hand, shushing him. "Yes, a Cloud-Buster, but with many modifications Wilhelm Reich never had the time nor the opportunity to complete. Still, I doubt, even his genius could have comprehended the true nature of his own discoveries!"

"No, I guess not," I said with a sneer, "that would take a man of singular genius."

"Like your ancestor, Miss West, I believe you are mocking me. Nevertheless, you are correct. The duality of Reich's beneficial *orgone energy* and its opposite, *deadly orgone energy* or *DOE*, which creates deserts, like the Mojave, is nothing new. Opposing forces or energies were the basis of Newton's Second Law of Thermodynamics: 'that for each force there is an equal and opposite force.' This principle also applies to Reich's *Orgone Energy* and its counterforce, *DOE*. The same with Richard Shaver's *Integrative Rays* or 'positive energy of the sun,' and his *Detrimental Rays* or 'negative solar energy.'"

Loveless picked up a bluish crystalline stone that looked like a blue diamond from the table and palmed it. "And this is *vrilium*, a positive form of its negative counterpart: radium."

"Its chemical symbol is Ra," Wills stated. "The ancient Egyptian Sun God; hence, a perfect fit for your faux-Egyptian cult."

"Indeed, my dear Mr. Wills," Loveless said with a slight bow. "Yet, it was but a coincidence. But back to *vrilium*... In its varied isotopic states, it has been known in the past by many names: *Orichalcrum* by the Atlanteans, *Element 115* more recently... A more recent isotope of *vrilium* was created by hydrogen fusion during the Hydrogen Bomb blast on the Bikini Atoll, and dubbed *bikinium*. I do not expect you to know anything about this event, Miss West."

"You'd lose that bet," I said, with my inner voice nagging: *Honey Girl, forget the fall-out, most men wants to see you in no bikini at all!* To Loveless: "The Bikini Atoll, part of the Marshall Islands in the Pacific, North of the Equator, is where, in March 1946, under the name of *Operation Crossroads*, the U.S. exploded the world's first hydrogen bombs, *Able* and *Baker*, both a thousand time more destructive than the A-bombs dropped on Japan."

"How do you know this?" a stunned Wills asked.

"It was a bad year for film-makers. For the test, the Feds used 18 tons of film equipment, and more than half of the world's motion picture stock."

"How droll, Miss West," Loveless said as he hobbled toward the other side of the observatory. "*Bikinium* was created via nuclear fusion, yet with a unidirectional magnetic field of 6,000 gauss. I, er, managed to liberate a large sample of it from the government's warehouse at White Sands Proving Grounds. And it has proven to be an excellent propulsion imitator, though it does have a nasty habit of leaking *Deadly Orgone Energy.*"

The laboratory—which Loveless pronounced as *la-bor-a-tory*—part of the observatory looked like something outta an old Universal *Frankenstein* flick, jam-packed with bottles and flasks bubbling, lights flickering, glass tubing twisting and flowing with various colored liquids glowing with brilliant phosphorescence, and batteries crackling.

"Oh, pretty," I couldn't help but say as I marveled at a small mesh cage of fireflies flashing.

"*Photinus pyralis,*" Loveless informed us. "Marvelous creatures. Their bodies produce ATP, which supplies the reaction between *luciferian* and the enzyme *luciferase...*"

"The Devil you say," I interrupted; I just could resist.

Loveless huffed in and out before continuing: "The light is *cold heat*, unlike the wasteful *hot heat* of the Edison light-bulb; or, more correctly, the one he is *credited* with inventing. The firefly's light is 98% energy-efficient."

"Cold fusion?" Wills asked, seemingly impressed.

"Yes," Loveless confirmed, then again with a sweep of his hand toward the glassware: "In recent years, Watson and Crick have unlocked the secrets of *deoxyribonucleic acid*, or DNA: its double-helix structure, held together by paired nucleotides. Again, you will note the duality of nature: a positive and negative, attracting one another, fulfilling each other. Matter and anti-matter complements one another, though in this case, they have a tendency to annihilate each other. As does *DOR* and *OR.*"

"The only *ante-matter*," I quipped, "I care about deals with *stud* poker!"

"Like your head, Miss West" Loveless said sarcastic ally, "Nature abhors a vacuum."

"But not as much as a cat!"

"I erred..."

"To err is human, to purr, feline."

"Why do I try?" Loveless mumbled, wiping his brow. But the urge—the need—to show off his genius compelled him to continue: "By using *vrilium* and *bikinium* crystals, I have created an *orgone* energy field which mutates DNA: replacing the *deoxyribose* sugar with a *vrilium* complex, which mutates organic matter. Immensely mutagenic, this *VNA* accelerates Darwinian evolution, creating hardier organisms with increased resilience to natural force, a greater adaptability to its eco-system. Or, in layman's term: exposed to a sensitive environmental niche, the host *VNA* will dominate it."

"That's layman's terms?" I pondered out loud.

"And," Wills said, avoiding my question (perhaps he understood all this voodoo-hoodoo) "you plan to use your *VNA* to create a super-race of the Aryan ideal, thus you are recruiting blonde, blue-eyed breeding stock as templates?"

174

"No, you idiot!" Loveless barked, his face beet-red. "I hate the Nazis, and everything they stood for! Their racial ideal! Their *super-men!*" After breathing in and out a few time, he seemed to calm a tad, before continuing, with a wave of his hand to encompass his complex: "When you entered *my* temple, you bore witness to what I have created with *VNA*... a garden... an Eden... a new Genesis... here, in the middle of the Mojave Desert, without any outside water or power. This is the *proper* use of genetics... not racial cleansing!"

"That's just fine and dandy," I said with mock-clapping, "you've created your Land of Milk and, well, Honey... your little taste of paradise in the desert... but for what? A gift for mankind? If so, why are we being detained? I mean, other than having broken a couple of your, er, toys."

"My dear, Miss West," Loveless said, repressing a snicker with his hand, "haven't you learned nothing from Gordon's ramblings? I am not known for my generosity!" He sighed before continuing: "I am utilizing my genius to reclaim the land of my ancestors, who had received a valuable land grant, here in California, by the Spanish Viceroy of Mexico, only to have it ripped from my hands when they found gold up North, and when California joined the Union!"

"According to Uncle Artemus' journals," I said, :"your original goal was to reclaim the lands you believed were your ancestral right, to create a haven for the financial and physical disadvantaged... to live in peace, away from the bigotry of society. Well, I guess that notion went down the drain, huh?"

"Yes. Thanks to the meddling of one James West!"

"But," I interjected, "you never gave up your dream. You've created this, er, *Utopia*—oddly, appropriate as it means 'nowhere'—out here in the desert, all for yourself and your robots?"

"Enough!" Loveless screamed.

"I am confident," Wills piped in, "that the U.S. government will reward you handsomely for your discovery, ah, creation of *VNA*, and the immense ramifications for desert agriculture: a technology requiring only sunlight and a minimal of moisture."

"Not interested," Loveless said with a manic laugh.

"Megalomaniacs rarely are," I popped in. "They all have the same blind obsession. I think you are what the story-book *Tinker Bell* called 'a sissy little ass.' But I guess it all comes down to the difference between insanity and genius... which is success! Something James West never granted you!"

"You are as impertinent as your father and other members of your, er, illustrious clan. Though the only member of that family tree with even a spark of genius was Herbert West; but, alas, he was slain by his own creations. Torn to pieces, if I remember correctly."

Honey Girl, you have to think of something, but it's hard to come up with a plan with those three Mech... what did Loveless call them? Oh, well, never mind... with those three Men in Black leveling heaters at your back. And Tom's face told you he was in the same boat, also without a paddle! Wait a minute...

"You knew my father?"

"Yes, my dear, Miss West. Your father, Henry West, became a thorn in my side in, let's see… 1941. After being humiliated as a background Lollipopper, I wound up in the overbearing Munchkin Town, on the Northern slope of Mount Soledad, in La Jolla. I kept my sanity writing about ray-guns and spaceship, at a fourth-cent to a penny-a-word, hoping a 20,000-word epic might net me one or two hundred dollars. Still, it was enough to finance my research on a method to divert the waters of Owen Valley to my parcel of land, here in the Mojave.

"Then your father came snooping around, investigating some 'illegal activities' for the A-1 Detective Agency, which had nothing to do with my plans of liberating the valley's waters. Yet, he was nosing around, getting to close to my plans. My only recourse was to send him a warning, where it would hurt the most; by threatening the thing he held most dear: you, Miss West! Thus I sent you the decapitated head of your Superman puppet, as a warning to your father to back off."

"That was you?" I gasped, my mouth hanging open for the longest time. "You scarred me for life, you maniac!" I tried to lunge forward, to get my claws on him, but was quickly restrained by my guardians. "Damnit, Loveless, face me yourself! But, no, you are but an impotent fool, relying on these mechanical Men in Black!"

"More melodrama, Miss West?" Loveless sighed. "Alas, my warning to your father became moot with the bombing of Pearl Harbor, and with the Germans invading Europe, imprisoning and slaughtering everyone who did not live up to their racial and religious ideals. I joined the French Resistance but was captured during a rescue mission." Loveless seemed to shudder at past memories. "I became the personal *pet* of Alfred Rosenberg, head of the *RRR*—the Secret Purpose Unit—the organization ruled over by *Reichsmarshall* Herman Goring, head of the *Luftwaffe,* and second-in-command after Hitler, himself. Rosenberg oversaw the 'Spiritual and Philosophic Training' of the Nazis; but his organization used dubious legal reasons to loot Europe's art treasures for Goring's private collection; that is, what he could hide from the *führer.*

"Rosenberg dressed me as a Court Jester… like an Organ-Grinder monkey with a pillbox hat. I looked like one of those damn flying monkeys in servitude to the Wicked Witch of the West. Yet, the Nazis were so much more wicked— they were pure evil! He led me around on a jeweled collar noose! Had me entertain for his Germanic 'Bread and Circuses', driving me mad—watch your tongue, Miss West!—playing *Deutschland Uber Alles* all the time! Since I was just their pet monkey, they never suspected my genius, especially related to anything mechanical. So, as my so-called master led me around, for his amusement and that of his flunkies, I paid attention… absorbed it all!

"At the Krupp's Works, I saw marvelous things: what appeared to be a space-rocket ship, giant robots… yet my attention was drawn to something those Nazi idiots could not figure out… did not understand what they had. They were

176

using Vandegraff's generators and Marconi's Vortex Dynamos, attempting to create a rotating electromagnetic field to reduce the effects of gravity via a *Thule Triebwerk* or *Tachyonator Drive*, which they tried to mount in a 25-foot diameter saucer-shaped craft. They never could get it to fly. The reason was obvious to me: their Tesla Magnetic Flux Capacitor was faulty, as was their Vandegraff accelerator. Their *Vril-Saucer…*"

"No more," I shouted. "Forget this trip down memory lane. Just tell us your scheme!"

"Impatient, Miss West? It must run through your family tree. Very well," he said with another wave of his hand, this time back towards the Cloud-Buster: "This, er…"

"Dohickey?" I offered.

"…instrument," he continued, ignoring me, "not only generates *vril* or *orgone* energies, to cleanse the atmosphere of *Deadly Orgone Energy*, but by reversing the polarity, it creates a form of *DOR* , reversing, degenerating, reverting organic matter to its primitive form. With it I will *de-evolve* you two meddlers!"

"Do something!" I screamed at Tom Wills as I wrestled and struggled against the iron-hold Moe had on me. Then, over my shoulder, I quipped: "We've established you never heard of Asimov's *Three Laws of Robotics*; so, how about *Klaatu Barada Nikto*? Ah, I didn't think so…"

"I'm open to suggestions, Miss West," Will said, struggling against the iron holds of Larry and Curly.

"You can't get away with this!" I screamed at Loveless, gritting my teeth.

"Why do they *always* say that? Not only can I get away with it, but I will!"

Honey Girl he's a maniac, true to form, mad at the world. After all, six out of the seven dwarfs are not Happy!

"And whom, do tell, Miss West, will stop me? An aging flunky for a once-great detective? Or a big-breasted, wanna-be detective trying to fill her daddy's gumshoes? A dim-witted, over-sexed, bleached blonde…"

That does it, Honey Girl, no one calls you a bleached blonde! And I exploded into action, reaching back, clasping Moe's metallic neck, kicking off, and propelling myself up and over my captor, landing solidly in a cat-like crouch five feet behind the MIB. Moe turned slowly, reminding me of Talos in *Jason and the Argonauts*, sans the creaking, and I again acted. Leaping forward, my palms slapped the floor, my arms coiled and sprung, sending me at Moe, my thighs locking around his neck, my ankles locking, and then dropping my body to bring him (it?) down.

Alas, the mass of its android body haltered all progress as my head slammed hard against his metallic body. My brain exploded like a H-bomb as I hung there, from his neck, my *naturally* blonde hair dangling loose, like a slab of beef in a locker, yet with no real beefcake in sight to rescue me.

Simultaneously, Tom Wills had swung into action, mumbling something about *aging flunky*, pushing back, crashing into his two restraining MIBs, Larry and Curly, sending them crashing into the beakers and other glassware, spilling, shattering, filling the room with misty fumes and flashing electrical sparks. In a mad scramble, Wills freed himself and sprang to his feet. The MIBs were slow to react; they definitely weren't the Pep Boys. Racing full bore, he crashed into the third MIB, dropping me into his waiting arms. And, without a moment lost, we fled from the observatory, to the manic screams of Loveless shouting: "Get them, you mechanized, tin-plated imbeciles!"

In a downward slopping corridor Wills stopped long enough to set me on my feet. "How are you, Miss West?"

"Shaken *and* stirred."

"Now what?"

"To quote Elvis: '*It's now or never!*' In other words: run like hell!"

Racing deeper down the corridor I could hear the echoing of the three MIBS goose-stepping swiftly behind us, Loveless screaming insults at them. Eventually, we ran out of corridor, facing a wide doorway, and the only thing flashing through my mind was from the *Classics Illustrated* edition of Dante's *Inferno…"Abandon all hope, ye who enter here…"*

Since there was little hope to abandon, we plunged into the darkness: a damp room, with the chill creeping into my bones as dripping water echoed around us with a *plink-plink* sound. My nose smelt the rancid odor of spoiled food and human waste as we cautiously proceeded further into the cave-like space, but we were stopped by a steel-mesh door. *A dead end*—and I hoped that wasn't an omen. We turned back the way we had come, only to find a heavy metal door slamming shut with the *wrack* of a magnetic lock, sealing your favorite Private Eyeful in total darkness. Then a slot in the door slid open and the grinning face of Doctor Loveless, boosted up by one of the MIBs, appeared:

"So, Miss West, you have escaped my *de-evolving* ray, but, alas, you have, shall we say, sealed your own fate. Now, you will face its *results!*"

"Loveless, what do you expect of us?" I pleaded.

"I expect you to die!"

"Not today," I screamed. "I may *dye* another day, but for the moment I will remain a blonde."

"As you wish, Miss West. Yet, to demonstrate my graciousness, I shall allow you to see the manner of your destruction."

The slot slid shut, again sealing the room in darkness. But I could still hear the maniacal laughter of Loveless, as grating as the mirth-machine at the Pike in Long Beach when it got stuck and wouldn't stop laughing until it was smashed to pieces. Nevertheless, a few seconds later, dusty and dim, sparsely spaced red bulbs flickered on overhead as the steel-mesh door slid into the wall, revealing a long descending corridor leading into the bowels of the earth. Lining either side was a seemingly endless row of cells, cages, like something out of a medieval menagerie. *But of what, Honey Girl?*

In the dim-red flickering lights appeared hundreds of floating red-globes, hovering eerily. Then came a sharp metallic clicks, echoing the distinctive sound of locks being popped. The floating, bobbing red globes seemed to inch their way toward us from the lower bowel of this dungeon, accompanied by echoing primeval mumblings. *Honey Girl, it's like the Minotaur's cave... or some other Devils in the Dark... or 'Uncle' Ian's tales of the Jamaican dragons. But, Honey Girl, this ain't no legend! They looked like something out of the front office of hell. Like something out of a* Batman *funny book...*

"An abomination... a bloody nightmare!" Tom Wills uttered as a humanoid stepped out of the shadows, dozens of others lurching behind him... *it*! It wasn't the *Terror from Beyond Space*, but something more real and grotesque: a hunched-back fitted in tattered rags, with long, dirty and greasy whitish-yellow hair matted with soil and god knows what else; a drooping face dominated by a longish tapered, jagged nose. Its fiery red eyes even glowed in the dim overhead red lights. It moved slowly, dragging one foot, its large atavistic claws slowly opening... closing... Its yellowed teeth—fangs!—drooling saliva.

"Holy Moly! Morlocks!" I screamed, suddenly realizing I was dressed similar to Weena, with the same blond hair and blues eyes, as in the recent George Pal film, *The Time Machine*!

"No, Shaver's *Deros*," Tom Wills corrected. "The results of Loveless' de-evolutionary ray. These are his de-evolved *Homo sapiens*; what he had planned for us! Because we do not fit *his* racial ideal!"

"As I said before, we're definitely not in Kansas anymore, Tom-Tom!"

Slowly, the Human Gargoyle inched nearer, saliva dripping, eyes brilliant red, yet vacant. It lifted its right hand, broken yellowed talons inching towards me. He must be the Alpha Male... as the others hung back, just barely in the shadows, peering out.

"Quick, Tom," I yelled as we backed up towards the steel door, "if they are anything like the Morlocks, they'll be afraid of fire."

"I appear to have left my Lucifers in my *other* space suit."

"Great. *Now* you get a sense of *humour*."

The other humanoids began to creep forward, circling us, and all I could think of was the witch doctor in *King Kong* chanting: "*Wa seha ani Maka, O Tarvey Rama Kong!*" It didn't help.

Then came a series of rapping sounds ont the steel door, which I recognized as Morse Code from my days as a Girl Scout: R-E-C-U-L-E-Z...

"Huh?" I said without taking my eyes off the humanoids.

"It is French," said Wills. "It means: *Step Back...*"

"Huh?" I repeated; yet the answer came quickly, as my tush began to warm, causing me to leap away from the door, among into the arms of the Dero.

But the humanoids had cowered away as the steel door began to glow red, then blue, then white, as a large circle appeared in the metal, bubbling, hissing, melting, issuing forth smothering smoke.

Honey Dear, are you dreaming? Is this just some nightmarish dream? Like something from Invaders from Mars?

The burning circle completed itself and was punched through, slamming to the floor with a bang. And who stepped through was definitely not a Martian, at least not like one from any of the movies I had seen. He was dressed in a white robe and turban, like something out of the *Arabian Nights*: medium height, broad-shouldered, handsome, with striking large, greenish-brown eyes, almost hypnotic. He appeared to be is his mid-forties. In his hands was a still smothering, futuristic ray-gun, like something straight out of an old *Flash Gordon* serial.

"Are you alright, Wills?" the stranger's baritone voice inquired. "And you, Mademoiselle West?"

"Oh, my god!" Wills managed to smatter, before regaining his composure, balling his fists and rushing at the man. "You damn Nazi!"

"More Nazis?" I mumbled to myself, glancing over my shoulder, relieved to find the Morlocks/Deros still cowered by the brightly glowing hole in the steel door.

Effortlessly the stranger grabbed both of Wills' wrists in his free steel-trap hand and applied pressure, forcing the detective to growl, buckle to his knees. "We have no time for this, Wills… Tom. Did not the CID fully brief you on my situation, *mon ami*?"

"I am not your friend!"

"Two years ago, President Coty pardoned me for all my alleged war offenses," the stranger said, releasing Wills with a shove. "Yes, I served France in my own way, but I never assisted the Nazis, nor partook in any of their crimes."

"Sophistry!" Wills hissed, rubbing his bruised wrists.

"In your heart, Thomas Wills, you know that I was not a Nazi, and so did your master. My involvement in certain activities were so sensitive that some people in authority, even after the War, were unaware of the scope of my activities during the War—and even to this day."

"Yet you fled to Argentina!" Wills snapped.

"Ah, guys," I interrupted. "Perhaps we can save this trip down memory lane for another day?"

"Mademoiselle West is correct, Wills."

"But," I said, "one question first: just who are you?"

"Pardon my manners," the stranger said, "I'm Leo Saint-Clair."

"The Nyctalope?" I gasped with awed surprise. "My daddy use to read me stories of your adventures."

"Some greatly exaggerated by my biographer, no doubt," he said with a flick of his wrist. "But I also knew your father, Henry West."

"*Honeeee…*," came a low, garbled voice.

We all turned, and saw the huddled mass of Deros/Morlocks staring at us, swaying back and forth, still cowering at the glowing, simmering hole in the door. Yet the one I determined to be the Alpha Male braved the metallic glow, shuffling forward, reaching out, and placing a clawed hand on my shoulder. "*Honeeee?*"

It asked it as a question this time and I replied: "Aaaah, yesssss..."

"Hon...nee... Child..."

I stared in the creature's red blank eyes and saw a glimpse, a twinkle of the true owner of these eyes. "Daddy?" I asked.

"Yessssss..."

"But... how... why?"

"No time," the creature said, "gotta get ya outta here..."

"We must get you help," I said, tears forming in my eyes. "And... and... the others."

"Nooooo... we ... better offfff... dead..."

And with that, my daddy growled a command, and his fellow captives began hopping back and forth on talonesque feet, hooting, rushing forward, only to again cower, shield their eyes from the harsh, naked light bulbs of the corridor.

"Pluck your magic *twanger*, Froggy," I said to Saint-Clair.

The Frenchman reacted, leveling his ray-rifle at the series of overhead lights, zapping, popping them with a reddish beam of concentrated light, until the only light visible was at the end of the corridor, in the observatory. Then he led his "troops" in a charge down the corridor, shouting: "*Par les yeux d'Aten!*"

"The Eyes of Aten, huh?" I mumbled, but had no time to ponder this as I followed forty or more transformed humans now amassed, hobbling down the corridor, with Wills hot on my naked heels.

Saint-Clair paused at the entrance to the observatory, took aim and zapped out all the overhead lighting, only to have the back-up generator pop on, illuminating the space in dull, low-wattage red light. The only other light was the glow of the full moon shining through the dome's portal.

The three MIBs stood in the middle of the observatory, waiting patiently, Tommy Guns at the ready. Beyond them, Loveless was at the Cloud-Buster adjusting dials, flipping switches, his blonde disciple at his side.

Without regards to the Three Laws of Robotics, let alone compassion, the three MIBs began emptying their Tommies, spitting out their venom into the horde of Deros, mowing down the first wave, who jerked about like puppets with their strings cut. Smoke and the smell of cordite saturated the air. Yet, they still came! They continued screaming hoots and grunts and eerie moans even as they were mowed down. Yet, they still came! And I realized I'd underestimated the number of de-evolved human. There had to have been hundreds!

With the Tommies emptied, the remaining Deros piled on the Larry, Moe and Curly, ripping them apart in a mad, pent-up frenzy, tossing legs and arms this way and that, their oily "blood" spurting everywhere.

I saw Loveless hopping back and forth, not pleased, simmering, his face beet-red, puffing hard, shaking off Hathor as she tried to calm him. It just made the evil genius madder! He pushed her aside; she stumbled and fell, but did not cry out, Loveless didn't even notice. Instead he yelled: "Release the hounds!"

Hounds? I didn't hear no hounds.

Loveless pulled a lever. A door slid open in the wall. Out sprang three *mechanical hounds*! Silvery, sleek, jaws filled with razor-sharp fangs! And the carbonized canine leapt! They tore... ripped... shredded... gnawed at the de-evolved humans, but these Deros fought with wild abandonment, without worry nor care for their own safety; or as my daddy remarked: *they were better off dead...*

From fear of zapping the humanoids and *not* the dogs of hell, Saint-Clair couldn't use his ray-gun, so he upended it and used its stock as a club against the beasties. He yelled to me and Wills: "Go! Get the maniac!"

So we high-tailed it after Loveless and Hathor, who had just ducked through a door, which shut before we could reach them. Turning back, I saw that the melee was over. The MIBS and the robotic Fidos had been reduced to heaps of metallic scrap, pseudo-blood mingling with the *real* greenish-blood of the Deros/Morlocks, the dead and the dying. The rest had escaped through a large hole in the wall, no doubt created earlier by the Frenchman's ray-gun.

Saint-Clair joined us. Suddenly, we turned in unison. From deep within the compound came echoing *puffffs* down the corridor leading to the garden area. We didn't have time to question the noises as I turned and glance at the slit in the observatory doom, and screamed: "Look! Up in the Sky!"

And there we saw, soaring through the full-moon lit sky, having erupted from the desert sand, a 30-foot diameter flying saucer, shooting skyward.

"*Vril-S* series saucer," Saint-Clair remarked. "Loveless has perfected the Nazi's *Victalew*—Frozen Smoke—most impressive."

"*Vril* energy," I mused aloud. "Isn't this Cloud-Buster supposed to cancel out the negative *vril* or *orgone energy*?"

"Even a blind squirrel finds an acorn now and then," Wills said, as he and the Frenchman stared at me. *Honey Girl, I think you have been insulted!*

"Of course, Mademoiselle West," Saint-Clair said, scanning the Cloud-Buster's control panel, noting the one marked: *DOE-NEGATE*. He twisted a couple dials, and flipped a few switches. The side tubes began to rotate, to revolve like an old Gatling gun, faster and faster, accumulating and electromagnetic charge—I was later told—sizzling, crackling, hissing. Then the central cannon issued forth a greenish-blue beam of pure-energized *bikinium / vril / orgone energy*. And, like a guided missile seeking a heat-signature, the ray locked on to the saucer's *DOR* emulations.

The ray engulfed the saucer as it was entering the ionosphere and it began to glow, filling the sky with a burning disc, flames shooting out from it like the solar rays of a dazzling sun burst!

"Aten," Saint-Clair mumbled as Loveless' saucer burst into fiery pieces, falling back towards the earth, crashing in the desert, sending up embers, sand and dust.

"You may wish upon a star, Loveless." I said, looking at the crashed saucer, "but not all your dreams will come true!"

"The Cloud-Buster did it!" Saint-Clair said.

"Oh, no, Leo, it was not the Cloud-Buster alone," Tom Will said, wrapping an arm around my shoulder, "'twas Beauty, Miss West's quick thinking, which brought down the beast."

We trekked out through the blast-hole in the observatory to the crash site, with Saint-Clair leading the way in the night, clouds obscuring the stars and moon. He seemed to be able to see in the dark—perhaps the legends were true, including the fact that he should have been pushing 65 or 70, yet looked no older than his mid-forties. Slowly we neared the crash, flames and smoke still issuing high from it, just beginning to abate. The saucer had split in half, the *DOR*-reactor, other equipment, wiring and circuitry spewed about. There was no sign of Loveless or the girl, Hathor. Not even footprints in the sand. As if they had vanished into thin air, just like in some of his adventures recorded in Artemus Gordon's journals.

"This Little Caesar," I quipped, "could this be the last of Loveless?"

Returning to the observatory Saint-Clair scanned the cordite-choked air, thicker than a London or Long Beach Port at dawn, counted the dead and the dying bodies, and quickly calculated that 26 or so had vanished into the night. He gave Wills a card, told him find a phone and call the number on it, and ask for *6221701*. They would send people to sanitize the scene; also, to tell them to bring a S&R team to corral the stray Deros and take them to Groom Lake for processing.

"Honey-child..." I heard my father call, barely a whisper. I searched the carnage and spotted him. I rushed to his bullet-ridden body, knelt and cradled his head in my lap, stroking his gangly hair, tears blurring my vision. "Oh, daddy..."

"Hoooney," my father mumbled between coughing up green-tinted blood, with a strong copper smell. "....remember to always be yourself. Only... when one fights to be human... and I, we, have been fighting for that... realizing how precious our humanity is. But we had lost that last bit of humanity until... until you and your friends showed up and gave it back to us... One last chance to be... human..."

"Mademoiselle West," Saint-Clair said, placing a hand on my shoulder, squeezing it. "You have given your father back his sense of purpose."

"But... we... thought you dead, Daddy... Where have you been all these years? Here?"

"Is that... you, Leo?"

"Yes, my old friend," the Nyctalope confirmed.

"I have so... so much to tell my little Alice... oh, did she love her tea parties," my father said, more goo leaking from the corners of his mouth. "Tell her why I wasn't there... for her... how I disappeared..."

"You knew," the Frenchman said to me, "that your father was in the O.S.S. during the war?"

"*Oui,*" I answered, managing a slight smile. "But he never discussed it with me—oh, so secret—as my 'Uncle' Ian Fleming might say."

"Commander Fleming," my father managed with a guttural laugh. "I understand he named his Jamaican estate after you... *Golden Eye*... The Golden-haired Private Eye. He was... all... always... so..."

"You remember our mailman, Mr. Ryder, Daddy?" I asked, wiping a tear from my blue—not *golden*—eye. "Well, Uncle Ian named a character after me and him: *Honey Ryder.*"

"Tell her, Leo..."

"Mademoiselle West, during October of 1943, a joint effort of the Allied Forces, including myself, Commander Fleming, Harry Dickson and your father, was undertaken in the Philadelphia Naval Ship Yards, utilizing the technical and theoretical papers of Nikola Tesla, obtained after his death. We conducted 'Eyes Only' experiments to render a ship invisible. This *Project Rainbow...*"

"Oh, yes," I said, "Tom mentioned it in connection with an annotated copy of Dr. Jessup's *The Case for the U.F.O.* He implied it was nonsense."

"Well, yes. Carlos Allende and the three alleged 'space alien' annotators were, er, a film-flam, as I believe you Americans would say. That was all 'Smoke and Mirrors,' but we learned a lot, especially the hazards, what not to do. But during the War research advanced by leaps and bounds, and U.S. Navy was ready to try again, a Project Bifrost or Iris, then..."

"Ship...," my delirious father mumbled, "...out of danger..."

"You saved them, you saved them all," Saint-Clair said as I mopped my father's feverish brow. Then to me he said: "You father was—is!—a hero, but the experiment failed. After the War, your father returned to his civilian life as a private investigator, opening his own agency. Unfortunately, we lost contact with one another after that, until 1952, when we were summoned to Washington for close- door hearings during a Congressional investigation into possible stolen technology, including that of *Project Bifrost.*"

So, my father wasn't ratting out the Reds in Hollywood; I don't know why but somehow, some way I felt relieved.

"Your father," Saint-Clair continued, "tracked a possible lead to a quantity of *bikinium* stolen from the White Sands Proving Grounds."

"Sure, Loveless mentioned this."

"Intriguing. It would help to explain your father's disappearance."

"But I thought all these years that my father had been slain behind the Paramount Theatre..."

"A deception, Mademoiselle. You never saw the body."

"Closed casket," I confirmed. "I thought it was because of his wounds...."
Then my anger came violently to the surface. "You bastards! My daddy was alive... all this time! And you let me believe... you bastards!"

"I imagine we are," Saint-Clair said, pausing, then: "But it was for his *and* your protection."

"My protection?"

"If the parties your father were investigating had discovered he was alive, they would have come after him for sure, and slain him *and* you, as retribution. Both of your lives were in constant danger."

"I became a detective because of my father's death. To search for his killer, to see justice done. I don't know now. 'There's no use going back to yesterday, because I was a different person then'."

"Since playing Alice in Wonderland," my father gasped out, in between coughs of his dying fits. "Don't blame the Frog... he's right. You had your entire life before you, I would've been there for you, if my old foe, Loveless, hadn't... *choke...choke...choke...* captured me. I'd tracked the bikinium to him... *choke...choke...* and in turned me into... *this*... with his fiendish de-evolution ray... to become one of his slave-laborers... to build his temple here with his other victims..."

Tom Wills arrived back and reported to us that he had called the authorities, and that those "*puffs*" we had heard were the cult members—all androids—being blown apart; no doubt, via a remote device Loveless had on his person.

"Daddy," I said as my father's eyes began to roll back, and I squeezed his taloned hand tighter, not wanting to let go... not wanting to let him go!

"Be a good girl, Honey... and God will protect you," he mumbled.

I looked up at Saint-Clair who said, "Saint Michael's remark to Jeanne d'Arc, before she left on her mission for God. Wise advice."

"I'll be damned if I'm going to cut my hair," I managed to quip through my tears, "and wear men's clothing! Yet, still my Hundred Years War is over. I found my daddy. And lost him, again. But the quest is over." The certitude seemed to have set me free. "Perhaps I can now quit being a P.I. and settle down. I know a certain Lieutenant who might want to marry me and have a brood of Western-Storms... or, perhaps, begin a cruise business with an all-girl crew."

"Or, Mademoiselle West," Saint-Clair said, "now you can discover who murdered your mother."

"What!" I exclaimed, looking down at my dead father in my arm, then back to the Frenchman. "She died giving birth to me."

"No. She was murdered."

"How? Why?"

"I do not know the details, but your father reported the situation to us, hoping that the C.I.D. could help find her killer. We had no such luck."

"All these years, I've suffered from Survivor's Guilt, thinking that my birth had caused the death of my mother. Why didn't my father tell me?"

"That, I do not know. We have the full file of the case at C.I.D.'s HQ, if you decide to pursue the case."

"I guess I won't be getting married anytime soon."

"*Comme vous voulez, Mademoiselle.*"

After the people from Gloom Lake had arrived and sanitized the place and rounded up the strays, and promised to release my father's body to me after processing, Tom Wills, Saint-Clair and I hopped into the rented Bel-Air, with the Frenchman behind the wheel, and drove East.

I was wedged in between the Nyctalope and Wills, who was rather quit for a chance. Well, at least, I had reconnected with my purse and trusty .22. I tried to question Saint-Clair about his various adventures, but he waved them all off as "exaggerations." I wasn't so sure.

The Nyctalope drove down a dark, seemingly abandoned pebble road, and I could barely see anything in the pre-dawn darkness, even with the head-lamps, er, headlights, on. Some of the legends about him were definitely true.

Saint-Clair was only forthcoming about why he was out here, in the Mojave Desert, and how he had come to rescue us. The how: he'd just returned from a mission, and the *CID* had asked him, since he'd be in the area, to keep an eye on us, which he had done—just in time! As for the why he was out here: When writing his memoirs, he'd recalled an assignment, an adventure from 1932, in Egypt, which had something to do with an insane Egyptologist. That had sparked an *epiphany* in him, about his ancestry and his destiny. It seemed that he was somehow ancestrally linked to something called *The Sacred Warriors* or *The Eyes of Aten*, something that had started during the time of Pharaoh Akhenaten. These *Warriors* had the power to see in the dark, and this ability had been passed down through the generation, for some 3500 years, to him.

"So, you can see in the dark?" I asked.

"Yes."

"To see the evil that lurks in the hearts of men?" I quipped.

Saint-Clair laughed.

"Are we here?" Wills asked, as the Bel-Air braked.

"Yes," the Frenchman said, killing the motor, stepping from the car.

"Where is here?" I asked, looking around as I exited the car. "We seem to be in the middle of nowhere."

"Appearances can be deceiving," Saint-Clair said, pointing to the gully between two buttes, the sunrise radiating the day's first golden rays. "*Ecco Aten!*"

The Nyctalope appeared mesmerized by the rising sun, before shielding his eyes. From within his robe, he retrieved a pair of ruby-tinted goggles, donned them, and turned back to the solar sight, now illuminating the desert before us in blues and reds. "Behold the Aten!"

The *dazzling sun*—the Solar Disk of the Aten—rose, creeping higher and higher into the sky, a red glowing ball illuminating an open-air temple before us, without the obelisks and pylons as in the picture books; just a plain flagstone floor, a square a hundred feet on a side. Tables were spaced about, laden with baskets of breads, beer and wine, and fruits. On the sun-shade altar were baskets of fragrance of flowers, mixed with the thick aromatic smells of resins and incense.

At the rear of the temple was a giant erect stone—I think it was called a stele—with the Solar Disk of the Aten shining its arm-like rays, ending in hands, holding the hoop shaped ankhs. Between the tables and the stele were a half-dozen women and an equal number of men, of various ages and hair-color, all with heavenly bodies, with plenty of "equipment," and very little clothing. They were dancing about, singing: "*Make holiday... Do not weary of it... None is allowed to take any goods with them... Lo, none departs comes back again...*"

Honey Girl, these are some wild guys and girls of the naked west waving their hands in the air. Wait, Girl, five fingers on each hand, who get it? Two fives makes... A Ten!

"I tried to get here as often as I can," the Frenchman said, removing his great coat, reveal a naked torso beneath, only clad in a brief loin-cloth and his goggles, "to, as you Americans say, recharge my batteries."

I couldn't help but notice that, for a guy who must be close to seventy, he was in remarkable sharp, not Mark Storm, but still, he didn't look a day over thirty-five... forty tops!

Then one of the female worshippers, a redhead, walked over, leading an ocelot on a leash, handing it off to him, bowing slightly, intoning: "The Aten is one..."

"...the Aten is all," he replied.

As the Atenist? Naturalist? Nudist? walked away, back toward the non-temple temple, I knelt down and petted the ocelot. "What a pretty girl. What's her name?"

"Nefertiti."

"Of course."

Saint-Clair turned towards the rising sun and temple, spreading his arms in greeting. "Aten is One... Aten is all! Aten is Everywhere. Aten is Universal. As Above..." He pointed upwards, then down, "...So Below! What happens in Heaven is reflected in its glory here Below on Earth! This is the Aten..." He turned and offered his hand. "Come, Honey West, and become as the day you were born."

I thought: *Well, when in Rome... er, the Mojave Desert....* I slipped out of my torn and soiled dress—I'd probably never get my deposit back from MGM—and revealed my body to the Glory of the Aten.

"Come, join us," I said to Tom Wills.

"I do not know what to say to a naked lady."

"Hi! I like your outfit?" I laughed, pulling my arms down parallel to my body, my hands extended at the elbows, and turning my face to the side. I began to shuffle, "Come, Tom. Come and walk like an Egyptian..."

Three days later, back in my Long Beach apartment, I was enjoying my first *real* shower, going in my head over the mail and messages which had accumulated in my absence. It felt good, soothing my sun-burnt skin which had begun flaking off.

My cousin Iris and Wally wished me a Happy Birthday. A solicitation from The Society for Indecency of Naked Animals, huh-hum. Some story and song idea from director Vic Kendall on his new play: *Private Eyeful!* It was based on me, with songs like: *The Brassy Blue-Eyed Blonde from Bellflower* and *Classy Lady with a Classy Chassis*. Also, there was a message from an aunt-twice-removed. Seeing as I was in Hollywood, she asked if I couldn't find a part for her struggling actor son, William Adam Anderson.

Then I thought of Saint-Clair's ocelot, Nefertiti, and mused on perhaps getting a pet ocelot and calling it, well, let's say, Bruce, after the secret identity of the once great detective hero, Batman...

After stepping from the shower, I dried myself off and wrapped myself in a towel and another as a "turban." I stepped into my office, lit only by the desk lamp, and I was not surprised to see Tom Wills sitting in the chair before my desk.

"You should lock your door," he said with a smile.

"I'm beginning to think the same thing," I said, sitting down behind my desk, where I noticed an ice-cold six-pack of Pabst Blue-Ribbon on the desk top. Using a church-key, I popped the caps on two, passing him one. Then I fired up a Chesterfield. After a few puffs, bluish smoke drifting to the ceiling, I held up my beer. "*Cul sec!*"

"*Santé!*" he countered as we knocked bottles together. He reached into his inner pocket, produced an envelope and slid it across the desk to me. I slipped it into my desk drawer, atop *Fanny Hill*, without counting the bills, knowing it wasn't a check for a million dollars from John Tipton.

"You are not going to count it?"

"What? After all we've shared. After all, we'll always have *Perris*."

"You are a wonder, Miss West."

"Honey, Tom... it's Honey."

"Er, Honey. It is jolly bad luck we were unable to capture that chap, Dr. Loveless."

"I was thinking about that. That's Loveless' messianic message was the hatred of Nazis, their idea of racial cleansing. Fair enough, not many people really like the Nazis. But in his zeal, he was no different in his blind hatred of blonde and blue-eyed folks than Hitler was of the 'degenerates.' Do you think hate is the only thing Loveless ever felt?"

188

"I don't know, but it's all he has left."

"And those poor innocent people… deformed, helpless slaves of the mad doctor… I felt sorry for those poor creatures… *people*. Even though I found my father, only to have him die in my arms. Though, to be honest, he did give me the *heeble-jeebles*. As for my mother, we'll have to see how that pans out." I took another puff from my cig and pull from the beer. "Well, Seth, looks like you finally got the best of Osiris."

"With a great deal of help from *Nekhakha-t*."

"Oh, yeah, you never told me what that name means."

"The 't' inserted in the middle or tacked on at the end of an Egyptian named denoted 'female.' Thus Rameses II's queen *Nefer-t-ari* translates as *Beautiful (woman) Companion*. While *Nefer-t-iti* is: *The Beautiful One (woman) has Come…*"

"Go on," I urged.

"*Nekhakha-t* literally translates as: *Woman with Large Breasts*."

"Oooookay," I said, looking at Wills, before letting out a full-body laugh.

Wills polished off his brewski and stood up. "It has been a pleasure, Miss West."

"Call me: Honey," I said, walking around the desk. "My brain keeps telling me we have unfinished business: that age in mind-over-matter if you don't mind, it doesn't matter."

"Huh?"

I kissed him, savoring it, my legs feeling like ribbons after a New Year's Eve party was over, and had to push back to catch my breath. *My, Honey Girl, this guy is no light-weight, second-rater!* "Yummmy."

"Miss… er, ah… Honey…" he mumbled, savoring his Taste of Honey.

"As Above…" I said, touch my index finger to my lips, licking it, then pointed it down between us, "…So Below…"

Epilog

In the 23th century geneticist David Marcus discovered Dr. Loveless' notebooks in a collection of old books. They contained data on *ZNA*, of creating "life from lifelessness." He incorporated the artificial *ZNA* into his mother's *Genesis Project*. Let's just say: he had to convince his mother, Carol Marcus, but the nightmare had already begun!

Matthew Ilseman is new to Tales of the Shadowmen, *and in this story, pays a Lovecraftian homage to Paris, the City of Lights, or rather, in this particular case, the City of Darkness...*

Matthew Ilseman: *Guided Tours of Famous Secret Places*

The group had gathered at the Rue Morgue. I looked them over. They looked like typical tourists from America and Britain. They stared with wide eyes at their surroundings. They took pictures on cameras and phones. They probably thought that the street was only existed in Poe's story. Then again, so did most Parisians. In certain parts of Paris, or really any other city, they would have stood out as a target for muggers and pickpockets

Those were not dangers on the Rue Morgue. There were other dangers, worse dangers, but not those. The sun was setting over the edges of the houses. It was what in Hollywood was dubbed the "golden hour." This was the earliest I could gather them and perform the ritual.

"I'll be your tour guide. I'm sure some of you were surprised to find that the Rue Morgue was a real street. Many people think it was invented by Edgar Allan Poe."

"Who?" said one of the Americans. I did not know how to answer that.

"Now, it does need to be said: you are not here just for a tour, but to participate in a *Working*. Given that we all share esoteric interests..."

"What?" said the man who asked who Poe was.

"Magick. We are all into magick."

"Oh, yeah, I am all about magick."

I sighed. "It is in the best interest of everyone involved to keep our names secret. Because of that, I have made name tags according to the place you are from." I handed out the tags. "Arkham?"

An old woman came up.

"Brichester?"

A middle aged man held up his hand.

"Derry?"

A young man with glasses came over.

"Ingersham?"

The man who asked who Poe was came over. He stared down at the tag like it was some kind of disgusting insect. Reluctantly, he took it. Him, I would not feel sorry for.

"Medicine Man?"

A guy who looked like he belonged to motorcycle gang came.

"Mud Creek, Texas?"

A middle-aged couple came over. I gave them the badges.

The first stop was the tavern of *L'Épi-Scié*, near the Rue Morgue. I had a deal with the owners. One of many, in fact. In this case, they gave me a discount on food if I brought my tour group here. I believed it is best to feed my guests first. Particularly, if the guests included Americans.

Then, we got on to the coach and drove to a mansion on Rue Thérèse. It was owned by the same people owned the tavern. Another one of my deals allowed me to use it.

I gathered them in the old, musty living room. There was a lot of ancient furniture, covered in sheet—the kind used in old ghost stories. The art on the wall was a bunch of old portraits and a few abstract designs. There was silver in mixed in with the paint of the latter. Old de Castries had taught me that silver and abstract designs kept his enemies away. Unfortunately, it hadn't worked all that well for him.

"You stand here in one of the hidden power centers of the world," I said. "This was, and perhaps still is, the meeting place of the *Habits Noirs*, or as you say in English, the Black Coats."

I looked at my guests. I expected to see their eyes widen with astonishment, but they seemed confused, instead.

"The Black Coats?" I asked. "You've heard of the Black Coats, right?"

The man from Derry said, "I have a black coat. I brought it with me, but my baggage got shipped to Frankfurt by mistake."

I decided to fill them in.

"For most of history, humanity has been manipulated by various secret societies. Groups like the Black Coats, the Si-Fan, the Illuminati, the Shin Tan, the Brotherhood of the Seven Kings, the Black Lodge, the Power House…"

The tourist stared. The woman from Mud Creek said, "Are we going to see the Eiffel Tower?"

"Not on this tour. There are plenty of others that will show you the Eiffel tower. I am showing you places that others don't even know exist."

"You're showing us an old room," said the man from Ingersham.

To be fair this was true. I decided it was best to move along.

"Well, I believe we can move on to the next place. I was going to regal you with the secret history of France."

"That sounds boring. Let's go," said Ingersham.

"Let him talk," said Mr. Mud Creek.

I sighed; this was going nowhere. I try to give people some culture, but do they want it? I decided to begin the ritual.

We made markings on the ground—all signs and sigils developed by De Castries. We chanted the names of the Old Gods. Then came the sacrifice.

The man from Brichester came forward with the lamb I had procured. Blood is the most common price for power. This is true both for magical power and for mundane political power. More so the latter, really.

I raised the blade. Brichester held forth a goat for my stroke. I brought it down into Brichester's neck. He gurgled and spat blood and fell over dead.

It's best the sacrifice does not know he's the sacrifice.

The Louvre seemed like a large cavern in the dark of night. The baroque style of the ornaments and paintings was hard to see in the dark. I would occasionally lecture on this or that piece of art. Some of the things I said were standard history; some I made up; some were what really happened.

We had yet to enact the ritual. There would be no more blood sacrifices. Everyone knew Brichester was going to be sacrificed. Well, everyone except Brichester. While a blood sacrifice at each point of the tour would make things easier, I could not go on sacrificing people. That would bring too much attention.

I took them to see the Mona Lisa. They always want to see the Mona Lisa. I told the story of its two most famous thefts. The one by Arsène Lupin; the other by some Italian.

"Lupin was very piqued that, after using a brilliant but complicated plan to steal the painting, another man would simply walk in and out with it. Lupin's trick was that he used a secret passageway, one also used by the notoriuous Belphégor, a.k.a. the Phantom of the Louvrer."

Ingersham raised his hand like a child in school. I asked him what he wanted. He said, "Isn't using a secret passage way, like, cheating."

That annoyed me. "How so?"

"Well, unless he built it himself, he was just using someone else's work. He didn't really think it up. He just found it."

"Finding it was difficult enough," I replied.

Harrisonville shrugged. "Whatever."

"As a matter of fact, Lupin had an entire block of houses built with secret passages just to use as a base."

"Seems kind of excessive."

"Shut up," I told him. "The actual truth of the matter is that Paris is covered with secret passages. There is the room in the *Dragon Volant* and the passages used by Erik under the Opera House, which we will see later, but first, I'll show you Belphegor's secret lair! Come this way!"

As I led the way, Medicine Man said to me, "You know, the eyes really do follow you in that picture."

I turned to look at the painting. The Mona Lisa had turned its head to look at us. My enemies were closing in on me. I made the Voorish sign and hurried everyone to the secret room.

As we walked through the Louvre, we passed by many statues. In the dark, they looked lifelike, but it was not just the dark. The unseen spirits of Paris were manifesting in them. The paramentals, as old De Castries called them, needed something to make themselves manifest. They were possessing the statues.

192

I hurried everyone to the Room of the Barbarous Gods. It was filled with strange idols. Giant stone statues of the Serpent-Men of Valusia that had been looted from the Middle East during the Crusades. A black idol from the castle of Joiry. And, of course, the statue of Belphegor.

This was to be the site of the second ritual. Just as in the house of the Black Coats, I borrowed the power of the blood shed in the name of money and domination; I could have borrowed from these ancient forgotten gods, but there was no time.

The paramentals had already come. The statue of the Serpent-Man hissed. Slowly, it slithered off its pedestal and came towards us. Medicine Man, either out of some missed placed heroism or simple aggression, charged it. Before he could do anything, its jaws had shut around his head. The decapitated corpse fell to the ground.

People screamed. I opened the secret passage and shouted for everyone to get inside. I spoke incantations while the fools took forever to go down. They did little to stop the statue. Before it reached me, I shoved Ingersham in and sealed the door behind me. I chanted an incantation and drew a pentacle. Then I sighed in relief. I guess we had a blood sacrifice after all.

We escaped from the Louvre through the sewers. I could not help feeling like Jean Valjean as we did so. My tour group was made up of amateurs in the occult, but they seem to be taking it well. I had expected them to freak out.

Eventually, we resurfaced not far from the Court of the Dragon. It is one of those parts of Paris that most people do not know of and cannot find. One of the Hidden Places.

"The Dragon from which it gets its name," I said, pointing to a stone dragon that overlooked the gate to the street, "is said to be the street's guardian. Just as it is said Notre-Dame once housed real breathing gargoyles to protect it."

I had already taken measures to protect myself from the dragon. What I feared were the other paramentals. The ritual was designed to protect me. However, each time I performed it, it seemed to get weaker. De Castries had been killed by San Francisco's paramentals not long after my tutelage under him had ended. I had used what I had learned to bind my life force to the city. It had kept me alive and young for a long time, but if I left the city, I would die. Well, I get nose bleeds if I go to the suburbs, but who wants to go to the suburbs?

The only major problem was the paramentals. These were the supernatural entities that lived in cities. They were the spirits of the buildings, streets, and lamp posts. De Castries had little protection and control over them. I had developed better ways, but over the years, my protection tended to erode. That was the reason I had to perform this ritual every so often. It seemed, however, that my control was eroding faster...

As I guided my tourists down the street, lecturing on this and that, I was deciding which one I would use as a scapegoat for the paramentals. I could tell that they had already found me.

We prepared for the third ritual. The slated roofs quivered. Faces appeared in the walls. Whispers came from storm drains. I alone noticed this. It was not hard to choose the scapegoat. Ingersham had been the obnoxious choice from the beginning. I could spare one for the final ritual. I always made sure to have spares.

I had in my pocket a clipping of my hair wrapped in a paper with spells written on it. I had already chosen him as my sacrifice. When he came close enough to complain about something, I slipped the paper into his pocket.

"This is the most boring tour I have ever been on," he was saying. Bits and pieces from a nearby building started to shake loose. "This is worse than going to a museum. I thought we would be going clubbing, and maybe to a casino."

There was a crunching sound from a nearby building. Cracks ran up the walls like veins. Ingersham finally turned to look what was going around him as the building collapsed. As the debris fell on him, there was a brief moment his eyes went wide and he said, "Bugger."

Then the debris hit him. He was crushed into pulp. Only part of a hand stuck out from the rubble. Well, that was that.

The secret passages beneath the Opera house were as always damp. How Erik could live here, I did not know. The old woman from Arkham had a hard time with it. She started having coughing fits. That did not bother me. As long as they lived until the end of the tour, I was fine.

I showed them the room that Erik had used to simulate the Punjabi desert. It had been a horrendous torture device that, for decades, had lay in ruins. Nowadays, it hads been fixed up and they sold tickets to it.

I then led them to the crypt where Erik lived. This has always been off limits. I imagine it is partly out of shame, and partly because someone with immense power made sure to keep it off limits. I told everyone this.

"Some say Erik himself is still alive! That is, of course, ridiculous. There was an imitator back in the sixties who came in conflict with Arsène Lupin's grandson, but Erik has been dead for decades."

I took them into the Phantom's lair. Erik had surprising good taste in furniture and paintings. Of course, he was French.

Arkham burst out in a particularly bad coughing fit. As I said, I did not care, but I could not continue my lectures like this. I told her to go outside. We performed the ritual without her.

After a while, she came back in and said, "There's someone outside who wants to see you."

It was then that I remembered I had forgotten to bribe the security guards. This was a big mistake. One can get away with not paying one's debts, but one must always pay one's bribes. It's what society is built on!

I went out into the dark. The security guard was standing at the edge of the lake. There was a boat drawn ashore. Like so much of the Hidden Places, the lake had become warped in time and space. Even I did not know where it led. I pulled out my wallet and walked up to him.

"Sorry about this. I put in a bit extra to make up for it."

Then I saw the guard's face. It was bone-white and noseless as a skull. The eyes glowed yellow.

"Oh, Erik. I did not know you would be returning so soon," I said.

"Did I not tell you that my sanctum was not to be disturbed?"

"Well, you were away. So I was sure you would not mind."

"That's when I mind the most! Are you the one who made it into a tourist attraction so that any Tom, Dick, and Harry could just walk right in?"

"No, no! That was the management of the Opera."

"Oh, I see. I will have a word with them. There is something in my boat I want you to see."

"Sure," I said, glad to be turning away from that ghastly face. I don't blame his mother for abandoning him. I would too. The worst of it was that there probably was some kind of plastic surgery that could now fix him, but no, he wanted to continue being a freak and outcast.

I walked to the boat and looked inside. It was the corpse of the night guard. He had been stripped of his clothes. His neck had been broken.

I put my right hand up just in time. The Punjab lasso had already fallen over my head. Without my hand in the way, it would have broken my neck, or at least strangled me. Instead, it crushed my hand to my Adam's apple giving me enough slack to breathe. Barely.

"I told you not to bring anyone here," said Erik. "This is my place."

I tried to call upon my powers to save me, but it did not work. This was Erik's dominion, as much as Paris was mine. According to the laws of magic, my powers were weaker here. Also, I was too busy being strangled to death to concentrate.

I managed to get the fingers of my left hand between the rope and my neck. With some slack, I might have been able to get it off my head. The problem was, the way the Punjab lasso was designed, the more you pulled the loop, the tighter it got. It dug into the back of my neck.

"Hey, let him go!" came a voice with a Texas drawl. It was the man from Mud Creek.

"Why should I?" replied Erik.

"I paid too much money to fly here from Texas to have my vacation ruined by some skull-faced hoodlum. This is my wife and mine's twentieth anniversary and I will not have you upset her. You let 'im go or I'll kick yer ass."

"Do you think you can defeat me? I was the Shah-in-Shah's personal assassin. I have trained in most of the arts of death. All of Paris trembled at my..."

Mud Creek kicked him in the groin and the Phantom let out a cry. Erik fell into the fetal position, his face even more wretched than normal.

I finally got the rope off my neck. Mud Creek helped me up. My neck and right wrist really stung. Mud Creek's wife came running over.

"See, I told you those Shen Chuan lessons would come in handy," he told her.

"Honey, you just kicked him in the groin. Anyone could do that,' she replied.

After I was done panting, I turned and saw that Erik had disappeared. I looked at the lake. The Phantom was on the boat. He looked like Charon on the River Styx, going back to whatever was on the other side.

Then we came to the Rue d'Auseil. It went up at such an angle that our coach could not climb it. We stopped by a foul-smelling pond and got out. Even in the day time, it was dark; at night, it was lit by archaic oil-burning street lamps. I mentioned the Hidden Places before. These were parts of the world that have been separated from the normal world by powers unknown, even to me. There was St. Beregonne's Lane in Hamburg, the cities of Selene and Xebico, entire lands like Lilliput, or the parts of the Sargasso that Hodgson wrote about.

They were separate, yet within the world. They should not be confused with journeys to other worlds like those of Randolph Carter or the crew of the *Mainz Psalter*.

They seem to be quarantined from the real world because they are dangerous. Whatever great powers did this, however, did not do a very good job at the Rue d'Auseil. Occasionally, like the poor musician Erich Zann, a person will sometimes find their way in. Someone like me can even find and use them.

So we marched up the street. I did not speak. There was no point. The old woman from Arkham huffed and puffed. The man from Mud Creek had to help his wife. The young man from Derry was fine.

Silently, I prepared the magicks necessary to sacrifice them. I was connected to the city. In fact, I helped make it what it is. I convinced Eiffel to create his tower to trap the spirits of the dead to use as my battery. The day will come when Paris will consume the world. Then I will be a god.

We reached the top. There used to be a boarding house there. It had a window that opened to the outer darkness. It was not there now. Zann's music had kept the gate closed. Now there was a gaping hole in the sky. It led into the realm of Azathoth.

I raised my arms and cried out words in the old tongue of R'yleh. The spell was ancient. It was a compact in which I sacrificed a few magic users to Azathoth in exchange for more power. As I shouted, tendrils stretched forth from the hole in the sky. They twisted around my victims lifting them up into the outer dark.

"I don't think so," said the man from Mud Creek. He shouted something in a language that I did know, making gestures with his hand. The tendrils retreated.

"In the name of Dagon and Cthulhu who dwells beneath the sea," said the woman from Arkham. Derry danced around, singing of the Black Goat of the Wood with a Thousand Young.

The tendrils disappeared in to the hole in the sky. There was a roar and the night sky seemed to shake. The hole itself closed up. Then it was quiet.

"Well, now that everything has settled down," said the Man from Mud Creek. "I believe I owe you an explanation. Now, we don't have a problem of blood sacrifice to the Outer Gods, though I don't particularly care to be sacrificed myself. The thing is, we know what you are up to. You grow stronger as Paris grows. If you have your way, it will grow until it consumes the world. Now, Paris is a nice city, and we appreciate you taking the time to show us around, but we like living in small towns. Emphasis on small. We can't have Paris covering the whole world, so we had to put an end to this."

"You've made a mistake," I said. "In Paris, I'm next to invincible. The city empowers me. You can't defeat me here."

"Then take a step toward me," said Mud Creek.

"What?"

"Take a step toward me," he said.

I did so. Or rather, I tried. My feet wouldn't move. It was like my feet were stuck to the tar. I looked down. My feet were *inside* the tar. I was sinking into the street as if it was quicksand. I struggled to pull myself out but I kept sinking.

Mud Creek walked up to me, "Well, you know that principle in judo about when fighting a stronger opponent, you use his strength against him? That's kind of what we did to you. We made your magical bonds to the city stronger."

I was down to my waist already. Mud Creek turned, put his arm around his wife, and walked down the street. The rest of the group followed after.

"You can't leave me like this," I shouted.

They paid no heed. I was down to my neck. I kept sinking. My chin met the tar. It rose up over my eyes.

Now, I dwell within the street.

No, I am the street.

There is nothing but dark.

In this story, Rick Lai continues to explore the myth of Fantômas, in particular the supernatural consequences of the Master Criminal adopting the alias of the Pallid Mask in his early career...

Rick Lai: *Phantom Masquerade*

Paris and London, 1888-92

It was Mardi-Gras in Paris. That evening in 1888, the streets were thronged with costumed celebrants. One man wore a white mask and a dark robe emblazoned with a curiously shaped yellow symbol.

"Who are you supposed to be?" asked a masked woman in Hellenic garments.

"A character from an obscure play. I am the Phantom of Truth. Are you a Greek goddess?"

"Actually, I'm a Trojan Princess. Call me Cassandra."

"If you really are Cassandra, you can foresee the future."

"I live in the Rue de Rennes. If you come into my home, I'll tell your fortune."

The Phantom did as she requested. Cassandra locked the door once they were inside. The living room of the house was lavishly furnished.

"Your mask is unnecessary, O Phantom. I see your past. You are Severn the artist."

Severn removed his mask. "Tell me my future."

"You have none. The Repairer of Reputations shall explain."

A grey-haired man suddenly entered the room. He wore a crimson robe bearing the same yellow symbol depicted on the Phantom's costume.

"You have blasphemed, Baptiste Severn," decreed the newcomer. "Only the Lord of Carcosa decides who wears the Phantom's raiment. The King in Yellow is not mocked."

The Repairer gestured with his hands. The luxuriant living room was transformed into a bleak stone chamber. Cassandra had vanished. Only the Repairer and Severn remained.

"Where are we?" demanded Severn.

"In a tower of Carcosa," answered the Repairer.

"What is that noise?"

"The flapping wings of the King in Yellow."

The owner of the wings entered the room through a window. Severn opened his mouth to scream, but his cry was stifled when a clawed hand ripped open his throat.

In London, Thomas Fane departed the Society for Psychical Research after midnight. As he prepared to hail a cab, he was seized and hustled into an alley.

"Have you found the Yellow Sign?" whispered the worm-faced intruder clutching Fane.

The occult scholar unsheathed his sword cane. The blade was swiftly thrust into the side of his attacker. The worm-faced man disintegrated rapidly into dust. Fane scrutinized his sword. Once again, the runes inscribed on the cold steel had saved him.

He quickly returned to his room at the Northumberland Hotel in London. There he found a telegram awaiting him. It was signed *Antonio*.

Grimoire located in Paris. Douanier can provide details.

The next day, Fane vacated his hotel and departed for France. The time for a reckoning with his persecutor had finally come.

"It is always a pleasure to meet an associate of Mte de Grandin, Mo n-sieur Fane."

As the occult scholar took a seat in the office inside the Sûreté headquarters, Chief Inspector Cardec scrutinized his visitor. He was a muscular man about twenty-one years-old. Fane had presented a letter of introduction from a retired prosecutor with a strong interest in the occult. The lawyer had met Fane the previous month while performing as a guest lecturer at the Society for Psychical Research in London.

"Remember a man named Jean Grimoire, Chief Inspector?"

"Alias the Repairer of Reputations. In 1878, I had the pleasure of arresting him for distributing pornography. His escape from a jail cell prevented his trial from proceeding."

"The pornographic work peddled by Grimoire was *Le Roi en Jaune*. Did you ever read it?"

"I would be a fool to read that cursed play. The Sûreté's files are filled with accounts of individuals destroyed by it. Some committed suicide. Others were confined to asylums. There are cases where readers have been afflicted with an inexplicable blindness. Worse yet, the play has inspired individuals to commit brutal murders. An admirer of the drama has even become a professional assassin known as the Pallid Mask."

"After the disguise worn by the Phantom of Truth in the play."

"I was under the impression that the Pallid Mask was worn by the King of Carcosa."

"No, Chief Inspector, it is only used by the Phantom to hide his true nature."

"Your statement suggests an intimate knowledge of the play."

"I read it four years ago."

"You must have been about seventeen at the time."

"I was a young hedonist sowing my wild oats in Paris. The play was a gift from a woman I desired. She purchased it from Grimoire."

"Did you read the text?"

"All of it."

"And you suffered no ill effects?"

"Grimoire traced me to London. He dispatched the Heralds of the Yellow Sign against me. Are you familiar with them?"

"They are merely hallucinations. Readers of the play imagine themselves to be pursued by walking cadavers with worm-like faces."

They are no illusion. The Heralds seek to coerce me to mortgage my soul to the King in Yellow."

"I can't assist you. Seek help from the Catholic Church. It deals with exorcisms. The Sûreté only has expertise in arrests."

"Your expertise can end my persecution. If you apprehend Grimoire, his incarceration would separate him from the mystical instruments needed to summon the Heralds."

"The Sûreté has no information about Grimoire's current activities."

"But I do! Grimoire is residing at 50 Rue de Rennes under the name of Johann Grimm."

"How did you come by such information?"

"From Marc Douanier."

"The printer who published *Le Roi en Jaune.* I arrested him the same time as Grimoire. He was sentenced to nine years."

"He's now free. Grimoire tried to persuade Douanier to resume their partnership. Instead, Douanier found it more profitable to sell his former accomplice's whereabouts to me."

"Thank you. Monsieur Fane, I shall pay a visit to the Rue de Rennes with a squad of gendarmes."

Although a decade had passed, the Repairer of Reputations displayed no signs of having aged since Cardec had last seen him. His appearance was exactly the same as it had been in 1878. He looked no older than fifty.

Jean Grimoire, you are under arrest!" announced Cardec.

"You are making a mistake," insisted Grimoire. "If we could meet in private, I shall explain."

"You shall have your private interview, but it shall be from inside the confines of a prison cell. Restrain him!"

Cardec's subordinates seized the Repairer of Reputations.

True to his word, Cardec visited Grimoire in his new cell.

"Is this ball and chain necessary, Chief Inspector?"

"You have only yourself to blame, Grimoire. You inexplicably escaped your prior confinement."

"Much has changed. My earlier apprehension was in compliance with the pornography laws of 1878. They were superseded in 1881 by the Law for the Freedom of the Press. That piece of legislation made it impossible to classify anything as pornography. You can no longer prosecute me for peddling *Le Roi en Jaune.*"

"There is still the matter of your unlawful flight from police custody."

"Even if you secured a conviction, how long would my sentence be? A year at most. I think it would suit our combined interests to reach an accommodation."

"What are you proposing?"

"My superior has a simple goal. He has a quota of individuals that must read the play every year. You desire to protect the law-abiding public from the play's effects. We can achieve both our ends. Arrange for *Le Roi en Jaune* to be given to condemned men awaiting execution. Any ill-effects they experience from reading the play will quickly be nullified by the guillotine."

"You must be mad!" protested Fane in Cardec's office. "How could you agree to such a Faustian bargain?"

"The Police Commissioner himself approved the deal," replied Cardec. "He felt that it was in the public interest."

"Public interest be damned! You and your Commissioner are unaware of the ancient lore. If a man is beheaded after reading the gospel of the King in Yellow, his soul is condemned to drown forever in the Lake of Hali."

"Such a grisly fate would only befall convicted murderers. I always believed they were slated for the fires of Hell. The substitution of the waters of Hali does not trouble my conscience."

Fane pointed to a photo framed on Cardec's wall. "Isn't that a picture of Joseph Clampin, the former head of the Sûreté?"

"It is. He devoted his life to destroying a criminal syndicate called the Black Coats during the reign of Napoleon III."

"Didn't the Black Coats believe in a doctrine called *pay the law*?"

"Yes, they arranged for their crimes to be attributed to innocent scapegoats."

"How can you be sure no condemned prisoner has been made to *pay the law*?"

"With the advent of the Third Republic, such miscarriages of justice have long ceased."

"For the sake of your soul, Chief Inspector, pray that you are correct. Since you refuse to help me against the Repairer of Reputations, I must pursue a different strategy."

"Do not take the law into your own hands, Monsieur. The Sûreté disapproves of vigilante justice."

"I plan nothing so elaborate. I merely intend to leave Europe and live under an assumed name in one of Her Majesty's colonies."

Four years later, Fane was back in Paris. It was now July 1892. The Paris newspapers were reporting the execution of Ravachol, the Anarchist bomber. There were calls in the French Assembly for new laws to prevent further Anarchist outrages.

Arriving at a house the Rue Austerlitz, Fane knocked on the door. It was opened by a rotund man with extremely round eyes.

"Professor Hern?"

"Yes."

"Antonio Nikola sent me a message that you wished to contract my services. My name is Thomas Fane."

"Please come in, Herr Fane."

Upon entering the abode, the Englishman noticed a young man with a pale complexion.

"I am Otto, the Professor's son. I function as my father's secretary."

Fane spied a device resting on a small table. "I see that you have a Remington typewriter."

"Using it is far more efficient than transcribing my father's correspondence in longhand."

"Are you familiar with my work?" asked the Professor.

"I've read *Verschwinden und Seine Theorie*," admitted Fane.

"Then you must be aware that the public outcry over that book led to my resignation from the University of Leipzig and my voluntary exile in France. Your familiarity with my work makes me curious about your activities as an adolescent."

Fane's eyes narrowed. "A rather cryptic remark. Please elaborate."

"In my book, I documented the regular sightings of two apparitions at End House in the English town of Appledorn. The current resident of End House, Captain Tobias, described the prior tenants, a widow with a son named Thomas. Tobias had forgotten their surname."

"Your suspicions are correct, Professor. My mother and I once resided at End House. Our former home was the first haunted house I investigated. However, my interest in your book extends beyond its allusion to my past. I found your theory that unexplained disappearances are caused by doorways into other dimensions quite fascinating."

"Further research has suggested that many of these gateways exist near lakes such as Lake Drummond in Virginia and Lough Derg in Ireland," revealed the Professor. "Are you familiar with Morryster's *Marvells of Science*?"

"A ridiculous book of wild speculations prevalent in the sixteenth century, but occasionally a glimmer of truth. Morryster characterized Lough Derg as a

Door to Hell. Another of Morryster's books, *Trauvells in ye Easte*, made identical claims about the Lake of Ghosts in China."

"Morryster attributed his assertions about demonic lakes to *The Fatality of Visitations* by Parapelius Necromantius."

"Translated from a Greek manuscript by Joseph de Quincey in 1680. All but three copies were burned in Massachusetts during the witchcraft trials of 1692. Morryster only heard of *The Fatalities of Visitations* from old records in Salem."

Professor Hern pulled a volume out of a bookcase. "Here is a surviving copy." He handed the tome to Fane. "I purchased it at a London auction months ago."

"It must have cost you a small fortune. Occult scholars like Antonio Nikola have long coveted this book."

"Dr. Nikola competed against me during the bidding on the book. That was how I met him. He graciously congratulated me when I won."

"That book nearly bankrupted us," interjected Otto. "If mother had been alive, she never would have permitted such an expense."

"Silence! Please forgive my son, Herr Fane. He forgets the size of the fortune that I inherited from my parents. Please turn to page 115 of de Quincey's translation."

Opening the text, Fane read the indicated page. "This is where Necromantius describes the Doors to... Hell."

"Hell? I detect a certain reticence on your part. You clearly see a different realm identified."

"Hali... the Lake of Hali."

"Adjacent to the metropolis of Carcosa, ruled by the King in Yellow."

"I have no desire to discuss such matters."

"Please indulge me, Herr Fane. After buying *The Fatality of Visitations*, I inquired at the Society for Psychical Research if anyone there was familiar with *Le Roi en Jaune*. Lionel Dacre mentioned your name. He had no idea where to find you, but he recalled your friendship with Antonio Nikola. In exchange for allowing him to verify the existence of a passage in *The Fatality of Visitations*, Dr. Nikola agreed to contact you."

"If you hope to have me reveal the play's damnable contents, you've chosen the wrong man."

"That is not my intent. I merely desire you to authenticate a copy offered for sale."

"Who is peddling that monstrosity? Is his name Douanier?"

"I know no such individual. Who is he?"

"A former publisher of the play. From whom are you buying *Le Roi en Jaune*?"

The seller is Sir George Burnwell."

"George!"

"You know him?"

"I met him in South Africa four years ago. He was a prosperous mining engineer with an impeccable reputation. Being my senior by more than a decade, George behaved like a mentor towards me. Inheriting a baronetcy upon his uncle's death, he moved to London and rapidly achieved notoriety as a gambler and libertine. George was acting like a totally different man. Your statements have confirmed a great fear of mine. I am responsible for his transformation."

"In what way?"

"On the eve of his departure for England, George visited my South African home. I had carelessly left *Le Roi en Jaune* lying on my desk. Before I could stop him, George perused it. The next evening, my home was burglarized. Only *Le Roi en Jaune* was taken. By reading the play, George's soul must have been corrupted. He stole my copy."

"You've read the play, but seem to have suffered no ill-effects."

"As a consequence of reading that infernal drama, I have endured a horrific persecution. I'm afraid, Professor, that you are dealing in stolen goods."

"Did you report the play's theft to the British colonial authorities?"

"No, I did not."

"Is there any way to identify your purloined copy?"

"I'm afraid not."

"Then I am well within my rights to deal with Sir George. Your accusations of thievery are mere supposition. Besides, he isn't selling me his own copy. He is arranging to have a new copy typed up from the manuscript in his possession."

"How did George learn about your interest in *Le Roi en Jaune*?"

"He has friends in the Society for Psychical Research."

"I assume George has a residence in Paris."

"He is renting a house in the Rue St. Claude."

"Perhaps I should pay him a visit."

"He isn't currently in Paris. After we agreed on a price, he had to return to South Africa to sell some of his property there. In his absence, I have been dealing with his charming young secretary, Fraulein Holder. She is typing the new copy of *Le Roi en Jaune*."

"I strongly advise against this transaction. That play only brings ruination."

"Listen to him, Father," pleaded Otto. "You've squandered enough of your money on volumes of arcane ramblings."

"Enough!" reprimanded the Professor. "I am convinced that occult lore is really a lost science. Possessing *La Roi en Jaune* shall provide the key to unlocking a fundamental truth of the universe. My disappearance theory shall finally be proved."

The Professor looked sternly at his guest. "Let us conclude our dealings, Herr Fane. I am willing to pay you a substantial fee to verify the authenticity of the manuscript that Sir George is offering to sell. Are you interested in my proposal?"

"I turned down Professor Hern's offer," stated Fane at the Sûreté headquarters.

"How was Hern able to contact you?" asked Chief Inspector Cardec.

"Since our last meeting, I've been living in South Africa under the name of Thomas Karnak. My real surname is a synonym for 'temple.' Karnak is the site of several ancient Egyptian temples."

"Such a name would raise the suspicions of anyone knowledgeable in mysticism. You take too many risks, Monsieur."

"Perhaps you are right. Only a few trusted friends in Europe know of my relocation to South Africa. One of them is a fellow student of the supernatural, Antonio Nikola."

"Maître de Grandin has spoken of this man. Nikola's researches into Asian cults have earned him an unsavory reputation."

"Quite true, Inspector, but Antonio is also a man of honor. He never breaks his word. Surely Maître de Grandin included that fact in his assessment?"

"Yes, he did."

"If not for Antonio, I would have fallen victim to Grimoire and his acolytes long ago. You must have noticed my cane."

"It is a sword cane."

"Very astute, Chief Inspector. Refitted from a Chinese sword given to me by Antonio, the blade bears the inscription of the Saaamaaa Ritual in the Yianese tongue. This sword has saved my life, if not my soul, more than once."

"Why did you come here? You cannot prove that Burnwell stole your copy of the play. There is nothing that the Sûreté could do to prevent this sale from being concluded."

"I was hoping that you would visit Hern and dissuade from purchasing the play. Years ago, you claimed that your files fully documented the consequences of reading *Le Roi en Jaune*. Share that information with Hern."

As Fane requested, Cardec paid a visit to Professor Hern. The academician arrogantly challenged the police official's assertions.

"How can you be so certain, Chief Inspector, that *Le Roi en Jaune* caused all those deaths? Did you ever read it?"

"No member of the Sûreté would permit himself to be contaminated by that accused drama. Any copies of *Le Roi en Jaune* found by us are quickly burnt."

"Then you and your colleagues are behaving like a bunch of superstitious savages."

"I fear this conversation has taken an ugly turn, Professor. There is no point in discussing this matter further."

Throughout the entire argument between his father and the police official, Otto Hern had listened in silence.

The next day, Mary Holder, Sir George Burnwell's secretary, was reporting on her progress inside the Hern residence.

"The transcription of *Le Roi en Jaune* is complete."

"Excellent," commented the Professor. "When will Sir George be returning from South Africa to finalize our bargain?"

"In about two weeks. As previously agreed, payment must be made upon delivery."

"The play will need first to be authenticated by an expert of my choosing."

"Authentication? You never mentioned this before."

"I shall be blunt, Fraulein. An acclaimed forger, John Clay, swindled an affluent scholar by selling him a fraudulent copy of the *Sigsand Manuscript*. I must be assured that a similar ruse isn't being perpetrated upon me."

"Who is going to perform the authentication?"

"A man named Douanier. He spent time in prison for publishing the play under the old pornography laws. I discovered his existence by pure accident."

"I feel thirsty, Professor. Could I pour myself some of your delectable Amontillado wine?"

"Of course."

"Would you or Otto like a glass as well?"

The Professor declined, but Otto was clearly delighted to have Mary pour his wine. The young man was clearly infatuated by the slender brunette.

"In the interest of time, Professor, Douanier could perform the authentication while we are awaiting Sir George's arrival," suggested Mary.

Upon Mary's departure, Professor Hern left the house to see Douanier.

At three o'clock in the morning, a slumbering Professor Hern was woken up. A gloved hand was shaking his shoulder. Opening his eyes, Hern beheld a dark-haired man with a mustache. It was a face well known to the Professor.

"Burnwell! What are you doing here?"

"Sir George Burnwell is but a mask. Now I shall wear another more appropriate."

Burnwell placed upon his head a white hood-like mask. With high cheekbones and thin lips, the countenance radiated an aura of cruelty.

"I shall be your guide to Carcosa. Behold the Pallid Mask!"

A cord tightened around the Professor's throat.

Registered at the Royal Palace Hotel under his Karnak alias, Fane received a visit from Emile Le Brun, one of Cardec's subordinates. Refusing to offer any explanation, Le Brun insisted that the Englishman accompany him to the Sûreté headquarters. Escorted by the young detective, Fane was ushered into Cardec's presence.

"Professor Hern died violently during the night," explained the Chief Inspector. "His son contacted the Sûreté in the morning after finding his father's body in the morning. Hern took his own life. A noose was tied around the chandelier in the dining room. Hern placed the rope around his neck. On the dining room table was this."

Cardec handed Fane a yellow folder. Inside were about forty pages. The first page bore the title *Le Roi en Jaune*.

"Burnwell concluded the sale."

"Not according to Otto Hern, Monsieur Fane. He says that Burnwell is still in South Africa. He was scheduled to return in two weeks to finalize the sale."

"Then how does Otto explain his father's possession of this?"

"He can't. However, Otto divulged that his father intended for Marc Douanier to verify the legitimacy of the text. Professor Hern left the house yesterday afternoon to see Douanier."

"You believe that Douanier provided this copy of *Le Roi en Jaune*?"

"From your own dealing with Douanier, Monsieur Fane, you know him to be thoroughly unscrupulous. He could have hidden away an old copy of the play from his days as Grimoire's printer. Hern could have seen an opportunity to undercut Burnwell's steep price by buying a cheaper copy."

"Assuming that the Professor made such an arrangement, why didn't he tell his son?"

"As you previously informed me, Otto objected to his father's book collecting. The Professor may simply have wished to avoid another argument that evening."

"This is all my fault. I inadvertently mentioned Douanier's name to Professor Hern. It's impossible to arrest Douanier. The Law for the Freedom of the Press protects him."

"There is a legal loophole. That law contains a vague passage about publications threatening public morals. Prosecutors have been reluctant to invoke it because the newspapers would protest against government censorship. Fortunately, times have changed. The recent Anarchist outrages have prompted cries for the regulation of literature promoting violence. I am authorized to invoke the loophole, but I aim higher than Douanier."

"You can't mean Grimoire?"

"Why not? Our 1888 agreement was a necessary evil. The charges concerning his 1878 arrest and escape were never formally revoked. If you help me provide the proper groundwork, the Sûreté would proceed against Grimoire based on his prior offenses."

"What do you want me to do?"

"Neither I nor any of my men have read this damnable document. I need you to testify in open court as an expert on *La Roi en Jaune*. You must authenticate the copy in your hands."

Fane began to read the pages. "This is a blatant forgery!"

"Are you sure?"

"Unquestionably. Instead of Carcosa, this play is set in the French city of Carcassonne during its occupation by the Moors. In fact, this document is actually plagiarized from a children's book."

"What is the name of this book?"

"*Cassilda or The Moorish Princess of Toledo.* The forger has changed the setting of the story from the Spanish city to Carcassonne."

"Isn't Cassilda a character in *Le Roi en Jaune*?"

"Yes, Chief Inspector, but the name also belongs to a Catholic saint, a Muslim princess who converted to Christianity. In the children's book, Cassilda is the daughter of Aldemon, the ruler of Toledo. The play ludicrously portrayed Aldemon as a tyrant who fed Christians to lions in the tradition of Emperor Nero. The forgery transplanted Aldemon from Toledo to Carcassonne, and bestowed the title of the King in Yellow upon him."

"Who wrote *Cassilda*?"

"I'm not sure. I stumbled across this oddity of juvenilia while researching possible literary origins for *Le Roi en Jaune*. *Cassilda* was published in America sometime during the 1870s. Written in English by a woman, it supposedly was a translation of an earlier French work."

"Le Brun, visit the Bibliothèque Nationale," ordered Cardec. "See if the archivists there can provide information about this children's book."

"Sir George shall be greatly disappointed by Professor Hern's death. The sale of *Le Roi en Jaune* would have provided much needed windfall."

Mary Holder made that admission to Cardec when he interviewed her at Burnwell's house in the Rue St. Claude.

"What exactly is Sir George doing in South Africa?"

"He is trying to sell an old diamond mine in Kimberley."

The police official held up the typed copy of *Le Roi en Jaune* that Mary had made.

"What brand of typewriter did you use to transcribe this?"

"A Hammond, Chief Inspector. It's upstairs. Do you want to see it?"

"Mademoiselle Holder, I shall do more than view your machine. I am temporarily confiscating it along with both your copies of *Le Roi en Jaune*. Certain forensic tests must be performed at the Sûreté headquarters."

"Tests? I don't understand."

"Have no fear, Mademoiselle. If you are innocent of any complicity in Hern's death, the tests will confirm it."

"You frighten me, Chief Inspector. You talk as if this is case of murder, not suicide."

"Perhaps it is. I have one final question. Where were you last night?"

"I dined with Boris Yvain, the noted sculptor, in his home. Regrettably, I drank too much wine. I spent the night in one of Yvain's guest rooms. I didn't return to the Rue St. Claude until this morning."

In Cardec's office, Fane verified the authenticity of the two copies retrieved from Mary Holder.

"They're both genuine, Chief Inspector."

"Is the older manuscript the play stolen from you in South Africa?"

"I'm absolutely convinced that it is, but I can't prove it."

"Then I have no choice but to eventually return your former property to Mademoiselle Holder."

"What happened to the title page of the copy typed by her?"

"It's being examined by probably the most brilliant member of the Sûreté, Alphonse Bertillon."

Emile Le Brun then returned from his inquiries at the Bibliothèque Nationale. Reading from a small notebook, the sleuth reported his findings.

"*Cassilda; or the Moorish Princess of Toledo* was published in New York by the Catholic Home Library during 1875. The translator's name was Madame Mary C. Monroe. Her text was derived from an 1872 French work, *Cassilda ou La princesse maure de Tolède: d'après une légende espagnole imitée de l'allemand,* by a priest only identified by the initials G. A. L. This French cleric actually adapted his story from an 1851 German novel by Ottmar Lautenschlager, *Cassilda, die Mohrenfürstin von Toledo.*"

Another member of the Sûreté interrupted the meeting.

"What is it, Juve?" queried Cardec.

"I have Bertillon's results." The newcomer handed a paper to Cardec. The Chief Inspector smiled as he divulged the conclusions of the forensic tests.

"Each brand of typewriter has its own unique characteristics regarding spacing, ink and so forth. The copy made by Mary Holder was typed on a Hammond. The forged copy found near Professor Hern's corpse was typed on a Remington. Gentlemen, let us review the facts.

"Hern was strangled by an assailant. The killer then made his death look like a suicide. Aware of the Sûreté's aversion to *Le Roi en Jaune,* the murderer left a forged copy near the corpse in the hope that none of us would read it. We were expected to burn it. Our alliance with Monsieur Fane has prevented the success of this ingenious scheme. The forgery was plagiarized from a work originating in Germany. The killer also originated from there. Furthermore, he owns a Remington typewriter. The murderer must be Otto Hern. His motive was to inherit his father's fortune before it was depleted by the purchase of rare books."

"I am innocent, Monsieur Fane," proclaimed Otto Hern vehemently inside his prison cell.

The occult scholar had asked Cardec's permission to question Otto privately. Due to Fane's assistance in the case, the request had been granted.

"Your father must have struggled with his killer. Yet you supposedly slept soundly while the murder was occurring."

"Feeling extremely tired after Fraulein Holder left, I went straight to bed. She must have put something in the glass of Amontillado she handed me. Holder must have drugged me."

Gazing into Otto's eyes, there was no doubt in Fane's mind that the pitiful prisoner was completely innocent.

Fane reported the results of his interview to Cardec. The Chief Inspector's response was to laugh.

"Drugged by Mademoiselle Holder? What a farcical story!"

"I believe him."

"Must I remind you that Holder's whereabouts at the time of the murder have been verified. Boris Yvain confirmed her alibi."

"You really believe her story of having too much to drink?"

"Of course not! She spent the night making passionate love to Yvain."

"She still could have drugged Otto. An accomplice could have murdered Professor Hern "

"Can you name this phantom accomplice?"

"Sir George Burnwell. His supposed presence in South Africa is an elaborate pretense."

"What motive could Burnwell have? The Sûreté made inquiries in London. He's on the verge of bankruptcy. He needed the sale of Le *Roi en Jaune* to transpire."

"When Professor Hern allowed me to peruse *The Fatality of Visitations,* I noticed a passage which might explain Burnwell's actions."

"I had that book confiscated as evidence. I shall have Le Brun retrieve it."

Once the book was delivered into Fane's hands, the occult scholar found the passage and read it aloud:

"*If a man reads the Yellow Gospel before being beheaded in the Festival of Death, then his soul is forfeit to the Lake of Hali. The tyrant of Carcosa desires the ravenous waters to be fed continually. A soul of innocence is valued more by the despot than a soul tainted with sin. If an acolyte provides such a morsel of purity as a Red Offering, the Disposer of Souls will grant favors on that mortal for thirteen years. Such a reward is granted in the Ritual of the Thirteenth Covenant, a ceremony that can only be performed by the King in Yellow himself or his earthly surrogate, the Repairer of Reputations. The favors bestowed by the*

Ritual can even be applied retroactively to prior years in order to pardon of-fenses against the King."

"That quote is meaningless gibberish," argued Cardec.

"No, Chief Inspector, it is a revelation. The Festival of Death is the cele-bration of the demise of a human being. In other words, it is a public execution. That is why Grimoire made that obscene agreement with you four years ago. As I then predicted, the blade of the guillotine is sacrificing condemned men to the King in Yellow. Somehow, Burnwell must have contacted Grimoire and learned of his truce with the Sûreté. He intends to use Otto's death to implement the Thirteenth Covenant. If Otto is condemned to death, you must not let Grimoire show him *Le Roi en Jaune.*"

"Monsieur Fane, my hands are tied by the accord reached with Grimoire. I am not disturbed by the consequences of a conviction. If anyone on this planet deserves to be damned for eternity, it is Otto Hern. I believe firmly in his guilt. He nearly made Marc Douanier a scapegoat. Hern is the worse sort of criminal. He hoped to use confidential information supplied by the Sûreté to make another man *pay the law.* How he must have secretly chuckled as he misdirected me with half-truths. It is poetic justice that Hern reads *Le Roi en Jaune.*"

"When you have me testify at the trial, Chief Inspector, be aware that I will shout my certainty of Otto's innocence to the high heavens."

"I have no intention of having you testify."

"Then who will prove the fraudulent nature of the play found near Profes-sor Hern's body?"

"Mary Holder and Marc Douanier."

"What about the history of the book *Cassilda*?"

"Any librarian of the Bibliothèque Nationale can easily testify on that mat-ter."

"I can still testify for the defense."

"If you do so, the prosecution will discredit you as a reclusive crackpot who has been living under an assumed name for the last four years."

Fane looked firmly into Cardec's eyes. "Promise me at least one thing. When Sir George Burnwell finally reappears in Paris, you will interrogate him vigorously about his alleged business trip to South Africa."

"I shall do so. I owe you at least that much."

About a half hour after Fane departed, Mary Holder requested to see Cardec.

"I just received horrible news," she announced upon entering the Chief In-spector's office. Mary handed the police official a telegram from South Africa.

Sir George killed in mining accident. Hendrika

"Who is Hendrika?" asked Cardec.

"Sir George's wife. He married her two months ago in South Africa."

When she had first met George Burnwell, Hendrika Pienaar had been a maid in the household of Colonel Beltham, a British officer stationed in South Africa. Romanced by Burnwell, she had become his wife. When her husband had revealed his activities as the international assassin feared as the Pallid Mask, she had promised to assist in his crimes.

It had been easy to find a tramp with the same physique as her husband. Convincing the tramp to don a set of her husband's clothes, she had bashed in his head with a shovel. Transporting the tramp's body to her husband's defunct diamond mine, she had lit an explosive. When the bomb had ignited, the shaft containing the corpse had collapsed. The police later concluded that George Burnwell had been fatally crushed in a futile attempt to open a new vein in the mine. Her husband was now free to adopt a new identity, and she would collect on a hefty life insurance policy.

An inscribed headstone had already been ordered for her "departed" husband:

GEORGE BURNWELL
(1855-1892)
The Truth Shall Set You Free

The trial of Otto Hern reached its inevitable conclusion. The defendant was sentenced to death. Awaiting his rendezvous with the executioner, Otto was surprised when a guard ushered in a visitor.

"My name is Jean Grimoire. I have a gift for you." The Repairer of Reputations handed the prisoner a manuscript.

"*Le Roi en Jaune!* What am I expected to do with this?"

"That's entirely up to you. Under the terms of an agreement reached with Chief Inspector Cardec, you are to be left alone with the play for three hours. At the conclusion of that time, the guard will take the manuscript away to be burnt. Farewell."

After Grimoire departed, the guard locked the door. Otto stared at the title. Fane and Cardec had warned of the consequences of reading the play. Yet his late father suspected that this text held the key to the secrets of the universe. He had become a pawn in a meaningless series of events. Perhaps this drama would tell him the reason why. His hand turned the title page. His eyes focused on the start of the first act.

When the guard came to confiscate *Le Roi en Jaune,* Otto was reading it for the sixth time. He felt like a God. Other mortals were mere insects. He could crush them just as the Tattered King had smitten the people of Hastur.

Otto had reached the height of ecstasy when he closed his eyes. When the nightmares commenced, he plunged into the depths of despair. In his dreams, the Phantom of Truth appeared and revealed the visage beneath the Pallid Mask.

Are you satisfied with my employer's Red Offering?" asked Marc Douanier inside the confines of 50 Rue de Rennes.

"Very satisfied," remarked Jean Grimoire. "Tell Sir George that his petition shall be accepted once Otto Hern is beheaded. Have your employer call on me after the execution. It will be pleasure to finally meet him."

"Sir George has an additional gift for you. There will be a man named Thomas Karnak attending the execution. You will recognize him as Thomas Fane."

The Repairer of Reputations was quite pleased. The outcry against the Anarchist bombings would soon lead to new censorship laws, and he would be forced to leave Paris. The sacrifice of a pure soul would be a fitting culmination to his temporary detente with the French authorities. An extra bonus would be the final extermination of the troublesome Fane.

Following Douanier's departure, Grimoire consulted a massive ledger whose cover bore the image of a peacock wearing a crown. Inside were detailed entries for countless individuals. On a page entitled "Fane, Thomas," Grimoire added these words: "Alias Karnak (Carnacki?)."

The man stood in Mary Holder's bedroom. Except for the white mask totally encasing his head, he was completely naked.

"My Phantom... my Master..." murmured the nude Mary Holder reclining on her bed. "Why do you wear the Pallid Mask?"

"I wear the Pallid Mask only when I decide whether to love or slay."

"What shall it be tonight?"

"I love."

His hands removed the Pallid Mask in order for his lips to touch her flesh. Mary's eyes beheld the face of Sir George Burnwell.

Two hours later, Burnwell was putting on his clothes. Mary remained on her bed.

"I'm not very happy with you, Mary. While you cleverly seduce Yvain to provide yourself with an alibi, you foolishly sold him another typed copy of *Le Roi en Jaune*. You made a substantial profit! Yvain paid the same price that Hern was willing to pay."

"But the copy you sold Yvain was typed on your hidden Remington typewriter! If the police learned of Yvain's copy, they would have had Bertillon examine it!"

"I made that extra copy while I was testing the Remington before making the plagiarized *Cassilda* version."

"An unnecessary risk!"

"You take risks too! You're attending Otto Hern's execution tomorrow. Someone might recognize you."

"No one will recognize me. I'll be clean shaven."

"I'll miss your mustache."

"I knew you would. That's why I didn't remove it tonight."

"Do you want me to attend the execution as well?"

"No, you will leave for London in the morning. A room has been reserved for you at the Northumberland Hotel. A woman named Orianne Coyatier will contact you with further instructions."

"Who is this Orianne? Another of your romantic conquests?"

"Merely a harmless flirtation like your fling with Yvain. She means nothing to me."

"You said the same about Hendrika. Yet you married her."

"Merely a ploy to gain her cooperation in faking my death. I have no intention of seeing her ever again."

"Why must you be present at the execution?"

"To remove a threat that has been dogging my heels."

"What is this threat?"

"A man from my past. He was the original owner of my printed edition of *Le Roi en Jaune*. Remember that object I told you to keep safe?"

"You mean the box you told me never to open?"

"Yes. Give it to me."

Reaching under her mattress, Mary pulled out a little box and handed it to her lover.

"What's inside?" she asked.

"The Yellow Sign."

It was an hour before Otto Hern's execution. In the halls of the prison overlooking the courtyard where the guillotine was erected, the footsteps of Chief Inspector Cardec and Thomas Fane echoed.

"I don't understand your presence at the execution, Monsieur Fane. Under the terms of the 1888 agreement, Grimoire is allowed to be there. He's sure to recognize you."

"I'll be disappointed if he doesn't. I may not have been able to save Otto Hern's life, but I might save his soul. There is a loophole in that passage from Necromantius. If my guess is correct, Grimoire shall insist upon my accompanying him to his house. I shall do so voluntarily. Promise me that you shall not interfere."

"I shall comply with your wishes."

"I may not survive this day, Chief Inspector. While we had our differences, you behaved like a man of honor throughout this entire affair."

Thomas Fane extended his hand. Cardec shook it.

At the appointed time, Otto Hern was led up the wooden steps of the execution platform by prison guards. "I've seen the face beneath the Pallid Mask!" he shouted just before the guillotine blade descended.

When Hern's head rolled into the basket, Fane was standing next to Cardec. Jean Grimoire approached them.

"Chief Inspector, I wasn't aware that you were acquainted with my old friend Thomas."

"Forgive me, gentlemen," said Cardec, "I have official duties requiring my presence."

As the police official departed, Fane's eyes met Grimoire's. "The time has come to settle accounts, Repairer. Do you have a carriage?"

"Yes."

"I suggest we ride to your house and conclude matters there."

"Agreed."

As Grimoire and Fane left the prison courtyard, another man followed them. The same individual hired another carriage to trail theirs.

"I remember you as a brazen youth," remarked Grimoire inside the vehicle "At our first meeting, your paramour bought one of my copies of Le *Roi en Jaune.* Whatever happened to that charming woman?"

Fane's grip tightened on his sword cane. "She died."

"Ah, I remember hearing vague rumor concerning her demise. She perished by drowning. Such a fate occasionally awaits those who read of Hali. Within the next hour, you'll be joining her among the ranks of the deceased."

The carriage arrived at its final destination. Just as Grimoire and Fane were preparing to enter the house, the other conveyance arrived. The passenger alighted and ran towards Grimoire.

"What are you doing here?" asked a stunned Repairer of Reputations.

"I have to perform an act of authentication," replied Marc Douanier. The ex-convict then whispered into Grimoire's ear. "Thomas Fane and Sir George Burnwell are one and the same."

"Thank you, Monsieur Douanier," interjected Fane. "You may go now. Perplexed, Monsieur Grimoire? Allow me to share the comforts of your home, and I shall enlighten you."

Inside the sumptuous living room, Fane sat comfortably on a coach.

"You didn't know my real name when we first met in 1884, Repairer, and I suspect you still don't. Suffice to say, shortly after reading the play, I was approached by a prominent criminal fraternity to be trained as an assassin. Do you know of whom I speak?"

"You're referring to Dr. Nikola and his associates. They are the current incarnation of the Black Coats."

"Let me commend you on your sources of information, Repairer. After three years of training, I began my career as a professional killer. I needed an alias that strikes fear into the heart of my enemies. I chose a name from a drama that had granted me an unforgettable sense of mastery and power. Of course, I'm referring to *Le Roi en Jaune.* My choice of the Pallid Mask seems to have offended your religious sensibilities."

"You blaspheme. Only the King in Yellow designates wearers of the Pallid Mask and the other vestments associated with the Phantom of Truth."

"In the course of my employment by Nikola and his colleagues, I established many false identities. In 1888, you were able to identify one of these aliases."

"You made the mistake of adopting the name of Thomas Fane in occult circles. 'Fane, Thomas' was obviously derived from the word 'Phantom.' You were clearly invoking the Phantom of Truth."

"My Fane identity has a complex pedigree. Professor Hern's book briefly alluded to an investigation of a haunted house by a bright young lad named Thomas. Performing my own inquiry, I learned that Thomas had the surname of Carnacki, which reminded me of the temples and fanes at Karnak. Modeled on Carnacki, the fraudulent Thomas Fane was born. As Fane, I sometimes took credit for Carnacki's own accomplishments."

"Word has reached me of Carnacki's exploits as a ghost hunter," said Grimoire. "I falsely suspected you of being the real Carnacki when Douanier cited your alternate surname of Karnak."

Reaching into his pocket, Fane pulled out the small box.

"To the London address maintained by my Fane identity, you sent me the Yellow Sign. Nikola was able to identify this symbol and its significance. He gave me this sword cane to protect me from the monstrous visitants that always follow the dispatch of the Yellow Sign. Locating you in Paris, I attempted to orchestrate your arrest. My stratagem was forestalled when you negotiated a truce with the authorities. My only recourse was to abandon my Fane persona, and replace it with another identity in order to move freely within London society.

"Since 1888, the real George Burnwell has been lying with a bullet in his brain inside an unmarked grave in South Africa. Due to Burnwell having lived his entire life abroad, it was child's play to pose as him in London. Using makeup to make myself appear twelve years older, I impersonated Burnwell over the next four years. Many of my subordinates even mistakenly believe that I am really Burnwell.

"A copy of *The Fatality of Visitations* surfaced in an auction. Nikola had heard rumors of a passage concerning the Thirteenth Covenant, a ceremony that could possibly negate my pursuit by the Heralds of the Yellow Sign. Although Nikola was unable to obtain the book, he verified the existence of the passage. Nikola also described the Hern household to me. Viewing Otto Hern as a potential candidate for the Red Offering in the Festival of Death, I initiated an elaborate scheme to make him *pay the law*. Despite having a radically different facial appearance as Sir George Burnwell, I couldn't risk a man with your powers penetrating my disguise. Therefore, I dealt with you by using Douanier as an intermediary.

"You told Douanier that my petition had been accepted. I am here to claim my reward. Blessed in the Ritual of the Thirteenth Covenant, I shall have the favor of the Tattered King for thirteen years. During that period, I am permitted to wear the Pallid Mask. Five of the thirteen years will be applied retroactively to my earlier activities as the Pallid Mask, and I can continue to use that *nom de guerre* until 1900. In that year, I shall be forced to adopt a new alias and mask. Personally, I'm leaning towards a black hood."

"Before the Ritual of the Thirteenth Covenant is performed, Monsieur Fane, a small matter needs to be rectified. You own a sword cane housing a blade stolen from the Shrine of Erlik in Yian. Erlik is another name for the Tattered King. I must insist that you surrender it to me."

"Do you think me a fool? Relinquishing this cane will leave me defenseless against you! I refuse!"

"Then your petition is nullified!" Grimoire waved his hands. The surroundings transformed into the tower room of Carcosa.

"Your sword is powerless against the King in Yellow. Listen to the flutter of his wings. Soon the Disposer of Souls shall feast on your flesh!"

Unsheathing his sword, Fane grabbed Grimoire and held the blade against his throat. "My sword can still slay you! I can make you an additional Red Offering to petition the King directly! Return me to Paris or die!"

The dark walls of the tower room dissipated. Fane and Grimoire were back in the house in the Rue des Rennes.

"Remove your blade," pleaded the Repairer of Reputations.

"Swear by the Kuen-Yuin Oath that my petition has been accepted!"

"You are worthy to don the Pallid Mask! I swear by the Dark Star of Yrimid and the Scarlet Lake!"

Releasing Grimoire, Fane sheathed his weapon. Following the consummation of the Ritual of the Thirteenth Covenant, the man known as the Pallid Mask exited the premises. The box containing the Yellow Sign remained inside the house.

The corrosive waters of Hali consumed the soul of an innocent man. As he was slowly erased from existence, the disintegrating intellect of Otto Hern was flooded with visions of his persecutor's past and future: "The Face beneath the Pallid Mask... Phantom... Mask... Fane... Thomas... Fantômas."

The last time we saw the Nyctalope, in Return of the Nyctalope, *he had flown to the planetoid Rhea on the outer fringes of the Solar System to reconnect with some of his family and old friends, before returning to Earth. By then, Leo was already back doing black ops for French Intelligence. This new story, taking place in an undetermined but slightly dystopian near future, follows on hat hppens next...*

Nigel Malcolm: *Tomorrow belongs to the Nyctalope*

"We learn from history that we do not learn from history."
Georg Wilhelm Friedrich Hegel

The Near-Future.

The place smelt—and almost tasted—of sulphur and diesel fumes, trapped in the dawn mist. The Nyctalope could just make out blurred images of buildings. He knew where he was going, and was more concerned with stepping around the mud puddles on the dirt-track road. Much easier to do with night-vision, as he was reminded when he saw one or two other locals trudging off to shift work. Many of them were speckled in mud, which looked like it was encrusted on their clothes after weeks of solid wear. The way they carelessly walked through the puddles seemed less to do with a lack of night-vision, and more to do with a slovenly disregard of the dirt. This town seemed monochrome, in spite of the mist—the color of dirty dishwater.

He arrived at the meeting point, a run-down bar, already open at this early hour. One or two customers were sitting at the counter, clutching glasses of beer as if they'd been there for hours already.

The Nyctalope walked inside and risked standing out by ordering a coffee instead, and sat alone at a high table. He wondered if he had jet-lag, because although he felt like he'd only got up less than two hours ago, the bar, with its sticky feel, cheap tobacco smell, and alcoholic barflies, looked like it was late at night.

Eventually, his contact walked in. They both exchanged a glance. The contact bought a glass of beer, and joined him.

"Are you the one they call the Nyctalope?" he asked.

Leo was cautious, but decided to take the risk.

"Yes," he replied.

"You wish me to call you that?"

"Yes, I would. What do I call you?"

"Just call me Stalker. It's best we don't know each other's real names in case one of us is captured."

"Of course," replied Leo, taking another sip from his coffee cup. "I take it you're an experienced guide in the Zone?"

"Yes," said the Stalker simply. "You're aware this is dangerous, yes?"

"Yes. I'm ready for whatever may lie inside that place."

The Stalker drank some of his beer, and looked at the table surface.

"I've taken many people into the Zone. A number of them showed great bravado before I took them on the trip. Some of them buckled before we even got past the guards. Some of them wanted to leave as soon as we were inside—or turn back half way. The most foolish perished just outside the Room itself. The Zone is formidable and to underestimate it is a big mistake. This isn't a day trip to the forest, Nyctalope."

Leo looked around. Through the grimy windows, he could see a grey dawn breaking. He had known all along that this was going to be another long day.

"Stalker, we don't know much about each other for good reason. But let me assure you that, over the course of my life—and, believe me, I'm much older than I look—I have encountered all kinds of dangers. Horrors even. Some of them in the furthest of places. I have faced things that would make your hair stand on end. They made my hair stand on end, too. But I have faced it all. So I can assure you that, although I may not have faced anything like the Zone before, I will face it without flinching or backing away."

The Stalker looked at him.

"I believe you," he said, before finishing his beer. As he drank, a freight train rattled past in the distance outside the bar, causing vibrations inside. "That train indicates that it's time to set off. Let's go."

The Nyctalope quickly finished his coffee, and they both left the bar.

Leo Saint-Clair looked out of the helicopter window. He was only twenty meters above ground, so the Parisian skyscrapers still looked impressively tall. Their glass and steel appearance were lent a pastel blue-pink by the sky.

Yet the ground level looked completely different. There were black patches on the roads that he initially thought were an unusually large number of oil patches, until he remembered that almost all motor vehicles in Paris were electric now. Then he realized that they were burn marks from the explosions.

Saint-Clair also saw traces of litter scattered over the boulevards, and a few isolated individuals running somewhere. Yet it was only when he saw a couple running together out of the shadows and across the Champs-Elysées that it made him wonder why they were running.

At the same height as the helicopter Leo was in, there were Police flying cars, apparently patrolling the area from the skies. One of them swooped down. He didn't get to see where it landed. Or why.

Saint-Clair had expected to be escorted to the HQ of the Service National d'Information Fonctionelle at Noisy-le-Sec. However, his helicopter landed on top of a thick-set skyscraper, making him realize just how long he'd been away, given that the SNIF had evidently relocated since he was last there.

Instead of a welcoming party of guards, he found himself greeted by a young uniformed blonde woman. This put him more at ease—about being brought back to the SNIF, and also the ending of his seventh marriage. She shook hands with him and they went inside.

The chrome elevator doors slid open and Saint-Clair found himself stepping into a large, fake marble and stone neo-Athenian office. For a moment, he felt too much a part of the aesthetic in his new sharp suit.

Colonel Auguste Pichenet stood, for a moment, with his back to the two newcomers. He was wearing a uniform, similar to everyone else's, apart from the rank. He turned round and faced him.

"Ah, Monsieur Saint-Clair! Do come in. That will be all, Mademoiselle Roche-Verger."

"Thank you," said Saint-Clair. Despite his rank, Pichenet did not seem much older than Leo, who himself still looked like a man in his forties. Saint-Clair was aware that, as he had got older, all his bosses and contacts seemed to get younger and younger, but Pichenet had also always appeared much younger than his age. Surprisingly precocious, prodigiously gifted, his brilliant career as an agent had eventually propelled him to the head of SNIF.

"Please sit down. I hope you've enjoyed your sabbatical, Monsieur Saint-Clair?"

"I did, while it lasted. And to be honest, I can't see why it had to be so abruptly ended with an armed escort bringing me back here."

"Well, you were becoming a difficult man to get hold of. Did you really go in search of that planet? What was it called, Rhea?"[4]

Saint-Clair decided to keep the events of his journey to the outer confines of the Solar System secret from these people. "Mainly just traveling around Australia," he said. He wasn't lying, because he had done that after he had returned to Earth.

"Yes, we knew we'd find you there," said Pichenet, as they both took their seats. "It must have been the only continent you hadn't explored."

"Yes," said Saint-Clair, whose suspicion was beginning to show. The Colonel grinned.

"You're wondering why we need you—again?"

"Well, most people, including here at SNIF, either haven't heard of me, and the ones who have must be retired—ordead." He decided not to add that he hadn't discouraged that perception.

"But I know better. The Nyctalope should be making a comeback. France needs you now more than ever before. We need you to act both overtly and covertly."

---

[4] See *The Return of the Nyctalope*.

All of this took a moment to process.

"I'm honored," said Saint-Clair, politely.

"For the time being, you will be acting covertly. Have you heard of the Kariven Archive?"

"I have even made some contributions to it—and Torchwood. So you'd like me to investigate an extra-terrestrial artifact?"

Pichenet pressed some keys on his laptop, and clicked a mouse.

"Forget Torchwood, that's fake news," he said. A big flatscreen TV on a nearby wall showed a pencil sketch drawing of a rundown building. "But there are several artifacts out there of extra-terrestrial origin. I want you to find them and either collect them for us, or destroy them so they can't be used by our enemies. This artifact here has ended up in the Russian Empire. It is in a zone protected by armed guards authorized to kill anyone who tries to get in. Inside it, there is a place simply known as the 'Room.' Anyone who goes inside is granted his greatest wish. You can see why this could be a potential threat to us?"

The Colonel picked up a touchscreen j-pad tablet and handed it to Saint-Clair.

"The Zone has been affected by radiation and does not follow the normal rules of reality," he continued. "Here is an interview with a physics professor who went into the Zone with a small atomic bomb, intending to blow it up. In the end, he chose not to. I know the Nyctalope will have more resolve."

"You want me to destroy that thing? It looks like it's been destroyed already. Why not retrieve it and bring it to France?"

"Appearances can be deceptive, Monsieur Saint-Clair. Anyway, logistically it would be impossible to move it. It has become a part of the area it's in. You have to see that it's blown up. The j-pad has all the background information you'll need."

Saint-Clair didn't feel he had any other choice.

"*Oui, Mon Colonel.*"

The Stalker and the Nyctalope stepped out onto the street, and walked purposefully up the road towards the edge of town.

"Are you fit, old man?" asked the Stalker.

"You don't have to worry about me. I'm in great shape—young man," replied Leo.

"Good," said his guide, "because we're going to climb a wall and do a lot of running away from armed guards who are authorized to kill on sight."

"Then it must be Tuesday," said the Nyctalope, drily.

They walked down a few more streets, which were becoming increasingly deserted. Eventually, the Stalker stopped and gestured at the Nyctalope to put their backs up against the wall of an abandoned-looking building.

"Wait," he commanded. He carefully peered around the corner. "Come!" he said.

Round the corner was a dirt track, beside a tall, barbed wire fence. They ran down the track. The only noise was the sound of their breath and that of their footsteps on the mud, or, occasionally, in a brown puddle.

At the end of the track, the Stalker stopped and peered around another corner. They went into a rudimentary courtyard, with another abandoned L-shaped building on two adjacent sides, and two other walls. The one ahead of them was made of concrete, and had clearly been put up in a hurry long after the rest of the courtyard, but still a few years before now.

The Stalker glanced around this square, before he and the Nyctalope jogged across to the far corner, where a wooden crate lay discarded under a rain-soaked blanket. The Stalker peeled off the blanket. It slapped onto the ground. He carried the crate along and up against the far wall. Leo realized that the Stalker had left the crate hidden there for the very purpose of scaling this wall. He looked around to make sure guards weren't already following them. There was a thin mist hanging in the courtyard.

The Stalker was now standing on the crate and peering over the wall. He seemed to be waiting for that train to go through some gates nearby, on its journey to a service station by the edge of the Zone.

As the train sounded like it was starting to move again, the Stalker turned to him.

"OK, let's go!" he said, before pulling himself up onto the wall.

The Nyctalope sprang on to the crate, grabbed the top edge of the wall, and swiftly pulled himself up. Seeing that his client didn't need any help, the Stalker jumped down the other side.

Just as the Nyctalope was on top of the wall, some troops ran into the courtyard. He landed on the other side just as he heard some harsh shouting and the firing of Kalashnikovs.

They now stood in a wide, muddy road with large warehouses opposite them, barely visible through the fog.

The Stalker was alarmed by the sound of gunfire. They both heard shouting from other guards by the railway gate, about a hundred yards away. The Stalker cursed, and they glanced around, looking for cover.

"The warehouse over there! Quickly!" said the Stalker, before dashing over the road. The Nyctalope followed him.

The Stalker ran up to the rusting doors and pulled them, but they wouldn't move. They were bolted on the inside. He pulled them all the more frantically as he heard distant footsteps getting louder.

"Stand aside!" said the Nyctalope.

The Stalker obeyed. The Nyctalope had a gun with a silencer on it. He shot at the bolt a few times, causing it to break. They then pulled the doors open, ran inside, and pulled them closed behind them.

They both stood there, trying to breathe as quietly as they could. They heard the footsteps of the guards as they ran past what looked to them like a long closed door. The intruders' breathing became more relaxed.

"If only it wasn't so dark in here," whispered the Stalker.

This was a surprise to Leo, but he knew to conceal it as much as he could. In this situation, he had to use his advantage to help them both survive.

"Which direction do we go from here? With our backs to the door, do we go straight on? Left? Right?" he asked.

"Diagonally left."

"Hold my hand. I'm good at seeing in the dark."

He took his guide's hand and led him carefully through the warehouse, around disused and abandoned vehicles and crates of ammunition. They eventually got to a door that was, fortunately, unlocked. They crept out into the open. The Stalker was blinking in the grey daylight.

"I can see why they call you the Nyctalope," he said. "How did you manage that?"

"I eat a lot of carrots," Leo replied dismissively, before quickly trying to change the topic. "Where do we go from here?"

"You see those railway tracks? We need to run across them and turn right. Look for an old, abandoned kiosk, just beyond."

"It's quite exposed, even in the fog," said the Nyctalope, doubtfully.

"If we can just get across the tracks unnoticed, we should be all right. From there, it's a straightforward run to the Zone. The guards won't dare to follow us."

Leo sighed. "Very well," he said.

"You go first, and I'll join you," said the Stalker.

"A little kiosk, just beyond the tracks?" Leo asked.

"Yes, run straight ahead, and once you're over the tracks, turn right."

"OK. Are you joining me?"

"Of course."

The Nyctalope did wonder. After all, he had met this black market guide only about half an hour ago. But his contacts had told him of this man's own connection to the Zone, that bordered on the spiritual. He'd heard that this talker" was taking people into the Zone for genuinely altruistic reasons. And even if he were just doing it for the money, he would be getting paid—very generously—only upon Leo's safe return. He had to trust this pale, thin man when he said he would join the Nyctalope at the kiosk.

They waited. There were no more guns or shouting to punctuate the silence.

"Go!" whispered the Stalker, who seemed to sense that it was safe.

The Nyctalope jogged up to the tracks, glancing around himself. It reminded him of the First World War trenches. Carefully hopping and skipping between the tracks and the sleepers, he then sprinted on into the fog, towards what he hoped was the kiosk. Still no gunfire. Total silence.

He found the kiosk, and went behind it. Like everything else around here, it looked like it was bombed out, and that it wouldn't take much effort to push it over. The Nyctalope would have leaned up against the wall, but there was something else propped up there, underneath a tarpaulin sheet. He looked further beyond the kiosk. The mist seemed to be thinning. He could make out blocks of abandoned flats arranged in street, like downtown Tallinn in Estonia.

He waited. The silence was getting uncomfortable. What if the Stalker had abandoned him here after all? Or he got shot coming across? The Nyctalope would have to go into the Zone alone and unaided. It would be exceptionally dangerous without local knowledge.

Suddenly, he heard footsteps coming towards him. He braced himself. It was the Stalker. They were both relieved to see each other. The Stalker took a moment to catch his breath.

"We're past the guards. They won't come after us now. They wouldn't dare come any nearer to the Zone," he said.

"So we're now inside the Zone?" asked the Nyctalope.

"Not quite. We're just outside it," said his guide, as he pulled away the tarpaulin to reveal three mismatched bicycles. "We'll ride these from here. We'll ride down that street, then we come to a forest. We'll go through it, and then we'll be there."

He wheeled a bike away by a couple of meters, before swinging a leg over it, and wobbling into motion. Aware he might lose sight of the Stalker if he wasn't quick enough, the Nyctalope uncoupled the second bike. It was poorly maintained, but it was up to the job. He mounted it and peddled after his guide.

Eventually, they were both just gliding along, as if it was just any Sunday morning bike ride. The mist was much thinner. As they passed an alleyway, Leo saw a large pack of stray dogs. Each seemed to belong to a different breed. They were all trotting along together as one unit. Presumably they had found food of some sort to live on around here.

At the end of the street, there was a main road. The two men weaved between the potholes, and left the town as the concrete beneath their wheels was replaced by overgrown grass and brown bald patches.

They peddled into the forest. After a few meters of carefully riding over the ground, negotiating roots and dead branches, Leo found himself remembering the Stalker's comments about how this *wasn't a trip to the forest*. It seemed very much like one at the moment. Being East European, it was a forest of pine trees, which made Leo think of old folk tales, which seemed apt, given that they were on their way to something that seemed to be magic.

Then, quite suddenly, they came to a clearing. The Stalker stopped, and so did Leo. He could now see the Zone itself. A large, unkempt valley with rusting tanks and trucks scattered around it. A foaming river flowed through its deep center in the distance. Oddly, birds were singing.

"We can leave our bikes here," said the Stalker, breaking the silence.

"Shouldn't we padlock them? No, stupid question, sorry."

The Stalker started to shudder, which erupted into the laughter of a man who hadn't had anything to laugh about for a very long time. The Nyctalope laughed too.

"Padlocks won't stop the Zone from stealing out bikesm" said the Stalker finally. "It just doesn't need to ride anywhere." He seemed much more relaxed. "Could you wait here for a moment, please?"

Then, as an afterthought, he took his bag off his shoulder and reached into it. He got out a handful of metal bolts. "I have some bolts here and some bandage strips. Could you tie the bandages to the bolts for me, please? Here you are."

He handed the items to his client.

"Where are you going?" asked the Nyctalope.

"I'll be back in a moment. There is something I need to do."

He walked down the slope a little way, and disappeared into the overgrown grass.

The Nyctalope sat under a tree, and began threading strips of bandage through the bolts, so that one end of the bandage was tied, and the other end flowed freely like a tail. He felt a sense of momentary peace. This simple task was quite therapeutic—almost like needlework or basket-weaving—which he found himself considering taking up as a hobby. But also he could breathe the fresh, damp air and listen to the birds singing. He didn't know why the Zone allowed wildlife to roam free here, but he was glad that it did.

He looked up at his surroundings, and his serenity shattered. The burnt-out army vehicles were there like a cancer. It reminded him of World War Two. Not only a dark moment in his country's history, but a dark moment in his own.

Saint-Clair scrolled through the newly uploaded file on the j-pad. He would look it over in more detail later. Colonel Pichenet, meanwhile, seemed to relax a little. He sat back and got out his own j-pad.

"You know that I've always been a bit of a fan of yours," he said, unexpectedly coy.

It had been a long time, but Leo recognized that glint in the eye and the sparkle of excitement in the voice. He wondered if the man was about to ask him to sign an autograph, knowing that he'd graciously oblige.

Pichenet was scrolling through his j-pad, before tapping an icon which evidently connected his personal photographs to the big screen on the wall.

He started flicking through the photos. It was a collection with a political theme. The photos flashed across the screen. The collection included campaign posters with pictures of a far-right party leader from the 1980s, and his successor, who also happened to be his daughter. A poster of that French President, who had been his grand-daughter and had closed the borders, out of concern to "protect"' French identity and values. She was laughing with that U.S. president with the strange hair. There were also a few photos of that shirtless Russian president hunting in some woodland.

"I've been collecting this stuff for years," Pichenet explained, as he searched through the photos.

A faint, distant tingle started glimmering away at the back of Saint-Clair's memory, before flashing into his consciousness and flooding it with horror.

"These are hard to find now. Not because the dealers are few and far between, but because so few of these collectibles left. The price is astronomical, but it's the pride of my collection," Pinochet gabbled on, excitedly. "Just look at *this...*"

A picture flashed up of a black and white photograph showing Saint-Clair standing side by side with Marshal Pétain flashed onto the screen.

"You *must* remember that day!" said Pichenet.

Saint-Clair was speechless for a moment, and very aware that he was shaking. The Colonel evidently didn't see the tremor in his hands.

He tried to work out how to respond to this man, who was expecting him to be nostalgic about a period in his life that he wished so profoundly that he could go back and change. He formulated words in his mind, deliberately keeping his voice even and his choice of words as diplomatic as possible.

"It is... difficult to explain to people who weren't there," he said, slowly. "France had been invaded—defeated. People had to choose the best way to survive. How to protect not only themselves, but also their loved ones. At the time, I had to choose how to do that, but also choose the best way to protect France. An accommodation seemed to be the best way to do it. In the process, I achieved some small victories, but also big defeats, all at enormous cost, to both myself, but also to others. So please forgive me if I do not reminisce about those times. They were truly horrific. If I had to make the same decision now, I would make a very different choice."

"I'm sorry, Monsieur Saint-Clair," apologized Pichenet. "I forgot that your generation relate to this stuff differently than mine. I know that what you did, you did for France. It was a heroic sacrifice, and I admire you for making it."

Saint-Clair was chilled by the fact that his generation *related to it different-ly*. That statement alone would haunt him for days.

"It's how you put France first that makes you who you are," the Colonel continued. "That's why we need you now more than ever. To protect us from foreign threats inside and outside the country. To help us reclaim our borders, regain our heritage. To make France great again."

Saint-Clair knew he had to finish this conversation somehow. At least, their business was concluded. He tried to smile as graciously as he could manage, and gestured at his j-pad.

"Then I should start by taking this and studying the Zone," he said, before standing up and saluting the conventional French way. "Mon Colonel."

He walked out of Pichenet's office, his mechanical heart pounding fast.

He hadn't felt too much remorse about it shortly after that time, because he'd insisted—to himself and others—that he hadn't got involved in any war crimes, but as the decades had rolled on, and more had come out about the Nazi regime, he had begun to see his guilt by association. He now realized that he'd lent his name to something truly evil, and that had influenced Europe for a very long time. He may have tried to justify his actions because of the small victories that he'd managed to achieve, but it was still a major failure.

The nature around him had lost its attraction. The greenery could be better described as off-green, as if the color had been drained out of the place. Why was he so unfocused? Maybe it was the effect of being in the Zone? He concentrated on threading the bandages to the bolts. He was here on a mission. He had a job to do. The introspection could wait until afterwards. He called on the mental disciplines that he'd learned in Tibet, all those years ago.

He quickly finished the job and chucked the bolts back into the bag. His guide had been a long time. He stood up and started looking downhill for him. He walked in the direction that the Stalker had taken. It took him down a slope from the forest on the hilltop. Not far down, he saw the Stalker lying flat on his stomach. At first, he thought his guide must have collapsed, but as he got closer, the Stalker moved, and got up off the ground.

"Are you OK?" asked the Nyctalope.

"I was communicating with the Zone," explained the Stalker. "Asking it to look upon us favorably."

Leo didn't quite know what to say to that. It seemed as if the Stalker had almost been praying to it. Maybe he saw the Zone as some kind of deity?

"I've done what you asked," he said, handing over the bag.

The Stalker took it, and looked at the bolts with bandages tied to them.

"It can sense if something is dangerous to it. You can see what it did to those tanks over there." He looked straight at Leo. "Get rid of your gun, Nyctalope. It would be more dangerous to you to carry it than to leave it behind."

The Nyctalope paused for a moment, then, reluctantly, took out the pistol that had been so useful to them earlier. He looked around. The bikes were only several meters away so, with an overarm throw, he lobbed the gun back up the slope towards the forest, hoping that it would land near enough to the bikes for him to find it again on the way back. But as he watched it flying through the air, the pistol simply disappeared. He was surprised.

"Did my gun just vanish into thin air?" he asked.

"Yes," said the Stalker, gravely. "Let's hope it won't hold it against you as we get nearer to it. Was that the only weapon you brought with you?"

"Yes," the Nyctalope lied.

"Good," said the Stalker, who then took out a bolt and cautiously threw it in the opposite direction to the gun. The bolt fluttered down nearby.

"Let's go." he said, before carefully walking towards where the bandage could be seen.

And Leo realized that the bandaged bolts were being used to help them negotiate their way through this unpredictable place.

They trudged further into the Zone.

They were having a rest before the final part of the journey to the Room. The Nyctalope was sitting, and the Stalker was lying face down, on the soggy peat ground just by the river. It was shallow enough for Leo to see the bottom of it. It might have been less shallow than it looked, because of a trick of the light reflecting on it, of course. However, he could see that the river, like the off-green land around it, was full of scattered objects. He could see coins; guns and ammunition; and, inexplicably, household items, like picture frames, photographs, and wristwatches.

Occasionally, little clusters of foam would drift past. Even if this area wasn't drenched in radiation, and abandoned to an alien entity, it seemed as if this place would still be a deeply unhealthy place to stay for too long. After all, the Stalker didn't look too good. He could even be terminally ill.

The Stalker stood up and stepped over to where Leo was sitting. He sat down next to him.

"I take it that you are familiar with the legend of the Nyctalope?" the Stalker said. "He was an Italian figure, a superman with a mechanical heart and eyes that could see in the dark."

"French. The Nyctalope was French."

The Stalker looked at him, with a rare, amused look.

"So you do know him."

"Well, I am French too—as you can probably tell."

"You must be something of an enthusiast to have picked his name."

"Not really. I just thought it would make a nice change for you, instead of simply calling myself the Tourist or the Visitor. You must have had dozens of those."

"No, actually. I've only had a couple of tourists. I've had professors, doctors, writers, travelers—even a vagabond once. You're my first Nyctalope though."

Leo could tell that the Stalker was still trying to find a way to subtly probe for more information. Very few people would have heard of the Nyctalope by now, and fewer yet would even suspect that he was still alive. He probably shouldn't have used it as his cover name on this mission, but he'd judged the risk to be low, and, well, he felt a sense of ownership about it. The name had been attached to him for a very long time.

Leo wanted to evade his guide's efforts to get any more information out of him, even though he couldn't possibly think that Leo was *the* Nyctalope. "So what's next?" he asked.

The Stalker sat there and looked at the river

"Your ability to see in the dark will be very useful when we get to the tunnel," answered the Stalker.

The Nyctalope got to his feet and stretched. He looked around.

"Is the tunnel far from here?" he inquired.

"It's just over there," replied the Stalker, gesturing. "Once we've gone through it—if we get through it alive—then, the Room is in the building just beyond it."

The Nyctalope looked over at a dilapidated mill house.

"It looks quite derelict for such a powerful place," he noted.

The Stalker clambered up and stood with him.

"Appearances can be deceptive. Besides, everything around here is derelict."

The Nyctalope brushed some of the damp soil off his pants. He noticed, not for the first time, that the Stalker didn't seem to mind the dirt and the damp he sat or lay in.

"Let's go." he said.

Leo followed the Stalker as he walked carefully up to the building and opened the cellar door. The guide peered wearily into it. So did Leo. All he saw was a tunnel with peeling whitewashed walls covered with dust and cobwebs. There was about a quarter of a meter of water on the floor.

"You go first," said the Stalker.

The Nyctalope gave him a sideways look. The Stalker handed him a threaded bolt. "Here. Throw one of these."

Leo took the bolt and tossed it well into the tunnel. It spattered into the water. He paddled slowly up to where it had landed. He couldn't see it through the murky water, and didn't particularly want to fish it out either. He wondered for a moment if the greatest wish of most of the people who made it to the Room was for a nice hot bath and some clean clothes.

He walked further on. It smelled powerfully of damp. By now, the Stalker had joined him. There were, once again, discarded things in the water. Some of them seemed to be weapons. Others were loose bricks and fallen masonry.

"The dilapidated state of this place is more dangerous than the Room," he said, dryly.

"Don't be so sure. If we are considerate, it will keep us safe."

The Nyctalope looked further ahead, and saw a heavy metal door. "Is the Room behind this door?"

"Not quite," replied the Stalker. "We pass through a steam that runs through on the other side of the door. Then we walk through this building, and finally get to a stable. The Room is the anteroom to that."

"How many people get this far?"

"Not many. It likes you, Nyctalope. It accepts you. At least, it has done so far. It can sense other things about you. It can see into your soul. It can see you as you really are.

This unsettled the Nyctalope. Surely, it would know what he had really come here to do. Maybe it knew that he would fail? Or maybe he was about to die? It might have been waiting for its chance to kill him. Or it wasn't as all-powerful as it was made out to be. He would soon find out.

He stood there, staring at the door. He realized that this could be where his life might end. He'd faced death many times before, of course, but this time, it somehow seemed different. Such a long life... Too long... He'd done so much. A lot of it had been good, but enough of it had been bad so that it still haunted him. And the losses as well... Good friends, who were now gone. And all the wives—Laurence, Sylvie, Véronique...—surely, no one living could have been as widowed as him. And the children... The twins, of course, were the deepest cut, given the circumstances of their deaths on Mars... But there was Petit Pierre, and Marcel, and others, too... Their deaths, and that of their mothers, were still keenly felt. His elder son, Pierre, had passed away too, on Rhea, but his grand-daughter Xavière was still alive, now married to Claude Marécourt. At least, Leo had been able reconcile with her. It was curious how she had recently developed the same night-vision as him.

Many were gone now, and he was about to join them. That was fine. He was tired, and ready to go. It didn't even bother him if it were a slow, torturous death, because he doubted that it would be any worse than the pain and torture of his life.

"Shall we go through?" said the Stalker, getting impatient.

The Nyctalope snapped out of his reverie.

"Sorry. It already feels like it's been a long day. Maybe that's what the Room senses about me."

"Maybe. And maybe also your lack of purpose."

The Nyctalope turned and looked at him. "What do you mean by lack of purpose?" he asked.

"Pardon me, but it is quite clear to me that you are lost and searching for meaning."

"I'm not lost," said the Nyctalope, sounding angrier than he intended.

"But that is why you're here, isn't it?" replied the Stalker. "You need something to believe in."

"Shut up!" snapped Leo.

Then he paused and struggled to regain his temper. He took some deep breaths and tried to remember those occult disciplines he'd mastered so long ago. He was an emotional mess at the moment.

"I am so sorry, Monsieur. You are probably right," he said to his guide, before correcting himself. "You are definitely right. I am a man without direction. Maybe this Room will help me to find it. Forgive me."

He braced himself and cautiously opened the door. They climbed into the next tunnel, waded through the chest-deep stream, and up into the building. The Stalker led the Nyctalope past a barn area full of rotting grain, and along several passageways through a stone building to a dilapidated, and partly flooded, stable.

They stepped into this place, and the Stalker gestured at the anteroom attached to it.

"The Room is just in there," he said.

The Nyctalope peered over. Not so far forward to actually be in the Room, but enough to see the place. The floor was made of cracked old tiles. There were gaps in the walls where windows used to be. There was no roof. It didn't seem like much after the journey to get there. Yet, there was some kind of aura about the place. Something so powerful it could crush even him without much effort.

"Clear your mind," said the Stalker. "Just be calm. Don't try to think of what it is that you most wish for, the Room will know."

Leo had spent much of this last leg of the journey mentally preparing for the final assault. He looked the Stalker straight in the eyes, and his own irises changed color:

"Go back outside, and wait for me by the river. Leave without me if I don't join you in ten minutes."

It was a simple mind trick he'd learnt in Tibet all those years ago. He had worried he'd be a bit rusty, and he'd done some mental exercises in the hotel the night before to make sure he was still fit enough for the job. He'd even considered practicing this trick on an unsuspecting member of the staff, just to get them to do something small and harmless, but his conscience made him decide against it. Good to know he still had some sort of ethical code.

But the mind trick worked. The Stalker wordlessly turned round and left the stable. Leo watched him go. He didn't need to worry about him, because the Stalker wasn't in any kind of trance; he had just been compelled to follow the Nyctalope's instructions. He was still alert, and able to use his own skills to get out of this place safely.

The Nyctalope reached inside his leather jacket, and under his jumper, where there was the belt strapped around his stomach, in which the flat or pen-shaped components of the bomb were. He was able to undo that utility belt, pull it off and drop it into the pool of floodwater. He knelt down on the floor and assembled the bomb. It was the latest in French military technology, light, easy to assemble, and yet extremely powerful. He fitted it together, just as the ammunitions expert had showed him. When it was assembled, it even had a timer and a dead man's switch.

His plan had been to set the timer and get out. However, after walking through the Zone, he realized that the dead man's switch was the only option to make sure it did the job properly. And he was fine with that.

He sat on the floor, looking at the bomb. It was made of plastic. Smooth, khaki and metal grey. The only clean and shiny thing in this rotting place. There was a moment of stillness—of a very intense awareness of the damp, dusty, stone floor, of the wet rubble around him. In the distance, he could hear the river flowing.

He gazed at the shiny plastic bomb that would finally stop his shiny plastic and metal heart. The Nyctalope would finally end here. He'd be remembered, of course, by historians and pop culture enthusiasts. And by a few friends, enemies and former lovers, who might still be alive—not all of them on Earth. Would he be "rediscovered" and again made into a national hero—posthumously—by he French government, for its own reasons?

Here he was, obeying orders again... Why destroy this place? It clearly had its own will, but it wasn't a threat to France. Any hostiles would probably be wiped out by the Room before they got near it. As the Stalker said, only the lost and the unsure could get this far.

Leo knelt forward and picked up the bomb. Then he dismantled it, scattering the components into the pool of floodwater. There seemed to be discarded things in there already. He'd read the account made by that professor who had also considered blowing up the Room with an atomic device, only to dismantle it and scatter its parts in this same pool. He was careful how he disposed of it in case any part might touch another and cause an explosion.

Then Leo stood up. Swaying slightly, he looked into the Room and walked inside.

Leo stepped into the foyer of his villa outside Paris. There was a party going on. The invitations must have been vague or misleading, because some of the guests were dressed for a black tie event, while others wore white tie and tails. The women all wore cocktail dresses, but of different period styles, as if it was a fancy dress ball, and the theme ranged the Belle Epoque to the present day. An orchestra was playing a jaunty tune he remembered he used to like back in the 1920s... What was it called again?

Everything in the room was pre- Second World War. He recognized the servants, gliding around the guests discreetly. He had hired them himself back in the 20s and 30s. They all looked younger than he remembered them.

Leo looked at the guests, and was delighted to see Vitto, chatting with Soca. They stood in the far corner of the room. He would have to make his way over to them later and reminisce about old times. They were talking to a woman who looked familiar. Who was she? Surely it wasn't Laurence. Maybe it was a relative of hers? No, it was definitely Laurence. He had to talk with her too, before catching up with Soca and Vitto.

Looking in the other corner of the room, Leo saw Gnô Mitang. He hadn't seen his Japanese friend since the Second World War. Life had taken them in very different directions. His Japanese friend was chatting with Véronique d'Olbans. What was she doing here?

This was all beginning to get a bit too much for him. All the people he'd lost—friends, girlfriends, wives—were gathered in this house he'd burned down before he had to go on the run after the war.

Maybe this was a second chance. Maybe the Room had sent him back in time to put everything right. Yet, this was not what actually happened…

"Leo!"

Leo gasped once again: "Sylvie!"

He ran over, nearly causing a servant to drop a tray. He kissed Sylvie Mac Dhul passionately. She tasted and felt and smelt just as she did all those years ago. He only stopped when he remembered that there was several other ex-wives in the room.

He stepped back slightly and put a hand on her face. She seemed to glow. So sparkling and joyful, banishing the image of the corpse in the morgue he'd spent a hundred years trying to forget.

"I cannot express just how much I have missed you!" he said, unable to stop himself.

"I am happy and free. That is all you need to know about me," she said, gently.

"You're free?" Leo replied.

She smiled back at him, a smile he recognized as conveying *you don't understand what I'm saying.*

"I am happy and free now," she said again, more carefully.

Leo thought he knew what she meant. "Good." he said. But she still smiled at him as though he didn't.

He noticed some children here, and his heart felt a twinge of joy—they might be his estranged children. "Listen, Sylvie, I have to speak with some other people here. Will you stay around? We can talk properly later." He looked around and smiled. "It's a lot like one of the parties we used to give," he added, before walking off in search of those children he had caught a glimpse of.

Who would have thought he'd meet her again, after all this time and yet leave her at the earliest opportunity?

"Father!"

"Marcel!" said Leo, fatherly joy mixed with cautiousness. This was one of Laurence's children—the son who had died in a retirement home, still angry at his father for cheating on his mother with Queen Mizzeia Khali. But now he was in his twenties again. Those beautiful eyes showing no signs of the dementia that had afflicted him during his final years. Were they still friends?

"It's good to see you, Father." said Marcel, smiling.

"And it is *very good* to see you," Leo replied, before taking a moment to formulate the words he wanted to say. "I know we've had our differences, but… well…"

"We no longer have any differences, Father."

"I am so sorry for everything."

"You don't need to apologize. I understand. All is forgiven."

This was balm to Leo's soul. They embraced. Then they detached themselves.

"I've got to talk to some other people. But we can talk more later."

Leo left Marcel and searched through the crowd for the children. He found the twins. He ran over and embraced them both. It was only then that he realized he should have approached them more carefully, given that he'd killed them. But they were both pleased to see their papa. Just like the last time. It cancelled out that last, evil, moment, when he had been possessed by the evil Martian intelligence. They were father and children once more.

"Listen, my precious ones. I am so sorry for what I did to you on Mars. Papa wasn't himself. I love you both very dearly, and killing you was the greatest pain I ever had to bear. I'll make it up to you both, I promise."

The two children both smiled and hugged him, and he knew he had been forgiven. It was a moment of perfect joy and peace.

As that moment passed, it occurred to Leo that the twins both smiled at him knowingly. Knowing something that he didn't know—like Sylvie. It was as if they knew he meant it, but that somehow, he wouldn't be able to fulfill his promise.

Then, he noticed the murky water soaking into his pants. He looked down at the floor—it was no longer marble, but those cracked tiles below a large puddle. People were replaced with crumbling walls, and the sound of the band music by the sound of rain. The twins had disappeared. Leo was just kneeling in the Room, covered in dirt and rain.

He started to weep. The weeping developed into howling, screaming, crying on his hands and knees. For a long, timeless, while.

When it went back to gentle weeping, he hauled himself up off the floor. He was in the here and now. All those people he'd loved were gone. Maybe they were in Heaven, but if so, he doubted he would make it there. Not with all the things he'd done. The people he'd killed. He should go to Hell just for collaborating with Vichy. That's probably the only thing he'd be remembered for.

Leo looked around the room. There was silence. Stillness. It just looked like a normal, run-down room in an abandoned building.

And now he worked for *that* government and he was going to become their mascot, just like he had been for Vichy. Well, not anymore! No more collaborations of any kind!

He reached into his pocket and pulled out a damp handkerchief, which he used to wipe the tears, snot and sweat off his face. Good job this handkerchief was just going to be thrown away after he got back.

He took a deep breath. As he exhaled, he noticed he seemed to whimper slightly. He realized that he probably hadn't cried for decades. No wonder he had been howling like an animal. He was so glad that no one was around to see him like this. Apart from the Room perhaps. He hoped it had witnessed other people do even more embarrassing things before now.

Leo Saint-Clair, the Nyctalope, stood up straight and made his way out of the Room and the building.

The Stalker lay on the ground by the river. *Please let this man find his purpose*, he willed.

He saw a figure come out of the building and walked towards him. The Nyctalope was tottering over the uneven ground. The Stalker could see that his client looked tired and old, but also happy and relieved. As though a huge problem had gone away. His eyes even twinkled in a way the Stalker hadn't expected. Those strange eyes.

The Stalker picked himself up and approached him, expectantly. "You found what you were looking for?" he asked.

"I didn't realize I was looking for it, but yes. I know what I want."

The Stalker became excited. This was exactly why he did this job. "What do you want?" he almost demanded.

The Nyctalope looked straight at him.

"Redemption." he said.

Christofer Nigro has already spun several tales featuring Paul Féval, fils' crea-tion, Felifax the Tiger-Man (available from Black Coat Press, ISBN 978-1-932983-88-0), in "Eye of the Tiger-Man," published in The Shadow of Judex, *then in "The Privilege of Adonis" (*TOTS *Volume 10), "The Noble Freak" (Volume 11) and "Justice and the Beast" (Volume 12). This is a direct sequel to the last installment...*

Christofer Nigro: *Kindred Beasts*

Paris, May 1937

Detective Cocantin stood solemnly before the grisly crime scene in an al-ley located in what was supposed to be one of Paris's better neighborhoods. He had returned to the dank passageway after the rest of the police had departed, pulling favors to keep the body of the victim right where her mutilated remains had been found, so that *someone else* could investigate the horrific tableau. Though the area was largely deserted so late in the evening, a cordon had been stretched over the alley's entrance to prevent contamination of the crime scene. The presence of the savvy young member of Paris's constabulary insured that the morbidly curious Parisians who may still be roaming about the city at this hour would not attempt to breach the flimsy cordon.

Cocantin leaned against the alley's grungy side wall to await the arrival of his old friend, whom he knew would have no difficulty getting there without at-tracting undue attention. He did not have to wait long.

"Justice demands retribution for this monstrous crime," uttered a chilling voice from a few feet behind the lawman.

Cocantin didn't jump with a start, as most people would have. He had ex-pected that unsettling but familiar voice to appear out of the dark without warn-ing. He was among the few Parisians who found its presence comforting. For the detective had worked beside the avenging Judex since the War to End All Wars, when he had been called the "Licorice Kid."

"Nice of you to make it, *mon ami*," said Cocantin, greeting his friend and occasional partner-in-crime-fighting. "With the Universal Exposition opening at the end of the month, the Police have their hands full—and two of these hands are mine! We most certainly do not need something like this on top of every-thing else—another Ripper on the loose."

"I commiserate with your overwhelming travails," Judex replied, "but what I see before me does not seem related to the Exposition."

"*Naturellement,* old friend. I mean, look at what was done to this poor girl."

The black-clad dispenser of justice stepped forward to take a better look at the gutted slab of human remains lying before him. His dark cape billowed in the air, making him resemble a shadowy apparition of death, his charcoal black hat concealing much of his upper countenance and creating a sinister-looking mien.

It was an apropos vision, considering what Judex was looking at. Moreover, his Grim Reaper appearance would become even more fitting when he would deliver the perpetrator of this heinous act to Lady Death; however, it would be done in the name of another personification, the more ethically discriminating but sometimes merciful Lady Justice.

The sight before Judex's gray eyes was one that almost choked him, even though he thought of himself as quite desensitized to brutality. A young woman—or what remained of her—lay on her side at the end of the alley, her stomach ripped open. She had been cruelly eviscerated, with her small intestine lying on the dirty ground like a discarded pink hose, her lower bowel splattered in a brownish pile beside it. Her rib cage had been pulled open, and her violated thorax was bereft of heart, lung, and liver.

The woman's right arm was missing, having been torn off with sheer force. Sizable portions of her shoulder and neck area had been ripped away, as if chewed off by powerful, sharp teeth. Her light brown eyes were wide open, her mouth still agape, as if she had spent her final moments screaming in horror—though no such sounds had been reported.

The victim's body was garbed in the tattered remains of what appeared to be a scarlet-colored Ramona dress. Its riffled circular flounce had been torn away by her attacker, apparently to get at the organs inside. Her cream-colored panties had been removed and were lying about two meters to her side. Her remaining arm had visible polish on the fingernails, indicating that, when alive, this young woman had tried to look like an attractive lady about the town. However, no other part of her body or clothing remained intact enough to provide any further indications of this.

"*Mon Dieu*," Judex said with little sign of emotion. "This resembles an act of… cannibalism. This woman's organs and missing limb were *eaten*. And those wounds on her shoulder blade and neck are bite marks. Unlike the Jack the Ripper murders, however, these mutilations do not display a surgical precision. This girl was literally torn open, not methodically cut; and her arm was pulled off, not hacked or sawed. This was not done in the style of a common madman, but rather with the vicious abandon of a wild animal."

"You aren't kidding. Our forensic experts said the bite and claw marks seemed like those of a large predatory animal, possibly a bear."

"There are no bears roaming about Paris, nor living wild in the surrounding woods. Beside that, such a huge and dangerous animal would hardly go unnoticed, even at night. Were there any sightings of such an animal, or were any of the bears from the Jardin d'Acclimatation reported to have escaped?"

"None on both counts. And it gets even stranger. Do you see how that poor girl's underpants were thrown to the other side of the alley? Our forensic experts checked what remained of her... er, lower parts, and it seems she was engaged in carnal activities. It must have been with her attacker, considering the copulation occurred shortly before her murder. As in, *minutes* before."

"*Incroyable.*"

"Wait, it gets better, though not in a good way, of course. The forensic men said this young lady wasn't a victim of rape. If so, there would have been tearing and other signs down there, but there were none. So, it seems..."

Judex gritted his teeth before finishing his friend's sentence: "...that this unfortunate woman went willingly for a tryst with whomever—or whatever—her attacker was."

"Based on what is left of her accoutrements, and her engaging in such an act in an alley, with the apparent intention of quickly concluding the encounter, we think she was a lady of the night," stated Cocantin. "Yet, it would seem carnal pleasure wasn't enough for the individual who purchased her services. He had to partake in, er, *culinary* delights, as well."

"I suppose that wouldn't be the most apt way to put it. There is actually no possible way you could say it that *wouldn't* turn my stomach."

"There are indications that whoever did the deed could not have been human, with all the signs pointing to a large beast. Nevertheless, the perpetrator was capable of engaging in the carnal act, much as a man would. I highly doubt this woman would have taken on an animal as a partner. But the forensic evidence says she apparently did that very thing. We found her purse, and it had seven francs in it. Whoever the perpetrator was, he evidently paid for her services. The poor girl had no idea, though, of the full extent of the kind of services her customer expected."

"Your mastery of the understatement never ceases to amaze me, Cocantin. But I am beginning to think of a possible suspect, and, if I am right, we need to take him down as quickly as possible, and by any means necessary, or many more streetwalkers will meet the same ghastly fate as this poor wretch."

"That wouldn't be Bertrand Caillet, the so-called Werewolf of Paris?" asked Cocantin.

"You know of this... creature?"

"I'm no dummy! I found out many things of this kind back when I was the Licorice Kid, and I've continued that fine tradition since becoming an officer of the law. I read the Gaillez Report, which that American student collected and handed it over to Guy Endore, who published it as a lurid Gothic novel entitled *The Werewolf of Paris* a few years back. Most of the public thinks it's just a disgusting fairy tale, but people like us... Well, we know more about these kinds of things than most folks care to admit, *n'est-ce pas?*"

"Then you must also know..."

"About Caillet's involvement in the fiasco during the India festival in front of Notre-Dame last year? The one where he was displayed as a 'wild man' or some such by a demented carny? Only to have him escape and go on a rampage, until that Hindu guy, Felifax, gave him a thrashing? Yeah, I know all about it! And we've both known about Felifax for years; you had a little tussle with him yourself when you went to India to get that rare plant that saved me from being poisoned. I know you must be annoyed to have been away when all the fun occurred at that festival last year, but don't worry, Felifax was there to save the day. No offense, of course."

"None taken. I was grateful he so happened to be in Paris to deal with Caillet in my absence. What you might now know, however, is this: when I ruined the plans of the Red Hand to operate their Horror Arena beneath the Louvre a few months ago, one of their 'gladiators' was another tiger-man called Felanthus. I found out that he was Felifax's sibling, but he rebuffed my offer to help him travel to India. He was determined to do it on his own, rather than trust another human. After we thwarted the Red Hand, he hastily departed into the concealment of the Bois de Boulogne, where he would have sufficient game and water to survive until he found a means to travel..."

"Wait a minute, old friend! You never told me that one of the Red Hand's gladiators had escaped alive! That tiger-man has been loose out there all these months, and you didn't tell the authorities, not even your good detective pal? Which would be *me*, in case you need a reminder."

"I confess I chose not to. He saved my life when I went into the Arena and fought at my side from that point onwards. He aided me in driving out Doctor Cornelius and Professor Tornada, who were responsible for that atrocity."

"Then how do we know this Felanthus is not responsible for the mess in front of us, instead of Caillet? I mean, from what you described, he does have the strength of an animal, but is still human enough to... well, er, copulate in a manly fashion. If he has the ferocity of an animal, maybe he has, er, the needs of one too."

"I believe you are mistaken, *mon ami*," said Judex. "Felanthus is indeed a force to be reckoned with, but only if attacked or provoked. He was entirely benevolent. His only motives are to keep out of sight and find his way back to India. Felifax would never have accepted a sibling who would prey on human beings. And I doubt Felanthus would be eager to return to his brother if his sibling was vehemently opposed to any of his habits. I further doubt that he would have had the money to pay a lady of the night. I also saw no evidence of his being able to take on a more human form, and our victim would not have been inclined to offer her services to a bestial individual."

"Are you absolutely certain of that? I mean, Paris does have all kinds!"

"Enough, Cocantin! This M.O. does not mesh with Felanthus, but it fits Caillet perfectly."

"But I thought Felifax had killed Caillet?"

239

"Beings of his ilk are notoriously averse to remaining dead. He is a troubled man, whose animal side makes him dangerous. I believe his intention was simply to pay for a quick tryst, only to lose control due to the phase of the moon and transform at the worst possible time. Likely, his mind is too addled to keep track of the moon phases—if he is even concerned about that anymore. You read the Gaillez Report, so you know his animal side has always been influenced by his human lusts. He needs to be dispatched—once and for all."

"I did read it, so I'm all too aware. And considering the location where this happened, you're probably thinking exactly what I am concerning where he ran off to...?"

"*Oui.* If the Bois de Boulogne can provide refuge for a tiger-man, it can do the same for a wolf-man. I must search the woods. If Felanthus is still there, I may be able to call upon him for assistance."

"You need look no further than this alley for assistance, pal. You can bet your silly dark hat I'm going with you. This is a police matter, and besides, you know you always needed me to watch your back."

Despite the seriousness of the situation, Judex almost smiled at his longtime friend's mirth. "Very well. Let us go and avenge this young woman. Lady Justice demands no less than Caillet's hirsute hide this night!"

The were-tiger called Felanthus drank deep of the fresh water to be found in the artificial lake known as the Grande Cascade, as he usually did after a day of hunting the plentiful small game which inhabited the Bois de Boulogne. The gentle but intense sound of the waterfall pouring down from the four thousand cubic meters of rock was oddly relaxing to his ears, which was one reason he favored the location. Peace of mind was what he sought most, besides food, water—and a way back to the jungles of India where his brother awaited him.

After assuaging his thirst, Felanthus lay on his back, the tannish-orange color of his natural striped coat contrasting with the green of the surrounding grass. There he stared up at the stars twinkling in the black evening sky, entranced by the sparkling pattern of these distant spheres. The great were-tiger released a contented sigh as he prepared to slip into a comfortable sleep, enjoying the tranquil expanse of the wooded park, but still yearning to ease the loneliness he felt there. The desire for the company of another like him, which would be fulfilled if he ever found his way back to his sibling, seemed to originate in the human aspect of his genetic make-up, as he preferred companionship to the solitary existence which was the natural way of life for most species of big cats.

Unfortunately, the tiger-man's planned reverie was not to last. Several minutes after his relaxing ruminations by starlight began, his pointy ears perked up upon hearing the sounds of a ruckus occurring a mere hundred meters away. The noise was clearly made by living creatures, and the incessant growling suggested several organisms of the canid variety might be involved.

Felanthus sprung into a crouched quadrupedal stance, ready to move at great speed if required. He then focused his acute hearing and sniffed the air, searching for distinctive scents to ascertain how many entities were involved in the fracas, and precisely where. The tiger-man knew from tumultuous experience how a nearby row could quickly and unexpectedly expand to affect those not previously involved. This placid region bordering the big city was his haven, and he wished to keep it as serene and safe as possible. He knew he had to tolerate the periodic encroachments of human visitors, but not any disruption that may threaten his well-being.

When he finally determined that the sounds were coming from a brush beside one of the ivy gardens to his left, Felanthus darted in that direction with such speed that he would have appeared a mere blur to the average eye. The tiger-man peered through the foliage concealing a clearing and finally beheld the source of the disturbance. The darkness which enveloped the park at night was no impediment to a vision that could detect patterns of heat.

What appeared to be a young man of average height and dark hair was cloistered against a large querus robur tree, threatened by a pack of ten slavering wild dogs. Such animals, captured and conditioned to be vicious, had recently been used by the Red Hand, and several of these dangerous canines had escaped captivity during the recent conflict.

The feral animals, consisting of several large-sized breeds, had instinctively understood they could not long survive seeking prey in the human populated city—they possessed a primitive understanding of how easily firearms could end their lives—so they had sought refuge in the Bois de Boulogne. However, these stringently territorial and mercilessly conditioned animals were not averse to attacking a stray human wanderer during the nocturnal hours.

"Stay away from me!" the raggedy man shouted at the canine pack. "I am warning you! I will kill you all!"

Felanthus was aware that a normal human being could never make good on such a threat. The unfortunate soul was but moments away from being slaughtered if the tiger-man did not jump to his defense. He knew, however, that tackling a pack of feral dogs would be a difficult proposition, even for him. The tiger-man considered surreptitiously moving off and minding his own business, as this pack had chosen to give him a wide berth since making the park their home. Conversely, humans had treated him very unkindly, to say the least.

But then, a thought occurred to him: Felifax, his brother, would never simply stand on the sidelines if a human was imperiled. The jungle lord would have risked life and the integrity of his limbs to save a person. Could he do any less? Could he act in a way that he knew would disappoint a sibling that the humans respected and considered a paragon of nobility? Did this not make it possible that, one day, he, too, might be accepted by humans, and even learn to care for and trust them as his brother did?

With his decision made, Felanthus moved through the foliage and prepared to pounce on the pack, hoping to use the element of surprise to take as many of them out as possible before the rest descended on him. The tiger-man prepared for the inevitable painful wounds he would receive, but which had to be endured to save a human life. What he wasn't aware of, however, was that the man backed against the large oak tree was no average human...

As Felanthus began his furtive approach, the angry human suddenly clenched his fists and gritted his teeth His body began to spasm while his mouth started foaming. His incisors became elongated, much like those of Felifax when he reached a state of animistic rage. The sheer fury emanating from the man was palpably tangible to the tiger-man's senses.

"I warned you to get away from me!" the man shouted furiously as his body underwent an astounding transformation.

The snarling canines instinctively took a step back as they found themselves startled by the radical metamorphosis they now witnessed. The sound of bones cracking and rapidly reforming accompanied the man's features taking on a canine appearance similar to his attackers', albeit in a morphological semblance to another, deadlier member of the canid genus.

Dark fur sprouted from every pore on his body, as his mouth extended to a muzzle filled with rows of razor-sharp teeth and his ears took on pointed contours. His entire body seemed to accrue well over a hundred pounds of sheer muscle mass, and the fingernails on his still human-shaped hands grew and sharpened into something resembling curved stiletto blades.

When the transformation had reached its completion, the monstrous lupine beast crouched down on all fours and opened his mouth to release a howling snarl, the magnitude of which surpassed the combined growling of the entire canine pack. This werewolf was ready to defend himself, and turn the would-be predators into prey.

Felanthus was no less surprised by the man's metamorphosis than the voracious pack of dogs. *Man became... like me. He not a man, but... a beast-man. He change like brother change... but into something more like... me. Like me!*

The tiger-man understood that, even a creature such as a *loup garou*, would have a difficult time facing a pack of that size on his own. Felanthus knew he had to help, and that two fighting side-by-side would greatly increase their chances of emerging victorious. Just as he and his brother had done when they had stood united against Professor Tornada's captured experimental subjects; or when he has joined forces with the mole-man Burrkos against the monstrous creatures set against them by the Red Hand.

Two of the bolder dogs were the first to overcome their initial astonishment, and they rushed the lycanthrope in tandem. The Werewolf of Paris put his incredible reflexes to good use by grasping one canine by the throat while it was in mid-lunge. The other clasped its jaw shut on the Caillet's free arm, sinking its teeth deep into its prey's hirsute limb. That move elicited a yelp of pain from the lycan.

The Werewolf responded by pulling the struggling dog in his grip over to his powerful gullet. The were-beast bit down on the canine's throat and tore it out with one mighty heave. The dog was instantly killed amidst a spray of blood.

The lycanthrope then turned his attention to the dog whose teeth were painfully locked onto his other limb, and plunged two of his sharpened fingernails into the animal's eyes. The blinded dog bayed in agony and released its grip on the Werewolf, rollig on the ground in writhing spasms. With a howl of rage, the lycan leaped upon the wounded dog and finished it off by ripping the viscera from its stomach.

In the meantime, Felanthus leaped upon the backs of two of the eight remaining members of the pack, taking them completely by surprise. There was no room for "fairness" or "honor" in the tiger-man's world, but only the fight for survival demanded by the laws of the wild. These required the taking of every possible advantage. Felanthus slit the canine duo's esophagi with a single motion of his arms, his retractable claws creating four bleeding gashes on both their throats, and puncturing their jugulars in the process. With scarcely a whimper of pain, both animals went still as they promptly bled out.

Two of the six remaining pack members turned and rushed at Felanthus, whose element of surprise had now run its course. The tiger-man responded by resuming his quadrupedal stance and meeting the attacking canines head on, doing his best to protect his own throat, lest one of them repay him in kind for what he had done to their pack mates. The anthropomorphic feline pounded one of the dogs directly atop its skull with his closed fist, his enhanced strength immediately crushing its brain into a pulpy mass.

The other attacking canine managed to clamp its teeth onto Felanthus' right shoulder, tearing into his flesh. The were-tiger roared in pain and rage, both spurring him on to a savage counterattack. He grasped the folds of hide on the sides of the dog's neck and pulled with all his superhuman might. The two folds of skin, along with the flesh underneath, were torn clear off the animal's body. The dog released its grip and yowled in agony as its lifeblood sprayed out of the gaping tears on each side of its neckline.

With that done, Felanthus looked up to see two of the four remaining canines tearing into his fellow beast-man, who was ripping back into them with an equal degree of fearsome aplomb. The Werewolf had many noticeable bloody gashes on his hide, though his two attackers were also bleeding in many places. The tiger-man determined their wounds would soon become terminal.

Felanthus still had the final two dogs to contend with. He stood up bipedally and roared a challenge, encouraging his slavering opponents to "bring it on." Both dogs charged him simultaneously, clearly intending to use their combined might to maximize their chances of taking their target down. He met their attack with his muscular orange-furred arms, but they clung and tore at him with a ferocity that impeded his ability to dispatch them before they could cause serious damage.

The tiger-man was suddenly granted a much-needed reprieve when one of the dogs was pulled off him. Felanthus held his single remaining attacker by its neck and took a brief second to see that the Werewolf had killed the pair of dogs he had been fighting, and had now moved to help him against the last two members of the pack. To that end, the wolf-man held the struggling canine by its throat with one arm and slashed the animal's stomach with a quick swipe of his claws. The hound's wriggling body went abruptly limp as its bowels fell out of its eviscerated gut.

At roughly the same time, Felanthus was finally able to focus on his attacker, and he held the struggling animal's neck firmly in his steely grip. Then, with a sudden twist, he snapped the dog's upper vertebrae in half. A stream of blood trickled out of the canine's mouth as all its movements abruptly ceased.

The tiger-man let the cadaver drop to the ground as he turned to see the Werewolf approaching him in bipedal stance. Felanthus stood his ground, keeping his limbs down to indicate he posed no threat, while remaining prepared for anything. The wolf-man stopped several inches away and tilted his head to scrutinize the strange felinoid. He seemed to comprehend his unexpected ally's altruistic intentions.

The lycanthrope then opened his muzzle and spoke in a gruff voice:

"*Merci... mon ami*. Do you... understand me?"

"I do," Felanthus replied in an equally gravelly vocalization of the French language.

"Good," the Werewolf said, as he partially reverted to human form and held out his hand. "My name is Bertrand Caillet."

"I am... Felanthus," the tiger-man replied. "Just... Felanthus."

He shook his fellow beast-man's hand, and it seemed as if a bond had been forged between two kindred spirits.

Over the next month, the two beast-men spent much time discussing their mutual predicaments. They also hunted small game together, and Felanthus was delighted to have a companion who didn't mind that he ate his food raw. He understood most humans would be disgusted by such a thing, as they insisted on cooking their meat. Caillet, on the other hand, had no compunctions about letting his inner animal loose in either hunting or eating.

The duo shared much of their oft-similar experiences, though Caillet wisely chose to leave out some of the more unsavory aspects of his past, specifically those dealing with his predation on human beings. He hated himself for those things, and he was unsure if his new friend would accept them.

The infamous "Werewolf of Paris" had, by now, learned the tiger-man bore no special love for humanity, but he did not yet know how far that dislike extended. The lycanthropic former soldier enjoyed having an actual friend who wasn't revolted by his animal form, and around whom he could release his wild side. He did not wish, however, to take too many chances in revealing the details of his past until he'd spent more time "feeling out" the benign felinoid.

So, he kept their late night conversations, during which they sat near one of the two lakes connected by the Grande Cascade, to more "acceptable" topics. Specifically, topics Caillet hoped would elicit further sympathies from his fellow beast-man rather than his possible ire. His form, at the time, was mostly human, save for lupine incisors that enabled him to eat raw flesh efficiently.

"I was placed in a few cages myself," Caillet said before taking a bite from a slain duck. "A prison in one case, and an asylum in the other. I must say I never ended up in the custody of a laboratory or a modern-dayl arena, however. They both sound truly horrible."

"Horrible... yes," Felanthus said while straining his not fully human voice to mutter comprehensible words. "Was experimented on. Forced to fight for life. Hated it. Hated people who did... things to me."

Caillet took another bite from the fowl and responded with his mouth full, something his fellow beast-man thankfully didn't seem to consider ill-mannered. "But I had my share of cruel captivity as well. Not long ago, I was kept against my will as a side show exhibit. It was right in front of Notre-Dame cathedral. I got loose, but some orange muscle-bound man almost killed me. Or whatever happens to me during the times I appear to be dead until I 'wake up' again."

Both were unaware of the irony in Caillet's recollection, in that it had been Felifax himself that had laid low Caillet's rampaging form on that occasion. But what the revelation of that information may have done to Felanthis and their budding friendship was forever destined to remain a mystery.

"That is... horrible. And people consider us... monsters. But *they* are the monsters! Them!"

"I most certainly concur, *mon ami*. One of the few decent souls I ever met among them was my beautiful Sophia. But she... took her own life. Because I was kept from her. She cared for me like no one else ever did—and will."

"I am... sorry to hear this." The were-tiger put a consoling palm on his friend's shoulder. "But not true... that no one cares for you. I am... friend. I care."

Caillet found himself moved to tears as he gently patted Felanthus' furry hand. "*Je te remercie*, my kindred beast."

That moment of strong bonding warmed the heart of a lycanthrope whose animal side was best kept in check by the power of love. Caillet felt closer to Felanthus than any other being since Sophie, the only other person who had accepted his animal side. Thus, he felt confident that the next evening he could reveal something else to his friend. It would be a decision with disastrous consequences.

The following night, Felanthus sat in their usual place near the lake with only the sound of the waterfall breaking the silence. There he waited for his friend's return, eager to see what type of "new treat" he would have for him, and why he had insisted that they didn't need to hunt the usual variety of small game that evening.

The tiger-man's keen hearing soon picked up a rustling sound in the brush, and his nose caught a familiar scent. Caillet was returning. He smelled another thing too, and that other scent carried a different type of familiarity. A type that the tiger-man found thoroughly unsettling.

Caillet emerged from the verdure carrying something in his arm. Felanthus' yellow-greenish eyes opened wide in horror once he saw what that "something" was: a severed human arm, clearly that of a woman, its long fingernails still coated with shiny polish.

"I saved this for a special occasion," the wolf-man said far too casually for Felanthus' liking. "I'd buried it in one of the rose gardens over a month ago. I had previously stolen a bushel of salt and hid it there too, so I was able to keep this morsel well preserved. I guessed you might want to taste this, and I had to eat it sooner or later anyway, so..."

"You... killed that woman!" the tiger-man yelled as he jumped to a bipedal standing position. "You ate her! And you want me... to do same!"

Caillet frowned, realizing he had just made a terrible mistake. However, he valued the friendship of Felanthus, and he hoped some quick talking could still salvage it.

"*Non*! I didn't! Didn't kill her, that is! I found her body in these woods already dead! The wild dogs had gotten her, and I was hungry, so I didn't think it would do any harm to make use of her... remains."

I hate lying to him! he thought. *I hate myself for doing this! But I can't lose his friendship! I won't...!*

"You... lie! I would have... known if girl came here. If dogs had... got her. You weren't here... long enough... or I would have found you... sooner. You spent most of time... in human city. Until you did... this!"

Damn it all to Hell! Thought Caillet.

"OK, I am sorry, Felanthus," he said. "I didn't want to lie to you! I hated doing that, just as much as I hated doing this! I didn't intend to, I swear it. She was a whore; she reminded me so much of my Sophia, I just wanted some... intimacy... I didn't mean to lose control, but I failed to account for the waxing moon... I am sorry... I made a mistake."

"You better believe it, wolfy!" came the voice of a young man from within the bushes behind them. Detective Cocantin had just emerged from the shrubbery brandishing a revolver. "And you can't imagine what a pain in my *postérieur* it was to stay downwind, so you beastly chaps couldn't detect our approach. Not that my friend here ever has any trouble in the stealth department. It took us almost a month of scouring this place to find you, but this park is like a thousand hectares large!"

"845 hectares to be exact," the "friend" said in a chilling monotone as he, too, stepped out of the darkness and into plain view.

The dark figure was likewise brandishing a gun, albeit a meaner-looking model. Judex had arrived and located his target, only to find an old friend alongside him.

"You..." Felanthus said as he recognized the vigilante. "Man who is called... Judex."

"Oh, dear lord, no," Caillet said as his teeth suddenly began elongating into fangs.

"Greetings, Felanthus," Judex said. "Now step aside while I deal with this creature."

"But he is... friend," the tiger-man insisted. "He only one who is... like me! Who cares!"

"That man is most assuredly *not* like you, *mon ami*," Judex responded firmly. "He has killed before, and also unlike you, he was caged for very good reasons. He will kill again, and more innocents like that young woman will fall victim to his lustful depredations. Justice demands an end to it all—with due prejudice."

Felanthus turned to Caillet, whose visage was now beginning to sprout dark hairs in addition to the fangs. "This true? Did you... kill and... eat other people?"

The wolf-man dropped his victim's dismembered arm and burst into a pleading diatribe, his voice growing rougher by the moment. "Yes I did! I did it! But I didn't want to! I lose control of the animal inside! But I do not want to hurt people! Only love keeps my animal side at bay, and you have given me that, Felanthus! I can be good now!"

"He speaks... truth this time," Felanthus said as he turned to the gun-wielding vigilante.

"Does he now?" Judex replied. "Then why did he keep that woman's arm? Why did he conspire to eat it rather than discarding it if he truly regretted what he had done?"

"And you should have seen what he did to the rest of her," Cocantin added. "That is, if you have a strong stomach. My friend here almost upchucked at the sight, and that would have been equal parts atypical and embarrassing if he did!"

Felanthus turned back to Caillet. "You did... as they said! You kept arm! You wanted me to... eat what left of her too!"

"I swear I am sorry, Felanthus!" Caillet continued to plead. "I do not mean to lose control! Please do not abandon me!"

Cocantin whispered to Judex. "Is it just me, or is that guy getting hairier by the second?"

"He is transforming," the vigilante clarified. "The change must be triggered by more than lunar energies. He will be far more dangerous in his lupine form." Judex turned his attention to the tiger-man again. "Felanthus, I need to act now! Either help me restrain him—or step aside!"

"No!" Caillet bellowed as the ghastly metamorphosis approached completion. "You won't cage me again! You won't kill me again! I will kill *you* first!"

The now fully transformed Werewolf sprung an incredible six meters in a single leap to land directly in front of Judex. The move was so swift that even the black-clad vigilante was caught unaware and brought to the ground before he could fire a single silver bullet. The former Licorice Kid was likewise taken by surprise.

"Will kill you!" the Werewolf howled as he held Judex down by the throat and raised his other hand to rip off the vigilante's face with a swipe of his talons.

Cocantin pointed his gun and fired a shot into Caillet's back—but it was a standard lead bullet and had minimal effect. Conventional bullets might cause a lycanthrope pain, depending upon the caliber and distance, but did nothing to abate the wolf-man's fury.

Though Judex could not match the Werewolf's strength, his skill as a fighter was still exemplary, and he hit the lycan in the throat with a brutal spear hand thrust. Caillet yelped and put both hands on his bruised trachea while Judex reached with his freed arm for his firearm. Unfortunately, the Werewolf recovered faster than any human could, and he grabbed the vigilante's extended arm before it could grasp the gun.

"No, you... don't! I'll kill you first!"

Cocantin pointed his pistol at the beast's shaggy back, preparing to empty its chamber in the hope that more bullets would cause enough pain to buy judex more time. It turned out not to be necessary, however.

The young detective blinked as an orange blur dashed before him and slammed into the wolf-man with a force that knocked the lycanthrope off his feet. Judex expertly rolled over the grass to recover his dropped gun. Felanthus had acted just in time to save the crime fighter. The two beast-men grappled with each other until the Werewolf kicked him off with his thickly muscled, legs. A minute later, the two beings stood face to face, in a deadly eye-to-eye confrontation.

"You no kill again!" the tiger-man decreed with furious conviction.

"He tried to... kill me... first!" Caillet rejoined.

"Only because you... kill innocents! You not innocent! You lie and betray me! You show me... we not alike after all!"

"No! I can't... help myself sometimes. I do not want to... kill innocents!"

Felanthus was certain he could see tears welling up in Caillet's glaring red eyes.

"I thought you... my friend!"

"And I thought... you were mine!"

248

The two beast-men then lunged at each other with rage. They traded blows and slashes with merciless abandon, their movements so fast the two humans could barely see them being thrown. The Werewolf slashed Felanthus across his face with a swipe of his talons, drawing spurts of blood. The tiger-man pushed past the pain and lashed out with his own retractable claws to inflict gaping lacerations on the lycanthrope's abdomen. Blood seeped out the wolf-man's stomach and he howled in pain, making another astounding leap towards his erstwhile friend now turned deadly foe.

Felanthus was taken down by the impact of Caillet landing on him. The tiger-man quickly reacted by using both hands to grab the Werewolf's throat in a choking grip. He quickly stood and lifted the gasping lycan into the air like a rag doll. The orange-furred then hurled the wolf-man against an oak tree several yards distant. Caillet's form slammed into the wood surface and slid down to the ground. Felanthus swiftly attacked again, but the lycanthrope had made a fast recovery and kicked out with his powerful right leg to strike the tiger-man in the plexus. The impact of that blow sent Felanthus sprawling backwards.

Nevertheless, he recovered and, in seconds, the two beast-men found themselves in yet another muzzle-to-muzzle confrontation. Both bared their fearsome teeth and raised their hands in preparation for more brutal slashes.

"You hurt me… by not being real friend!" Felanthus roared.

"I *was* your friend," Caillet bellowed back. "I needed you, and you betrayed me…"

The wolf-man's sentence was cut off by the loud reverberation of a gun shot. A hole appeared in the Werewolf's throat. Caillet put his hands over the wound as blood spurted like a small crimson geyser. The bullet had passed clear through his throat, and a wound inflicted by a silver projectile would not heal quickly. The pain-ridden beast-man howled in agony while Judex pumped another silver bullet into him, that one penetrating his gut.

The terminally injured Caillet shed tears of loss along with streams of blood as he turned and used the last of his fading strength to run towards the nearby lake. A third and final shot struck him in the spinal cord just as he leapt into the water.

The ruby-colored tint that immediately permeated a wide swath of the surface served as a grim indicator of the damage inflicted upon the were-beast. Several minutes of silence passed, and Caillet never emerged. The beautiful lake had become his ugly grave.

After the Werewolf's demise had become a certainty, Felanthus turned to see Judex standing a few yards behind him with a still-smoking gun in his hand. Cocantin ran up to join his longtime friend and ally.

"Into the drink he went," the detective observed aloud, "and into it he stayed. Please don't take offense to this question, but exactly how pure were those silver bullets?"

"As pure as a substantial amount of money can buy," the vigilante interjected.

"Of course."

Felanthus approached the vigilante, whose dark attire failed to prevent his natural heat emission from registering his presence to the tiger-man's slit-shaped irises. He stopped a few inches before the crime-fighter, saying nothing. During the stare-down, Judex was certain that he saw what must have been tears dripping down the tiger-like face of the noble beast-man.

"I am sorry," the vigilante said as gently as he could muster. "It had to be done. Justice demanded no less."

"He was... only friend," Felanthus replied in a somber voice. "Was the only one... like me... here."

"His resemblance to you was only superficial. Caillet lacked the most important trait you possess. And he is not the only one like you on this planet. Please accept my offer to fly you to India and reunite you with your brother."

However, Felanthus' despondency at the human-dominated world was beyond succor.

"I told you... no! Maybe you had to kill... wolf... But you humans always kill! Nevere... understand... Be gone... leave me alone!"

The tiger-man dropped to all fours and dashed away into the darkness with astounding speed. Judex could only watch with a sorrowful glare as Cocantin stepped up beside him.

"I really feel bad for that cat guy," the detective said. "What he had to do, and what he saw you do, sure mustn't have been easy for him. I'm also sorry for suspecting him. He's OK in my book."

"I know," were the last words uttered by Judex before he turned and headed back towards the city lights.

The forner Licorice Kid quietly followed his grim ally back to Paris where he knew they would both spend every day of their lives meting out conflicting, but strangely complementary, forms of justice.

In a departure from his usual stories about Jean Kariven or the Frankenstein Creature, Frank Schildiner takes us to 19th century Japan when the first great French pulp icon, Rocambole, a masterthief who later became a do-gooder, meets a local icon...

Frank Schildiner: *Dice, Pearl and Sword*

Yokohama, Japan, Early 1850s

A shirtless gangster landed in the muck three feet from the approaching Rocambole. The fallen man moaned, a red blood bubble forming on his lips. He collapsed and none on the busy street paused to help, or even glance in his direction. Such was the way of the sailors' quarter of the port city of Yokohama.

Rocambole stepped around the gambler, heading towards the squat wooden inn called the Green Tiger Palace. Sliding inside, the tall Frenchman believed that the name was obviously a bit of irony on the part of the owner. The Green Tiger was slovenly, smoky, and filled with foreign sailors looking for a good time. Heavily powdered slatterns slithered about the room, whispering suggestions in a variety of languages. Their potential customers guzzled down heavy bottles of watered rice wine by the barrel. A long scarred wooden table dominated the room, surrounded by yelling Japanese and foreigners. Three tattooed men, dressed only in cloth pants and sandals, presided over the area, waving the gamblers to silence before the start of the next turn.

Rocambole was well-aware of what was occurring, a popular dice game known as Cho-han. The game was simple enough: the dealer placed two six-sided dice into a bamboo cup. The cup was shaken and the gamblers bet whether the sum was even (*Cho*) or odd (*Han*). This was the favorite sport of the gangsters in the port cities of Japan, and an easy method of removing a sailor from his cash.

There were dozens of ways of cheating in these games, all of which were basic training for Rocambole. He'd learned such skills when most boys were hoping for their first pair of long pants, but he needed to play and lose some money tonight, a small loss for a greater gain. Why else would he have dressed his body in cheap cotton and allow a three-day growth to cover his chin?

Taking a seat at the gambling table, he cashed in a few Ryo coins for some wooden blocks. The gamblers around the table were howling and yelling, swilling down the cheap alcohol and smoking small pipes which stunk of the noxious tobacco of the East.

"One, even." Rocambole turned one betting block straight, indicating his choice. Others slid their blocks forward, shouting and turning their direction of choice.

The man shaking the dice cup was a thin man with tattoos which crawled across his arms and chest like a nest of colorful insects. His possessed a pointed, face that resembled that of a predatory bird, and a mean, thin mouth. Rocambole knew such faces from his travels, angry men who hated the world and happily stole from all, to even imagined slights. Language, dress, or race were unimportant. Such men could be found in any city around the world.

"Bets stop!" the large man at the dice holder's side bellowed. He was a head above his compatriot, with rolls of fat covering his form and tiny dark eyes. His tattoos were less colorful, cruder and, in Rocambole's estimation, probably completed in prison. This man cracked his knuckles often, snarled constantly, and appeared to be daring everyone to start a brawl. Rocambole knew that type of man too. Large as a child, a bully to all those smaller, who solved all problems with a blow of his fist. An even more typical criminal, one available in most villages and cities across the world.

"Five and two! Han!" The dice-shaker yelled above the crowd. A third character, a tall, muscular man with a square face, scooped up the losing bets and paid the few winners. The handle of a short sword protruded from the sash around his waist.

Rocambole quickly estimated that this gang won on an average of ten times for every one loss. Very good odds in their favor. However, that wasn't why he was here, in this hellhole. What he sought was somewhere in this building. The question was, where?

After a second loss, a new player dropped heavily into the seat by Rocambole's side. He was heavily built, with razor cut gray hair and a large fleshy face. His eyes were closed and he clutched a long wooden cane in one hand. The man kept his head lowered and it was obvious to all present that he was blind.

Placing both hands on the table, the blind man chuckled and turned his blocks. "Odd!" he called as the fat man opened his mouth to stop the betting.

"Two and one! Han!" the dice-shaker called out. Most of the gamblers, Rocambole included, lost. The blind man continued to chuckle as his winnings were placed in front of his place at the table. His large hands gently straightened the wooden blocks in a pile and he pushed the entire group forward.

The dice-holder began to shake the cup before slamming it down on the table. The betting grew louder and, just before the fat man called for an end, the blind man called out, "Even!" and turned his blocks accordingly.

The first gangster lifted the cup up and said, "Six and four! Cho!"

This time, the only winner was the blind man, who took a long slurping gulp from his wine and continued to guffaw quietly. Once again, he neatened the stack and pushed the entirety forward as his next bet.

"Quite a gamble," Rocambole remarked, grateful he'd used the boat trip from India to learn Japanese.

"Yes, yes. I like wine and gambling and never get enough of both." The blind man tilted his head Rocambole's direction and appeared to smile. "You speak Japanese well for a Frenchman," he added.

"Is my accent so bad you can tell where I am from?" Rocambole asked, turning his blocks and saying, "Odd."

"No," the blind man said and waited to the last moment a third time before saying, "Odd."

"Four and one. Han!" The dice-shaker yelled and stared daggers the blind man's direction. The stack of blocks easily added up to ten Ryo, a great deal of money.

Rocambole scanned the room again, trying to act like he was examining the prostitutes that appeared to work en masse at this low dive. He missed the next bet, but turned around in time to see the sword-carrying gangster pushing another set of blocks in front of the grinning blind man.

"I think you've won at least eight Ryo," Rocambole remarked, watching as the latter straightened the blocks into a small square pile. The French adventurer was aware this was about a month's salary for a person in this city.

"I have good luck, eh?" the blind man guffawed lightly, sliding the pile forward. At the last second, once again, he pivoted the pile and yelled, "Odd!"

"Five and one! Cho!" the dice-holder yelled, his face a mask of rage as they paid off the blind man once again.

"You are looking the wrong way, Frenchman. The doorway behind these bastards, back there, is where Boss Yamikubo is, with five men and a gun. What are you trying to steal?" the blind man spoke in a matter-of-fact tone, lost to all but Rocambole in the raucous atmosphere.

"Are you truly blind?" Rocambole asked, sliding his blocks forward to the even position. The blind man did the same and they both won, much to the fury of the gangsters. Rocambole had heard that these men were known as Bakuto to the people of this country.

The Blind Man opened his eyes, showing milky white orbs that stared without focus. "What are you trying to steal?" he repeated.

"A small treasure. This group killed a Chinese messenger secretly working for a warlord. The warlord was executed by the head of a tong and the treasure has been forgotten," Rocambole explained as he lost and the blind man won again. He had at least fifteen Ryo now, a huge amount of money for this bottom-feeding gambling parlor.

The blind man nodded and smiled briefly. "Good. If you'd just wanted money, I'd tell you to go hell. I want something in Boss Yamikubo's big safe. You help me, I help you. Agreed, neh?"

"How will you help me? You are blind... forgive me, I never asked you for your name." Rocambole was astonished by this bizarre conversation. This blind man was very unusual, behaving in a manner unlike any Rocambole had ever experienced, despite living an unusual, adventurous life.

"Zato-no-Ichi. I have my ways. Are you any good with that sword in your coat, Frenchman?" the blind man replied, closing his eyes and straightening the blocks once again.

"Zatoichi?" Rocambole wasn't sure he heard the name properly. He wasn't surprised the other knew that he was carrying a small sword in the lining of his pea coat. This Zatoichi possessed senses far beyond the normal man. Having lost his sight did not appear to be a hindrance.

Zatoichi grunted. "Close enough. What about the sword?"

Rocambole was about to nod, but stopped himself in time. It was easy to make that mistake with this strange Japanese man. "Yes, very much so."

"Good. Get ready to use it," Zatoichi chuckled and then his face suddenly transformed. Before he appeared a genial man, head lowered with humility, shoulders bowed by age. Now Zatoichi straightened and stared at the Bakuto with open fury across his broad features.

"Cheating bastards! This game is false!" Zatoichi snarled, standing and pushing away for the table. He held his cane in one hand and his voice silenced the whole room.

"Shut up, you blind fool!" the dice-holder snapped back. "The Green Dragon always runs the best games!"

"Oh yes?" Zatoichi asked, smirking slightly. His hand appeared to slash out at the dice-holder, who shrieked in pain. Across the table spilled four of the man's fingers and two sets of six-sided dice.

Rocambole was unsurprised to see a sword in Zatoichi's hand, blood dripping across the edge. The blind man's cane was a sword—a clever ruse that appeared to surprise all present. The blade was approximately three feet long, single edged and as straight as the cane which held it moments ago. Zatoichi held the sword in a reverse grip, the sword pointed downward the way most men held a dagger. His grip was secure and his movements, seconds earlier, were nearly impossible to track with the naked eye. Something else also impressed itself upon the mind of the French adventurer. Rocambole had viewed many sword canes in Europe, but none were as capable of such clean slices as the one in Zatoichi's hand.

"Two sets of dice! Cheats!" A filthy English sailor named Mugridge howled. He grabbed a bottle of rice wine and threw it at one of gangsters.

Yells of "Cheat!" filled the air and a pair of massive Norwegian sailors jumped into the fray. Moments ago, they'd been arguing, the dark-haired one accusing the blond one of acting like a "wolf" at sea. Now their disputes were put aside and they battled against all comers, gangster and gambler alike.

Rocambole drew his sword and stepped around the table, heading towards the back. The fat bully gangster stepped in his path, a heavy club in his hand. He grimaced and raised his club, screaming wordlessly as he ran towards the French adventurer. Rocambole lunged, smallsword extended, and pierced the Bakuto's heart. The huge man collapsed to the ground with an audible thud, club spilling from his nerveless fingers.

On the other side of the table, Zatoichi faced off with the sword-wielding gangster. The blocky faced man drew his weapon and exhaled loudly as he dropped into a fighting pose. He roared and swung his sword down towards Zatoichi's head. The blind man blocked the blade with the sword sheath and sliced once. The gangster moaned and fell, dead before he hit the ground. Zatoichi stepped over his dropped sword and dead body and headed towards the back room.

"Remember," Zatoichi stated, "five men, Boss Yamikubo, and one gun."

"I remember." Rocambole was slightly aggrieved by the superior attitude of the blind man. The five tattooed gangsters, each of whom carried long curved swords, wiped that irritation from his mind.

"Zatoichi! I know you, you blind filthy monster!" A round-headed man dressed in a silk kimono yelled. He had a bald head, a surly expression and a long mustache that made him look slightly sinister. This man was obviously the leader, standing at the rear of the five men, a Pepper-box revolver in hand.

Zatoichi threw back his head and released a bark of mocking laughter. "Is that you, little Yamikubo?"

"It is!" Boss Yamikubo stepped forward and raised his revolver. "You killed my father!"

Zatoichi nodded and smiled again. "Dark Lord Yamikubo? Yes, I killed that bastard. He was a great swordsman but true garbage. He'd be embarrassed by how little you've accomplished. He was blind and twice the man you were, little Boss Yamikubo!"

"You…you…" Boss Yamikubo spluttered and raised his revolver.

Rocambole sensed Zatoichi had a method of dealing with the gun. But the French adventurer didn't wish to take that risk. Pulling a dagger from his sleeve, Rocambole threw it at the gangster boss. The blade sliced across the Bakuto's right eye, causing him to yelp in agony and drop the gun. He clutched his bleeding eye and screamed in pain.

"Kill them! Cut them to pieces!" Boss Yamikubo shrieked.

The five sword-wielding gangsters surged forward, their yells mixing and merging to an unholy chorus. Zatoichi stepped aside as one sliced towards his head. His blade slashed across the man's back, killing him instantly. A second stepped in, swinging for the blind man's neck. Zatoichi parried the attack with the wooden sheath and sliced the man across his body. He screamed and fell, blood spraying across the wooden floor.

Rocambole knew better than to try and parry these Japanese swords. Though light weight, they were as deadly as a saber and capable of shattering a lesser blade. No matter, the French adventurer was unafraid of such weapons.

Moving lightly on his feet, Rocambole leaped over a slice aimed for his legs. Landing lightly, he slashed out and cut the attacker's throat with the lethal point of his smallsword. The gangster fell away, gagging and coughing blood. He would be dead in mere minutes.

A second gangster took the place of the other, shuffling forward and keeping his blade extended in a two-handed grip. Not a bad strategy while training, where the stakes were to learn. But in a street fight, this was a foolish maneuver. Feinting to his left, Rocambole smiled to himself as the gangster flinched. The French adventurer sliced downwards, cutting across his opponent's knuckles. The man screeched in pain and dropped his sword, his hands feeling as if they were on fire. Rocambole cut off the yells of agony by lunging and sinking his sword deep in the man's throat. He too would die in a short time.

The fifth gangster ran at Zatoichi, swinging his sword wildly. The blind man cut him down in two sift slices, stepping over his bleeding body and approaching Yamikubo. The gangster boss was still dancing about searching for his gun and moaning in pain.

Zatoichi sneered at the screaming gangster for a moment. Then his sword slashed the air and Yamikubo screeched even louder. He grabbed his other eye and stumbled backwards, falling to the ground.

"There! Now you're blind like your gangster father and me. Maybe you'll make something of yourself. Or you'll die. Up to you now, Yamikubo." Zatoichi intoned as he reached into the man's kimono and pulled out a key.

Following Zatoichi through another curtained portal, Rocambole stepped into a small office. A heavy wooden and metal door lay in the rear of the room, resembling the door of a jail more than a safe.

Zatoichi nodded towards the lanterns which lit the office. He walked over to the door and, after a minute or so of fumbling, the lock snapped open. "Take one."

Rocambole grabbed one and followed the blind man into the dark space. The room was rectangular, made of stone and metal and filled with racks of goods. Rows of swords, pieces of armor and flintlocks filled one side. On the other were three heavy metal boxes. Zatoichi opened the first and felt inside. He shook his head and moved to the second. Nodding he pulled out a handful of gold Ryo coins. Counting fifteen, he placed that small pile in his robe and dropped the rest inside.

"My winnings. What are you looking for? The first box felt like jewelry and the like. The second is money. The third will be opium." Zatoichi asked, stepping away from the boxes.

Rocambole considered the first box and inhaled deeply. There, on the top of the small pile was the object of his search. The size of a pigeon's egg and perfectly round, the object glittered in the spare light. It was perfectly white and unblemished, the most perfect pearl in the world other than the one formerly held by the Borgias.

Scooping it up, he placed it in a handkerchief and then buried deep in his jacket. "I found it. What do you seek?"

"You see the swords and weapons? Find me a sword cane, just like mine. Is it there?"

Rocambole pushed aside several curved blades, but found the one Zatoichi sought a moment later. It was tossed aside into a corner, a forgotten, ignored item. The cane-sword was as a little over three feet long, sheathed in black wood and possessing a carved wooden handle. The sword within was narrow and appeared to glitter when Rocambole examined it briefly. "Yes, I found the weapon."

"That is what I seek." Zatoichi appeared to grip his sword a little harder and stood in a crouch.

Rocambole smiled, understanding the man's concern. Had he been interested in betraying the blind man, this was the time. But that was unimportant to him, as was this weapon. He merely pressed it into Zatoichi's hand and led the blind man towards the now-visible rear door.

A moment later, they were in the street, walking several blocks before stopping in a far more respectable tea-house.

"What did you take?" Zatoichi asked after slurping down a cup of hot tea.

Rocambole reached into his jacket and placed the pearl in the blind man's hand. "This was known as the Emperor's Pearl. It was a gift from the Persians to the Tang Emperor. It is priceless."

Zatoichi felt it for a moment and nodded. "I've heard of it. They say it was stolen by Genghis Khan and he wore it in his hat."

Rocambole placed the pearl back in hiding. "Why that sword?"

"This sword is the only straight sword made by the mad swordsmith, Muramasa. A Muramasa blade won't break and could slice a god. I'm teaching an idiot boy how to protect himself. He's blind too. Needs his own sword." Zatoichi placed the cane sword next to his own.

"Your son?" Rocambole asked, finishing his tea and rising to his feet.

Zatoichi shrugged and chuckled. "Who knows? Plenty of ladies warmed my bed, neh? Unlike me, this young idiot was born blind."

"Good luck," Rocambole stated. "It was good to meet you, Zatoichi."

"You too, Frenchman. Oh, and if you want a fast way out of Yokohama, go to the docks. Look for a Struan ship named *Dancing Cloud*. It's headed for England." Zatoichi poured himself another cup of tea.

Rocambole smiled and shook his head, unwilling to ask how the blind man knew so much. "My thanks again."

An hour later, he stood on the deck of the ship, watching Japan vanish in the distance. Though his visit to this mythical land was short, he'd never forget his adventure with the blind gambling swordsman named Zatoichi.

As was the case with Matthew Baugh's story, the presence of Madame Atomos looms large in this story from the future...

Michel Stéphan: *The Odyssey of Madame Atomos*

I. The Dawn of Man

Moonwatcher looked at the warthogs shambling down the path, panting and growling. At the approach of twilight, he and his companions had gone back to their cave without killing a single prey. Moonwatcher was an ape-man, living in the desert on a continent that would one day be called Africa.

At dawn, on the other side of the river, they saw the mutilated body of the antelope and Moonwatcher was suddenly aware that his day had come. His day—and the day of his people. The corpse of the antelope was proof that the leopard was not far, and it was going to make a mistake.

Growling and switching its tail with arrogant poise, the wild cat finally showed up. Thinking that the ape-men were caught in the trap, the animal was already rushing at them when it suddenly realized that something was not right. An object had pierced its side. Once, twice, three times. The leopard ran around, suffering unbearable pain, but it could not escape the hailstorm cast by the clumsy hands of the ape-men. The animal's roars expressed a whole range of emotions from pain to fear, then dread and terror. The ruthless hunter had become the hunted and was desperately trying to run away.

That morning, Moonwatcher and his tribe had won, thanks to intelligence and cunning.

Moonwatcher swaggered up to his victim, feeling like he was the master of the world. By using his skill, he had conquered—and, in the future, he would be able to tame the forces of nature. By domesticating fire on this earth, he had laid the first foundations of technology and left his animal origins far behind.

Before him now hundreds of ape-men bowed. Moonwatcher had become a demi-god, and was going to rule the world.

While he was staring at the bodies bowing before him, he realized that these creatures belonged to him body and soul from now on.

That was when he saw one of them not acting like the rest. It was not an ape-man like the others. It was standing straight up, stubbornly refusing to bend to the rules of this ludicrous ceremony. And it stared back at Moonwatcher so intensely that he thought for a moment that he was the one who was going to bow down.

It was a female. Who not only refused to compromise, but also seemed to be questioning Moonwatcher's authority over the rest of their kind.

Moreover, she was not part of their clan.

Moonwatcher had never seen such eyes before. This female's eyes were different, a little slanted. Her body breathed heavily. And her whole attitude exuded contempt. Moonwatcher knew that by proclaiming himself chief, he had signed his death warrant.

II. Carl 12000

Explorer-3 had now passed Jupiter's last moon. Inside the vessel, which was as big as several cargo ships put together, there was only one man and a computer. A man who was always wondering if he was the only one to understood that he was going to die.

The astronaut had taken off his suit. He walked stark naked down the long, empty corridors of the ship, aware of his solitude and his imminent death. A true end of the world for this expedition that had left Earth three years earlier and was traveling through space to reach the orbital station X2 on the rim of Saturn.

What was, at the start, just a simple, routine flight had completely mutated into disaster. And this had been a long time coming. The onboard computer, a technological wonder called Carl 12000, had gradually taken control of the ship and changed its course. The multitude of scientists and specialists on Earth had struggled to keep in contact, at all costs, with the doomed expedition, all the while pretending that a rescue was still possible, and that the best experts were working night and day to find a miracle solution.

The astronaut had a different view of things. With nothing left to lose, rather than find comfort in spirituality on the eve of the great plunge into darkness, he preferred to console himself with excessive drinking, especially since the computer had given him access to the supply room. And there were plenty of supplies. The *Explorer-3* was supposed to deliver six months of supplies to the X2 base around Saturn.

The man was wearing his dirty shorts and sat tipsy in a comfortable seat in front of a giant screen that showed the image of a huge, three-dimensional chessboard. As if all this technology was of any use! Instead of complaining and crying over his fate, he had decided to enjoy one last game of chess against this demented computer that had taken control of the ship and was hurtling him to his death.

On Earth, it was a different story. Since the announcement of the unbelievable and tragic news, astonishment had given way to a highly active search for data over which a very few engineers apparently had a monopoly. New men came to mission control. Strange men who seemed to hold some pieces to the puzzle. The top official at the base was forced to submit to the authority of these newcomers, whose close connection to the government was unquestionable.

"Let's sum up," the governmental envoy said. "*Explorer-3* is out of your control."

"It's still heading straight for our Saturn space station, but it's taking a course that it shouldn't be on, which is putting it on a distorted curve. The computer won't be able to adjust for a good approach, so the ship will crash right into it."

"There won't be any survivors out of the 500 colonists on the station."

"Are you joking?"

The envoy did not react to this last remark.

"Has the computer completely taken over the ship?"

"I think so. Even though it seems impossible, right now there's only one commander on board and it wants to crash the ship into X2."

"How's the astronaut doing?"

"He's understood the situation for a long time. I don't think he's expecting much. He spends his time playing endless games of chess with the computer."

"That's exactly why we have a chance."

"I don't understand where you're headed," the engineer said, standing up from his chair.

"Sit back down. I'll explain. It's a long story and you have to hear it to be able to make up your mind and be of any eventual use."

The astronaut had just lost another piece, this time one of his rooks getting captured. He looked at the screen. The computer sometimes answered him because it had a voice—its designers were aware of the need to give a semblance of social contact to men isolated in a hostile environment. The astronaut knew very well that the computer was the cause of his desperate situation, but he was not mad at it, because a machine, as powerful as it might be, was still a machine, designed by men and certainly not endowed with its own intelligence.

But what annoyed the astronaut the most was that every time the computer won a game—and it won practically all of them—the female voice came over the speakers—Carl 12000 had a sensual woman's voice—to tell him:

"Check and mate. With the compliments of Madame Atomos."

Most of the engineers on the base were gathered together in the main room in the middle of the building, the place where all communications with *Explorer 3* took place. The man who had started to talk with those in charge had quickly called for silence to tell his story, an incredible story that was about to carry his audience more than 200 years into the past.

"Do you remember Madame Atomos?" he told his listeners, who were not expecting such an opening. "The woman is now a part of History. Everyone pretty much knows the terrifying events that scarred the 20th century. I won't remind you of them, but rather mention certain things that you surely know nothing about. As you do know, the Japanese woman is supposed to have died in the early part of this 21st century. I say 'supposed to' because we never found her body. Which still, even if she's no longer with us, gave her exceptional longevity. In short, it would seem that, one day, she decided to drop out of sight. Of course, during the last decades, there were other people who tried to use her identity, but the fraud was always discovered, and, despite some people's protests, despite the woman's exceptional aura, I think that Madame Atomos was, above all, human. I also think that, like every human being, she must have thought about the end of her life, and a way to continue her work after her death. So, gentlemen, the question you have to answer tonight is this: was the computer on board *Explorer-3* tampered with by Madame Atomos—or is it Madame Atomos herself?"

The astronaut ended up finding his outfit a little inappropriate for Carl 12000, which he considered a woman. He decided to stop drinking for the moment and put his pants back on.

"Tell me, Carl, why do you keep saying 'with the compliments of Madame Atomos'? Do you want to talk about that Japanese woman who sowed so many years ago?"

There was no answer from the machine.

"OK, you've messed things up good on the ship. I looked at the flight plan. In less than 30 days, we're going to crash into the space station with all the colonists still living there. And apparently, I can't do anything about it. So, my dear Carl, the question is: do you have any particular reason for screwing with me or do you have a more subtle goal?"

"*With the compliments of Madame Atomos.*"

"Damn it! Is that all you can say? The end of my life, meaning the end of *our* life, doesn't look like it's going to be much fun…"

"A long time ago," the man continued, "an engineer came to us. Cobb Anderson—I think the name means something to you—was one of the best in his field. Thirty years at NASA. He had his own department there, working on computers. He came to see us at the end of his life to tell us that he had made a pact with the devil. We didn't really believe him because we couldn't shake the idea that we were dealing with a senile old man, so we set aside his information. It was absolutely unbelievable. So unbelievable that we treated him a little rudely and way too casually… Cobb Anderson confessed that he'd had a visit from Madame Atomos. She knew her days on earth were numbered and wanted to find a way to continue her work and make one last big splash before it was too late. She asked Anderson if his work was advanced enough to transfer her mind into a machine."

"You mean she wanted to actually transfer her mind into a computer?"

"That's right. She asked Anderson to keep her alive through a super sophisticated intelligence so she could keep terrorizing the United States. Anyway, that's what he told us."

"That's utterly impossible!"

"It happens that for Anderson it was an opportunity to end his career with a bang as well. Of course, we thought it was so crazy that we didn't believe him, but he admitted that the experiment went forward and worked so well that he was sorry for it, which was obviously why he killed himself soon afterward. We were left with his notes, but didn't know what to think. However, we did know that there might be an infected computer at NASA somewhere, a computer that might have found its way onto one of our spaceships to cause a mission to fail. Unfortunately, we didn't take this seriously enough and here we are today."

"It's not possible! I'll admit that he could've tampered with a computer, but you can't expect us to believe that our astronaut is up there with the spirit of a long-dead Japanese woman!"

"We'll find out. And that's why I came here. We've been living in uncertainty for years. We've looked at the problem from every angle to see whether Carl 12000, if it turns out to be the cause of the disaster going on up there, should still be considered a machine, or should we be preparing to face Madame Atomos once again."

A deadly silence loomed over the room now. All the engineers were hanging on the words of the government envoy.

"We've cooked up a plan that I'll explain to you briefly. How much time is left before the ship reaches the point of no return?"

"We've got one hour to get around the computer and put our man in manual control. After that, *Explorer-3* won't be able to stop its deadly course toward the space station."

"I guess we've tried everything else to incapacitate the machine?"

"Carl 12000 is unresponsive to all contact. It's got total control over the ship."

"There's still one weak point. It's in Carl's gaming system. The computer was initially programmed to have no vulnerability concerning the flight crew's safety and security. At the same time, it was designed to leave some freedom of action to its adversaries. You see what I mean?"

"You mean its adversaries in games?"

"Exactly. Particularly in chess. The computer was programmed to let its adversaries win about... let's say, 25% of the time, so that the game wouldn't become too boring. There is, therefore, a weakness in the computer's program. Certainly, a tiny flaw, but it's our only chance of getting back in control."

"I don't really understand how you plan to...?"

"Well, I've brought with me two of the world's greatest chess masters. They're going to get in touch with our astronaut and lead him in a game against the computer. Carl 12000 was designed for pre-programmed games, games that are certainly complex, but remain perfectly logical for a machine as advanced as it is. Through the astronaut, our two chess champions are going to start playing against Carl. Then they're going to start cheating. Not in order to win, but rather to lose. Very subtly. Too subtly for our computer to catch anything because the necessary information for this kind of game hasn't been programmed into it."

"And you think you can get it to break down?"

"We think we can find something. Either we're dealing with a real machine, and in less than an hour, its circuits will go haywire thanks to our trick. Or we're dealing with Madame Atomos, and we should probably start wondering if it's not too late."

"When she learns the truth…"

"Right. Put me in touch with the astronaut right away."

"You're going to show me that you're nothing but a brainless computer," the man said to the machine.

The game was started in less than ten minutes. The astronaut was staring at the on-board clock. He had less than an hour now, which is what the base had told him, seeing that the computer was no longer able to give him any reliable or coherent information. The astronaut was also letting his game be played. By chance, the communication system with Earth was independent of Carl 12000 and therefore perfectly secure.

From the start of the game, the man had already lost three important pieces, one of which was a rook. Every time, the computer had greeted the capture with the words, *"With the compliments of Madame Atomos."* Then the game continued. They were now less than half an hour from the point of no return.

"Good God, what the hell are you doing down there? The game's getting totally stuck."

The astronaut did not understand what was really happening. The computer felt something was wrong and was answering his moves much more slowly.

At less than 15 minutes from the point of no return, the ground control was starting to panic. The engineers were pacing around the chess masters who were saying it was impossible to cheat against a machine that did not want to move back.

"With the compliments of Madame Atomos," the computer declared as it picked a fourth piece off the board.

"Who are you really?" the astronaut asked in a daze. "Are you still Carl or are you really possessed by the spirit of that Japanese woman?"

"I am Madame Atomos."

"Well, I don't see it. You're a very well designed machine, Carl. You might be tampered with, but you're still a machine. I can't believe that a human mind is living inside of you."

The astronaut had heard the signal from Earth. He had less than ten minutes to free the computer.

"Don't waste any more time," the engineer shouted. "There are only two solutions. Either this computer is a machine and we've failed. Or we're dealing with Madame Atomos and you have to tell her the truth."

263

"Did you hear that?" the astronaut said. "I have to tell you the truth."

The computer was silent for a moment. It had, however, just snatched the second rook from the board, but it did not seem to make any difference. The astronaut started talking in a calm and quiet voice, even though he knew that he was probably living the final hours of his life. And he told the truth.

After a minute, a voice echoed through the speakers, "*You're lying*," the computer said.

"I'm not lying, Carl. Or should I call you Kanoto Yoshimuta? Everything I told you is absolutely true. There are exactly two minutes for you to free the navigation system so we can get back on our programmed trajectory."

"*You're bluffing! What you're saying is impossible! The game of chess was a trap to cheat me. And so is what you're telling me.*"

"Are you ready to take that risk, Kanoto? Hurry up and make up your mind. You only have thirty seconds left."

"*I am Madame Atomos.*"

"Yes, you've already told me that. If you repeat yourself, I'm going to end up not believing you. You've got fifteen seconds to free everything up, scumbag!"

Without thinking about it, the astronaut raised his fist and smashed it onto the control panel. He knew, however, that it was completely pointless. Everything was wrong in this spaceship, all the way down to Carl's voice.

The astronaut looked at his hand. There was a slight cut, but it did not matter much now. The deadline had passed and the man knew he was condemned. Nevertheless, he kept on insulting the computer.

All of a sudden he calmed down. And the ship was silent.

The man was ready to accept his fate. He knew that the point of no return was long past, and that here was no chance of going back. In a few hours, the spaceship would end its crazy race, with a trajectory stuck on space station X2 and the 500 colonists living there. It would be the greatest astronautical disaster since the beginning of the conquest of space.

In seeking to bring the United States to its knees, the madness of the Japanese woman had ended up turning against herself.

In seeking to fight against Madame Atomos, in seeking to spend huge sums to repair the damages caused by the sinister Japanese woman, America had no more money to spend on the conquest of space. Madame Atomos had already jeopardized this conquest with her flag planted on the Moon.

When the formidable Japanese woman had contacted Cobb Anderson, he was working for NASA and the computers that he was supervising were working on all kinds of American projects. The computer series Carl 200, 1000 and 12000 were assigned to spaceships, but, in time, the United States abandoned almost all of its space program in order to rebuild what had been destroyed on its own territory.

It was Japan, China and Russia that were sharing the space race and sending ships farther and farther into the galaxy. Thus, the Carl 12000 series ended up on all the vessels of the Empire of the Rising Sun.

The astronaut was ready to accept his death. In his family, as far back as he could remember, there were always heroes, men who knew how to die with dignity. Ichiro Anaki knew that many of his ancestors had been kamikazes and he himself was going to try to prove himself worthy of his ancestor in honor of their memory.

As for the ship that had kept its American name because it had been built in the huge factories in Nevada, when America could still afford it, it was hurtling right now toward space station X2, where 500 Japanese colonists lived, chosen from among the best people from the Empire of the Rising Sun.

Translation by Michael Shreve

Another short vignette by one of our French contributors, bringing together two of the most fearsome representatives of...

Artikel Unbekannt: *The Yellow Peril*

1980

Brooklyn, Williamsburg, a non-descript building.

"I am extremely upset."

Not bothering to hide her anger, the woman who had just uttered those words in a voice that was both sweet and menacing was standing against a large window, her back to her visitor.

She was silhouetted against the light and gazed through the glass as if seeking to derive a sense of calm from the sublime Japanese garden extending across the roof terrace.

The scene unfolded on the top floor of a mansion, which no one would have suspected of housing such wonders. Indeed, no external signs suggested that its huge loft had been converted into a jungle of sorts. Dozens of tropical plants bloomed from floor to ceiling under the building's heavy metal structure, inherited from its industrial past.

The man stared at the woman's back with admiration mingled with unease.

"How dare you return to me with no information?" said the woman, still without turning. "Did I not impress upon you the importance and urgency of your mission?"

An awkward silence floated about the room.

"Orgonetz, you have lost your way. Your impotence forces me to take a radical decision. I shall have to leave. And you know how much I hate that."

As she spoke, the woman finally turned around. Like a heavenly vision stepping out of a masterpiece, she pulled away from the darkness. Her long shapely legs were sheathed in black leather. She took a few steps toward the coffee table near which stood the visitor. He could at last regale himself with the sight of her stunning beauty.

She was dressed in a tight black shirt emphasizing the curves of her body and the satiny tan of her skin. Her perfect oval face was framed by ebony hair with highlights that shone blue; her eyes were two finely cut black diamonds, their expression showing a fierce nobility, a timeless heritage of warrior princes and indomitable amazons.

Miss Ylang-Ylang looked disdainfully at Roman Orgonetz, cruel lights dancing in her eyes. The Eurasian woman's melodious voice matched her stunning physical beauty. It was suave and smooth, yet coldly authoritative if circumstances required. This was the case now.

"I haven't yet heard the sound of your voice. Do I terrorize you so much? Like those idiots who seek to blame me for crimes I did not commit?"

The man in front of her opened his thick lips, but no sound broke through the barrier of his gold teeth. He merely shrugged in a gesture of utter helplessness.

"I see. Your silence is a confession," said the female leader of the powerful espionage cartel known as SMOG. She pressed a button which caused a portion of the wall to swing open. "I shall not detain you any longer. As for me, I'll be leaving the U.S. tonight. We shall meet again soo," she concluded ominously.

Meanwhile, in Chinatown...

After the latest terrorist attack, the authorities appear to be helpless. The enemy seems to be everywhere and nowhere at once. Nothing can stop him. The question now is, what will his next target be? And when will he attack?

The Mongol turned off the television. The giant screen stood in a stark contrast with the decoration of the apartment, a veritable Eastern museum. Japanese prints, Chinese vases, lacquered dressers, coffee tables surrounded by embroidered pillows... All was in exquisite taste with a subtle sense of proportion. An adjoining room was reserved for wonderful hand-crafted bookcases made of rosewood, harboring the complete works of Mishima, obscure philosophical treatises and martial arts, as well as countless anthologies of haiku. An impressive collection of antique swords took up an entire section of wall.

The man looked at the weapons with amber eyes that never seemed to blink. His head was fully shaved; he wore a black clergyman suit, the cut of which suggested an impressive musculature beneath. A carnivorous smile revealed two rows of gleaming teeth. He was the dreaded Ming Tsai Tsou, a.k.a. The Yellow Shadow.

His interlocutor was a young Japanese woman with a ravishing face.

"Thank you for responding to my invitation, Madame. You are what I think might be called a local celebrity, and I suspected that the Americans would blame you for my latest, er, initiative. However, I had not imagined that SMOG would be, er, associated with our festivities. But I confess that this unexpected rapprochement does not displease me. The more, the merrier, no?"

The man paused, then continued:

"But that is a mere detail, because I succeeded in my goal. You were in retreat, after the losses suffered by your own organization. It was essential that a structure like the one I run come to your assistance to give you time to lick your wounds. Our interests are the same. You dream of destroying America, and I the whole western world. Consider, therefore, my invitation as a token gesture of friendship."

The woman indicated her approval with a slight nod of the head, then invited her host to continue with a gracious gesture.

"There could be other opportunities in the future. Since you are now, er, acquainted with Miss Ylang-Ylang, feel free to contact her again. For the proper fee, SMOG can render you many useful services. For now, our paths will separate, but I am sure we will meet again. No matter what, the Western powers will not soon forgive these attacks, nor will they forget the name of she whom they arbitrarily hold responsible for them. But do not get me wrong: I do not intend to let you carry this burden alone. You can count on me to keep their fear of the so-called 'Yellow Peril' alive by stepping out of the shadows myself."

"Are you suggesting some kind of association, Mr. Ming? I thought you preferred working alone..."

"Better than a mere association; a partnership. To our best—and their worst!"

Did Madame Atomos appreciate the witticism, or was she relishing the pleasant prospects ahead? In any event, a radiant smile suddenly lit up her face. A smile full of promises.

Translation by J.-M. & Randy Lofficier

A new Tales of the Shadowmen *would not be complete without a story featuring that wonderful rogue, Arsène Lupin, and we can always count on David Vineyard to provide one. The following tale takes place rather late in Lupin's career (the "André de Savery" pseudonym is from* Le Dernier Amour d'Arsène Lupin, *written c. 1936 and only published very recently) and manages to bring in several characters from Sax Rohmer's oeuvre...*

David L. Vineyard: *The Third Eye of Osiris*

Egypt, 1938

Beautiful as the view was standing on the Cataract Hotel's large veranda, beneath the red and white awning, watching the wide-flowing Nile and scarlet poinsettias on the island opposite, all bathed in the deep red light of the dying day, the Bimbashi Baruk could neither appreciate the cool evening breeze, nor the view. There were more important things to think about. The message from Sir Denis Nayland Smith had been concise and clear:

Meet me Aswan. Stop. Sir Lionel Bart's reception Cataract 6pm. Stop. Stakes are highest. Stop.

The message was typical of Sir Denis, now roving Commissioner with Scotland Yard, formerly of Burma and points East. Annoyingly typical; terse, uninformative, and assuming the half-English officer of the Camel Corps had nothing better to do than drop all his duties in Cairo, hop in a borrowed military plane, and fly to Aswan at the last moment to attend a cocktail party as the guest of a famous archeologist. But then, that was Nayland Smith, and soldiers, even bright and upcoming ones from the Political Intelligence division of the Camel Corps, ignored him at their peril.

Not that it wasn't an interesting guest list. Major Baruk, or the Bimbashi as he was known, had noted that. To begin with, Sir Lionel himself was larger than life—a brash but brilliant man with the manners of a hungry lion and the temperament to match. Then, there were the guests: the mysterious club-footed German with the orange Prussian haircut spiking from his grotesquely large head, Graf von something or other; John Solomon, the sprightly little Cockney in the red tarbash and white dinner jacket, a businessman with a hand in every pie and the best private intelligence network in the East; the guest of honor, the Danish archeologist Professor Tör Andersen—who had yet to arrive—who had been digging nearby and was known for his eccentric theories about Ancient Egypt; and, last but not least, the tall, slender elderly French archeologist, André de Savery, about whom there was talk that he secretly worked from the French Ministry of the Interior.

There were other guests as well, local celebrities and civic figures, a few well-heeled tourists, soldiers, various Consuls, elegant ladies in sleek evening gowns, larger matrons sporting glittering jewelry, and a tall, rather mysterious Arab who kept his eyes hidden behind dark-green glasses, and his face behind his burnoose. He had only been introduced as Mr. Hamid. Nubian waiters in red fez and long white caftans navigated effortlessly among the guests with trays of champagne, canapés, and martinis

Baruk, a tall, bronzed young man with striking blue eyes that only betrayed his origins by the lids that, when half closed, displayed a Mid-Eastern cast, was drinking a Club Soda from a cocktail glass. Something had told him this was a night to stay sober. Suddenly, he noticed the Graf standing beside him. The man was off putting, to say the least, and something about him put Baruk on his guard. Perhaps it was the piggish eyes? The clubfoot was merely a physical deformity, but there was something about those eyes, the bristly orange hair, and the ugly countenance that made the hair on Barouk's arms stand on end.

As chief political officer for local intelligence, Baruk had been informed that the Graf had entered Egypt on a German diplomatic passport, but so far, despite close observation by his many agents, the man had not been observed doing anything more suspicious than visiting various local tourist sites. It had been a busy season for German tourists, many of them no doubt seeking one more season in the sun before the inevitable war brewing in Europe.

"Egypt... Your country is quite beautiful and very ancient," the Graf said in English.

It was a statement, not a question. As an opening ploy for conversation, it was good enough, Baruk decided, if a bit condescending, but then condescension was to be expected from a Nazi. The Graf wore a white summer uniform with a red armband sporting a Swastika. Turning around, the Bimbashi acknowledged it was indeed a beautiful country.

"And to truly know Egypt," the Graf continued, "the real Egypt, one must leave Cairo and its cosmopolitan European sham behind and travel to Luxor, or here on the edge of the Nubia desert. It is here that the real mysteries of Egypt can be found. Of course, so much of ancient history is misconstrued. We in Germany, have devoted much time and expense to rooting out the true history of the Ancient World, as you have likely read. It is absurd to believe the great edifices of Egypt's past were erected by sand fleas and Jewish slaves, wouldn't you agree?"

As a half-"sand flea," Baruk was aware of the challenge being presented. Whatever else he was, this German was not a boor. He was probing.

"I'm only a poor soldier, better suited to riding a camel than investigating the past," he lied. "I read no more history than was required of me in school—Egypt's or anyone else's. I'm much more interested in the modern world."

The Graf nodded, but it was clear he didn't believe the handsome young man in his white dinner uniform. "Some feel that way in my own country, but luckily, the Führer is a visionary in this as well. He wishes to trace the history of our race in the distant past, and he has shown great concern about preserving the artifacts and wonders of the ancient world. That is why I am so excited to meet Professor Andersen tonight. You know that he searches for one of the lost treasures of your country's pas—the Eye of Osiris."

"I should think that it is quite difficult to find," a third voice said.

Baruk turned around to discover that they had just been joined by André de Savery. "Once Set murdered Osiris, he had his body cut into pieces and scattered to the seven winds as I recall," added the Frenchman.

"You are too literal," the Graf said, seemingly angry at being interrupted. "We do not believe in literal gods of the pagan past. No, we speak of an artifact of untold power, at least over the minds of men; that is the Eye sought by Professor Andersen."

"I see," de Savery demurred softly. "It is just as well, then, that we aren't speaking of fairy tales."

The German made a sound like "pfaugh" and lumbered away.

"I believe I offended him," de Savery said, sounding quite pleased with himself. "Forgive me for interrupting, but you looked as if you needed rescuing. By the way, I am André de Savery, archeologist, and you need not introduce yourself." After a pause, he added: "Sir Denis has already spoken very highly of you to me."

The hairs on the back of Baruk's neck stiffened as those on his arms had earlier. It seemed to be that kind of night.

"And how is Sir Denis?" Baruk asked noncommittally.

"Nearby," de Savery replied.

"Have you known him long?"

The Frenchman smiled, recognizing Baruk's ploy, but didn't seem much concerned about it. "Much longer than even Sir Denis himself knows."

Before Baruk could question that odd remark, a servant appeared at their elbow. "Sir Lionel requests that you gentlemen should join him in the reception hall, if you please?"

They followed the tall Nubian to the reception hall. Two great doors were closed. The Nubian knocked, then answered a whispered request from the other side with more whispers. A second Nubian opened the doors and ushered them in, then closed and bolted them, standing with his back to them.

At the bar on the far side of the room stood three men: the rotund Cockney John Solomon and the leonine Sir Lionel Bart were unmistakable. The third man was the mysterious Arab, Hamid, still wearing his green glasses, and, much to Baruk's surprise, nursing a whiskey and soda. It was an odd choice of beverage for a follower of Muhammad.

"Major Baruk, Monsieur de Savery, join us and have a drink, Sir Lionel is buying," said the tall Arab, speaking in the clipped accents of an Englishman of a certain class and background.

As he did so, he whipped back his burnoose to reveal tight iron-gray curls and a ruggedly attractive face, the bronzed skin dyed even darker with some sort of stain.

Nayland Smith removed the green eyeglasses; his gray eyes twinkling.

"Sir Denis will 'ave 'is little jokes," Solomon said in a strong Cockney accent. "Always good to see you Bimbashi, and you too, A.L. H'im elected to play Mother tonight, so w'at'll it be gentleman?"

Baruk stuck with club soda to the twinkling amusement of Nayland Smith's sharp eyes. The Frenchman asked for a brandy.

"I believe we all know each other in one way or another," Smith began, full of that nervous energy that so marked his character. "As the latest arrival in our little conspiracy, I should introduce Mohammed Ibrahim Brian Baruk, Major in the Camel Corps, assigned to political intelligence and quite adept at it. His friends call him B.B., I'm told. He rounds out our little group for this night's activities. I suppose you are all interested in why I've sent for you? Suffice it to say, there is villainy afoot this night. First-class villainy. Before morning, we may all need something more substantial than alcohol if we are to keep our scalps and claim the prize. First off, Bimbashi, how did you find our German friend? I noted his interest in you."

"Quite curious. He plays the boorish Nazi well, but there is something about him. Whatever else, I wouldn't take him for what he seems."

"Excellent," Smith snapped. "What did I tell you, Sir Lionel? The lad has brains. What would you say if I told you that our Graf whatever he is calling himself is, in reality, none other than the notorious Adolph Von Grundt?"

"The clubfoot," Baruk said. "I should have... But I thought he was on the outs with Hitler?"

"There would seem to have been a reconciliation, or a truce. Even Hitler isn't mad enough to do without the benefit of a man like Von Grundt. Desmond Okewood has kept a close eye on the man ever since they met in the Great War, and he believes Von Grundt is with the Wehrmacht, German Military Intelligence, but working with Himmler and the SS regarding that little troll's fascination in ancient relics, particularly those of power, such as the Spear of Longinus or the Holy Grail. The Germans have the Spear, at least they think they do, and the Grail is safe for now, as is the Ark of the Covenant, if only just. The Americans have the latter. Probably buried in a warehouse somewhere."

"And what is it the Nazis want here in Egypt? My country is a living relic, but as far as I know, the only power is monetary."

"There is more than one kind o' power, lad," Solomon interjected.

For the first time, Sir Lionel spoke. "And more than one way to wield it. What do you know of Osiris, Major?"

"Father of the gods, brother of Set, he was murdered and torn to pieces and his body parts scattered over the whole land, but he was granted new life and gave birth to the gods. The usual resurrection myths of the region."

"And what of the Eye of Osiris?" Sir Lionel asked.

"The Eye... wasn't that one of John Thorndyke's cases back in the twenties? A jewel, wasn't it?"

"That was *an* Eye of Osiris, not *the* Eye of Osiris," Smith said.

"The ancient priests of the old faith kept many secrets," de Savery began. "Of course, I am only an amateur compared to Sir Lionel, but objects of great power, whether real or imagined, were often embodied with the aspects of the Gods. The Eye of Osiris, in this case, may be an object of great reverence..."

"A call to arms," Solomon finished and the Frenchman nodded. "H'i dare say, you all know H'i keep me finger in a good many pots. Egypt h'is sort of my backyard, my 'eadquarters is in Port Said. Lately, h'i've been 'earing of talk. Funny kind of talk. Not just the loose talk of rebellion and revenge, but talk about a symbol to gather h'an uprising around. A symbol of Egyptian mystery and ancient sorcery and power. There is some sort of society, the Sons of Osiris, making claims and making plans."

"Egypt is always full of such rumors," Baruk said. "I've picked up rumors about these 'Sons of Osiris' myself, but it's mostly mystical mumbo jumbo conjured from kif dreams and hemp nightmares."

"True," Smith said. "I've read your excellent reports. But if, as you say, these are kif dreams and hemp nightmares, what brings Adolph Von Grundt here? He's no dreamer, and what is it that Dr. Fu Manchu is looking for in the guise of Professor Tör Andersen in the sands nearby?"

"Fu Manchu?" Sir Lionel barked.

"Sorry, old friend," Smith said. "I couldn't let it slip out. The real Andersen is dead. I saw his body myself in the sewers of Paris where the Si-Fan murdered him. Fu Manchu has taken his place, determined that the Nazis will not have this treasure, and the East will. So, you see, our little intrepid band has its work cut out for it. Tonight, Fu Manchu will break through the temples of Osiris and Horus, Osiris' son, and when he does, Von Grundt and his men will descend on him to steal the relic. The town and nearby region are swarming with SS officers in disguise, and natives they have either bought as mercenaries, or to whom they made extravagant promises."

The Bimbashi thought of all those young German tourists making one last winter in warm climes.

"I could call on the Army to outgun them both, but in the confusion of a three-way gun battle, either Von Grundt or Fu Manchu could sneak away with the relic, and I can't take that risk. Nor do I wish to cause more harm to the sacred sites of Ancient Egypt than absolutely necessary. Instead, I've gathered this little band of trusted men to strike, seize the relic, and get away in the confusion. We take the prize while Von Grundt and Fu Manchu each believe the other has seized the day."

"Or," John Solomon added, "we die trying."

Later, Smith and Baruk went up to Mr. Hamid's suite while the others attended other matters arising from the coordination of the evening's plan. Smith had drawn Baruk aside and asked him to join him in his room. There, the Englishman had flung himself down on the bed while the Major chose to sit in a deep chair near the curtained window.

"It's good to see you again, lad," Smith said as he tapped tobacco into his disreputable old briar pipe. He paused a moment to light up. Then puffed a blue gray shroud of strong smelling smoke about his head.

"So, what do you think of our little group?" he asked. "Be truthful now."

"Personally, I think I'd rather have a tank," Baruk said, taking a cigarette from a gold case and lighting it. "I know of Sir Lionel—Doctor Petrie has spoken highly of him, but he's not young, and while I'm sure he is a good man in a row, I have to assume he is here more for his expertise than his fighting skills."

"Go on," Smith said, pipe removed from his firm lips and then returned, as he lay back on the bed, his back propped up, arms akimbo with one hand loosely holding the pipe bowl.

"Solomon, I know of course. Who in Egypt doesn't at least know of him. He doesn't look it, with that red nose, white hair, and cherubic cheeks, but he's a good man in a fight, courage, and brains. Solomon's all right."

"And," Smith's gray eyes flashed in Baruk's direction.

"This André de Savery, the Frenchman, he's a puzzle. He must be sixty at least, with that white hair, and he looks like a caricature of a French academic. But I've heard rumors about him. Someone mentioned he once served in the Foreign Legion, but that was back before the Great War. It just doesn't add up. Either that, or I've been in intelligence too long and grown suspicious of everyone." The eyes were half-lidded now and the Mid-Eastern aspect was striking.

"Around sixty, yes," Smith said," though with *him*, it's hard to tell. I know a little more about *him* than you do, but he is why we're here, and it felt safer to have *him* with us than on the outside."

Smith stood up and began pacing nervously while he puffed on his pipe like a train engine leaving a trail of blue gray smoke.

"Three weeks ago, I was in Berlin," Smith said. "I had heard a rumor than Fu Manchu was interested in the Spear of Longinus—a false lead, as it turned out—but at dinner, one night, a man sent me his card, asking if he might join me to both our advantages. I was bored and alone, so I thought, why not? That man was André de Savery.

"What he proceeded to tell me was fantastic, but told so calmly and with such details that I was convinced on the spot. He said that Professor Andersen was dead in a Paris sewer, and that the man who was in Egypt making the dig in his name was none other than Fu Manchu. He added that Fu Manchu was behind the secret society of the Sons of Osiris and all the recent troubles, and that he was seeking this Eye of Osiris, the key to starting a full-scale revolt in Egypt. It sounded preposterous, even given my experience with Fu Manchu, but then de

Savery told me exactly where to find Andersen's body. When I checked later with my old friend Gaston Max, sure enough the body of Andersen was in the sewers where de Savery had indicated, and showed signs of having been murdered by the Si-Fan. Still, I couldn't take him on trust; after all, he might well have murdered Andersen himself. That was when he produced the key that I could not ignore."

"And what was that?" Baruk found himself leaning forward to hear more.

"I have to preface this part a bit. Back in '05, when I was in Saigon nosing into the Si-Fan's activities, the local head of its Saigon branch was a crippled former Chinese governor of Northern Annam known as Hanoi Shan. As luck would have it, I blundered rather badly and ended up in his clutches. There wasn't much hope and, frankly, I was in pretty poor shape when someone broke into Shan's compound, rescued me, and apparently notified the local gendarmes, because, by morning, they were swarming all over the place. Shan got away, though he finally met justice in France on the guillotine, but I never knew who my rescuer was…"

"And it was de Savery?"

"That's the damnable part, lad. I still don't know. But I do know this. Only a handful of men know what happened that night, or that a valuable jade Buddha was stolen, and fewer still knew I was working under the name M. Lenormand at the time, and there was one other thing… De Savery brought a small ivory elephant out of his pocket and handed it to me, asking if I recognized it, and I did. I had seen it among Shan's collection before I tripped up. That and Andersen's corpse convinced me."

"So, de Savery's motive, his relationship to this business, none of that is clear?"

"Nothing ever is when Fu Manchu is involved. I learned that early, and I trust my instincts. Whatever de Savery wants, he plans to stop Fu Manchu first, and those are *bona fides* enough for me tonight. After the game is played, we will see what de Savery's hand is. Frankly, that's why I brought you in. This little business needed another professional in the mix.

"Now, I've had a suite booked for you and your uniform for the evening is waiting there. Get some sleep, we may be late, and if you know any prayers to Osiris, say a few for all of us, for we may need them later."

With that, Baruk found himself ushered out the door with little more information than he started with, other than a firm conviction to keep his eye on André de Savery.

Bimbashi Baruk lay on his back looking at the stars.

Only minutes before, he had been on his stomach looking down onto the site of the Andersen dig—no, make that the Fu Manchu dig, since there was little doubt that the tall robed figure they saw below them was indeed Dr. Fu Manchu, impressive physically even at a distance, and likely more so in person.

Smith had relieved him of his watch, and now he had moved back down from the rocky outcropping they had chosen as their observation point, and lay back studying the sky. Too bad it was the wrong time of evening to see Osiris.

"I think our business will be concluded long before the archer puts in an appearance tonight," de Savery said, as if reading his thoughts. Not a feat, he supposed, that was difficult to achieve under the circumstances, but unsettling in the Frenchman's accuracy at doing so.

"Aye," Solomon said, checking the Browning semi-automatic he carried at his side. "We shall 'ave to be content plotting h'our course by the Polar Star tonight."

"Just wondering," Baruk said. "I was supposed to be in Cairo at the Gezireh Palace dining with a most beautiful young lady before dancing at the Mena house. Instead, I'm in my bloody uniform sweating under Arab robes about to deliberately step into a crossfire between two of the worst actors on the planet for a mythological relic that may not even exist. Which is why I was wondering if old Osiris still had enough pull with whatever gods there be to keep us safe tonight."

"I suspect even the *Bon Dieu*, as we call him," de Savery said, smiling. "would have second thoughts about our chances tonight. I am at least grateful those two Nubian waiters from the hotel proved to be agents of Sir Denis. They look capable with those Lee Enfields."

The two men did look murderous in Arab robes with the rifles and other gear they carried. That was reassuring. The Nubians were good soldiers, Baruk had found, intelligent, generous, brave, and savage in battle. Little wonder their kind had risen from slave to kings in this land. He didn't know these two were; they were rifleman from a fort in Sudan. But that Smith trusted them was enough for him.

Sir Lionel, who had been up at the top of the rock formation with Smith, came scrambling down. "Better get ready! It looks as if they're about to break through to the temple any minute." His version of a whisper wasn't all that quiet, but they were too far away to worry about that. Anyway, he was a veteran of Smith's past actions and they weren't.

The five men gathered at the top with Smith, who was watching the events below through his binoculars. The Nubians stayed back to watch their rear in case Fu Manchu or Von Grundt had put out scouts.

The scene below was well lit by large klieg lights powered by several generators that whirred noisily and belched exhaust. Baruk fished out his own binoculars to see better. Even up here, the wind carried the stinging scent of kerosene from the valley below.

On the perimeter of the dig were numerous men, Arabs, or at least in Arab garb, well-armed, and looking out from the site as guardians. Inside, in a smaller circle, there were fewer men, some arabs, others in loose black pajamas and headbands—Dacoits, the personal guard of Dr. Fu Manchu, all carrying large curved blades, and, according to Smith, a virtual Pharmacy of deadly drugs.

Beyond that were the tents which housed the sleeping, cooking, and supply units, then an inner circle which consisted of several men, including the tall figure of the Chinese Doctor. Directly in front of them was a large excavated area, a wide pit carved out of the side of a rock, which showed what could only be the entrance to a temple. Numerous workers were busy around a central opening removing rock and sand, as the gigantic lights cast bizarre shadows on the walls.

It had the heightened reality of a film, something out of Lang or Murnau. It only needed Tesla coils and lightning flashing in the sky to complete the surreal scene. It would not have been surprising if Osiris himself had emerged from the temple to complain about his sleep being disturbed.

Baruk focused on the tall Chinese, but he could only get brief glimpses of the side of his face. He remembered Smith commenting about the bust of Seti, but he could make nothing out for his own judgment. Besides, he could not honestly say he remembered what the bust of Seti looked like.

Suddenly, one of the workers scrambled up the wooden platform leading into the excavations and prostrated himself at Fu Manchu's feet. Whatever his message, and it was clear from the Doctor's actions what that message was, Fu Manchu stepped forward and descended into the pit, the worker scrambling away to avoid being trod on.

Though his dignity never slipped, Baruk could feel the tension and excitement rising in him. Beside him, he felt the tension in the Frenchman as well. He seemed gripped in some sort of thrall, as if they had uncovered a great treasure and the chest was about to be opened. Baruk himself felt some of that, but also trepidation for what was soon to follow.

"Remember," Smith whispered hoarsely, "we don't move until Von Grundt arrives. We can't afford to take the brunt of fire from Fu Manchu's guards."

Afford, nor want to, Baruk agreed, though he wished he had a company of his old Camel Corps troops with him, not the mechanized modern ones, but the true cavalry, charging down these slopes with swift-footed beasts that looked like Satan's own creatures when they charged, with their flaring nostrils and large square teeth.

Now, Fu Manchu stood in the center of the light while one worker, naked save for a loin cloth and headgear, worked carefully but quickly clearing away the last debris blocking the entrance to the temple. Such was the power of Fu Manchu's presence that they could almost feel him mentally urging the man to hurry. Then the worker stepped back.

Fu Manchu stood alone under the bright light, his enormous shadow cast over the temple entrance like that of some great bird of prey, malign and voracious in its appetite. A long slender hand, showing cords of muscle as it touched the entranceway, moved and probed, sending even more menacing shadows along the white walls.

"This is the moment," de Savery said so softly that only Baruk caught it. "The very moment..." The rest trailed away.

Through the binoculars, Baruk watched as Fu Manchu's hand paused over a hieroglyph of Horus. He rested his palm on the stone, then leaned forward pressing his weight on it. The stone slid in, slowly at first, then with sudden rapidity. There was absolute stillness. Even the generators seemed to hold their angry breath.

A groan came from the earth. A groan like a living being unhappy at being awakened. It was a deep rumbling sound and it shook dust and sand off the front of the temple, lightly showering the Chinese Doctor who made no move to protect himself. As the great stone pivot swung inward, time itself seemed to turn backwards.

A fine crack appeared in the temple wall, then, as the groaning grew deeper, it grew wider until the noise could now be heard to be stone grinding against stone, the fat used to grease its movement long dried with age.

The workers had prostrated themselves on the ground and were trembling. Baruk trembled a little himself.

Before the unmoving Fu Manchu, the earth seemed to open, the very gates of Hades.

Baruk stiffened.

Fu Manchu signaled for a torch, and one of the men who had stood up top with him came running down to provide it. Lighting the electric torch, Fu Manchu shone it inside the temple, too dim to allow Baruk to see anything, even with the binoculars.

Fu Manchu stepped forward into the darkness. And all hell broke loose.

Smith had been terse in his instructions: "Von Grundt is subtle for a German, but he won't be tonight. He'll try to distract Fu Manchu's forces and get to the temple first with his own expert. We'll work our way down into the fray, picking off both sides to sow further confusion, then make for the temple.

"Major Baruk and Monsieur de Savery will see Sir Lionel reach the temple, while Solomon, our two Nubians and I will give you cover. Remember the Eye itself is as good to us in fragments as safe. We're spoilers in this fight. Our goal is to keep that beastly thing out of more dangerous hands. If we can save it, fine, but that isn't what we are here for."

Brutal, typically Smith, the Anglo-Saxon mind bereft of sentiments or illusions, but he was right. This was no time to get sentimental. Egypt at best was a powder-keg, and with rumors of war and men like Fu Manchu and Clubfoot sewing seeds of unrest, it was no time to throw ancient religions and superstition into the mix. Osiris' eyes would have to remain lost, or be destroyed.

The journey in the shadows of the valley was harrowing and dangerous, with stray bullets popping all about the little group. It was even hotter once they reached the edge of the fighting, though there was something exhilarating about plunging into battle right and left, with no regard for who was struck, as long as he wasn't an ally.

Baruk felt a certain wildness struggling to the surface, and could not say if it was his Egyptian blood on some Saxon berserker trying to awaken. He only knew that keeping his head was half the job, and a damn hard one. He laid on his Webley, bullets and butt on either side, men sprouting wounds as they fell aside or succumbing to cracked skulls. Black-clad dacoits and Arabs in different colored robes fell along with Von Grundt's blonde stormtroopers.

Somehow through all the cordite and smoke, fire and fray, Baruk and de Savery managed to get Sir Lionel to the entrance of the temple. They had not seen Von Grundt in the battle, but he could easily have made it to the temple before them, and Fu Manchu, deadlier than any asp or scorpion, was already inside.

A few feet in, the three men paused to let their eyes accustom to the darkness. They had torches, but were reluctant to use them, for fear of making themselves targets for knife, garrote, or gun.

"Ahead and bear right," Bart whispered. "We don't want to wander into Horus temple when the action is in his father's."

Keeping that in mind, they followed his instructions, and it was soon evident they had chosen right. They heard voices, shots, and saw the flickering torchlight ahead, just past a passageway that must have led to the temple of Horus. Von Grundt had indeed made his way into the temple.

A few feet further, they stumbled over a body. Baruk used a match long enough to determine he was white. It was Von Grundt's expert.

The passageway opened into a large space, and from the glitter of gold and jewels sparkling in the light of the torches, it was clear no tomb nor temple thief had ever penetrated this sacred place during all the ages since it had been sealed. Carter and Carnarvon would have been salivating. Even de Savery caught his breath from his place in the rear.

Against the far wall lay the great figure of Osiris, and one of his eyes had been stolen from a socket. Ten yards distant, behind a sarcophagus of gold and jewels, Von Grundt was crouching, machine pistol in hand, shining a bright torch at the base of the figure.

"Come out," Von Grundt commanded in German. "All I want is the Eye. I have no argument with you."

"Ah," Fu Manchu replied, his voice as sinuous as a snake, but betraying no accent, "but I have an argument with you, Herr Von Grundt, and all your kind. Your prancing, stiff-legged, murderous kind. Your Führer's crimes make my actions pale in comparison. Aryan indeed! My people had built a great civilization when you were still living in caves dressed in animal skins.

"In any case, since neither of us knows who has prevailed outside, it is premature to call for my surrender. I am quite willing to bide my time until there is a definitive answer. Unless you wish to attempt to cross that open space between us on the gamble that I am unarmed."

A soft laugh chilled Baruk's spine.

Von Grundt had chosen his hiding place well, protected at the back and front. Baruk was a crack shot and still doubted he could do more than crease the German's pith helmet from their passageway.

"Fu Manchu is right," de Savery whispered. "And we can't afford for either side to prevail, since our numbers are too few. Eventually one or both sides will notice what we're doing if the fighting continues."

He was right. A standoff was untenable.

"If you have an idea...?" Baruk began.

"That earlier passageway leading to the temple of Horus... It might connect to this one, and if it does, I may be able to get behind Fu Manchu, grab the Eye and have the two in a crossfire between us."

"It wouldn't be unusual for the priests to have secret passageways from one temple to another," Sir Lionel whispered, for once tempering his roar.

"All right," Baruk said, "but I think I'll let them know they aren't alone. That should shake things up and allow you more freedom." And with that, he leveled the Webley and fired into the chamber, gouging a considerable chunk of gold from the surface of the sarcophagus behond which Von Grundt was hiding.

The German jumped back.

"This is Major Baruk of the Egyptian Camel Corps," he announced, trying to sound like every Sergeant-Major he had ever heard berating troops in the field. "Surrender and come along quietly, and this will all be settled back in Aswan."

Von Grundt swore and fired a wild burst towards the passageway, harmlessly, but Fu Manchu merely chuckled.

"A fine imitation of a policeman, Major Baruk. I take it Nayland Smith has made his presence known—a blunderer, but useful at times. Still, he can't have gathered sufficient forces without showing himself to make much of a show outside. You have Sir Lionel with you, I take it?"

"Aye," Sir Lionel spoke up. "I'm here as well."

"A reunion then. How many times have we been at arms like this, my old colleague. Only Doctor Petrie and young Greville are missing,"

"Prattle on, you fools," Von Grundt said. "My forces are crack troops and will soon have that Oriental rabble out front in hand. You are both trapped."

"Then you should know, O Clubfooted One, that trapped animals are the most dangerous. Is that not so, Bimbashi?"

"So I've been told, but I have nothing to worry about. Sir Denis is even now flying in troops he had on standby in Luxor. He knew you would be keeping too close an eye on local movements, both of you."

There was silence for a moment as both Von Grundt and Fu Manchu weighed that bluff.

"I should not wish to play your Western game of poker with you, Bimbashi, though you should be an excellent chess opponent, I suspect. Still, wisdom dictates that a retreat of sorts is in order. Farewell then, gentlemen."

Baruk saw a yellow hand curve over the base of the statue, then an object tossed halfway into the chamber.

"Flash-bang," he shouted at Sir Lionel, pulling them both down and turning their backs to the temple. The light and explosion still deafened them both and, as they struggled to recover, Baruk felt himself almost bowled over.

It was Von Grundt escaping.

"Who...?" Sir Lionel sputtered.

"Von Grundt."

Sir Lionel leaped up to follow, but Baruk stopped him. "Nothing we can do and he doesn't have the Eye anyway. He's got diplomatic immunity. The worst that can happen is, he gets shipped home in faux disgrace. But Fu Manchu..."

'The Eye..."

"He must have taken one of those priest holes de Savery was going on about," Sir Lionel said. "If we look, perhaps we can..."

"No time. We have to get out and hope Smith and Solomon can cover our escape."

"But Fu Manchu... De Savery...?"

"They will have to fend for themselves."

And with that, Baruk caught Sir Lionel by the arm and dragged him into the passageway.

When they had arrived back at the hotel, Sir Lionel had begged off and returned to his villa a defeated man. Solomon excused himself when told that a letter was awaiting him at the desk. Smith and Baruk consoled themselves over large whiskey and sodas.

"My own damn fault," Smith said. "Everyone did splendidly, but as usual I was too late. And poor de Savery... Manchu won't be kind if his men found him. Worse yet, that fiend now has the Eye, and God knows what deviltry he will get up to with it. I don't envy you your job, Baruk. I fear I've put the torch to your powder-keg."

Baruk was about to reassure the older men when Solomon returned.

"So despondent, gentlemen? Aye, well ye 'ave no need to be. H'i, 'aven't played fair with ye H'i fear. Not entirely. You see h'i've known about André de Savery for a good many more years than either of ye. H'i knew 'im back when 'e was Don Luis Perenna, in the Legion, puttin' down a rebellion in Morocco. He even had 'is own personal submarine, ye know. H'i know lots of fantastic things about Don Luis Perenna."

Solomon had poured a bubble glass of brandy and sat down as he swirled it around and sniffed the aroma.

"He's alive then?" Baruk asked.

"Aye, and more. But 'afore H'i go farther, H'i better read you the letter that was waiting for me when we came back."

Solomon sat forward, placing a pince-nez on his nose and withdrew the letter with a flourish.

"My dear, Solomon, (he began to read) *By now, once again, you will have surmised that my death has been again exaggerated to the point even Mr. Clemens might be amused, and you will know that, when I left Major Baruk and Sir Lionel, it was not entirely for the purpose I stated. By then, I had observed and had time to exercise a bit of logic, and the numbers were not adding up. All I know of Dr. Fu Manchu—and I have had run-ins with the Si-Fan before—told me that he would not allow himself to be cornered by a man as unsubtle as Von Grundt without another exit—those very same priestly passages I claimed to be looking for—but why play out that little game in the first place?*

I admit, this puzzled me for a moment. Then I recalled something that happened earlier, when Fu Manchu first opened the temple, that seemed as strange to me. You recall that he hesitated before pushing the pivot stone in; then, quite deliberately, he pushed in not the hieroglyphic for Osiris, but for his son, Horus, which opened the temple. But why? The treasure was the Eye of Osiris... Blind Osiris...

Who indeed was the keeper of the Eye of Osiris, the blind father, or the one-eyed son? Fu Manchu must have had the same revelation, but he could not have known of my presence. He simply planned to divert Von Grundt and slip away, remove the Eye from the Horus temple, and escape, regardless of which side won the gun battle being waged outside. No doubt, his fanatic followers were happy to die for him to do so.

Now, the Eye is safe in my keeping, and will remain so among my treasures, being safer there than in any vault or museum, whatever may come in the dangerous days ahead. I knew Fu Manchu had executed his plan when I heard the flash-bang and saw the light. I guessed that the sensible Major Baruk would get Sir Lionel to safety rather than pursue the rabbit down the hole.

Myself, I made my way to an upper chamber of the temple where I could cover your retreat, then simply waited for a quiet moment, and escaped to my own little safe-house, which I have now departed after having this letter posted to my old friend John Solomon.

My regards to you all.

"H'it's signed of course," Solomon said, "not by André de Savery or Don Luis Perenna but by..."

"No," Smith barked a laugh as he rose with a burst of energy from his seat. "For once, I don't want to know. Whoever the fellow is, he has the Devil's own nerve, and I will sleep better knowing that he has the damned third Eye of Osiris in his keeping, rather than some underpaid museum guard. God knows, I've seen Fu Manchu get around enough of that breed!

"No, gentlemen, tonight I feel my age, and if you don't mind, I'm off to bed. I still should pretend that I'm desperate to find Fu Manchu come morning, if only to keep this chap's bluff going until he is safe away. Good night, gentlemen."

Smith rose and walked stiffly from the room, his wide shoulders a bit bowed for once, but his pace steady and sure.

Baruk, not rising from his chair. merely extended his hand toward Solomon. "I'm not half so sanguine as Sir Denis," he said. "Let me see who our sneaky benefactor was."

Solomon handed the letter to Baruk. The missive was initialed only, *A.L.*

"*A.L.*? Who the bloody hell is *A.L.*?"

Solomon took the letter and returned it to his pocket. "Some would say a myth, others a legend. Sleep on h'it, and H'i'll tell ye in the mornin' if ye still don't know."

It was about three in the morning when Solomon heard a whoop of surprise from the direction of Baruk's room just down the hall from his own. It seemed he would not have to reveal the name of the letter's author in the morning after all.

Credits

The Lights on Haint Mountain

Starring:	Created by:
Silver John	Manly Wade Wellman
Mari & Ken	Matthew Baugh
Isao Matsumoto	Based on André Caroff
Atomos Institute (Kano, Mitsui, Demura, Ishiyama)	Based on André Caroff
Hannah	Matthew Baugh
The People (Jeremiah, Daniel, Jerusha)	Zenna Henderson
Co-Starring:	
Kanoto Yoshimuta (Madame Atomos)	André Caroff
And:	
Haint Mountain/Witch Mountain	Alexander Key

Matthew BAUGH lives and works in Albuquerque, NM. He is the pastor of a small church and an editor for Permuted Press. He is also the author of *The Vampire Count of Monte-Cristo*, a mash-up of the classic story of adventure and revenge with vampires, ghosts and Faustian bargains, the co-author, with Win Scott Eckert, of *A Girl and Her Cat*, which continues the adventures of classic TV heroes, Honey West and T.H.E. Cat. He is a regular contributor to *Tales of the Shadowmen*.

The Curse of Orlac

Starring:	Created by:
Stephen Orlac	Maurice Renard
Sâr Dubnotal	Norbert Sevestre
Feodor Orloff II	John Argyle
Richard Marlowe	Robert Charles
Richard Vollin	David Boehm
Blind Jake	Edgar Wallace
Jan Compton	Rex Carlton & Joseph Greene
Bill Cortner	Rex Carlton & Joseph Greene
June Talbot	Ben Pivar, Francis Rosenwald,

	David Duncan
Dr. Paul Talbot	Ben Pivar, Francis Rosenwald,
	David Duncan
Dr. Alberto Levin	Gino De Santis, Alberto
	Bevilacqua, Anton Giulio
	Majano, Piero Monviso
Vernon Paris	Newt Arnold
Duncal Ely	Fred Mustard Stewart
Damien Ludlow	Bill Rebane
Eugene Ludlow	Ralph Murphy & Lora Baxter
Dracula	Bram Stoker
Feodor Orloff III	Fred Gebhardt
	& DeWitt Bodeen

Co-Starring:

Dr. Cerral	Maurice Renard
Vasseur	Maurice Renard
Count Feodor Orloff	John R. Carling
Paul Cressingham	John R. Carling
Princess Barbara	John R. Carling
Dr. Dionysus Orloff	Jesus Franco
Melissa Orloff	Jesus Franco
Dr. Genessier	Jean Redon
Conrad Jekyll	Jesus Franco based on Robert
	Louis Stevenson
Mason Zimmerman	Jesus Franco
Morpho	Jesus Franco
Inspector Tanner	Jesus Franco
William Tanner	Edgar Wallace
Paul Kelton	Ed Wood
Alan Hacker	Jesus Franco
	based on Bram Stoker
Erik Usher	Jesus Franco
	based on Edgar Allan Poe
RAF flyer (Bob Morane)	Henri Vernes
Tania Orloff	Henri Vernes
General Orlov	George Macdonald Fraser,
	Michael G. Wilson,
	Richard Maibaum
Captain Gogol	Christopher Wood
Byron Orlac	Peter Bogdanovich
Leonard Orlac/Orlok	Jean-Luc Godard
Dr. Orlac	Guillermo Calderon
	& Alfredo Salazar

Professor Dearborn	Walter Summers
	based on Edgar Wallace
George Lorenz	Harvey Gates, Sam Robins,
	Gerald Schnitzer
Eric Vornoff	Ed Wood
Lobo	Ed Wood
Orlok	F.W. Murnau
Julian Karswell	M.R. James
Hazel Hexen	Adam Mudman Bezecny
Frankenstein	Mary Shelley
And:	
Alphaville	Jean-Luc Godard
Incomputare	Adam Mudman Bezecny

Adam Mudman BEZECNY is a graduate from the University of Minnesota Morris. His previous publications include the novel *Tail of the Lizard King* and the online stories *Dieselworld* and *Words from the Inner Circle*. He is the editor-in-chief of a fiction magazine, *Odd Tales of Wonder*, and he also writes movie reviews for the blog Adam Mudman's A-List, which sometimes publishes his fiction (mudmansalist.blogspot.com). He is a regular contributor to *Tales of the Shadowmen*.

Hero of Two Worlds

Starring:	**Created by:**
Zachiel	Marie-Anne de Roumier Robert
Also Starring:	
Gilbert du Mortier, Marquis	
de Lafayette	
George Washington de	
Lafayette	
And:	
Barsoom	Edgar Rice Burroughs
Malacandra	C.S. Lewis

Nathan CABANISS has had short stories appear in various publications, in English and in French. 2016 saw the publication of his first collection of short fiction, *Mares in the Night*, an anthology of horror, dark fantasy and science fiction. He can be found online via his newsletter *Notices from the Abyss*, where he publishes his serialized novel *Alamud Ahab and the Great White Werewolf*, and his blog *Girls, Guns & Cigarettes*, where you never know what sort of nonsense he'll be musing about this time. He is a regular contributor to *Tales of the Shadowmen*.

A Case of Mistaken Identity

Starring:	Created by:
Teddy Verano	Maurice Limat
Connor MacLeod	Gregory Widen
Mike Pearson	Don Coscarelli
Reg	Don Coscarelli
Colonel Bozzo-Corona	Paul Féval
The Marchef	Paul Féval
Co-Starring:	
The Tall Man	Don Coscarelli
John Winchester	Eric Kripke
Yellow-Eyed Demon	Eric Kripke

Matthew DENNION lives in South Jersey with his beautiful wife and daughters. He currently works as a teacher of students with autism at a Special Services School. Matthew writes giant monster stories for *G-Fan* magazine and he has recently published three giant monster novels, *Chimera: Scourge of the Gods*, *Operation R.O.C.: A Kaiju Thriller* and *Atomic Rex*. He is a regular contributor to *Tales of the Shadowmen*.

The Death of Von Bork

Starring:	Created by:
Boris Liatoukine	Marie Nizet
Von Bork	Arthur Conan Doyle
Polly Bird	Paul Féval
Irina Petrovski	based on Arnaud d'Usseau
	& Julian Zimet
Co-Starring:	
Sherlock Holmes	Arthur Conan Doyle
Irene Adler	Arthur Conan Doyle
Irma Vep	Louis Feuillade
Venenos/The Vampires	Louis Feuillade
The Golem	Gustav Meyrinck
And:	
Selene, the Sepulchre	Paul Féval

Brian GALLAGHER has a BA in Politics and Society and lives in London. He works in the media and for many years has written on the politics, economics and many other aspects of Croatia and has been quoted in Croatian and international media. In relation to that he has written extensively on Croatian-related cases at the International Criminal Tribunal for the Former Yugoslavia. He has always been interested in science fiction, classic horror, comics and is proud to be a lifelong *Doctor Who* fan. He is a regular contributor to *Tales of the Shadowmen*.

Princes of the Universe

Starring:	Created by:
Solomon Kane	Robert E. Howard
Baroness Phryne	Paul Féval
Lord John Cleverly Cartney	Brian Clemens
The Taferals	Robert E. Howard
Connor MacLeod/Adrian Montague	Gregory Widen
Co-Starring:	
The Libertines	Marquis de Sade
Ramirez	Gregory Widen
Doctor Omega	Arnould Galopin
Captain Kronos	Brian Clemens
Hyeronimus Grost	Brian Clemens
Maciste	Giovanni Pastrone & Gabriele D'Annunzio
Telzey Amberdon	James H. Schmitz
N'Longa	Robert E. Howard
And:	
Selene, the Sepulchre	Paul Féval

John GALLAGHER is a freelance artist living in the North West of England. He divides his time between working on his own comic strip projects and painting fantasy subjects. Amongst other things, he has published, in collaboration with 'Archaic' Alan Hewetson, *The Complete Saga of the Victims*; a graphic novel compilation of the old Skywald *Horror-Mood* comic strip. He is a previous contributor to *Tales of the Shadowmen*.

Rouletabille at the Old Bailey

Starring:	Created by:
Joseph Rouletabille	Gaston Leroux
Benjamin Bates	Derek Marlowe
Harry Dickson	*Anonymous*
Sir Wilfrid Robarts	Agatha Christie
T.C. Rowley	John Mortimer

Edward Leithen	John Buchan
Impey Biggs	Dorothy L. Sayers
Justice Wargrave	Agatha Christie
Gustav Schellenberg	Martin Gately
Mavis Blythe	Martin Gately
Dr. Rupert Grierson	Martin Gately
Sherlock Holmes	Arthur Conan Doyle
Sexton Blake	Harry Blyth
Seaton Begg	Michael Moorcock
Victor Drago	Chris Lowder & Roy Preston

Martin GATELY is the author of the official prequel to Philip José Farmer's first novel, *The Green Odyssey (Samdroo and the Grassman* in *The Worlds of Philip José Farmer 4 – Voyages to Strange Days)*. His writing career commenced in 1988 when he wrote for D C Thomson's legendary *Starblazer* comic book. He is also a contributor to the UK's journal of strange phenomena *Fortean Times*. For Black Coat Press, he has provided stories for the following anthologies: *Night of the Nyctalope, Harry Dickson Vs. The Spider* and *The Vampire Almanac Vol. 1*. His latest work is an adaptation of Edgar Rice Burroughs' *The Mad King* into comic strip form – drawn by Enrique Alcatena and available on the official Edgar Rice Burroughs website. He is a regular contributor to *Tales of the Shadowmen.*

Beneath the Mount of Divination

Starring:

Aramis (René d'Herblay)	Alexandre Dumas
Brom Cromwell	Micah Harris
The Barbusquin Order	Jean Ray
Françoise de Bretigny /	Micah Harris
Françoise de Foix	*Historical*
	based on Robert E. Howard
The Scurvamhites	Thomas Pynchon
Baal	Renée Dunan

Co-Starring:

Maciste	Giovanni Pastrone &
	Gabriele D'Annunzio
Trystero	Thomas Pynchon
Natvilcius	C.S. Lewis
Dark Agnes	Robert E. Howard
Abhoth	Clark Ashton Smith

Also Starring:

Mazarin

290

Father Joseph (Grey Eminence)
Richelieu
Orazio Morandi

Micah S. HARRIS is the 2016 Pulp Ark Award winner in the category of best novel *for Ravenwood, the Stepson of Mystery: Return of the Dugpa*. He is also the author with artist Michael Gaydosof the graphic novel *Heaven's War*, a historical fantasy pitting the Oxford Inklings against Aleister Crowley. His most recent publications are the mystery novel *Murder in the Miracle Room* and an in-depth article, published in *Little Shoppe of Horrors*, on the "lost" sword and sorcery movie of the early 1980s, *Thongor in the Valley of Demons*. His out-of-print *The Eldritch New Adventures of Becky Sharp* recently became available again as an e-book. His other publications include *The Frequency of Fear* (also available as an electronic book), *Jim Anthony: the Hunters* (with Joshua Reynolds) the Image Comic book *Lorna, Relic Wrangler* (with artist Loston Wallace) and his short fiction collection, *Slouching Toward Camulodunum*. He is a regular contributor to *Tales of the Shadowmen*.

The Case of the Remains to be seen

Starring:	**Created by:**
Etienne Camparol	André Laurie
Stella Astarte	Alfred Driou
Spiridon	André Laurie
Doctor Ox	Jules Verne
The Radar Men	Ronald Davidson
Co-Starring:	
Professor Brainard	based on Bill Walsh
	& Samuel W. Taylor
Inspector Juve	Pierre Souvestre
	& Marcel Allain
Fantômas	Pierre Souvestre
	& Marcel Allain
Professor Cavor	H.G. Wells

Travis HILTZ started making up stories at a young age. Years later, he began writing them down. In high school, he discovered that some writers actually got paid and decided to give it a try. He has since gathered a modest collection of rejection letters and had a one-act play produced. Travis lives in the wilds of New Hampshire with his very loving and tolerant wife, two above average children and a staggering amount of comic books and *Doctor Who* novels. He is a regular contributor to *Tales of the Shadowmen*.

The Night of the Dazzling Sun

Starring:	**Created by:**
Honey West	G.G. Fickling
Aunt Meg (Honey West)	Gwen Bagni & Paul Dubov
Tom Wills	*Anonymous*
Miguelito Loveless (Osiris Prime)	John Kneubuhl
Hathor	John Kneubuhl
Leo Saint-Clair	Jean de la Hire
Henry West	G.G. Fickling
Co-Starring:	
Lt. Mark Storm	G.G. Fickling
James West	Michael Garrison
Artemus Gordon	Michael Garrison
Harry Dickson	*Anonymous*
Herbert West	H.P. Lovecraft
Bob West	Willis Cooper
Wally West	John Broome
Iris West	John Broome
Sue Storm	Stan Lee & Jack Kirby
Johnny Storm	Stan Lee & Jack Kirby
David Marcus	Nicholas Meyer & Harve Bennett
Carol Marcus	Nicholas Meyer & Harve Bennett
Also Starring:	
Gene Roddenberry	
Julius Schwarz	
And:	
Vril	Edward Bulwer-Lytton
Bikinium	Jack Du Brul

Paul HUGLI has a degree in Zoology, and has written for everything from *Cracked* magazine to general interest pamphlets, and for most of the first, second *and* third tier adult magazines. He is the author of three published "adult fantasy" novels, and the acclaimed *Traci Lords Companion*. He has also been employed as a science/math instructor, and as a "Floor Manager" at a local "Gentleman's Club." In addition, he once owned/managed Destiny Bookstore, which dealt in SciFi, comics and adult "fantasy" magazines, for 30 years. He now has three novels in the works. He is a regular contributor to *Tales of the Shadowmen*.

Guided Tours of Famous Secret Places

Starring:	Created by:
Rue Morgue	Edgar Allan Poe
Arkham	H.P. Lovevraft
Brichester	Ramsey Campbell
Derry	Stephen King
Ingersham	Jean Ray
Medecine Man	Gene Wolfe
Mud-Cree, Texas	Joe Lansdale
Erik	Gaston Leroux
Azathoth	H.P. Lovecraft
Co-Starring :	
The Black Coats	Paul Féval
The Si-Fan	Sax Rohmer
The Illuminati	Robert Anton Wilson
	& Robert Shea
The Shin-Tan	Henri Vernes
The Brotherhood of the Sev-	L.T. Meade
en Kings	& Robert Eustace
The Black Lodge	Talbot Mundy
The Power House	John Buchan
De Castries	Fritz Leiber
Belphégor	Arthur Bernède
Arsène Lupin	Maurice Leblanc
Jean Valjean	Victor Hugo
Randolph Carter	H.P. Lovecraft
Erich Zann	H.P. Lovecraft
And:	
L'Épi-Scié	Paul Féval
House on Rue Thérèse	Paul Féval
The Dragon Volant	Sheridan Le Fanu
Voorish Sign	Richard A. Lupoff
Room of the Barbarous Gods	Arthur Bernède
Valusia	Robert E. Howard
Joiry	Cartherine L. Moore
The Court of the Dragon	Robert W. Chambers
Rue d'Auseil	H.P. Lovecraft
St. Beregonne's Lane	Jean Ray
Selene	Paul Féval
Xebico	H. F. Arnold
The *Mainz Psalter*	Jean Ray
R'lyeh	H.P. Lovecraft

Dagon	H.P. Lovecraft
Cthulhu	H.P. Lovecraft
Shub-Niggurath	H.P. Lovecraft

Matthew ILSEMAN was born in Texas and currently lives in Colorado. He started writing before he could actually write. His mother would write down stories he dictated to her. He has been writing ever since. He contributed a story to *The Many Faces of Arsène Lupin* and this is his first contribution to *Tales of the Shadowmen*.

Phantom Masquerade

Starring:	**Created by:**
Baptiste Severn	Robert W. Chambers
Thomas Fane (Carnacki)	William Hope Hodgson
Cardec	Goron & Emile Gautier
Fantômas (The Pallid Mask)	Pierre Souvestre & Marcel Allain
The King in Yellow	Robert W. Chambers
Jean Grimoire (John Grimlan)	Robert E. Howard
Marc Douanier	Rick Lai
Sir George Burnwell	Arthur Conan Doyle
Mary Holder	Arthur Conan Doyle
Professor Hern	Ambrose Bierce
Otto Hern	Rick Lai
Emile Le Brun	Arthur Conan Doyle
Juve	Pierre Souvestre & Marcel Allain

Co-Starring:	
Morryster	Ambrose Bierce
Parapelius Necromantius	Ambrose Bierce
Maître de Grandin	Seabury Quinn
Joseph de Quincey	Evangeline Walton
Lionel Dacre	Arthur Conan Doyle
John Clay	Arthur Conan Doyle
Cassandra	Rick Lai
Hendrika	Rick Lai
Orianne Coyatier	Rick Lai
Colonel Beltham	Pierre Souvestre & Marcel Allain
Boris Yvain	Robert W. Chambers
Phantom of Truth	Robert W. Chambers
Heralds of the Yellow Sign	Robert W. Chambers

Antonio Nikola	Guy Boothby
The Black Coats	Paul Féval
Joseph Clampin	Paul Féval
Captain Tobias	William Hope Hodgson
Also Starring:	
Alphonse Bertillon	
Ravachol	
And:	
Le Roi en Jaune	Robert W. Chambers
Verschwinden und Seine Theorie	Ambrose Bierce
Marvells of Science	Ambrose Bierce
Trauvells in ye Easte	Ambrose Bierce
The Fatality of Visitations	Rick Lai
Saaamaaa Ritual	William Hope Hodgson
Sigsand Manuscript	William Hope Hodgson
Thirteenth Covenant	Robert Bloch
Cassilda or The Moorish Princess of Toledo	Historical
Carcosa	Robert W. Chambers
Lake of Hali	Robert W. Chambers
Yian	Robert W. Chambers
Lake of Ghosts	Robert W. Chambers
Shrine of Erlik	Robert W. Chambers
Kuen-Yuin Oath	Robert W. Chambers
Dark Star of Yrimid	Robert W. Chambers
Scarlet Lake	Robert W. Chambers
Royal Palace Hotel	Pierre Souvestre & Marcel Allain
End House	William Hope Hodgson

Rick LAI is an authority on pulp fiction and the Wold Newton Universe concepts of Philip José Farmer. His speculative articles have been collected in *Rick Lai's Secret Histories*: *Daring Adventurers*, *Rick Lai's Secret Histories*: *Criminal Masterminds*, *Chronology of Shadows: A Timeline of The Shadow's Exploits* and *The Revised Complete Chronology of Bronze*. Rick's fiction has been collected in *Shadows of the Opera*, *Shadows of the Opera: Retribution in Blood* and *Sisters of the Shadows: The Cagliostro Curse* (the last two titles are available from Black Coat Press). He has also translated Arthur Bernède's *Judex* and *The Return of Judex* into English for Black Coat Press. Rick resides in Bethpage, New York, with his wife and children. He is a regular contributor to *Tales of the Shadowmen*.

Tomorrow Belongs to the Nyctalope

Starring:	Created by:
Leo Saint-Clair	Jean de La Hire
The Stalker	Arkady & Boris Strugatski
Auguste Pinochet	Vladimir Volkoff
Mlle. Roche-Verger	Vladimir Volkoff
Co-Starring :	
Pierre Saint-Clair	Jean de La Hire
Xavière de Ciserat	Jean de La Hire
Xavière Saint Clair	Jean de La Hire
Claude Marécourt	Jean de La Hire
Sylvie Mac Dhul	Jean de La Hire
Laurence Païli	Jean de La Hire
Queen Mizzeia Khali	Jean de La Hire
Véronique d'Olbans	Jean de La Hire
Marcel Saint-Clair	Jean de La Hire
Vitto	Jean de La Hire
Soca	Jean de La Hire
Gnô Mitang	Jean de La Hire
The Professor	Arkady & Boris Strugatski
Jean Kariven	Jimmy Guieu
Torchwood	Russell T. Davies
And:	
The Zone	Arkady & Boris Strugatski

Nigel MALCOLM lives in Kent, England. He works as a teacher of English as a Foreign Language. He is a long-term *Doctor Who*, *Star Trek* and *Prisoner* fan—long before all the new-fangled versions came along. He is still working on that elusive steampunk novel and various short stories. He is a regular contributor to *Tales of the Shadowmen*.

Kindred Beasts

Starring:	Created by:
Judex	Arthur Bernède & Louis Feuillade
Prosper Cocantin	Arthur Bernède & Louis Feuillade
Licorice Kid	Arthur Bernède & Louis Feuillade
Felanthus	Christopher Nigro
Bertrand Caillet	Guy Endore
Co-Starring:	
Felifax	Paul Féval, *fils*
Dr. Cornelius Kramm	Gustave Le Rouge

Professor Tornada	André Couvreur
The Red Hand	Gustave Le Rouge
Sophie de Blumenberg	Guy Endore
And:	
The Galliez Report	Guy Endore

Christofer NIGRO is a writer of both fiction and non-fiction with a strong interest in pulps, comic books and fantastic cinema, and a regular contributor to *Tales of the Shadowmen*. He may be known to some by his websites *The Godzilla Saga* and *The Warrenverse*, as he is an authority on the subject of *dai kaiju eiga* (the sub-genre of cinema specializing in giant monsters), and the characters featured in the comic magazines published by Warren. He has recently revived and expanded Chuck Loridans' classic site MONSTAAH, and has since been published in the anthologies *Aliens Among Us* and *Carnage: After the Fall*. He is a regular contributor to *Tales of the Shadowmen*.

Dice, Pearl and Sword

Starring:	**Created by:**
Rocambole	P.-A. Ponson du Terrail
Zatoichi	Kan Shimozawa
Yamikubo	Shintaro Katsu,
	Takayuki Yamada
	& Kan Shimozawa

Frank SCHILDINER has been a pulp fan since a friend gave him a gift of Philip Jose Farmer's *Tarzan Alive*. Since that time he has written his first novel with Black Coat Press, *The Quest of Frankenstein*, with a sequel, *The Triumph of Frankenstein*, due out next year. Frank has been published in *The New Adventures of Thunder Jim Wade, Secret Agent X* Volumes 3, 4, 5, *Ravenwood, Stepson of Mystery, The Black Bat Mystery, Pride of the Mohicans, The New Adventures of Richard Knight* and *The Avenger: The Justice Files*. Frank works as a martial arts instructor at Amorosi's Mixed Martial Arts. He resides in New Jersey with his wife Gail who is his top supporter. He is a regular contributor to *Tales of the Shadowmen*.

The Odyssey of Madame Atomos

Madame Atomos	André Caroff
Moonwatcher	Arthur C. Clarke
CARL	Arthur C. Clarke
Cobb Anderson	Rudy Rucker

Michel STEPHAN was born and lives in Brittany with his wife and two children. He has been a fan of science fiction, fantasy and horror since age 10. He loves Universal monster movies (especially the *Frankenstein* series), sci-fi serials and collects Aurora model kits. He has recently written new *Madame Atomos* novels for Black Coat Press's French sister imprint, Rivière Blanche, and is a regular contributor to *Tales of the Shadowmen*.

The Yellow Peril

Starring:	Created by:
Miss Ylang-Ylang (SMOG)	Henri Vernes
Roman Orgonetz	Henri Vernes
The Yellow Shadow	Henri Vernes
Madame Atomos	André Caroff

Artikel UNBEKANNT (not his real name!) lives in Berlin and is the author of several short stories published by Black Coat Press' sister imprint, Rivière Blanche, as well as a horror novel, *Bloodfist*, released in 2013.

The Third Eye of Osiris

Starring:	Created by:
Bimbashi Ibrahim Brian	Sax Rohmer
Mohammed Baruk	
Sir Denis Nayland Smith	Sax Rohmer
Sir Lionel Bart	Sax Rohmer
Dr. Fu Manchu	Sax Rohmer
Dr. Adolph Von Grundt	Valentine Williams
Desmond Okewood	Valentine Williams
John Solomon	H. Bedford Jones
André de Savery/Don Luis Perenna/Arsène Lupin	Maurice Leblanc
Co-Starring:	
Desmond Okewood	Valentine Williams
Dr. Thorndyke	R. Austin Freeman
Gaston Max	Sax Rohmer
Dr. Petrie	Sax Rohmer

David L. VINEYARD is a fifth generation Texan (named for his gunfighter/Texas Ranger great grand-father) currently living in Oklahoma City, OK, where the tornadoes come sweeping down the plains. He has useless degrees in history, politics, and economics, and is the author of several tales about Buenos Aires private eye Johnny Sleep, two novels, several short stories, some journalism, and various non-fiction. He is currently working on several ideas while battling with a three month old kitten for household dominance and the keyboard of his PC. He is a regular contributor to *Tales of the Shadowmen*.

WATCH OUT FOR

TALES OF THE
SHADOWMEN

VOLUME 15: TROMPE L'OEIL
TO BE RELEASED DECEMBER 2018

www.ingramcontent.com/pod-product-compliance
Lightning Source LLC
Chambersburg PA
CBHW060432030726
47495CB00003B/839